The
WOLF
TATTOO

Other books by Kenneth Fore

MOSSBACK

Award Winning Short Stories

HOOKED

SWEETNESS IN THE HUNT

For more information visit
www.KennethFore.com

The
WOLF
TATTOO

By

Kenneth Fore

Odell Books
ATLANTA, GEORGIA

Odell Books
Atlanta, Georgia

Copyright Kenneth Fore 2013
All rights reserved

Printed in the United States of America

Library of Congress control number 2013902990

ISBN: 978-0-9890320-0-1
EBook ISBN: 978-0-9890320-1-8

Publisher's Note

This is a work of fiction. Names, characters, places and incidents either are the product of the author's imagination or are used fictitiously, and any resemblance to actual persons, living or dead, events, or locales is entirely coincidental.

Dedication

Dedicated to my two grandsons, Kalen and Weston,
and to my granddaughter, Sophia.

To, Judith,
the lady who puts pieces of the heart back together.

In memory of,
Larry Allgood
Michael Bell (Shad)
Adon Bell
Jerry Boutwell (JB)
Ricky Hendrix
Larry Powell (LP)

ACKNOWLEDGEMENTS

I wish to thank acquaintances and friends for their encouragement and enthusiastic support. Many friends and acquaintances have generously given their time to listen, to read, to offer their opinion on what they liked and disliked. You know who you are. Thank you all; you always had my back and you were always there when I needed you.

Special thanks and deep gratitude go to Terry and Arlene Robinson for their advice, patient guidance, encouragement, and useful critiques of this story. Their unwavering support and encouragement went a long way in keeping me sane and on track. Thank you both for your enthusiasm and support.

Thanks to Duncan Long who designed the book cover.

Thanks to Magic Graphics for their web site design and typesetting of this manuscript.

Finally, to the readers, thank you. I hope you enjoy this story.

CHAPTER 1

The cab let Clayton out at a remote cabin about fifty miles from Fairbanks. The split-log building with its pitched tin roof nestled like a Tibetan monastery in the forested hills. Eight metal canoes had been stacked, one atop the other, outside Wilderness Outdoor Riggers. A half-dozen or so outbuildings surrounded it. Clayton had no fear but felt out of place just the same.

He paid the driver, told him not to wait. The driver nodded; he'd heard this before. Then Clayton stepped onto the cabin's porch. No breeze stirred the dry air, but a flock of black-winged birds did. He felt a chill on his neck in spite of the late-summer warmth, turned around to see the cab's taillights as it sped away, leaving him alone at the entrance.

The door opened on quiet hinges. A long mahogany counter with a cash register came into view. No one was behind it. On the wall behind and above the counter, a trophy moose head and bear head flanked a mirror and a massive painting of Custer's Last Stand. The painting looked as off-kilter as Clayton felt. He went inside.

He hadn't traveled to the Alaskan wilderness to disappear, or to hug a tree, or to commune with nature or for other such nonsense. He'd conditioned his body and mind for the journey, had read all he could find. He wasn't worried about survival, exactly; he'd already been to hell and back.

There was time to change his mind, though doing so meant a long night and day in the Fairbanks airport, waiting for the next flight out. Not the real question, he realized. What worried him most was that once he went forward with something, he finished it.

He walked to the center of the long counter and pulled his arms through the straps of his backpacks. They dropped onto the rough plank floor. He allowed his eyes to rest on the painting. Not a print, definitely not a garden-variety work of art. Probably the best rendering of the event he'd ever seen.

He'd thought no more before his attention was taken by the subjects' faces. The expressions in their eyes. The terror of knowing that lightning bore at them, about to strike them down.

A nervous sigh escaped him. Avoiding the soldiers' eyes, he forced his mind to the colors. What wouldn't he pay to become an artist like this artist? Money wouldn't help; and he knew it would take more than hard work to raise his so-so talent as a landscape and wildlife artist to this level. More like divine intervention, because he could no longer distinguish between some colors. Especially greens and blues; they looked much the same to him. He refused to delve into how this misfortune could have happened to him. It did. And he didn't believe in miracles.

General Custer leaned forward in the painting, revolver in the air, a tattered gray 7th Cavalry flagstaff gripped in the other hand. The artist had balanced Custer at the edge of the canvas.

By design or accident?

2

Clayton also wondered if Custer had gone into a state of madness at that point. Most men did. To admit it can serve no good purpose, he believed. He stared at his watch, then closed his eyes, but still saw faces, heard thunder that couldn't have come through the split log walls.

"Whoops!"

Clayton opened his eyes.

"Sorry, didn't mean to startle you. Can I help you?" The man who'd appeared behind the counter had light blue maybe green eyes behind gold-rim glasses and white hair neatly trimmed, combed straight back. Not tall, maybe five feet eight, but stocky under his golf shirt and with a healthy round face. A man who looked retired and happy doing what he liked.

"Yes, you can. I'm Clayton Spears. I'm here to rent a canoe we've been faxing about." He offered a grin he didn't feel. "To float the Yukon River?"

"Yes. Mr. Spears, yes, been looking for you. I'm the one you've been talking to." As he spoke, the man extended his hand. "Joe Gibbs, glad to finally meet you. We have everything you requested. Fifteen-foot canoe, foodstuffs, cooking utensils, medicine, extra bootlaces, slacks, insect repellant, sweaters, sleeping bag, I believe you're ready to go."

"Great," Clayton said, and reached for his wallet. "How much I owe you?"

"Let's see now, including taxes, it'll be two-thousand five-hundred fourteen-dollars and fifty-three cents. And that includes picking you up at Shell's Landing afterward, like we talked about. And oh, I put an extra paddle under the foam seat at the front of the canoe. No extra charge for that, just a precaution."

Clayton patted his pockets. Where was his wallet? "It seems I've lost my wallet. Had it in my hands a few minutes ago—"

"Take your time, son," Gibbs said.

Clayton hurried outside and was relieved to see his wallet on the ground where he'd paid the driver. He hurried back inside and counted out the bills slow onto the counter.

"Keep the difference."

"Thanks." Gibbs' features brightened as he adjusted his gold-rim glasses, picked up the money and shoved it into his trouser pocket. "First time in Alaska?"

"Flew in from Seattle three days ago," Clayton said, and nodded past his shoulder. "Nice painting. Those words on the bronze plaque below it? Can't quite read them."

Gibbs glanced around at the plaque with the casualness of someone who didn't need to. "That's Latin, I believe it's pronounced, duke et delcorum est pro patria mori. It means it's sweet and right to die for your country." Gibbs smiled.

Uncomfortable, Clayton wasn't sure he had grasped the Latin quote correctly. Gibbs said it fast. He nodded thanks and forced a return grin.

"A marvelous painting you've got there."

"We get lots of compliments on it. Believe this or not, I used to take it to the middle school, for the children to admire. Had to stop though. Some kids said their teacher said it wasn't true about Custer's Last Stand." He smiled politely, "So, you thinking about fishing, exploring, prospecting, or sightseeing?"

"Maybe all the above."

Gibbs nodded and walked out from around the counter. "Let's get you on your way, then."

Clayton grabbed up his backpacks and let Gibbs lead him out the door. As soon as they stepped off the porch, Gibbs stopped and turned. "Mr. Spears, something we talked about and I know you won't forget, but, it's the third week of July. Not too late to make the trip. You've got everything you ought to need and it's easy to see you've done that conditioning I suggested. But you'll have to finish by the last week of August. When September comes it'll snow, when it snows you won't see the ground again until spring."

Clayton nodded. "I understand—"

"I've lived here all my life and I know you think you do, but we lose at least a dozen people along the Yukon every fall. And every one of 'em thought they understood too. Most of 'em we find, but-" Gibbs looked down a moment, then lifted his eyes back to Clayton's. "Mr. Spears, even the locals'd be fools to stay out in the kind of cold and snow we get up here, at least in a canoe tripped out for summer. And remember, in about a week, you'll be at least a hundred miles from the nearest living soul. It'll be that way for a long while. Cell phones are of little use here, as I mentioned in one of my faxes. Don't venture far from the river."

Clayton nodded, wondering if he should share his thought: that he didn't give a rat's ass about any of that. Except maybe that here, at the top of the world, he'd discover something worth knowing.

They walked to the river where a canoe was moored, its camouflage color not glinting in the sunlight as the flowing water behind it did.

"Oh! One last thing," Gibbs said, and smiled. "Nothing to worry about. There's an old Eskimo who lives along the riverbank. Don't know exactly where, he won't tell anybody. Don't pay him any mind. Don't know his name, he won't tell anybody that either. He's a nut. Harmless. Just ignore him—"

Clayton opened his mouth to answer, but stopped when the lightness faded from Gibbs' face and he added, "Except, for him, be very suspicious of any stranger on foot. Even though everyone needs a little help along the way."

Gibbs stood, awkward, until he realized Clayton wasn't going to reply. Then he said, "Well, that's it. And we'll see you at Shell's Landing the last three days of August. Telephone by landline when you arrive—And oh, I need a phone number, just someone to contact in case of emergency—"

"There's nobody," he said.

Clayton put the backpacks in the front of the canoe; it bobbed from the weight. He grabbed a paddle and sat down on the shiny and warm metal seat in the canoe.

"I appreciate all you've done," he said.

"Have a safe journey," Gibbs said. "And peace be with you."

"Thanks and peace to you, sir."

That was the first time, in a very long time, someone wished him peace and it came from a stranger. It felt as strange and incomprehensible as the wilderness around him or the river pushing against the rocking canoe, eager to take him when Gibbs heaved the heavy craft out into the water.

Clayton wriggled to the center of the metal seat and crunched his shoulders to ward off the chill, shoved the paddle in the water and pushed back. The water swirled, gurgled and boiled. The canoe rocked, then slipped forward, broke free of the eddy and gained speed.

He never looked back.

Eight hours later, he glanced at his wristwatch. He doubted he'd sleep tonight. He rarely slept more than an hour at a time anyway. Maybe being alone and isolated would have an influence, just like sleep that would help a tired body and give power to the head. Finding this out mattered more right now than anything else.

Ahead, suspended twenty feet above the river to his left, a grayish precipice stretched over the water like a beveled spear point. Slopes on both sides led to the riverbank. On its top, a figure crouched in a ball adjacent to a thicket of brush.

At his first glance, he figured a bear sat on its haunches. But it wasn't a bear. Remembering Gibbs' caution about strangers on foot, he squirmed to the center of the canoe seat, shoved the paddle in the water and pushed back. The water swirled, the canoe lurched while he sculled it toward the center of the river to avoid floating underneath the overhang.

An outline of a man's wrinkled face came in view. An Eskimo, lost in contemplation. Long white hair straggled down over the dark brown and gray animal pelts covering the man's shoulders. He could've been easily mistaken for a hundred-thousand-year-old cave dweller.

Ignore him, Joe Gibbs had said, but Clayton found that impossible when the old man stood, knock kneed, bent double with a fit of coughing, shaking and trembling.

He fought to keep the canoe from rocking, unable to stop watching when the man's coughing stopped and he hurried to the overhang's ledge at a trot.

Just when it seemed the old man would go over the edge, he stopped, raised his arm and pointed a bleached bone, the femur of some large animal, directly at him.

"You there!" the man said. "I say you there! Beware the blows!"

That's what Clayton thought he'd said anyway. The man's form dissolved into another coughing fit and for a second, he thought the old man would spread out his arms and glide to the canoe.

He shoved the paddle in the water and pushed back. The water whirled and the canoe lurched forward. Best to get on the other side of the overhang and on his way. But what if the man was trying to warn him about something real?

He cupped his palm over his ear, "What, old man?"

The man jerked his arm up and waved the femur bone as if it were a wand to cast a spell. "Beware the blows don't be a fool!"

Clayton never took his eyes off the man and kept paddling. "Blows? Is that what you're saying?"

The old man's arm shot up and he shook the bone at him again, "You there! Get away! Leave! You still got a chance! You hear them they'll come. Run! Don't be a fool! Run away when you hear the blows!"

Clayton guided the canoe with the paddle until he was finally on the other side of the overhang, still mystified about the word the man had shouted. "Blows" didn't make a hell of a lot of sense to him. "Run away" did.

The canoe drifted like a ghost away from the overhang. Clayton glanced back.

The old man's head drooped forward now, drool falling from his mouth. On unshod feet, he shuffled away from the overhang's edge, mumbling to himself. But then he stopped. He jerked the femur bone up and pointed it, "You there! I say! You there! Beware the blows! Don't be a fool! Run! Run away!"

Still puzzled about the old Eskimo's words, Clayton allowed the canoe to take its own speed. While it drifted like a cloud on the surface of the water, he stood. The canoe rocked but held steady while he stretched his arms, rolled his shoulders to release tension and glanced back.

The old man had come down one of the slopes and scampered along the riverbank now, hiding behind a boulder, then a tree trunk, peeking at him all the while until he disappeared behind one bush pile.

Deciding his question wouldn't be answered here, Clayton returned to paddling and the darkening water suddenly looked peculiar as it swirled.

CHAPTER 2

Early morning three weeks into the journey, he sat on the bow of the canoe with his journal on his knee, sketching a boulder in the middle of a small stream that ran off the Yukon River. Though he didn't need to shave here, he was clean-faced this morning. After he finished the sketch he would hunt gold for a while, then continue his journey.

A speckled brown eagle glided and rocked its wings above the cool stream before it extended its legs down and clutched a bare limb. Once settled, it tucked its four-foot wingspan into its body and perched like the sculptured eagle on a totem pole. But then, it cocked its head and peered at him.

It was the first eagle Clayton had seen in the wild. His artistic juices flooded through him. Grasping his pencil, he abandoned the boulder for now and sketched the eagle. Once finished, he put the pencil to the page to write in the journal: "Today's like yesterday and tomorrow will be like today."

A passing shadow on the page told him the eagle had flown to wherever it intended to go next. He lifted the pencil from the page and closed the journal, replaced it and the pencil in a waterproof pouch in the backpack, pulled on his jeans and boots, grabbed his prospector's pan and walked along the sandbar.

The quantity of gold flakes he'd found so far wouldn't cover the bottom of a pill bottle, weren't beautiful in shape, but discovering them had added a little sweetness to his day. He never wore rings or any piece of jewelry, didn't care for the big-spender diamond rings or earrings men wore and didn't believe jewelry like that belonged on American men. He planned to keep the gold flakes and any nuggets he might find, for that special woman. If she came into his life. Maybe in time, he could hope, but it would require divine intervention now. And how could he blame her? He'd pushed his former girlfriend out of his head a little farther each day and wondered why God had made hearts with so much space.

He squatted and dipped the lip of the pan into the water, sand and gravel, then lifted the pan. A round jade with beveled edges appeared half buried, a rainbow in clouds among the brown sand, pea gravel and foam.

He stared in wide-open disbelief until he had the presence of mind to grab up the jade as though it would disappear if he didn't. He rose, grinning, examined it, turning it over in his palm, wiping it clean on his jeans. The silver-dollar-sized jade shone as if polished by a jeweler, as if some skilled craftsman had flaked and beveled the edges smooth. An outline of a wolf's head was on one side of it. The outline in the jade had a dimple for the wolf's eye and it gazed back at him.

"Kind of like my tattoo."

He'd gotten the wolf tattoo on his left shoulder not so long ago, in what seemed another life. And now, here, he'd been gifted with its priceless cousin.

A tiny round hole at the beveled edge indicated someone had worn the jade as a medallion, but the stone fit in his palm nicely, assuring him it belonged to him now.

He never had rhythm to dance or he would have. Grinning wide, he shuffled his boots in the sand and pea gravel anyway. Until an unexpected alarm sent chills through him. Unexpected, but familiar: a sniper prepared to take a headshot at him.

He raised his head slow, held his breath to hear clearer, but made out nothing but the scant sounds he'd heard these past three weeks. His eyes roved the brush, eyeing the evergreens for movement or a color shade out of place. As he did, he stretched out his hand and grabbed the prospector's pan, sprinted to the canoe. There, he jerked his pistol out of its holster, a .357 magnum that could stop a car engine running.

Standing by the canoe's bow, he listened and scrutinized every tree on the ridge, every brush pile, every boulder upstream, downstream, every facet of every object studied in detail.

After two full minutes of this, he reared back and roared with all his might. The roar echoed until it dissolved into the dry air, returning only silence.

He felt satisfied that an animal low to the ground lurked nearby and he'd scared it off. Or maybe he'd roared more from excitement about his lucky find than anything else. He strapped on his holster, shoved the pistol into it and focused his attention on the jade again.

He ran his fingers over the jewel, admiring the blue and green prisms. He guessed, believed they were blue and green. He wondered about the shape of the wolf head and how the shape could have been forged without chipping or fracturing the fragile stone.

He'd seen enough art in his life to recognize its value, but already knew he wouldn't sell it for any price. An extra bootlace made a fine lanyard and he proudly positioned the stone so it lay flat against his sternum, turned so the outline of the wolf's head looked out.

He wasn't certain, even later, but he thought several minutes passed before he heard a knocking, far away, like an axe chopping wood but not quite.

Simultaneously the songs of birds hushed, as if knowing an intruder invaded their space. Branches of trees quaked, but they, too, made no sounds. Not even the drone of insects could be heard. A quiet overwhelmed the proximity, some unseen deadly fume that killed every living sound in an instant.

For a moment, he felt he was the last being on the planet that wasn't rooted. Pulse thudding behind the jade, he held his breath, raised his eyelids and listened to orient the sounds.

No, not an axe chopping. More like two logs banging together. But again, not quite like that. The knockings echoed from up the stream to his right. A quick glance revealed nothing out of the ordinary in that direction, until he saw a dark animal a long way off, maybe a bear, slipping across the shallow bed of the stream.

He stood very still, counting off the seconds. The knocking continued for two minutes, but not in a predictable pattern. The sounds silenced. Only then could he tell the knocking's direction: the high ridge above the river.

Moving his head as slightly as he could, he looked to his right and left, front again, then finally, slowly, up to the top of the cliff.

There were trees and boulders, the slide from the cliff to the water's edge and nothing more. Logic told him at least several hundred miles of wilderness existed between him and the nearest human. That didn't matter. His bones told him other people might be nearby.

Several minutes more and the wilderness had revived with the pleasant sounds of birds. An eagle's screech farther down the stream declared all clear. And all he could feel was disappointment.

A conversation with anyone about anything would be good medicine right now, a welcomed change. Just in the past day, he'd caught himself twice, babbling like the wilderness idiot he'd met on the journey's first leg. Loneliness and boredom did that to a man; human company was the cure. At least he didn't babble in third person. Well, he didn't believe he had.

He returned the pistol to its black canvas holster. With only a passing thought, he grabbed his binoculars and hung them around his neck before climbing the steep rocky slide, leaning forward in the effort.

When he reached the top, he stopped. It frustrated him that he couldn't make out their full colors, the difference between various blues and greens being muddled now, but he knew with certainty that he was gazing down at thousands upon thousands of treetops, rolling away to meet what he was certain was a bright-blue sky. White clouds stretched to meet the earth far out on a heaving, folding green sea of treetops.

Nothing he'd read or seen captured or described with any sense of breadth the vastness of the wilderness. The weight of his binoculars against his chest made him think of his camera back at the canoe.

But photographs wouldn't be enough. He had to frame and lock away the panorama in his head, to hold it until the time was right to recall it to paint one day. If he could get up the courage. If some miracle allowed him to ever tell the difference between green and blue again.

He leaned against a tree, lit a cigarette and puffed out smoke that floated aimless as a bird. *Sometimes they're not enough words and not enough paints anyway.*

At the bottom of the mountainside, about a half-mile or better, nestled a glimmering lake in the shape of a teardrop. A meadow abutted the lake. The meadow was five, maybe eight acres, heart-shaped, wider at the northwest section. Its green grasses sparkled in the morning sun.

He raised the binoculars and aimed the lenses at the lake, increased the magnification with his nervous finger.

The water shimmered under a wavy line of mist that hovered at the lake's upper end. The lake was too small for an outdoor rigger to fly a plane into. At last, he understood what he'd read, that over a hundred thousand lakes dotted the Alaskan wilderness and most had never been fished.

A single emotion swept through him when he saw the lake alone, isolated like him. He knew he shouldn't. Gibbs' warning had been clear on that too.

He lowered his binoculars and took a deep breath, raised them again and peered through the lenses, increased the magnification, relaxed his fingers. Then, he knew he would.

Why not? He hadn't let up since the trip started, yet his mind still hadn't found the peace for which he'd hoped. A break from routine might bring order, put things in his mind on the right shelves. His canoe would be an easy walk away, a terrific place to camp, scout for artifacts and rest.

The water's clear, cold, deep and plenty of wood to build a fire. Yeah, why not?

He returned to the canoe and assembled articles to carry with him in his backpack, from food to bottled river water, to his wallet and journal in a waterproof compartment. Disassembled, his gray graphite fly rod tied neatly to loops on the pack.

He secured the canoe so it couldn't float away while he was gone, made sure his lucky blue-and-white baseball cap was snugged firm on his head, then laced up the best snake boots money could buy, ones that went halfway to his knees. He knew no snakes were in the wilderness this high up. Something he'd read about, but he didn't want to be the first person to find out otherwise. He feared snakes.

He checked the pistol's magazine though he already knew it had nine brass-case bullets with hollow-tip copper points, the kind to stop an elephant.

He lifted the pack, put his arms through the straps and leaned forward, holding the bottom with two hands and headed up the ridge. At the top he took his bearings, realized the backpack was heavier than he'd thought. The return trip, he'd worry about that later.

He descended the sloping terrain, glad for tree trunks and small limbs to grab down the thick forest of the mountainside. By midway down, the crush of timber, brush piles, ferns and moss-climbing vines were like gated barriers to keep back or lame the most determined from descending farther.

An unearthly stillness permeated the area. He listened for the finest sound, on guard for any assassin with fangs to rush out from underneath brush piles like a mad crawlspace dog.

He wiped his face with his shirtsleeve and continued to walk down the steep terrain, wishing Abby were with him. She would alert him if danger lurked nearby. He'd never own another dog like her. He shook thoughts of Abby away, wondered again why hearts were made with so much space.

Sudden exhaustion took him over. He removed the backpack, glanced back at the direction he came from. The gray-barked trees, evergreen brush piles and shadows seemed to conceal all proof anyone had walked through there. He dismissed his nervousness as being in an unfamiliar place, heaved the backpack up, pulled his arms through the straps and continued down.

After a short time, the meadow came into view through the wide-girth trees, but he stopped his advance toward it when his peripheral vision revealed a vertical gray rock on his left. He studied the formation, whose tallest section evoked a massive spear point stuck into the ground.

A covering of climbing vines and what he figured to be green moss shaded the entire formation. The rest of it, twelve flat-topped, washtub-sized boulders about waist high, made a quarter moon out from the vertical statue. His hunch: the boulders weren't positioned that way by natural forces. His curiosity piqued, he jumped over a log and walked to the formation.

The petroglyph of a woman's nude body was finely shaped, but with a wolf's head. Her right leg appeared ready to step out of the granite to the ground, yet her posture wasn't threatening. The eyes of the wolf woman gazed out, a spear in her right hand. In her left she held a leash or rope, as if she held to something that had been defaced from the granite.

Astonished, Clayton ripped away the climbing moss and other matter from the granite, exposing geometric symbols and lines that looked burned into the hard granite. The lines were wide, scorched black as though some hot finger had drawn them, the perfection of detail artistically done. On the backside of the granite were the same symbols and designs, spirals, circles, triangular shapes and horizontal lines.

The lone wolf heads on the round boulders were similar and pointed in the same direction, toward the meadow. Most amazing, the outlines of the wolf heads had similarities to the wolf on the jade medallion around his neck. In particular, the snouts were quite similar, in shape and in form, even on the wolf woman.

He'd seen the Pyramids in Egypt, studied and read about the ancient Mayans. The interest he'd picked up in college had never left him. The etchings looked prehistoric, but he didn't think stone tools could make designs so flawless in hard granite. "This is crazy," he muttered.

With regret that he hadn't thought to bring the camera, he removed his journal from the backpack and sat on a boulder, sketched the wolf woman and the spiral symbols, filling an entire page. As he lifted the pencil and prepared to turn to a fresh page—he had to sketch just the woman's face this time, to get all those marvelous details—he felt a light breeze against his neck, accompanied by a chill. Trying to not show alarm, he stood and scanned the area, listened for a full minute before he sat back down, rolled his shoulders to shed the chills that kept coming.

The sketch took form and Wolf Woman's eyes weren't peaceful or in harmony, as the engraving might in a glance indicate. Believing as he did, he idly sensed some of the spiral designs and circles possessed a warning. As the sketch took on more details, a breeze through the forest cast a shadow that brightened then darkened the wolf woman's face in rhythm. *Like she's telling me something, like maybe she's telling me to run like that old man did.* He scrunched his shoulders in defiance and hurried to finish his sketch.

Done.

He returned the journal to the waterproof compartment in his backpack, along with the binoculars, lifted the pack onto his shoulders and walked toward the lake, chastising himself when he gave in to the urge to glance over his shoulder. As he did, a crack echoed through the woods a hundred feet away.

He froze. He held his breath. Slowly, he gripped the pistol. A slow minute, then three went by. Not another sound, odd or otherwise. He decided the noise was a limb that cracked when it fell and hit the ground.

His worries calmed and he left the monolith and walked toward the meadow, decided if he had time he could return, explore and search for artifacts around the formation for keepsakes. If the fish were biting, he'd know soon enough.

It took a few minutes to reach the meadow's edge. He stopped to catch his breath and to survey it, but first glanced back at the mountainside, concluded it took an hour to walk down excluding the time he spent sketching. Figure that, plus maybe half-again, back to the canoe, longer than he'd estimated, but not a worry.

Then he took his bearings and tied two three-feet-long trail markers on a tree limb above the chest-high grass at the meadow's edge. The tapes could be spotted from any location on the other side, he believed. It was important he find the route he traveled down the mountainside so he could return on the same route. He didn't intend to be one of Joe Gibbs' statistics.

Much of the thick grass grew chest high, parting at the many game trails that spooled out across the weeds. A breeze blew, tall and short grasses and assorted-colored wildflowers leaned and swayed with barely a sound.

Across the meadow, in an open space through the timber, ripples glimmered on the lake. The urge came to sprint to the lake and get butt naked, jump in. He shivered again, not from anxiety but enthusiasm. He maneuvered slow and quiet on a game trail that meandered through weeds toward the lake.

Water oozed around the soles of his boots with each step he made. That was when the sense of peril riveted inside him, the kind you got when you were about to step on a rattlesnake. He froze midstride and looked down.

A human skull gaped back. Grasses grew out of round eye sockets, the mandible too, but moss covered the top of the cranium.

He shuddered, swallowed, stepped back slow. He couldn't believe his eyes, closed them. Opened them and peered again, scanned the vicinity. Looked back at the skull. Couldn't think past the sight.

A brown bird flew up from the grass and tweeted with all its might as it flew across the meadow. A cloud of brown birds blasted up and after it, swarming around like a devil's twister in a bleating, tweeting chorus.

The shock made his heartbeat, already galloping, jitter. It took thirty seconds, maybe more, before its rhythm calmed. His peripheral vision caught a movement of brown in the parting weeds. A thousand feelings rushed over him. The most wearisome: *Oh, hell, a moose—*

A broad head snapped up, level and then above the grass. A Kodiak grizzly peered unflinching at him from forty yards away.

Don't bat an eye, he warned himself, even as his legs wavered and tried to run without his consent. In this microsecond, he understood the encounter wasn't just beginning. The grizzly had stalked him down the mountainside. The sounds, the feeling a sniper had him in his sight, all the signs were there. He'd failed to put the signs together.

He recognized the grizzly as a blonde-tip Kodiak, a mature grizzly with a mane that stood like a heap of rusty pig iron. Nine hundred pounds, maybe more, eight feet tall minimum, its eyes were like dull-brown buttons.

The grizzly's short round ears rotated. Its broad head merged into its wide shoulders. Its front paw, the span of a concrete block, rose while it elevated its nose to sift the scents in the air. It dropped out of eyesight in the tall grass.

Then its head snapped up again.

Clayton knew he was nose to nose with the lord of the wilderness. One misstep, he'd be dead. But the ammo in his pistol could kill a grizzly. Slow, he got his fingers around the .357's ice-cold grip.

The impulse to run was strong. He would have prayed but he stood alone. He wondered who would back down first. If the grizzly let him, he gladly would.

The grizzly huffed and grunted, aggressive gestures, then it lowered its head slow and rolled its ears back.

Clayton swallowed panic, dry and hard to force down. For the first time in a long time, he tasted fear. He was a good shot with his pistol, but not that good at forty yards away through thick weeds.

A blade of grass could deflect the bullet in spite of its knockdown power. But he'd read that a bear could run at bursts better than thirty-five miles an hour, that it had the endurance of a buffalo. So running would be last-ditch, only if the bear made the first move.

Something else he'd read: a heart shot wouldn't stop a grizzly in its tracks. A bear's heart beat less than forty times a minute. A headshot or a broken back would do it, but the risks were too great to allow the grizzly eight or ten yards away should it decide to charge him.

The grizzly dropped out of sight, Clayton breathed in. Before he could breathe out, the grizzly's head snapped up again and its spine leveled out as it took a frightful leap. Weeds popped like firecrackers as the grizzly crashed through them, a brown torpedo hot for the kill.

Clayton's cap flew off as he sprinted through the grass.

The grizzly grunted and huffed with each stride as it narrowed the distance.

Its noises fueled the panic in Clayton's legs. Blood pumping, elbows swinging, he sprinted like an Olympian in a hundred-meter dash. Then he realized he still carried the backpack. Panicked, he pulled his arms out of the straps. The backpack dropped to the ground. He never lost stride.

With his backpack gone, head thrown back, arms swinging, he ran at rabbit speed through the brush, ducking limbs and pushing foliage out of his way. Brush, twigs and limbs snapped and cracked like bones as he leapt erosion ditches and undergrowth in the scramble to escape.

The grizzly's huffs and grunts abated.

Clayton shot a fearful glance back.

The grizzly was slinging the backpack side to side with its jaws. A water bottle catapulted through the air.

He looked back to see where he was running, at the thick, tangled forest before him. He had to put more distance between him and the grizzly as fast as he could.

He heard a noise and glanced back again. The grizzly had ripped the canvas backpack open and it chomped on cans as it grunted.

Clayton turned back around and sprinted for his life.

CHAPTER 3

Clayton's pistol holster rode his hip, moved in perfect rhythm with his body. He ran through tangled vines, hurled, darted and dodged everything that tried to slow him. His breath came fast and short, lungs strained until he felt his consciousness begin to slip. He slowed his pace down to a jog, then a walk. Then he stopped, faced the direction he'd run from, leaned over, grabbed his knees and breathed fast.

Sweat burned the corners of his eyes and dripped off his chin. When he could, he took his shirtsleeve and scrubbed the sweat off his face. His head turned this way and that, eyes and mind alert the entire time, vigilant until he got his wind back.

Could the grizzly have lost his scent, maybe? Or better yet, forgotten about him? One thing was sure; he couldn't be drawn into an endurance contest. If it caught up with him again, he had to outsmart it, or kill it. Pissed about getting into an encounter with a grizzly after all he'd read, all his preparation, he looked up through trees that nearly obscured the sun with the thickness of their canopy.

Rough guess, a solid ten or twelve hours of sunlight remained. Plenty of time to either escape or, if need be, kill the grizzly. He removed the medallion from around his neck and shoved it into his jeans pocket. The leather loop caught on a limb while running from a grizzly would not be his undoing.

By the time he caught his wind, he was swamped by swarms of flies, gnats and mosquitoes that hummed in clouds around him, attacking every part of his body and biting through his shirt, damp from sweat. Near the river, the insects were an occasional nuisance but nothing compared to now.

A crosswind jog through the woods left the insects to their own devices and took him into a hollow. He'd jogged the length of maybe a football field before he decided to turn right. The sun was at his back while he jogged deeper into the woods.

He'd traveled well below the lake and the meadow, but he could find his way back as long as he could see the sun. Around him were waist-high ferns, huge logs, boulders smothered in fungus that looked pale yellow to him but might have been lime green, climbing moss that rendered him mostly blind until he could rip it out of his path. Though difficult to maneuver, the rolling terrain provided cover.

He stopped and leaned against a tree to think through a plan and catch his wind. Pages from the grizzly book he'd read flipped back and forth in his mind's eye.

Climbing a tree was an option. Gravity, combined with a bear's weight, prevented a mature bear from climbing high up a tree. But the grizzly might linger around the tree until Clayton became too exhausted to hold on. Moreover, he saw no limbs near the ground stout enough to hold his own weight. To reach those required that he shimmy up fifteen feet or more. But then, the papery bark of the tree trunk would cut him like razors. He dismissed the notion.

Looking around, he wondered if the grizzly was a threat anymore. Known as a determined tracker among animals, the grizzly couldn't be too interested or he'd surely know wouldn't he? Remembering his vow, he continued to walk quiet, guarded, while he hunted for a hiding spot to bushwhack the grizzly should it come after him.

Turn the tables, take back the advantage ...

It wasn't a long time before he found an ambush spot, one he thought would provide good concealment and protection. He watched, listened. He waited for the grizzly.

The forest was as quiet as a graveyard at night. He allowed himself to think. He knew if he walked in the direction of the sun, he'd come out on the Yukon River or the side stream his canoe was on. Yet, if either river turned in another direction, he could walk for miles and never find either one before dark. He decided against attempting to return to the canoe that way.

As he waited for the grizzly, each minute stretched longer than the last one. After an hour, he thought it a reasonable assumption the grizzly no longer hunted him. He decided to return to the lake and meadow. Once there, he'd know exactly the path back to the canoe. If he had time before dark.

He was always confused about the time of day here. The sun rose up each morning and went along the horizon, then moved just below the horizon, twilight, then night. The sun never got higher than an eleven o'clock sun did in the lower forty-eight. It was hard to get used to the sun that way and this had kept him disoriented about the time of day.

He looked around, listened. Still nothing. Kept telling himself not to underestimate the grizzly. Silence meant keep listening.

Now all he had to do was walk back through the forest like he was in an urban park in the bad part of New Orleans on Friday at dusk. No problem.

He thought that no man could feel a stronger emotion than one who, for the first time, finds himself hunted by a grizzly. He left the ambush spot and began to slip toward the meadow in a crouch, consumed with stealth, not speed. He stepped careful and tried to avoid making any noise and that was impossible.

Stepping slow and quiet made him anxious and the torment was endless. He felt at any moment and from any direction something in the woods would charge out and attack him before he knew it was out there.

Little by little, daylight crept out of the wilderness. He had lost his sense of time. Hours had gone by and he still hadn't found the lake or the meadow. Either he'd wandered in the wrong direction, or he'd run much farther than he thought. He couldn't retreat to locate his original ambush spot and start over. Not enough time for that.

For a moment, he didn't know what to do and the powerless feeling he felt made him so anxious he sat down and took a deep breath. He controlled his breathing to calm the jitters. He was taught that while in the Army. It did help yet he hated the powerless feeling.

He sat there and reasoned that dead reckoning for directions using the sun's position was accurate. He knew this. He had to trust the technique or he'd be lost forever.

The forest was becoming darker. The wide logs, boulders and tree trunks once covered with climbing moss were changing to dark things. Small boulders covered with moss pushed up through ferns, looked like hippopotamus heads. The bare branches made soft creaking noises. It was becoming a challenge to keep his imagination from seeing shadows shift.

In a short time, he came upon two piles of strange-colored fungus, or perhaps hair, among the ferns and leaves. Upon closer examination the stuff didn't feel or look like hair, more like monofilament line.

It was a hell of a shock when he realized that each pile of fungus was in a circle the size of a bed sheet. At first glance, the matter looked like an animal had dissolved and left only its hair, no hide or skin or even bone fragments. The fungus seemed dead but its color was orangey, white, black, and a rust color. Nevertheless, he was stunned by the feel and by the sight of the stuff and unable to identify it or associate it with anything he'd ever known.

He left the stuff on the ground and quickstepped out of the area. He realized he had to locate the lake or meadow within an hour, or search for cover to spend the night. Thirst was starting to drain his strength. He went forward with every fiber and muscle in his body prepared to fight to the death in hand-to-hand combat.

When he saw a glittering that could only be water, relief surged up and engulfed his aching body. The relief felt great. He could hardly stand it.

On shaky legs, he emerged from the woods into a clearing at the lake's lower end. The open space had thick moss beds to his knees, boulders and thickets too.

Most important, all the water he cared to drink.

A small brook drained away from the lake. Narrow, less than knee deep, the water wiggled over sand and stone. The water's color seemed lighter than the surrounding moss, but darker than water, maybe the color of celery.

Damn, can't even tell the color of water anymore.

With an anxious heart, he snuck through the ferns to the brook's edge, dropped to the prone position and pushed his face down to drink, guzzled deep and swallowed hard. Lifting his head to breathe, water dripping from his chin, his head moving slowly to scan the area. His eyes fixed on tree limbs just up the streambed.

The limbs were covered with brown silt, algae swaying with the water's flow, like fish. Then he saw the white patches, realized he wasn't looking at tree limbs. Not at all.

He drew back, sprang to his feet.

Shuddered.

Shuddered again.

What the hell was this place? A serial killer's burial ground?

That was all he had time to think before he realized he'd been drinking from that same water. He dry heaved and it felt like an orange caught in his throat and he was choking to death. He put his finger in his mouth to vomit but couldn't.

Finally, he overcame the dry heaves but he was deeply shaken by the sight. He did not look at the bones again. He had to get out of there to return to his normal state of mind. Should have stayed focused on his first destination, would have avoided this scene. He surveyed the woods again, and began to step quiet in the direction of the lake's upper end.

So quiet were his steps, he was able to hear pops and snaps drift through the shadows and brush, like dark clouds scudding.

Stepping quiet next to a tree, the nearest cover, he slid his pistol out of its holster and let it hang relaxed at his side. Ten yards behind him was the lake, and he was grateful to be on the side of the lake he needed to be on.

Only his eyes moved while he familiarized himself with the shadows so if they altered he would observe the change from his vantage point.

A series of snaps shocked the quiet but nothing moved until an abrupt shift in the shadows forced his focus to snap slightly left. A patch of cinnamon brown at first seemed to be a shadow, until a muscled shoulder came in view, instantly followed by a broad head.

The grizzly stopped. Head raised, alert, it sniffed the air. Its broad head seemed fixed, intent on something across the lake.

Clayton's heart pounded. He felt ill. He managed to remain motionless. He sensed the grizzly hadn't scented him or spotted him by the way the grizzly acted. Though it would. He couldn't determine if this was the same grizzly but it made no difference. His best weapon was staying quiet and still until he got a clear line of sight for a headshot.

The grizzly didn't move. Then it began to move slowly with no traces of sound, a stocking-faced stalker with a switchblade.

Clayton held his breath, waited until without warning or reason, the dark shadow vanished in the thicket. Only a muted snap in the shadowy, vines, brush and limbs in the woods betrayed its location, then stillness.

Stillness.

With his thumb, he eased the hammer back on the pistol until it locked without a sound. He put his finger, feather light, on the trigger. He watched. And he listened.

In minutes the gnats, mosquitos, and flies found him. He was downwind from the grizzly, but didn't know how long he could hold out. The slightest move and the grizzly wouldn't need his scent to find him. Worse, there were no traces of sounds to betray the whereabouts of the grizzly.

He remained a statue braced against the tree until the insects' torments became unbearable. With a sinking heart, he accepted he had to do something.

If the grizzly was in the area it was less than fifty feet away. He squinted and searched the thicket, couldn't find the grizzly or hear any sound to locate it.

Then muted snaps in the thicket slowly faded away and downwind of him. It was not enough. He never saw the grizzly. He waited without moving.

Only the drone of insects stirred the air. No other sound in the thicket not even a breeze stirred. The insects were biting, stinging him. He couldn't wait any longer. He felt the grizzly had moved out of the area.

The odds were in his favor, trying to ignore the agony of the bites and stings on his flesh he resumed stealthy steps until he walked among the thick undergrowth under the tall trees.

He kept a constant vigil at his back until he emerged from the woods into a clearing at the upper end of the lake. He was jubilant.

He rushed headlong toward the meadow, not stopping until he reached the perimeter of a thicket at the meadow's edge.

Panting from the run, he holstered the pistol and stepped up on the wide end of a fallen tree, needing a better view of the meadow and to locate his trail markers.

The white ribbons swayed in the breeze, directly across the meadow. The fatigue, even the fiery itching of his flesh, fell away like dust.

A wavelike crash of branches snapping and grunts came from the brush at his back.

Startled, he jerked around, yelled in open terror and reeled backward, off the log and several feet into the thicket, landing on his back with a thump.

A brown mass bulled through the limbs and brush straight for him.

He twisted in wild distortions and his eyes narrowed to the point his vision blurred.

He pumped his boots nonstop at the blurry mass, simultaneously grappling with his holster.

The grizzly grunted, then huffed and pinned his leg with its paw. Its fangs sank into his thigh and lifted him off the ground.

Crushing jaws jerked him side to side. He was certain the grunts, cracks, and pops would be the last sounds he'd hear. He strained with all his might to free the pistol, then his head slammed against something. Leaves spiraled in a motion of boiling, tumbling arrays, direction and time vague in his shock.

At the precise instant he began to see flashes of gray limbs in his vision, the pistol came free of the holster. He pumped his right boot again. Again. Connecting, thudding against taught muscle and hard bone. The jerking and shaking continued undeterred.

He strained to raise the pistol. His right arm came up. The pistol fired once, then a second time from recoil.

The grizzly paused, let go of his leg. With a grunt, it chomped down on his leather boot. Bones popped like chicken bones.

He kicked, strained to pull the trigger. The pistol fired.

The grizzly flipped onto its side, staggered upright. Grayish-purple entrails ballooned out its side. It growled and lunged for his face.

A surge of strength shot through his right arm, shoved the pistol up from underneath, pulled the trigger.

The barrel spat fire as the grizzly's head burst open. Its legs buckled, its head and neck plummeted to the ground, pinning his waist and chest.

Wet-hot blood mixed with spongy brain matter splattered his face.

"Got ya, got ya."

Then he gasped for breath, but breath didn't come. Uncontrolled trembling overtook him and he had to fight to remain awake, to breathe. He strained to move his arms, hands and legs, fought to stay conscious, couldn't.

A roar assaulted his ears. The sound came louder, but he couldn't run. "Incoming. Incoming."

Then he came to.

One mass blur was all he could see. Before all his senses had gathered, a bug or a fly tried to crawl inside his nostril. He couldn't make his hand reach up to swat at his nose.

Hearing a twig snap, he turned his head, saw three apparitions appear. He smelled carrion breath and at the same time, a snarl of cold indifference at his face.

CHAPTER 4

The growls and snarls, low and slow at first, heightened in fervor, aiding his realization that three wolves were nearly on top of him. Thoughts clearing, his mind grasped that based on the numbers of growls and snarls, a half-dozen wolf packs were somewhere near him and the grizzly.

The grizzly's head and neck had him pinned and helpless. He stiffened, expecting the wolves' eating frenzy and his death, prayed for a quick and merciful bite to his throat to end the misery of the wait. Hardly had he breathed when the wolves turned away from him and onto each other. He'd been right; multiple wolf packs fought all round him.

They were fighting over the bear.

And me ...

The growls and deathly squeals sounded across the wilderness and swamped over his body while he fought for each breath.

An eternity passed as the chaos and bedlam of the fighting moved away from the thicket, through the meadow and into the forested timber, their initial goal apparently forgotten.

But for how long?

To stay sane, Clayton ticked off the seconds in his head, counted sixty-seven before the fighting sounds dissolved into silence. The quiet that settled over the wilderness was just as unnerving as the fighting had been. He waited for the peace of death.

Something moved. Something walked in the stillness. The steps were like the sound conveyed by a chilly breeze through branches and weeds, slow as though an animal slinked through them. The breeze crept, the leaves shuddered, the weeds quickened. The breeze quieted until silence shrouded the vicinity in a strange stillness.

Then a breath sneaked over and around his body, like the nose of a wolf gathering and debating his scent.

He was shocked by how quick the enigma stood over him. His heart hammered. He lay still, certain a wolf gathered his scent. He remained rigid and waited for his throat to be ripped out. He listened.

It seemed an eternity before the enigma slipped away hiding its exit among the rattling weeds and darkened shadows.

It seemed a long time, before his heart, more optimistic than its owner, pounded with relief. He hadn't heard any more wolves or strange sounds. He wondered if fate had dealt him a lucky draw. He felt no one could be so lucky. But he was alive. Barely, but he was breathing still.

His relief ended when he realized the alpha wolf pack was simply distracted by the need to show dominance. In time, they would return to claim their spoils.

He lay still and tried to listen, to occupy his mind with his thoughts, to keep him away from the pit of nothingness. Then he heard buzzing, humming, buzzing in the air. The insects returning for their meal, surely.

He knew he was badly injured. He could hardly breathe, couldn't see clearly and it was a safe bet he'd be eaten alive by predators within the next twenty-four hours, no more.

But what frightened him most were the buzzing sounds in the air around him coupled with the sensations he felt in his right thigh that told him the flies had turned on him. He'd seen a human body ravaged by maggots.

His panic worsened when the light-headiness came. If he passed out again he might not wake up and the flies, which went for the soft tissue first, could get to his eyes then.

There was nothing else for him to do, nothing else he could do but fight with all he had against the embrace of nothingness. He tried to move his arms, hands and legs, but they felt nailed to the ground.

Then he smelled a foulness that pulled him back from the sensation of drugged awareness. Each breath reeked with putrid vapors of pungent musk and rancid guts. Each breath dragged him back up, each one fouler than the last. He floated up, then opened his eyes, smelled the grizzly's brains and heard flies swarming, busy with their chore. His stomach churned. After a series of spasms, each deeper than before, he choked his guts out.

Yet, he was fully conscious now. In that sense, the grizzly had saved his life though he was fully aware his body had been weakened by injury and shock. But his distorted vision concerned him the most. He wondered if maggots had fouled his eyes, his sight was so profoundly blurred. Somehow, blind or not, he had to move away from the grizzly, else he'd be another pile of bones in the wilderness.

He tried to move again, forgetting the beast's head lay on his diaphragm, pinning him. He gritted his teeth and strained to shove the head off, and did. It was immediately easier to breathe and each breath brought more clarity of thought.

Next, he had to leave the dead grizzly before its blood scent charmed every predator's nose in the wilderness. Now that he could move a little, he wasn't worried about the wolves, or as frightened of them. He suffered no illusion though. If he didn't move, if he appeared dead or helpless, they'd put their fangs into his flesh as quick as they would the grizzly's.

It had become quite simple to him once he put all the facts together. Either he lived or he died; the choice was his to make. He would fight to live. What he did in the next minute, the next hour, the next day, that's what truly mattered. Not even his past mattered, even if it would never yellow and fade with time, as he'd hoped when he started his trip down the Yukon.

Blinking his eyes repeatedly brought no improvement to his sight. His vision was like peering under light but murky water without a facemask and he couldn't attribute that entirely to the nearing nightfall—lighter spots in the blur told him it remained bright daylight. He remembered it was almost late evening when he was attacked. He must've been out longer than he'd thought, maybe a full day, maybe two.

Perhaps time would bring his sight back, perhaps not, but he didn't have time to wait. He had to make a plan and then act on it.

His first attempt confirmed he wouldn't be walking out of here. He could crawl, though, discovered by rolling into the prone position.

Once the pain from that lessened, ten seconds later, he'd moved four, maybe five feet forward. With practice and luck, he might be able to get up on his right knee. Dragging the left leg, the worst wounded, would slow but not stop him. He could move now.

But to where? He had to figure that part out now, while he could at least guess at where he was. Getting turned around and disoriented while crawling to the canoe, without vision, would be a death sentence. Less odds of surviving than of shooting a BB through a half-inch circle from a hundred yards on a windy day. He couldn't make that shot in a lifetime.

He spent thirty precious minutes evaluating and sorting through a plan, a route out of the thicket where he lay. During the process, he exercised his arms and neck, his right leg and torso. His left ankle was the breath freezer and the heart taker, but the exercises loosened the remaining stiffness in his muscles and gave him back his body. Maybe that would make the crawling easier.

The bite wounds in his left thigh had light prickling sensations, but a little investigation told him they came from maggots already ingesting the bad flesh. In his mind, that enemy had become a friend; he'd read somewhere they were beneficial for getting rid of dead tissue and infection. He decided to permit them to coexist with him until he evicted them in the cold water of the lake.

As soon as he could figure out in which direction it lay. Unable to see it, he decided to find the log he'd stood on before the grizzly's attack. He recalled that the log's bulky base pointed at the lake and that the lake was no more than forty yards away. Not only would the water aid his wounds, but maybe also his eyes. The water could be a fortress against predators.

With a lot of straining, he struggled up to lean his back against a slender tree. It took at least five minutes before the sensation of rocking and floating left his head. His headache didn't feel as bad as it did an hour before and he was thankful for that little gift of hope.

He felt the ground and found his pistol, shoved it into its holster. He wasn't sure how many bullets remained, but figured a case of them might not be enough. So he didn't delay to count them, just felt around until he located the log, dragged himself along it until he found the widest end. In the prone position, he stretched out his hands to grab brush, sticks and grasses, anything he could grab hold to while he pulled and dragged himself forward inch by inch.

Although crawling was tough and frustrating work, he felt his body grow stronger, not weaker as he'd expected. His muscles responded and cooperated well. He began believing he could walk if he had support, but first things first. He had to get into the water of the lake, if for nothing else than to soothe the aches and soreness, and above all, the water might shock his vision clear.

At times, the gash in his left thigh caught on branches or sticks. Grit and plant matter got into all the wounds and his eyes. Limbs snapped and whipped against him like bee stings. The insects found him, bit and stung every exposed part of his body.

Every inch of each yard he crawled was earned and paid for with heart-stomping pain, freezing grimaces, freezing breath, tears, sweat and grass burns on his bare skin. Sometimes the pain in his left leg and ankle was so agonizing it pickled his brain. Each time, he had to still his body for five or ten minutes just to catch his breath.

Once he recovered his strength, he'd crawl another foot or two, knowing the pain he felt five minutes before would strike again. Yet each foot he achieved raised his optimism and breathed life into his endurance. After what seemed a month, he thought he was nearing the lake, grabbed a handful of weeds to pull himself forward.

A twig snapped in the weeds ten yards out from him, to his left.

He froze, uncertain. Listened.

What he was sure about: he hadn't made the noise.

Something, something large, slipped in the weeds. It walked slow and careful, then stopped again. Twenty seconds passed this way before he made out a hulking, blurry enigma that slipped forward, then stopped again. He held his breath, reached down and eased the pistol out of its holster, brought it forward.

CHAPTER 5

The weeds rattled as the enigma slipped forward … and stopped again. The distance and his blurred vision prevented him from learning anything more than he already suspected. The animal was either a moose or a caribou. Any move he made could trigger its charge, it would stomp his guts out before he could get off a shot. He felt certain the animal had already spotted him. A predator behaved with randomness, unless it had identified an easy meal.

The blurry animal stepped forward. A thunderous whooshing snort announced its presence. At the sound, a jolt vibrated Clayton's body.

But then, the animal wheeled and ran through the brush. Swishing weeds, cracking limbs and splashing water sounded the unknown animal's path. The assorted noises trailed out of hearing. His anxiety released its grip. The animal was a moose, he was certain now.

Two minutes passed before he realized the splashing sounds pinpointed the lake, it was ten yards ahead. Unhurried, he leveled himself onto his hands and raised his head above the weeds. From this position, he made out a wide gap between the sky and two blurry jagged lines of treetops. He listened to water lapping on rocks along the shoreline, the sounds were as pleasant a carol as any bird could sing.

With the renewed strength of hope, he shoved his pistol into its holster, stretched out his hand to grab anything he could hold to pull himself forward. He hadn't gone far when a light breeze pushed against the weeds and the stalks rattled lightly. For a moment, there was deep silence, then the stalks moved and seemed to band together ten yards to the right of him.

He froze in place, listened intently for an animal's stealthy steps, for sounds of rattling weeds. Nothing, yet he felt an undercurrent warning him to stay still and tried to ignore the irritating insect bites. His neck hair prickled and sweat formed on his brows and scalp.

After another minute, he hadn't heard any more noise of movement, no rustlings, nothing. He eased his hand back to grab the pistol. During the process, he felt a smooth stone in the weeds. His first notion was the stone could be a weapon, to bash or break bone.

Scarcely had he grasped the stone in his palm than his fingers and his palm sent a message. The object didn't feel like a stone. It was smooth, light and hollow … another human skull.

In panic, he rose off the ground hobbling, stumbling forward in a scramble to reach the water. Pain struck his head and he felt faint. At that moment, a gale force wind crashed through the weeds and attacked him.

He yelled as he lost his balance and fell among the weeds. Simultaneously his flesh was twisted, pulled and yanked as his torso was dragged from side to side. Blurry silhouettes growled and legs trampled on and off him. Pungent musk flooded his nose.

He felt pain, but wouldn't accept it, refused to become Joe Gibbs' next lost traveler in this unforgiving place. A man ablaze, he rolled, punched and kicked wolves amid the noises of growling and crackling weeds.

Before he realized it, he was on his feet stumbling forward, dragging wolves in a frantic scramble to reach the water. He grappled for the pistol, but dropped it.

The loss of the pistol didn't matter. He couldn't, wouldn't allow the wolves to hold him back from the water. He dragged them through the weeds along with him until the ground gave way, then gasped as the free-fall sent him down the bank to splash into the water.

Wolves jumped into the ankle-deep water with him but they weren't as aggressive now. He pushed up, sloshed and stumbled forward, splashing face down into the water again. Just as quick, he pushed up and hobbled after the blurry images.

The images scurried up and onto the bank. He dropped to his knees in the water, panting for air. A group of wavy gray-and-black images appeared on the shoreline, moved along the water's edge and stopped. Warning snarls wove through the air, as though the bandits wanted him to know they watched from the weeds and timber. The images moved along the shoreline, merged into one murky enigma of phantom snarls that glided, then vanished into the quiet.

Shaken and terrorized, he was suddenly stricken by the idea that the apparitions had laughed, and still laughed at him. He felt a budding inside him, a choking power that rose from the depths of his being. He fought to restrain it, clinched his fists until he felt he would implode. In his vision came the memory, of groping around, in pain, on a filthy floor in a lightless room that reeked of sweat, urine, concrete dust, pungent powder, burnt skin, of fish. And laughter. Laughter, while he wrenched in agony.

He shook his head to dislodge the odors and the laughter, but something inside him had popped like a ruptured water pipe and the memory kept coming. At that instant, he would've struck the devil had the devil stood in his way. Only one thing drove him now, the knowledge that he'd become a wild and dangerous man that only a headshot could stop.

Blood from the bites trickled from his face, mouth and nose. Spurred on by rage instant and recalled, he struggled to his feet, sloshed and hobbled forward toward the shoreline and toward the apparitions, intending to rend them to pieces with his bare hands. But his trembling body wouldn't allow him farther. The phantasms were gone and his rage flamed higher. With his feet anchored on the lakebed, he boiled in oil. He roared.

Several minutes passed and the fire burned itself out. He closed his eyes and leaned his head back to gaze up, not at the sky he could no longer see, but at the memory. He had ruptured a volcano inside him that had bulged for two years, a boiling caldron of what was done to him in war. He had always suppressed it, but not this time. He wasn't aware of the breeze in the trees or the water lapping rocks on the shoreline, yet he was aware of where he was.

After some time, sweat dripped off his chin and water dripped off his fingers. He didn't know how long he'd stood there in the water, eyes closed, when he felt the last of the anger hemorrhage from him. When it left, it was replaced with surprise.

He couldn't imagine how he lost control like that. He hadn't been raised to lose control. Quite the opposite. He was taught that only a foolish man loses control, or their temper. He had no explanation for his behavior and didn't want to go through it again. As much as anything had so far, it frightened the hell out of him.

His mind sobered, now he could feel the tremors swamp his body, from the cold as much as the release of remembered rage. Knowing the water would offer some protection, he limped back, slow and quiet, until he stood in water to mid-calf. His throat was dry and scratchy. He cupped his hands and sipped the cool water, found it clean and refreshing.

The tremors at last calmed to twitches in his mauled hands and fingers. Though growing weaker, he felt lucky. Yet he needed more than luck to survive now. He needed a good hiding place until his blurred vision improved. He needed to survive the next minute, the next hour, the next day. That mattered to him now. It mattered a hell of a lot. No other consideration mattered.

His left boot had kept his broken ankle in line and restricted the swelling. The water almost numbed the ache now, but the bracing cold didn't help his eyes. That caused him to worry some and he didn't want to worry, because he had made it to the water.

He held on to the left side of his face and shuffled into knee-deep water. At the same time, he realized there were more bite wounds on him than he'd expected. He wasn't angry at the wolves. Wolves did what's natural for them to do. They'd only claimed the dead grizzly and as nature intended, saw him as their next prey. With his fingertips, he tenderly rubbed the bite wounds, tiny anthills on his face and arms, cupped his hands and splashed water on them until the cold numbed them.

He knelt and ducked his face underwater, swallowed the icy liquid until his cheeks bulged, rose up, rinsed out his mouth and spat. Ducking his face under water, he blew air through his nose again and again. Each time he opened his eyes they still burned. His vision had to improve. Without good sight, the lake could be his tomb. Still he pushed the notion out of his head, not wanting to think about anything that could discourage him now.

The throbbing in his bad ankle returned. Soon, he'd be back to crawling. Another memory nudged at him, but this one didn't cause the rage to return.

He took what was left of his shirt and tore it apart, wrapped his thigh and made a bandanna for his forehead, for safekeeping of the extra cloth. He wrapped cloth around his left hand, his left bicep, with what cloth remained he made a hand-sized pad. This, he soaked in the cold water and pressed against the bite wounds on his face, then cocked his head against the pad, relishing the easing of the pain even when it made his breath hitch.

And suddenly, his sight cleared. Not wanting to waste good fortune that might end any second, he blinked and looked around, deciding where he could go next. More luck: for the first time in memory, he could see colors, sharp and clear. The miracle lasted maybe ten more seconds before a hodgepodge of neon lights blinked inside his head. Then a flash and his vision sank into distorted grays and blacks worse than before.

He sighed and whispered, "Well, at least you saw a little." Along with that came an important perception. Even if he couldn't see blues and greens, there were sights to be enjoyed. Now, he regretted that he'd damned his once perfect vision just because he couldn't distinguish between blues and greens anymore. If his vision ever returned, he wouldn't wish to see colors again, no, never. He'd enjoy the sights just as they seemed and be thankful.

He remembered the jade medallion, pulled it out of his pocket and pulled it over his head and around his neck. The jade rested against his chest. The smoothness of the jade, such a little thing, lifted his spirits. He tried to see the jade's colors in his mind's eye but that eluded him. No matter. That he could see it at all, was alive to feel it, was enough.

After he sorted through a hundred options, he decided the south end of the lake with the brook would be the best location to hide from predators until his vision improved enough to make the trek out. The area around the brook, as he recalled, had plenty of floral matter such as ferns, moss, thickets and brush piles to hide in. Even with his blurred vision, he could construct a temporary shelter.

Grateful his broken ankle was still numb and secured by the boot, he waded knee deep along the shore until he reached the lake's lower end, a laborious and breath-freezing process.

More strenuous work, he crawled up a five-foot bank onto the shore. There, he groped and felt the ferns all round, located a few limbs and moss. From them, he made a miniscule lean-to and made a bed out of the mulch as best he could. Under the circumstances, the shelter had to do. Then he spread mud over his exposed skin to keep the insects off him, something he'd read the Indians and ancients had done and wished he'd remembered before now.

For several minutes he assessed his physical condition and the more wounds his fingers felt, the less he felt, except a knowing that he'd reached the end of his endurance. He lay in the sun's waning warmth and tried to fight off exhaustion, but what little strength he had siphoned off quickly and he went unconscious.

It seemed only a second passed before thunder cracked as if artillery had fired over the valley. The ground trembled and rain fell hard through the lean-to's branches, cold droplets hit his flesh. A rush of pain hit in his left ankle. Then a flash came in the pitch black and the ground quivered again. The wind, rain and darkness frightened him. Blind or not, he knew he must leave the wilderness at first light.

If he didn't succumb to hypothermia first.

If the wolves didn't find him.

CHAPTER 6

He was clean-shaven when he entered the wilderness and now his beard was at least six inches long. This, he knew. And he knew he had to remain very still. He listened as two animals sneaked into the weeds, held his breath until they stopped.

In a painful grunt, he lashed out with a short, stout limb and clobbered only the weeds. As happened each one of the past eight attempts to take the grizzly away from the wolves, the animals escaped unharmed and scampered through the weeds, out of his hearing.

The wolves were savvy now to his efforts to lure them in close, yet to some degree feared him now. His belly had become frightful, ready to devour anything and everything that crawled or walked. He felt his entire body had become the belly of a locust, ravenous and unrelenting. His hunger pangs had created a dungeon in his mind, one containing a dragon without conscience, without remorse, without pity. Hunger cramps controlled him like iron constraints. He realized now that the most dangerous were those whom were hungriest. And that desperate people made unpleasant choices to stay alive at times. The time had come for him. At no time in his life could he have imagined the choice he made. But he made them.

He groped blindly to grab weeds to pull forward. His fingers and palms no longer felt the stings or burning cuts of the weeds were callused and tough. The odors of the grizzly's carcass swamped all pleasurable scent, now each breath was a dismal boom box of putrid sickness.

He stopped to rest and pinched his nose.

The snarls of wolves around him sounded more of disdain for him than anything else. They tolerated him and had for some time, he could tell they'd let him closer to the dead grizzly each of his past attempts. In spite of his blurry vision, he knew the area in the weeds at the upper end of the lake almost like the cuts and sores on his fingers and palms, could visualize the jagged tree line, the proximity of the lake, knew the stench of rotting flesh.

Even after many attempts to find his pistol and articles from his backpack, he had managed to survive without them. Barely, but he was still alive and swinging a club. And in the night, it was the fights, the strange howls, snaps and swishing of weeds that assured him he was alive for another minute. The decision to leave his shelter and try for the grizzly was second best.

All attempts to crawl out and back to the canoe had failed in the fear of getting lost forever. Yet he had to somehow overcome what fate had dealt him. He had to eat, or starvation would take him, as it had the owners of those skulls and bones. The arctic cold had run off the insects, so he'd consumed worms, grubs, centipedes and flies, any insects his fingers felt, whatever his hands touched that wiggled or moved. He had subsisted on slimy algae in the lake, but it made him sick and nauseous now. If he could kill one, just one wolf, he could eat enough to stay alive. But, the wolves were too cagey.

He pulled closer, hearing sounds that had tormented him for days now. He didn't want to eat the grizzly. He wanted to eat the fresh meat of a wolf.

Please ... please wolf come in closer ... please Mr. Wolf, just a little closer please ... please a little closer ... will you please ... please ... help me ... just come closer and smell me ... I smell like you ... please ... please—

He lashed out with the stout limb.

The wolf sprinted away unharmed. He knew the wolves were full from eating on the grizzly or from other prey, was glad for this. Hungry enough, they would have made a meal out of him. Yet they denied him access to the grizzly. His grizzly. It belonged to him and he planned to take it from them soon, one way or another.

His legs betrayed him constantly. His left ankle and his leg below the knee had numbed days ago and stayed that way. The wetting and drying of his leather boots did nothing to help, but the tight boot kept the swelling down and his left ankle in line. He hadn't removed that boot since the grizzly hurt him. He was afraid to.

He waited for a wolf to approach him, lashed out again with the short limb. And hit nothing but weeds. He chided himself for having considered the predator-prey dance as some marvelous poetic death struggle. He'd never think about it like that again. If he got his vision back, he'd paint without the greens and blues, instead use reds, violent reds. And grays too, to show the true cruelty of Mother Nature's beauty. He'd paint her that way, if he survived.

Although he'd changed with the discovery of a new type of hunger, he knew his situation couldn't be defeated by the discovery of a new way of thinking. It would take more than an idea to save him now. It would take a fresh kill of a wolf or a miracle and he didn't believe in miracles and never would.

He raised his head to peek over the weeds. Something whooshed over his head. He jerked his head to the ground.

Another whooshing, like a boomerang's whizzing.

What the hell was that?

Suddenly, the air he breathed filled with the fragrance of basil. He was mystified for moments then he felt he was becoming delusional. No. He smelled basil. He was sure the fragrance was basil. No mistake.

Finally, he shifted his position, too unnerved to assess what was going on and crawled back toward his shelter, to rest. Then, whooshing noise or scent of basil or not, he'd go back and test the wolves' resolve once more.

The mud he caked on his skin to keep off the insects started to feel sticky. He had become feverish. Sweating, he went to sleep, woke in his fragile shelter with the notion that something wasn't right. He heard the familiar rattling, swishing of weeds, but then, all went still.

Through the spaces in the foliage, a blurred enigma that seemed to sparkle moved furtively among the timber, stopped next to a tree.

He blinked sleepily at the image, certain it wasn't real but the product of the fever.

The enigma seemed like a mirage of autumn leaves through smoked glass. It made jerky movements, then, the enigma became stationary. It remained stationary half hid behind a tree for a long time before the enigma seemed to vanish in the shadows without a sound.

Perhaps a kind of animal he hadn't seen before. His mind worked in a fury trying to decide what it was but it did no good. He watched and listened for sounds for a long time.

Finally, his apprehensions waned, though he'd shaken the hand of fear many days ago and had become acquainted with it. It amazed him how he so naturally accepted the malevolent sounds in the night, accepted his blurred vision, the nuisances of animals sniffing his hiding place; he accepted the pain in his left leg and foot and the agony of the festering bites on his face and hands.

He had made a hundred adjustments in mind and in body. It would take more than a blurred image to frighten him now. Some might say he was insane, maybe he was. His hunger pangs had seen to that.

When he came to a second time, it was dark, cool and windy. He cramped up, vomited and lay back wincing in pain and heat that burned his entire body. The fever flattened his scant optimism of survival. He stifled his disappointment by going back to sleep.

* * *

Even at the first moments of daylight, the surroundings were darker than when the sun was out; clouds blocked the sun. The wind still blew, but the temperature had dropped dramatically. He told himself it was the mud on his body, not the fever that helped keep him warm to some extent. There were no drones of insects, only the cold wind lashing at his hiding place. And the hunger he'd thought couldn't get worse was ten times worse.

He put the jade medallion back on and prayed it would bring him luck. The jade had become his friend, his best friend. He felt the lines, the edges of the pendant, thinking how it brought him hope every time he palmed it and put it on. It was the dearest thing he owned, though he could never see the colors in his mind.

Now, he resolved to roll the dice. This time, he would take that grizzly away from the wolves or he would become another pile of bones in the wilderness. It was a slow, laborious process to crawl a little way. The fever was what finally stopped him. He lay rigid on the ground, quaking with chills. No more need to ponder his chances of making it out now. He would know soon.

He hadn't lain long when he heard confusing sounds in the weeds. He raised his head and listened. From a distance came a jingling like tiny Christmas bells. Then silence, but one that lasted only a moment before the strange musical chimes filled the air of the meadow and the nearby forest.

He listened, disbelieving, for a long time, hearing nothing more, rolled onto his back, unable to think of one explanation why that sound would be in the wilderness. It had to be the fever, or the pain in his body, or perhaps the final stage of starvation setting in.

A stealthy blur loomed over him, on him before he knew it was there. He froze but his right hand moved, trying to locate the stout limb.

Twigs snapped and cracked underfoot. Tall, wavy apparitions appeared, separated, merged like dark gray images in a photographic negative. A wide and strange rust-colored mirage loomed, then stooped, walked around him. The odor of spoiled meat and leather permeated the air, together with noises. The only one he recognized was the warning snarl of a wolf.

Bewildered, Clayton watched what he could see in his blurred vision. Or what he thought he saw. The enigma seemed to have arms and it walked upright. That couldn't be true, though. It was the fever, or the starvation working on his mind.

The image loomed above him and swayed, seemed other than the distorted illusion. Then, the image dropped toward him, but before he could move out of its way, warm breath flowed lightly over his lips, nose and cheeks.

"Don't be frightened," mumbled a feminine voice.

He didn't breathe. He didn't dare to breathe.

He listened.

He knew the words weren't made by the winds, couldn't have been. He blinked, blinked again. No help. He breathed. He felt sure at that moment he was dying and his mind was making the process pleasant.

For a fierce minute, the image was at his face and its breath swept over his lips and cheeks. He couldn't determine if the face was human. The image rose, looking to him like an orangutan with gangly arms and auburn fur. Then leaves crunched, the wavy-orangey silhouette loomed over his face once more, bringing the tender breath flowing over his face again.

"Don't be afraid," the feminine voice said, with breath full of sweetness in this fetid place.

His mind was so turbulent now, he scarcely believed or fathomed what he had heard. It was certainly a woman's voice, one that carried a soothing quality in tone.

Although fearful, he was more afraid of being in a nightmare. That meant he might wake up. He did not want to wake up, hell no he didn't want to wake up.

"Don't be frightened," said the voice.

Dare he speak and risk this being a dream that would end at the sound of his voice? He tried, a gurgle flew wild from his mouth. He listened to soft mumbled chatter in reply, knew it wasn't the wind or his mind.

His blurred vision created more mystery when it seemed the images were placing something on his left leg. Not placing, forming something on his left leg. He felt nothing.

Through the haziness, he saw what looked like a saint out of the Bible, floating in umber glow. Mysterious sounds he recognized as voices came, other voices, their garbled nature confounded him as thoroughly as his blurred vision had. He fought it, but unconsciousness suddenly wanted to take him. He fought back, harder than at anything he had struggled against so far.

After what seemed a lifetime, he realized he wasn't in a nightmare and that was good. And that someone, maybe a rescue party, had found him. No one could have known where to look for him. And yet, someone had found him.

But who ...?

He thought back to the old Eskimo at the river, back to the odd noises he'd heard before. Joe Gibbs' warning assailed his mind. Were those who found him his saviors, or worse?

It didn't matter, he decided.

The voice continued, he clung by his fingernails to each word that stirred over his cheeks and lips. His mind pleaded it not be a dream, his grip tightened to each word as he went unconscious listening to the sweetest voice.

CHAPTER 7

Snow freewheeled among branches and covered the ground. Treetops quaked and leaned, as if to pull up roots to run with the wind. The gray clouds seemed a troubled sea.

Clayton blinked repeatedly, gradually became aware he wasn't dreaming. That he could see.

He could see clear as ever.

Thank God …

A set of emotions sailed through him. In exhilaration, he braced and strained to push up. At the same instant, a violent streak of pain shot through his head. He grabbed his head and slumped back.

Hardly had he settled back when he realized his right ankle was bound to a stake in the ground. Scarcely had he frozen in disbelief at the stake than a graveled testosterone voice rumbled, "Can you see me?" and mingled with the noises of the frigid wind. Startled, Clayton turned to the voice.

Before he could reply, he found himself staring at a heavy broad face and near slanted dark eyes. An Eskimo sat on the snow, his back against a leafless tree, legs folded, wide gray mittens resting one on each knee, below a fur parka that displayed a profusion of black, gray, white and orange shades.

Clayton's heart pounded with a hundred questions, but he nodded and blurted. "Yes." The man's question not fully realized in his head.

The Eskimo pulled off one gray mitten and scratched his leathery neck nonchalantly. Then he smiled.

"Do you hurt?" he asked while he shoved his thick hand back into the mitten.

With Clayton's strongest effort, he mumbled hoarsely, "Don't know exactly. My body feels numb all over."

The man considered this in silence, then grinned. Finally, he said, "It's probably because of your fever. My name's Nokatuhuma, pronounced Nock-CU-Too-Ma. You can call me Tuma. And I believe you're Clayton Spears, it's hard to say from the picture in your wallet. You have a black beard and long brown hair now. My daughter found a wallet and knives and a book with drawings on the ground near the spot we found you. We believe the belongings were yarned."

Yarned? Clayton wondered what yarned meant, but his curiosity was overwhelmed by wondering about the last item the man had said.

Book. My journal. He hoped they hadn't read it. He shook away all thoughts of the journal. He would think about it later. His fear waned, but not his apprehensions as he remembered Gibbs's warning about strangers. That his leg was tied to a stake didn't help ease his mind. He couldn't crawl anyplace in his condition. He resented being tied, the last time he was, the consequences were bad. Yet until he figured out this man's intentions, he had to be calm and polite. He nodded and said, "Thank you, Tuma. Yes, I'm Clayton Spears."

Tuma grinned and stared thoughtfully with brown eyes as flat, fierce and quick as his smile. On his right cheekbone was a purple scar the size of a golf ball. The scar sunk into his tanned skin, the wound had healed poorly. The taut skin of his cheeks made the scar appear a decoration, some bizarre badge of courage. His right eyebrow was lower than his left and his right brow wiggled slightly with each word he spoke.

Clayton didn't wish to seem impolite or ungrateful but he had to return to his canoe with his journal. If he was tied to the stake because Tuma feared Clayton would harm him, surely the man would be happy to be rid of him. He sighed nervously and said, "Tuma, could you help me to my canoe?"

Tuma stared. Finally, he said, "Where's your canoe?"

Clayton felt reluctant to volunteer any more information than he had to, but to get back to his canoe, he needed help. He said, "On a small stream off the Yukon River."

Tuma nodded, looked at the snow on the ground and then looked up. "We're far from the Yukon River," he said, unemotional. "All the water is freezing, so you wouldn't go anyplace in your canoe. If you tried to, you would die in a day or so. When my daughter comes back, we must leave here before the snow blocks the mountain pass out. We must travel to our winter campgrounds. You're safe with us."

"Winter campgrounds?"

Tuma nodded.

Clayton tried to hide his shock. He'd felt certain he was still near the lake where he'd lost consciousness, but now he wasn't sure where he was. Nothing seemed as he remembered it. The timber here was wide and thick as corn, the ferns waist high, he couldn't make out the valley's rim or the mountain range as before.

Yet, the last time he'd seen either, it was late summer. The snow all around him should have already told him that more time had passed than he thought. Though he didn't care, he asked the first question that came to mind, "How far are we from the winter campgrounds?"

Tuma surveyed the darkening forest and glanced over his shoulder, as if he'd heard a noise above the wind and snow.

"A long way. The journey will go fast though."

Now, he cared. He wanted to demand to know exactly where he was, insist he be taken back to the river so he could take his chances getting out of the wilderness. But though he had no reason to, he trusted Tuma's assessment.

Maybe he didn't have to go with Tuma. Perhaps there was a village somewhere around, maybe close to here, somewhere he could stay until his bearings returned. Buoyed by that possibility, he said, "Uh, I'd really like to get back to my canoe if I can. Is there a village nearby?"

Tuma's eyebrow twitched, "The nearest village is where we're going. We have many pelts to keep you warm. You can ride in my daughter's sled."

Clayton sighed and rubbed his brows. He felt miserable, knew the fever was wreaking havoc on him. He had no strength to resist, only to endure.

"Thank you," Clayton said. "How did you find me?"

Tuma looked around, distracted by the wind in the trees. But after a moment, he turned his intense brown eyes back to Clayton. "My daughter's pet wolf found you when we were passing through on our way to the mountain pass. I thought you were dead, but when I told my daughter that Snow Wolf found a dead man, she wanted to see for herself and saw you breathing. I was sad I had left you. The jade-green rock you had around your neck is in my pouch and your billfold, knife and book are someplace, I know not where, my daughter Palafox has those things."

Clayton glanced at Tuma's neck, saw him clutching a teardrop-shaped brown leather pouch nestled among three colorful trinket necklaces. He wouldn't ask for the jade's return now, though he wanted to. But he wasn't leaving the wilderness without it.

Tuma stood and went to Clayton's right leg, unsheathed his knife and cut the leather strip that tied his leg to the stake. As Tuma shoved the knife back into its scabbard, he said, "I did that so you couldn't crawl away."

Instead of returning to the tree, he sat and folded his legs next to Clayton's shoulder.

Tuma said, "You tried to crawl away all the time while you slept."

Clayton listened, wanting to believe him.

Tuma leaned forward, "Brother, your reasons must have been good for coming into the sacred valley of the wilderness. How did you find the sacred valley?"

Sighing, Clayton looked at Tuma. "I don't know what you mean. I saw a lake from a mountain and I couldn't resist the urge to fish it. I almost made it."

Tuma looked keenly interested, "What happened?"

Clayton closed his eyes. "I was attacked. A big grizzly."

Tuma sighed and leaned back, "Good reasons are just as dangerous as bad reasons for coming into the wilderness. Was anybody else with you?"

Clayton opened his eyes and shook his head side to side.

"Did you kill that grizzly I found near the lake?"

Clayton thought a long moment. He felt unsafe and worried. In preparation for his trip, he had studied the laws. The law for killing a grizzly in Alaska without a permit could get you more time in prison than armed robbery. An overzealous prosecutor could trump up a scenario whereby killing the grizzly was an unnecessary killing. But, in his condition he had nothing to lose. He leveled his eyes at Tuma, nodded, "Yes. I killed a grizzly near a lake."

Tuma grinned wide and shrugged, the scar under his eye seemed to glow. "That grizzly would've killed anybody on sight. That grizzly always behaved like it had a broke tooth in its skull. He almost got Palafox and me three seasons ago. Twice! I still dream about that grizzly."

"The grizzly nearly killed me," Clayton said. "I'm lucky to have survived this long. I was attacked by wolves there as well."

Tuma's eyes opened wide, "Wolves! You've had very bad luck and very good luck in another way. Did you kill a wolf?"

He stared at Tuma's dark eyes. "No. Not because I didn't try to kill one, to eat." He would have said more, but a coughing fit overcame him. When it ended, he saw Tuma grinning.

Tuma leaned forward, "If they were arctic wolves you wouldn't be here. The arctic wolves would have eaten everything, your dungarees, boots and belt. Palafox's pet wolf is an arctic wolf. Powerful wolves. Always hungry. It's early for arctic wolves. They don't come into the sacred valley until the first snows at right about this time of the season. I'm happy that grizzly's gone now. That grizzly was a mean, tough old bird. I kinda thought that grizzly died from the pain of its broke tooth in its skull."

Clayton's stomach muscles tightened in a wave of nausea and lightheadedness.

Tuma leaned back, "You should eat food for strength. A long journey to shelter needs much strength, brother."

He braced his right mitten on the snow-covered ground, rose with a soft moaning grunt, then brushed back his hood and casually slapped snow off with his mitten, exposing thick white hair to his shoulders and parted in the middle. Clayton hadn't noticed it before, but several pelts with short and lushly plumed gray tails hung off the arms of Tuma's parka. The tails swayed and lifted in the wind. The parka seemed handmade, dropped below his knees almost like a sack dress, but a better fit.

He watched as Tuma snapped off a leafy branch, went to Clayton's left leg and knelt, lifted the heavy brown hide that covered Clayton to his knee. Clayton hid his astonishment at what he saw: what appeared to be a wad of plant matter where his lower left leg should be.

With the branch, Tuma fanned the smooth but bulky mass on Clayton's leg. Then he leaned forward, tapped Clayton's left leg between the knee and where the mass began.

It's a cast ....

Clayton thought in amazement that quickly turned to worry. He didn't know exactly how or when the cast was formed on his leg. How badly hurt, how close to death had he been while the cast was placed on his leg?

"You feel that?" Tuma inquired, tapping while looking at Clayton.

Clayton gave a nod, though his left leg was numbed to his crotch. In fact, his entire body didn't feel like his. The only thing he felt were awful shots of pain in his head. He wiped his sweaty bearded face and pushed back his damp hair, looked at his hands and was appalled at the scabs full of pus, at seeing his hands pitted like the surface of the moon, his fingernails long and grimy.

He thought for a moment, and then looked up at Tuma. "I'd like to thank you for what you've done, keeping me alive. How long have you tended to me?"

Tuma stood, tossed the leafy branch in the fire, turned and went to a small stack of wood. "Brother, you've been sleeping and talking in your sleep, two cloudy days now."

"Two days!"

Tuma nodded while he grabbed two logs and put them in the fire.

Clayton stared at his back in disbelief until Tuma swiveled back around, smiled and said, "You want trout or moose meat? We have to fatten you up, get your strength back."

Clayton paid scant attention because he was trying to reconcile the days missing in his life.

Had he suffered an embolism, seizure, or amnesia ....

No way. Granted, he wasn't in the best of health, but did he lapse into a coma? He noticed Tuma waiting for him to reply.

He shook his head, "No, no. I'm not hungry, thank you." He looked away and tried to keep focused.

"Brother," Tuma said, "you must eat something. Moose meat or trout?"

"Moose, I guess. I'll try it."

"Brother, how do you like your moose?"

"Alive," Clayton said, and grinned.

Tuma chuckled, but quiet respect colored his reply, "This moose we're about to eat lived a long time. It injured itself and it was too weak to travel to its winter grazing grounds. One cloudy day a short while ago, this great animal jumped off a high cliff so we could have food. I just don't understand the ways of great animals anymore, nor can I explain them. I hope its spirit dwells in happy grazing grounds."

Clayton felt Tuma's words were a prayer for the spirit of the deceased moose. He nodded, "me too."

Tuma walked less than five yards to another tree. Hanging from a bare limb were two large hindquarters and other red meat. Clayton figured it was meat from the moose. He hadn't seen the meat hanging there before. But then, an image came to him, fuzzy, so fuzzy he had to struggle to recall it. Now he did recall the sight, though in what context, he couldn't be sure. He sighed. He'd have to let the two missing days work out naturally or else he'd worry too much. There were other things to consider now.

Tuma returned to the campfire and carved the liver-colored meat off the hindquarter with a knife. When he turned back, he was smiling.

"I will not feed you like my daughter Palafox fed you."

Confused, Clayton asked, "Your daughter? How did she feed me?"

"With her mouth."

"Ah, yeah. Yes, I think I can eat by myself now."

The air was easy to breathe and he found he was becoming fond of Tuma. Naturally, he was troubled about the prospects of not returning to his canoe and the loss of two days. But he'd at last accepted he was too sick to go anyplace alone.

Tuma cut the meat into bite-size bits, shoved a slender stick through each one and let the sticks hang over the yellow-orange flame. He returned the larger piece to a sling hanging from a tree limb, high off the ground. He returned and sat near the fire, stoked it with a log. Red sparks flew up and swirled in the wind.

Clayton studied him. "Do you stay in the wilderness all year?" he asked, more to keep his mind away from the missing days, his fever and trying too hard to figure out a way to get the hell out, which was pointless right now.

Tuma leaned back, "Our home belongs in the wilderness. We arrive at spring's thaw and stay until the snowfall each year, like our people have done since the sky formed. We call this valley the sacred valley of the Great Spirit. Our clan keeps most of the ways of our people who came before us." Tuma shook his head slow, "Though we don't understand our fathers, mothers, sisters, daughters or brothers or sons, or their ways, very much anymore."

Clayton was sweating and he squeezed his eyes closed, tried to ignore the discomfort of the fever breaking. He opened his eyes.

"Who are your brothers and mothers?"

Tuma straightened his shoulders, "All people are our mother, father, daughter, son, sister or brother."

"So. You travel here every year. What do you do here?"

"We trap and hunt animals for food in the sacred valley," Tuma answered with a secretive smile, then stood up slow, came around and knelt on the snow next to Clayton. He stretched out his left hand to grab the hide on top of Clayton. He hadn't noticed before, but Clayton realized that his covering was from a fresh moose kill. The hide was limp and still wet with blood.

Tuma pulled the hide up higher on Clayton's chest. On the inside of Tuma's left forearm was an outline of what looked like a wolf head. The wolf head's snout pointed at Tuma's palm.

Clayton bit his lower lip to keep from blurting out his astonishment; perhaps only an artist could tell, but the wolf's shape was quite similar to the drawing of the wolf woman. The unique shape of the snout especially. The wolf outline wasn't a tattoo though. The lines seemed to have been stamped by a hot iron or a brand. Seeing the wolf sent strange chills through him, he quivered.

By the time he'd fully composed himself, Tuma was kneeling in the snow near Clayton's left shoulder. He grasped Clayton's left hand with a firm grip. Before Clayton could object or even question why, Tuma bent over, placed his forehead against Clayton's forehead and pressed down. Then Tuma drew back and smiled proud.

"Now we're brothers," he said. "You killed a grizzly with medicine. Only a warrior can kill a great grizzly like the one you killed. The grizzly's spirit is proud. It will save your life many times in this life. You and the grizzly's spirit will become great friends and proud warrior spirits in the next world, when your spirit returns to your other spirit's life. The grizzly's spirit will be the first spirit to greet you. Together, you'll battle all *Tonaquasim* spirits."

Responding to Clayton's confused look, he continued, "*Tonaquasim* spirits are all forces of evil, but especially those with marks on them. Your appearance here, your conquest of the grizzly, are great things. I'm glad you're now of our clan. It honors our people."

Clayton had read of them, but wasn't expecting a kow-tow ceremony. Of course he was a religious person and believed in the afterlife, but he didn't want to fight anything. He wanted to get out of the wilderness. Yet Tuma had been quite reverent in the way he performed the confirmation and the way he spoke. As far as the confirmation went, it had been easier than Clayton imagined while reading about it on the Internet. No ritual sayings, chants, pledge, or Latin gabble that only the prigs cared about. Just a head butt, a symbolic greeting, a meeting of the minds and a vise grip of the hand meant they were now bosom brothers. He liked that.

He smiled and said, "Thanks."

"This is our way now that we are brothers." Tuma said quietly. "Now, you're a hunter, a fisherman, a warrior and man of the clan."

Little by little, the conversation moved through the weather, the journey to the winter shelter and about his leg and how he had survived after the grizzly attacked. The campfire brought warmth to the air in spite of the cold wind, snow and dark clouds. Tuma asked him many questions, some of which told Clayton the Eskimo was familiar with cultures far outside his own, but the talk was pleasant and he felt at ease. Tuma was kind and sensible and probably the gentlest man he'd ever met. For the next half hour, he didn't feel cold or ache. He did sense a mystery about Tuma, one that had him curious, though he didn't want to disrupt their tenuous bond to ask about it now.

They'd been speaking of something so inconsequential Clayton couldn't recall it later, when Tuma grinned and asked, "Where did you find the green-jade stone with the wolf's head that you wore?"

Immediately, Clayton wondered how Tuma could've known he had found the jade jewel, rather than brought it with him on the trip. Wary, he decided the best course was the truth.

"On a gravel bed, at that stream off the Yukon River."

Tuma nodded, but said nothing else for several moments while his eyes turned glazed, as though caught up in a daydream beyond reach of this world. Clayton felt Tuma's expression showed defeat and he was wondering what he could do.

Tuma looked down, then fixed his eyes on him, "You find anything else?" Tuma's scar seemed to pulsate as he asked this.

Clayton thought a moment and squinted in concentration. He shook his head, "No".

For several moments, Tuma looked pensive. He sighed. Then he rose with a moan in his bones and stretched out his right mitten to grab a clay bowl. He put the roasted meat into it and laid the bowl near Clayton's left arm.

"I let the food cool, so you can eat, brother."

Tuma smiled as he spoke, but his brown eyes were at another place while he went back and gathered his food. He seemed slower in the way he walked and put food into his own bowl, and he didn't sit next to Clayton this time. Rather, he sat with his back turned, eating slowly in the hurried wind and snow, looking out into the darkening forest.

Clayton took a finicky bite; the meat was tender with a strong earthy flavor, like the odor of half-spoiled meat. After he ate several tidbits, he felt satisfied and filled, but then a queasy and unsettled feeling came over him. He was finding it a strain to keep his eyes open too. His fever was making him sweat as the wind chilled him. Once, as he forced his eyes open, he saw the back of Tuma's head dip. It sounded as though he was growling while eating the moose meat.

At the same instant, Clayton saw a huge wolf, assumed it was Snow Wolf and Tuma was feeding it. He never saw the frightful-looking wolf come into the campsite. It must have appeared out of the wide timber and ghostly swaying ferns at the edge of the shadowed forest. He felt he would have surely seen the wolf if it had walked up to Tuma, but admitted his eyes weren't always open.

Tuma turned, smacking his lips lightly, "Brother, you want more food?"

"I've had plenty, thanks," Clayton said, and watched Tuma tease the huge, fluffy wolf with a piece of roasted meat, then pat it on the head.

Snow Wolf was buckskin colored with splashes of white, brown and black. The wolf had jagged patches of black around his frighteningly big, honey-hued eyes. The wolf stared steadily at him, ignoring the noises in the treetops, the whirling snow and thrumming flames on the logs, seeming caught in a trance. Its only movement now was to slowly wag its fluffy tail, as if contemplating him. The big wolf's gaze caused a foreboding inside Clayton that made him uneasy and he couldn't explain it. He was grateful when the sounds distracted him, intrigued; the sounds of Christmas jingles and chimes were what he recalled hearing when he couldn't see and were nearby again.

Tuma stood and looked in the direction of the sounds. He couldn't decide if the man smiled because of the jingles, Tuma always seemed to have a smile.

Then an eight-foot-long sled drawn by Huskies or wolves, it was hard to tell which, bounced into view.

From a distance, the person behind the sled looked like an auburn-colored wolf, but he assumed it was Palafox, Tuma's daughter. If what Tuma had said was correct, he was about to meet the person who'd saved his life.

CHAPTER 8

Clayton watched the woman pull her parka snug and walked to where he lay and forced a short grin. She sat down on the snow, folded her legs and pulled her mittens off, rested them on her lap. Her brown eyes were as alive as a wolf's.

She pushed back the parka's hood. Her black hair was bowl cut midway to her ears, parted in the middle and her bangs hung almost to her eyebrows.

She lowered her chin and fumbled with one of the three necklaces draped around her slender neck. Color-coordinated beads, clamshells and other trinkets dangled from the necklaces. He heard their soft tinkling while she adjusted the necklaces in a triangular pattern. Tanned claws of some animal, three inches long, swayed from her earlobes.

The woman reminded Clayton of Cleopatra, an impression that disappeared when the dim light added a strange aura, of a wolf hunched with fierce eyes staring an unflinching stare. He stared back at her, transfixed, as if she'd metamorphosed into his darkest nightmare.

In a rush to greet the woman, he garbled, "Palafox?" He had no explanation for why her name burst from his lips as it did.

She raised her face but not her eyes. Even under her eyes, her tanned skin seemed smooth. "Um, yes," she said. "I'm pleased you're talking sense and look good now." Her voice and words gave no trace of emotion or inflection.

"Wished I felt as good as you think I look," he said, and grinned.

Her brown eyes slid away from him. "You look all right."

Teasing, he said, "You're an awkward liar, too."

There was an audible gasp as her eyes cut to him, as if to say, "How dare you." She squinted, as if she couldn't stand him all at once in her eyes. For a moment, he felt she might go into a fit of rage and attack him.

"You look like a shaggy wolf, and stink just as bad."

"We all stink at the end."

"I didn't mean it that way."

"It's okay."

"I'm sorry."

"It's all right." He felt his fever coming on now. "Mind if we drop my look and odor as a subject?"

"All right," she said, softer, still with no detectable emotion.

Definitely not the sort of first impression he wanted to make. It wasn't the time for him to make an adversary, it was the time to have a friend. Clearly, people who were generous and kind were paramount to his survival, to him getting out of the wilderness. She and Tuma were the only people to whom he could turn for help. No doubt, a change in the course of the conversation was needed. Mostly, to steer it away from himself. But there was something frightening about her, he felt it from the beginning.

After they stared at each other for several moments more, he said, "Thank you for what you and your father did for me, Palafox," he said, and grinned the best he could.

Palafox continued massaging her arm slow. "How did you know my name? Did I tell you?"

He looked at her, puzzled, and said, "Your father told me."

For an instant, her face softened, "He's not my father, he's an elder. All people are his relatives. I need to feel your temple if that's all right."

He nodded and brushed oily strands of hair off his forehead. Her palm felt cold on his temple. She pulled back her hand and scrubbed her palm on her thigh.

As she pulled on her mitten, she said, "You gotta shaking wilderness fever and it's hot. We gotta do something about that."

"I've had worse," he said, then felt ridiculous for saying that.

Her expression seemed to agree, but she shrugged, "It's a mystery to us how you hurt your foot and leg, wearing them strapping boots and all. What exactly happened?"

Clayton wondered how he could explain what happened without sounding like a buffoon. In truth, he didn't want to think or recount the terror of the attack. He'd hoped that Tuma already told her. Finally, he managed, "A grizzly mauled me."

Palafox's mittens covered her mouth so fast, he almost didn't see the movement. Abruptly, she lowered them and her expression softened as she leaned forward, "You killed that grizzly near the lake?" The corners of her lips slightly curved, "That mad grizzly killed my blood sister four seasons back."

"Such a pity," he said as he shook his head. "A pity."

After a few moments, she said, "You now own the distinction of killing the one that many have tried but failed to kill. Only a brave man or a complete fool fights a grizzly."

He didn't reply to her scoff right away. He thought about what to say. "You flatter me," he finally said, and shook his head. "But I'm not brave. Or a fool."

A tense silence ensued, until she said, "Well. Aren't you a noble one?"

"No." He shook his head. "I'm not noble, either."

She lifted her chin and said, "I'm curious. That continuous purple scar from your shoulder straight across your chest to your hip. And those ugly slashing scars across your back. Did that grizzly claw you like that?"

He couldn't answer. His pulse had quickened and a peculiar rawness gripped him.

"What are your thoughts?" she said.

"Nothing that's important."

"Do you think about the scars?"

He shook his head, "No."

"I can see by your frown your scars must trouble you."

Startled, he turned away from her and looked up at the sky. The snow appeared to circle him, the swaying ferns seemed stressed by the snow's trivial weight. He sighed and closed his eyes.

God in heaven ....

"Are you troubled about your scars?"

He opened his eyes and peered at her in silence, wondering if she'd read what he wrote in his journal or was simply tapping her intuition.

She looked suddenly uncomfortable, "Don't let the scars trouble you."

"They don't." He shook his head, "They don't."

She massaged her left parka arm, then casually adjusted her necklace, all without looking at him. The claws on her earlobes swung back and forth.

His eyes felt grainy and heavy. He blinked them repeatedly and finally closed them with a sigh.

"Do you brood about your scars?"

Clayton felt she understood damn well he didn't want to think or talk about his scars, her questions made him uncomfortable. He opened his eyes and stared at her.

"I was thinking about the last person who asked the same question a year ago."

"What did you say to them?"

There are questions he let go by at times but not this time. Finally, he said, "Nothing. I ripped out their lungs instead."

Palafox snickered and scrubbed her thighs with her mittens.

"My, aren't you a bad man." Then her grin left her lips, "I'm sorry," she said, and her tone seemed sincere.

He felt she might've been put out by his answer. That wasn't all he intended to say, but her expression seemed to indicate she'd heard enough. He felt relieved. What happened to him in the war made him angry. No good could be served by dredging it up.

He wanted to change the topic of conversation. He squeezed his eyes to cleanse his mind of the fever. Then he got a whiff of a peculiar odor. He sensed he'd smelled the odor before, the scent too brief for identification. It puzzled him, seemed foreign. A chill coiled inside his head and disturbed his thoughts. After several moments, he pushed the odor to the back of his mind and got comfortable the best he could.

"Thank you for keeping me alive and for the hospitality," he said. "I feel like I'm, imposing."

Palafox studied him and a shadow split her face. She sighed, "We couldn't abandon anyone in the wilderness who was injured and alive." She looked up at the darkness, then lowered her chin and her eyes seemed dull until the campfire gave them life.

"Look. We must hurry to shelter before the snow gets too deep here." She glanced over her shoulder in the direction of Tuma, who to Clayton, seemed to be working on the sled in the falling snow. Then she looked back at Clayton.

For the first time, he saw uncertainty in her eyes. Then her voice lowered below the sounds of the wind, "It's bad luck to be in the sacred valley during the first snows. The first snows are the beginnings." She peered over her shoulder in another direction and he followed her gaze.

At the edge of the light where the fire's illumination ended, waist-high ferns swayed with barely a sound, like cattails. He suspected some animal crouched in the ferns and it watched, waited for an opportunity to pounce. The wind made the fur rise on Palafox's parka, which didn't help his frame of mind. The same wind cooled his exposed flesh. He felt no ache, no fever or scratchy throat, as he had before. Yet he realized he was irrational and should be thankful he was alive for one more minute. And he was. He was also grateful they'd sacrificed their time to aid him. He most certainly would be dead by now if they hadn't. This reminded him of something he wanted to ask Tuma, but figured Palafox would know.

He asked, "How exactly did I get to this place?"

She brushed back her bangs, but slowly, then rolled her shoulders as if to roll off the chill. "Rode in my sled, all bundled up. Don't you remember?"

In spite of the pounding in his skull, he tried to think through his fatigue. "No. I don't recall anything."

"When we lifted you up to put you in the sled, you fought us. And swore at us every time."

He knew he was prone to say words that could offend just about anyone. He wasn't proud of it but had grown accustomed to it in the military. He'd worked at avoiding the habit since he became a civilian, but cursing remained a kind of second language.

"I don't remember a thing," he said. "I apologize. I hope I didn't offend you or your, the elder."

She whipped her head back to face him and narrowed her eyebrows, "Of course not! I know a few words myself and say them quite freely—" She abruptly stood. "Curses! I've gotta shoo a rabbit, so don't crawl off, we'd never find you."

She spun around and walked away and the snow crunched.

What a damn bizarre woman, he decided, but couldn't help the grin he sent after her. His fever made him dizzier by the minute and it made him tense. After a few moments, the pounding seemed gentler and he felt a little more at ease. Most of all, he wished he were in better spirits and could keep his eyes open.

After what seemed several minutes, he heard snow crunch. Palafox appeared out of the dark, and he saw her bend down and gather snow in her mittens. With it she shaped two snowballs, came over and knelt by his shoulder. She handed him one snowball.

"Eat the snow and rub it on your face and neck," she said, "It'll reduce the heat of the fever." She grinned and her eyes fell demurely while she munched on the other snowball.

"Thank you," he mumbled hoarsely. He bit off a small chunk of ice and chewed it slow. Though it was still hard to swallow, the snow cooled and soothed his scratchy throat. His back teeth felt loose. He bit off another chunk of ice. Wanting anything other than a conversation about him, he said, "Can I ask you something?"

She glanced at him, "Why not?"

"I hope I'm not being rude, but who named you? Palafox, I always thought that was a Spanish name."

She leaned forward, wiping snow from her chin with her mitten, "A man and a woman taught the Tacoma clan how to read and write a long, long time ago. My mother loved to read books. And like my mother, I also love to read. My mother read the name 'Palafox' in a book and liked it. My name doesn't fit like other Eskimo names. You can say, well, I'm plain different."

Another grin came, this time he didn't try to stop it.

"Palafox is a beautiful name." And Palafox, he believed, with those coffee-brown eyes that seemed innocent and trustworthy, wasn't beautiful or ugly, but just right for most men in the looks category.

But instinct told him it would take a certain type of man and she would have much to say about who that man would be. Even with his fever, he sensed that much about her, or at least felt he did. But what the hell did he know after a brief conversation with her about absolutely nothing.

She was right; the fever that had addled his mind till now was receding. He took another bite of the snowball, chewed and swallowed.

"Did you really feed me with your mouth?"

She froze with the snowball against her lips, only her eyes slid to his. She lowered the snowball, "Of course I did!" Her tan lightened on her cheeks. "Feeding someone with their mouth is not like you're kissing them, you know. It's nothing to be embarrassed about or ashamed of. Not so long ago, when elders lost their teeth or were sick, we fed them by chewing food and blowing the food into their mouth so they wouldn't starve. When our people become old, we take care of them very well. How can we ever repay the old?"

He was silent for several moments, contemplating a respect for the aged he'd never seen in his culture. Sudden pain made his body stiffen as he pulled the hide higher on his chest.

He nodded, "We can never repay them."

She smiled in agreement and started to babble about the snow, how cold it would be in the blizzard and how the wind made it much worse. Even when he closed his eyes to rid his mind of the painful throbbing in his head, he felt her watching him. His thoughts were as distorted as an image on a carnival mirror. When he could bear that unease no longer, he opened his eyes and looked up at her again, blinking.

Palafox grinned. She said, "I saw your sketches in the book. The one with the crow on the limb, the woman with the wolf face and spear, how you signed your name. If you don't mind, I'm curious where you went to find the woman with the wolf face and spear to draw."

A crow ....

He wanted to yell, "It's an eagle." But he didn't let her see how much her question disturbed him. At that instant, he intuitively sensed he'd be better off if he didn't, sensed without understanding why to be guarded. He put his arm over his brow and rocked his head.

Palafox bent so close to him he smelled her breath, which carried a scent similar to pastrami. Before he could open his eyes, she quickly whispered, "Did you show your drawings to anybody, Clayton?"

The arctic chill clamped his head with the abruptness of a bang. In spite of his grogginess, he squinted to see her clearer, and air shot into his lungs as if it were his last breath. When he moved, it felt as though his limbs moved underwater. She drew back, eyes wide, as he shuddered, choked, coughed and doubled over and gasped for breath. He felt his fever spread to the small of his back, where it escalated into the worst pain he'd had since the grizzly attack.

"Jesus!" he said, the only word he could speak.

There was silence between them for a long while, but the silence had no calming effect. Palafox sat, seemingly empathetic, fidgeted with her necklace, not once breaking eye contact with him.

She wanted an answer to her question. That was easy to sense now that fever and pain were no longer his companions. His gut was honed to a decent edge, the one that had kept him out of line-of-sight of windows, told him places to not step, narrow alleys to avoid and rooms to toss a grenade into before he entered. In a flash, his instinct had gone to his finger and decided life or death. More than once, his instinct saved the lives of his men and him too. Now his instinct warned him to be careful of everything he said and did from this moment on.

Yet reason mattered too. In spite of the pounding in his head and distraction of pain, he spent the silence considering the likelihood that the motivations of Palafox and Tuma might be menacing. He couldn't recite one incident where their actions toward him were other than benevolent. Perhaps the fever had brought paranoia; that could happen. Was her question innocuous, then? He didn't believe so. Regardless, he wouldn't answer her question until he had some answers of his own. The problem was, the fever had drained him so much, he couldn't think of a question to ask her for his own peace of mind.

"Where do you hurt?"

Startled when she spoke, he opened his eyes and looked at her. Her tone sounded sympathetic, but how could he know if her effort was to make him feel at ease, easy enough to get the answer she wanted? That wasn't going to happen.

At least she'd given him a question that would allow him to ignore the one before it. He cleared his throat.

"I don't hurt, now," he said. "My fever makes me strange. Comes and goes."

No sooner had the last word floated out of his mouth than he smelled a foul garlicky-cheese odor. Then, puff, the odor that had startled him as a clap of thunder would, gone.

He was, he didn't know, just as there is a moment when you're about to sleep and be inaccessible, that moment in the late night when you're asleep and unreachable at the ringing of the telephone, your eyelids fly open. Gradually, he sensed that he wouldn't be the same again. He couldn't explain it and didn't know why.

He immediately peered at Palafox.

She stared back and said, "I wanna look at your leg and foot, all right?"

A sharp and inexplicable refusal fought to emerge from his mouth. After several moments, he nodded to her and closed his eyes. Seconds later, he felt her unwrapping the organic matter that encased his foot and leg.

He sighed.

He opened his eyes.

In a few moments, she stopped. She quickly covered her mouth and nose with her mitten. Her shoulders crunched and her body seemed to roil and convulse.

He became aware that he was holding his breath and forced air from his lungs. He asked, "Is it that bad?"

She leaned back, and lowered her mitten. She turned and stared at him. Her dark eyes seemed weak. She swallowed. She nodded.

He braced his elbows on the ground and strained to push up. The effort exhausted him and he fell back. Palafox's eyes held sympathy as she watched him struggle. It took three attempts before he got up on his elbows. At that point, she grabbed his shoulder and helped him up.

The toes on the left foot were stubby and miniscule appendages. Brown fluids oozed from blisters and flowed down the side of his ankle. The foot and half his lower leg was no longer the color of flesh. Though it seemed impossible, a darker-than-black shadow lay on the moist, split flesh of his foot and half his leg. And he knew.

His experience about the types of gangrene, what the symptoms were and how to care for gangrene in emergencies, came from his training in first aid in the army. He remembered that bacteria caused gas gangrene and its toxins. The smell, blisters, brown fluid, bloody discharge and his moist flesh signified gas gangrene. Worst of all, gas gangrene was as deadly as its name; it spread as much as six inches in an hour. If he went unconscious, he'd never wake up.

He studied his leg for several moments. A kind of catastrophic disbelief washed inside him, blinding him for a moment. Maybe his self-diagnosis missed the mark. When he was able, he looked again. His foot seemed the size of a football, an unbelievable girth. He couldn't believe it. But he couldn't deny it either. He looked again. His will to live to the next minute seeped out of him. He slumped back.

Oh God, no.

He gazed toward the campfire but didn't see it because he'd fallen into a pit so deep no light could reach him. He wished he hadn't come back to reality and then, that he hadn't survived in war. He thought of the moment when he stood peering through his binoculars at the lake. Since that moment, he hadn't known peace, happiness, or contentment. And he didn't have many hours to live.

If he wanted to live. Feeling lost, alone, depressed, he knew what had to be done. Time could not be wasted. He had to move at rabbit speed.

"Clayton. Look at me."

He inhaled, the volume of air didn't seem quite enough to inflate his lungs. He tried again. With all he had, he said, "We have to cut off my leg below the knee right away."

"What."

"I won't survive the night."

Palafox stammered, "But, the bleeding."

"A tourniquet."

She groped for words. Finally, she said, "What's this tourniquet?"

Her eyes and lips grimaced while he summarized what a tourniquet was and how it worked. She didn't seem to hear after that. It seemed she could only imagine what a tourniquet looked like and not what the device prevented.

"That's unheard of," she said as her eyes strayed to his foot. "Your spirit will be harmed." She threw her head back and gazed away from his foot, now her face seemed optimistic; even her eyes were wider. "I'll make soup. After you eat, we'll wait until light so we can leave. Then you'll be better and feel better."

Clayton shook his head. "No, we can't wait."

She rubbed both her thighs back and forth with her mittens, never losing eye contact. "We'll wait until light," she said, but her tone didn't hide the plea hid in her voice.

"No," he said, and at the same instant, the wind thrummed the flames and they stuttered and returned to idly burning away the logs. "My leg has to go now, or I won't see another sunrise."

She didn't move, just stared at him. Finally she said, "The body is sacred. It's forbidden to maim your body, it'll blight your spirit in the next world, I'll make soup, it'll cut the fever and cure your foot and leg-" Clayton put his hands beneath the moose hide to keep her from seeing his hands tremble, "then you'll be better and won't talk about this tourniquet, only a fool could think of such an obscene thing."

He deliberately showed no surprise at her revelation because within moments he felt sick. He would go through with the amputation. He had to. He knew anything other than cutting off his leg would doom him. He had nothing to lose by being defiant. "I know what to do," he said, and half smiled to reassure her, but he knew his eyes betrayed him, they always did.

She brushed the hair off her brow with one fast stroke. "No, you cannot do such a thing," her words softer now.

In her eyes, he caught a reflection in the campfire's glow of a ghostly image covered with a moose hide, lying on a makeshift nest of limbs and matted debris. And he tried to read her body language. He considered the possibility that her inner debate wasn't about cutting off his leg. No. Her refusal seemed because her customs or religious convictions strictly forbade maiming the human body. Or was it something else? He decided Tuma might be the same way. In spite of his leg, he had a fear of and respect for their convictions. Yet he couldn't do the amputation by himself.

She looked at him for long moments then abruptly drew her head back. She scrambled up.

"I have things to do," she said, her voice faint and strained.

She wiped snow off her parka as she walked away. A loose, fluffy pelt dangled sideways, whipped by the wind and slapped against her body. With a coldness that froze Clayton's spine, she whipped out her knife and whacked off the dangling pelt, pulled the parka hood over her head and hurried to where Tuma stood against a tree trunk fifty feet away.

Clayton sighed and glanced up at the dark sky, wishing he had her faith the infection would burn itself out in a couple of days. He couldn't deceive himself; he had hours to live.

CHAPTER 9

"Wake up, no, no, don't sleep, wake up."

"Huh," Clayton said, and wondered why she was talking so loud.

"Wake up."

Feeling as though he'd been drugged, he groaned when he heard her voice again, but lifted his hands, swiped his face as if he could rub his trouble away. He opened his eyes.

Snow whirled around Palafox, who sat massaging his arm with snow. When his mind cleared, he knew what had to be done. He rocked his painfully throbbing head and sighed.

The churning snowflakes didn't obscure her smile, "It's your fever, it's nothing to be bothered about. I've dealt with wilderness shaking fevers before."

He nodded and tried to speak, didn't have the strength, gave her a weak smile instead. His vision blurred, but not colors.

She leaned forward, "I'll stay next to you until the soup's ready, then you can eat and sleep."

He couldn't believe what he'd heard. What was she talking about? Could he have become delirious again?

"No. No soup, no sleep. My leg must be cut off right now."

She nodded, seeming to understand, but her next words put the lie to this. "It won't be long before the soup's ready. It will rid the fever and heal your leg. You'll feel much better."

Clayton eased his arm away from her. He knew enough to know his leg wasn't likely to heal by osmosis. But proving this would take more energy than he had. Instead, he said, "I don't have a lot of time, all right?"

She stood without a word and went to the campfire, returned with a clay bowl between her mittens, lowered the bowl to the snow near Clayton's left shoulder.

"Clayton, soup's ready. You must eat all of it, then you'll sleep."

Her dark eyes believed every word of what she'd just said, and confirmed his suspicions that he was speaking to a mindless Eskimo woman who had no inclination of the peril he faced.

"This can't be happening," he said.

"Don't be afraid."

"What a nightmare."

"You're angry."

He raised his arm and laid it across his chest. He looked at her, "Let me say this as practically calm as possible. I'll be dead by sunup unless you help me cut off my leg—"

"Don't say such things. You're too weak. It'll blight your spirit."

They exchanged glances for awkward moments.

"Can you fetch me a knife? And a piece of rope or string? Will you at least do that for me?"

"If you'll just eat the soup."

"Please, please listen, I can't eat soup. I have to cut off my leg, right away. Not in an hour, but right now, all right?"

"You mustn't say that," she said. "Why are you so set on cutting off your leg? Just eat the soup."

"We can't waste time here, please, don't you realize how serious this is? Please, a knife."

For two minutes, he tried his best to persuade her. Her face remained expressionless and each time he made the request, she shook her head in a slow, defiant gesture. The only time her expression changed was when he said, "If you're not going to help me, then promise you'll bury me deep."

Even then, she remained silent. Finally, with no strength left, he refused to guzzle the concoction of dark gruel out of that clay bowl. Knowing that gruel would be his last meal on the planet, he couldn't eat. He'd probably vomit it right back up. He barely could swallow his own saliva. His eyes burned and were growing heavy. He fought against the unrelenting pressure to sleep. If he slept, he wouldn't wake up.

Their heads turned at the approaching footsteps on the snow, both watched, stoic, as Tuma sat down beside him.

"Brother," Tuma said, "You must eat the soup. It'll make you better amongst other things. The soup will cure your fever and infected leg. Take the soup."

"I ask you, Tuma, to give me your knife. I have no chance to—"

"No! It's not right." Both men turned to Palafox, who said, "He's too weak!"

Tuma gave her an impatient wave, then lowered his arm.

"Daughters sometimes interfere when they shouldn't be speaking a'tall," Tuma said calmly. Then he removed his knife from its sheath and handed it over.

Clayton accepted the knife and smiled, "Thank you. Thank you, Tuma." But even as he struggled to sit up, he wondered if he had the strength left to do what he must.

"Help me, please," he said.

The campsite spun. He leaned his head over onto his knees and rested that way for a moment.

He looked at Tuma and his vision blurred. He blinked his vision clear, again. "I need some rope or a strap—"

Suddenly, he felt a tug and the knife disappeared from his hand and when he lifted his head, he saw the knife in Palafox's mitten. She held the knife like she wanted to stab someone.

"Daughter, no-" After a brief struggle, Tuma overwhelmed her and seized the knife. Above her protests, he pointed her a place near the campfire, where the snow whirled in a nervous energy.

"Daughter, go over there and sit."

Palafox cowed, likely out of respect for Tuma, but shook her head, "No."

"Go." Tuma said, paused, then firmer like a father to a child, "Go!"

"No," Palafox said, stubborn resolve clung to her words.

As though working against an unseen weight above him, Tuma stood, his shadow fell against her.

"Daughter, don't interfere in matters between brothers, again."

Pain that Clayton couldn't figure out, but which seemed as great as his own, flickered across her face.

Palafox stood and walked to her designated spot on the snow. The snow seemed to protest with each step she made.

Tuma left, but returned quickly, holding several leather straps. Wordless, he helped Clayton affix and tighten the rough tourniquet. A few times, Clayton glanced over to where Palafox sat, her face sullen, her mouth closed.

Tuma leaned forward and whispered, "Brother, your leg, once it's gone it won't grow back. It won't make life simpler. You sure this path is the right path of life for you?"

He looked at Tuma, then at his foot, then his leg. The cold air was heavy on his body, everywhere except his leg. He didn't need a doctor's opinion and he didn't know an alternative, though he most certainly would've preferred one. He barely got the words above a mumble when he said, "Yes, it's vital."

Tuma went to the campfire and heated the knife blade until half the blade had turned ash white. Seeing this, sensing the finality, Clayton felt his heart bang in his chest, thinking of the words he couldn't share with Tuma. *Just what the world needs, another man with his leg gone.* Yet he would worry about his handicap at sunup, if he saw another one.

Tuma grabbed a red fox pelt and wrapped the knife's handle, then took measured steps across the packed snow to where Clayton lay. There was no hesitation in his motions as he handed Clayton the knife.

"Don't!" came Palafox's soft entreaty as she walked back and sat down several feet in front of him.

Tuma whirled around to her, "Daughter. Don't interfere."

She covered her face with her mittens, yet her mittens widen and she was peeking through them.

He looked down at his leg but hesitated, to get a better view of the site on his leg to cut. He couldn't swallow, his throat was dry and he tried to swallow but couldn't.

The knife was a lot heavier than he figured it would be. This surprised him. All kinds of apprehensions jumbled up inside his head and he got all tangled up. He was glad Palafox sat far away but in another way, he wished she'd taken the knife and stabbed him in the heart with it.

The knot in his stomach was paralyzing him, so he concentrated on the progression of the amputation. Once started, he'd have to finish. He identified a spot just below his knee, what he judged a safe distance above the ruined part of his leg. He braced himself, moved the knife to the site on his leg. He gritted his teeth. His vision blurred and his hand began trembling. He grabbed his trembling right hand with the other hand. He took a deep breath.

What if I change my mind after, after the cut?

The prospect scared the hell out of him. He concentrated to push the notion out of his mind. If he made the cut, he had to finish. It was that simple.

At the last moment, he looked at his unsteady hand. In shock, he lifted the wobbly knife and stared at a small incision on his leg, already welling blood. He'd never felt the cut. Now, he had to finish.

Maybe his father was right. Maybe he was too soft in the heart to do what a man had to do. He knew his chances weren't even fair, with or without finishing what he'd inadvertently just started, he didn't have the courage to face either outcome. His heart in turmoil, fighting bile rising in his throat, he put the knife on the ground with the blade pointed at his foot.

A shadow shifted beside him and Tuma peered at him. He grabbed his necklace and held it up. "Brother, can you recite the colors you see in this necklace I hold?"

Clayton's eyes blurred and he said, "I can't see colors, my vision is blurry."

Tuma's eye brow twitched as he reached down for the knife. Tuma didn't speak, knife in hand, he sat with his jaw open, staring at Clayton as though at a venomous viper inches from his face.

After a while, he didn't know how long, Tuma helped him remove the tourniquet. Tuma never took his eyes from him during the process. He was certain Tuma watched him as if he would suddenly grab the knife and slash Tuma's throat.

Though Tuma didn't speak, he stood up slow, nodded, and went to his bedding spot, his back to Clayton. He stood a moment over his bedding then he gave a casual glance over his shoulder. Tuma's face seemed mystified before he turned away.

Clayton remained sitting up, staring at the campfire, knowing that soon, he would give up the space he now occupied on the planet. As hard as he'd fought to live since the ambush by the grizzly, he now fought for acceptance.

Several Hail Marys and all the prayers he knew and he didn't feel at peace, just a strange calm when he realized he could still see. No flashes of his past life entered his mind. Then he recalled an Indian adage he'd read while preparing for his ill-fated journey: A man fears three times: when he's born, when he learns his spirit must be returned intact and he must learn the last fear alone. He never understood the last fear, until now.

A shadow approached and became Palafox holding a clay bowl. "You must eat the soup," she said.

Her brown eyes seemed understanding he was ready for the process to be over with, but didn't wish to waste his last few hours sleeping or eating. He would sleep soon enough. She persisted though and for her sake, not his, he agreed to eat the awful stuff to silence her so he could go to sleep and not wake up.

She tilted the bowl so he could sip the warm soup. The sleeve of her parka slid back, a wolf symbol, inside her left forearm, identical to the one on Tuma's, came into focus in the weak firelight. They stared at each other in silence. She adjusted her parka sleeve to cover it up. Her eyes grew darker.

It's a birthmark," she said, and her voice seemed to come from a long way off.

Did you show your drawings to anybody, Clayton?

He felt the cold rise in his soul.

Moments passed, he kept staring at her trying to avoid the slightest hint that he'd heard what she had said. He returned to sipping the watery soup.

The soup tasted nothing like he thought it would. It had a bite like raw garlic and smelled of raw potato. Though only warm, it burned his throat.

His resolve ended when he was struck with a fit of coughing that made tears come to his eyes and made his head feel like it would split.

Able to think again, he wondered if she'd done him a kindness and laced the gruel with hemlock.

The bowl empty she grinned and said, "Good. The soup will cure your foot and fever. You'll see, you'll sleep and dream."

She turned and walked back toward the campfire, he imagined an irrational scene, a house falling out of the sky and landing on her. A strange hilarity giggled inside his feverish mind.

"Just what the world needs, another Rip Van Winkle," he said, and not loud enough for her to hear it.

She stopped and turned to him, "Huh?"

"Nothing," he said. "Nothing."

He remained resigned and scared, but not as frightened, though he couldn't have explained why. The one positive thing, she'd left him alone. A little thing, but he was thankful for that.

In spite of his resolve to not sleep until eternal sleep took him, it seemed after only ten minutes or so, he was fighting to maintain consciousness, again and again.

Snow Wolf had come into the glow of the campfire and in one period of wakefulness, he decided the wolf's reflective eyes were ones he never wanted to see glowing in the dark.

He watched Tuma, who sat against a tree next to his bedding spot. Though the light was dim and perhaps it was the fever, it seemed to Clayton that Tuma wore a grin, that his posture was as if he were waiting for prey; not moving, just watching intently.

The campfire wavered continuously before his eyes, until it seemed dreamlike rather than real. It would've seemed like that until he passed on, except at one point, he began hearing, *Clayton, Clayton, Clayton,* echoing in his head.

Maybe it wasn't hemlock in her soup, he decided, but some other potion or drug, one with the side effect of numbing and paralyzing euphoria. Or maybe it was poison, just one kinder than the drug that ended Socrates' life. He felt neither good nor bad, just locked in a surreal fuzzy wakefulness, drifting.

Palafox stood over him, peering down.

"He's sleeping," he heard her say. Before he could correct her, she turned and looked at Tuma, then went out of his vision and he decided it didn't matter.

From faint noises and moving shadows in his side vision, he wondered if they were engaged in some task out of his sight. Curious, he shifted his head just enough so if he squinted a bit, he could see them.

Palafox took a position at his legs while Tuma removed two short logs from the smoldering fire, holding them by the unburned ends. He stood above Clayton and looked down, then began bumping the logs together above Clayton's head. As he did, he chanted like someone speaking in tongues, or perhaps a foreign language. Just as well, Clayton thought; if he'd been speaking English, whatever had numbed his senses would've kept him from sorting out the words. Tuma repeated the maybe-chant, banging the logs in rhythm, pulsating sparks sprang off the logs and spiraled down, smoldering, on top of the moose hide that covered Clayton.

While Tuma did this, Palafox sang a cryptic chant. He couldn't make out these words either, but to him it sounded almost like Latin;

he thought he heard "culpa." Her brown eyes changed to blinking bright, almost like the reflection in an animal's eyes. The sight didn't frighten him, only puzzled him, he knew he was under the influence of the soup's euphoric feeling.

He noticed her hands clutched some kind of leafy-fern plant, she pulled the leaves along and over his left leg, fanlike, until she bowed her head and repeated a chant, then drew a circle in the space above his bad leg, below his knee, and put her right hand to her chest, then raised her hand level with her shoulder and clapped both hands several times, making the plant leaf shudder and rustle. She looked up, but then bowed her head again, repeated the routine twice.

Having lost a sense of time, he simply watched while Tuma and Palafox placed an animal hide around the rotting flesh of his left leg, then packed snow on the pelt until the leg and pelt were encased in snow. He didn't feel it, realized he couldn't feel his headache or the effects of the fever either, which he found astonishing.

Once his leg looked like a cast made of snow, Tuma knelt by his shoulder and pressed his forehead against his feverish brow. He felt Tuma's head butt, the kowtow, but managed to not move. Again Tuma chanted as though speaking in tongues, but now his plaintive tone reminded Clayton of a penance, or perhaps an attempt to summon a spirit. But then the Tuma's voice rose and fell, not in a predictable rhythm, but as if the severity of one sin required a higher or maybe more intense throat vocalization than the other.

Hardly had he reminded himself to stay calm than a sensation of being adrift washed over him. Seeking an anchor, he focused on Tuma's throaty words. No sooner had the words distorted than he drifted out of sight, out of hearing, out of all recognizable consciousness. Clayton realized, suddenly in this last moment, he would never be the same again.

CHAPTER 10

While the elder prayed, Palafox knelt by Clayton's shoulder and kept her position, watched him sleep with not even the slightest movement, the only noise from him the wheezing with each breath.

At that moment, she realized not once did she see him brood, or believe him afraid of dying. He seemed more afraid of cutting off his leg. That troubled her, because he had the right to be afraid of dying.

She never once believed he wouldn't cut off his leg, she couldn't have exactly explained why, but she'd lost respect for him as a man because men do what they say they're going to do, didn't they? At least, the men she knew did what they said they would do.

She wondered what it was that she found fascinating about this round eye. He seemed different from the other round eyes she'd met. All she knew about Clayton was that he had walked into the sacred valley of the wilderness and killed a mad grizzly that killed her blood sister and he didn't cut off his leg like he said he would.

She wondered if the Great Spirit had helped Clayton realize the soup would help him. She didn't feel sorry for Clayton, instead she felt glad because she cared, but not in a special way. She already had a man, and he would be disappointed in his heart when she didn't return with the others.

If she could get through one single day without thinking about her bad decision to stay, she would have a better outlook about things. Yet how could anyone have a good outlook in a blizzard, in the sacred valley?

When the elder stopped praying to Clayton's spirit, he leaned back and peered at her.

Made embarrassed by his gaze, she asked, "Why did you give him a knife?"

The elder frowned. "Because the brother asked."

He peered at Clayton as if he couldn't make up his mind whether to look at him or not. The elder's face showed something she had never seen before: uncertainty. She didn't know why the elder acted so strange. She'd known the elder all her life and had never seen him this way.

"You knew he wouldn't cut off his leg," she challenged.

He glanced sideways at her, "No, I didn't know. He's a brother. Fearless brave warriors are good, but brave warriors are better. He couldn't be an Akkikiktok warrior until he did what he did. All the Tornuaq devil spirits with marks on their heads will fear him now."

She wanted to scream *Ah-yo-koo*-chett—*oo-a,* because she didn't understand what the elder spoke about. She wondered why only a man could understand unsaid things, why a woman never understands these things about men, the stupid things men do to prove they're worthy to be men.

The elder stood and glared at her, "Did he say?"

She didn't answer right away, but after a moment she shook her head and looked up, "No. He didn't say, he was too sick."

The elder looked at her with disapproval in his eyes, "We must know. We have to know, Daughter. Wait until he's better. There can be no mistake in his answers."

She wanted to say what was going on but she didn't. She was worried more about something else and voiced her concern, "He might remember."

"That crossed my mind, but he cannot ever know, ever. It's forbidden to speak about, say a wilderness fever, not a word more."

"I know," she said, clearly resented him reminding her as if she were still a child. He must believe she'd run off and speak about matters that are best not spoken about. No one could go against the trust bestowed upon the people of the Tacoma clan.

She glanced back at Clayton, who slept with his mouth opened and still labored in his breathing. His breaths came short and long, almost as noisy as the wind through the trees.

Something had changed her notions about Clayton though, she couldn't explain it. Looking up at the elder, she said, "If his spirit leaves we must bury him with his book. It was his wish."

The elder turned and stared at her.

"He will be sacred and give back like our people if he's—," the elder caught himself. He sighed heavily. He looked around.

"The wind and cold are in my bones, they will be stronger by light. We must rest."

That's when she knew the elder had made Clayton Spears a person of the Tacoma clan for killing that mad grizzly. She was afraid

Clayton might remember. She reached down, pulled the moose hide over Clayton's shoulders and under his chin. She peered at him.

He can't remember. What can they say he'd believe, where, where did you go Clayton?—

"Daughter!"

Startled, she looked up at the elder. He grumbled something, then spat in the fire, cracked his knuckles in his mitten, a habit she always found irritating.

"You must make the tribute to the grizzly's spirit," he said. "The grizzly's spirit won't be restful, we'll have very bad luck until the tribute is made. You must see to it that all the colors are used, every one."

She looked back at Clayton. She nodded, "All right."

In truth, she had an urge to grab the elder and shake him senseless for talking about a tribute to the grizzly's spirit. An offering to the grizzly's spirit was an age-old custom, but even though that grizzly had killed their people, they still had to make a tribute to its spirit with all the colors? But it was pointless to argue with the elder.

She wanted to ask the elder why, but she didn't. Curious about something else, she asked, "Did you believe his explanation?"

The elder adjusted his parka as he turned away from her and began a slow walk over the snow to his bedding.

"I don't know. He found nothing else." The elder never looked at her.

This side of the elder she'd not seen and she'd known the elder since she was a girl. She wondered if the elder's strangeness had to do with the medallion Clayton wore and where he found it. The elder's woman wore the medallion when she went missing four seasons ago. She wondered if that was a bad omen where Clayton had found it and the elder hadn't yet told her about it.

She didn't know if the Great Spirit had something to do with Clayton appearing in the wilderness like he did. Then it hit her like the cold wind against her face. She leaned back.

He shall bear a gift of a another, walk into the sacred valley, kill a great beast. He shall ... The scroll warned there shall be five temptations sent by the force of evil to seize the gift. No one could interpret the symbols after the first five statements, or could they? Granted, the council had knowledge of many things, but customs forbid the elders from sharing certain knowledge with the people.

Before she agreed to help, she thought it silly to go through the trouble to risk their lives to save a man almost dead. That could explain the behavior of the elders toward Clayton, why the elders decided to give Clayton the soup medicine. The elders had to have known something, but what?

If her guesses were right, Clayton wouldn't leave the wilderness alive. What worried her, mistakes had been made in the past and the prospect of it happening again troubled her. She felt helpless, the same feeling she had when the elders came and said her mother had died. She wasn't very strong that day.

She had difficulty reconciling the idea that Clayton could be a temptation, or that he'd been to the sacred forest. Something about the events and Clayton, didn't seem in the right places. The matters must be coincidences. Or could it be?

Could it be that he was sent by the force of evil to seize the gift? That could explain why he didn't seem afraid of dying. Aside from all else, it couldn't be true that his flesh was warm like hers.

Not wanting to think about it anymore, she pushed her mind away from the Temptation Scrolls and watched Clayton sleep, until she realized the air had turned colder. She put two logs on the fire so it would burn hotter, returned to a spot near him.

Though his eyes remained closed, he trembled at times.

"I'll sleep next to him, he's restless," she said, loud enough for the elder to hear.

The elder glanced at her, then at Clayton. "His spirit battles now," was all he said.

Without acknowledging the elder's words, she sought out Snow Wolf with her eyes. "Snow Wolf, come, come Snow Wolf."

"Don't let Snow Wolf call to the spirits," the elder said as he lay down on animal skins. "It will keep my brother from rest. He needs rest, much rest."

"Snow Wolf, come, come here," she said as she closed her eyes to sleep. And couldn't sleep. She lay and watched dark shadows above her swaying. Finally she slept, until sometime later when she awoke not knowing what had disturbed her rest.

The wind rolled the treetops back and forth. The flames on the logs seemed to ignite anew. Scarcely had she breathed, a strange coldness came over her, then she sensed fish scales had covered her skin.

Shivering, she jerked the animal skins off her and sat up, rubbed her arms. Her hair blew across her face. She held her breath, listening.

Far away in the dark forest came sounds of chop-chop-chopping, then bump-bump-bumping. Then there was croaking, which drew other croaks that rose out of the snowy, windy dark of the forest. The croaks seemed to have come out of a hollow log like belches.

The noise vibrated the air in the wind and trees. The Alaskan Huskies tied at the sleds barked, squealed and jerked against the reins that tied them to the sleds.

The elder leaped to his feet, grabbed his spear and hurried to where the campfire's weak glow met the darkness. On his way, he grabbed a log from the fire and raised it above his head.

She knew what the bumps and croaks were as well; she and the elder and Clayton were in danger of being killed. Her alarm grew as the elder stood, but she didn't move otherwise until Snow Wolf leaped up, ears perked. Before she could restrain Snow Wolf, she bolted for the dark forest.

"Catch Snow Wolf," she cried.

The elder dropped the log and the spear and turned to grab Snow Wolf, but was too late. Snow Wolf raced toward the croaking sounds and disappeared in the dark.

The elder snatched the spear off the snow, grabbed the log he'd dropped and chunked it in the fire. The flames sputtered and snapped back as the elder spun around.

"The Mueumonds always hunt in killer packs at the first snows. But the Saluuette wolves will greet them. We'll have to make a run for shelter."

The Saluuette wolves the elder spoke of were bigger than the arctic wolves, the fiercest of all the wolves. Snow Wolf, an arctic wolf, had run toward the croaking to attack the Mueumonds.

She said, "The man's too weak, he might die."

The elder looked at her with the same resolve she wished she had seen when she and the others suggested Clayton was too far gone to waste their time to keep him alive. If he had, they would've left too.

If it hadn't been for the medallion Clayton wore and the drawings in the book—

"We must hurry, Daughter," the elder said. "We must hurry."

"Why didn't we leave yesterday? Why?"

"Something we had to do."

"What about Snow Wolf now?"

The elder looked at her, his face now reddened with unaccustomed anger.

"We can do nothing to bring her back until she wants to return to us," he said. "She'll catch up if she can. Wrap up our brother good. We have a long journey in this hawk."

This hawk, meaning the arctic-cold wind and snow. She didn't reply, but wondered why if the cold and snow mattered now, why it didn't yesterday.

"I've already taken the wheels off the sleds," he said, ignoring the judgment on her face. "I'll hitch the Huskies to them. Don't forget to take the meat hanging from the limbs. And leave some meat piled on the ground and scatter some meat all over this campsite."

The elder breathed deep. He dropped the spear, but quickly snatched it off the snow and stood stiff and erect. He looked all around, as though searching every shadow.

In all her memory, she had never seen him drop a weapon unless it was a meaningful action. And it alarmed her to see the urgency on his face become tinged with panic. She started to speak; he stopped her with a raised hand.

"We must hurry, Daughter, we must hurry. We've stayed too long. The Mueumonds will hunt us until we're safe out of the sacred valley."

A growl of wind tore at her parka. She felt a chill and caressed herself as, with slowness born of trepidation and cold, she pulled herself to stand, listened.

CHAPTER 11

When Mr. Wilbert Gin heard the first sound, he was gazing ahead of the lead dog pulling his sled and thinking how bright the moon's light reflected off the snow to give a glimmer of twilight to the wilderness. At first, the throaty belching seemed to come from one of the hundred sounds caused by the wind. An experienced wilderness hunter, more often than not he could identify the noise, but not this time. The second belching noise, louder than the first, was eerily deep and almost like the cough of a bull moose in rut. But no moose would be in rut in the winter and the sound wasn't fully like that anyway.

Still, the strangeness of it made him slow the speed of his sled until it stopped. He removed his parka hood and listened. The wind bumped, squealed, wailed, whistled and gushed through the trees, but it didn't make a belch through a bullhorn. He wondered if what he'd heard was his imagination or if he'd gone mad.

He'd been a trapper near fifty years in the Alaskan wilderness, he'd heard many a strange sound, but this was the first time he heard a belch–grunt, especially in winter and in the middle of the night in the deserted upland region of the arctic.

Wilbert turned to his grandson Lewis, who was visiting from Boston. At six-two, Wilbert had to look to the side and up to even see him in the gathering dark.

"Lewis. Did'ya hear anything strange, or was it my imagination?"

"Heard *something* freaky." Lewis said this while he turned and strolled into a small moonlit clearing to relieve himself.

As much to consider his answer as for modesty's sake, Wilbert turned his head back to face forward. Lewis was a Marine sergeant who'd returned from his second tour in Iraq and the first thing he did was grow a beard. Unlike Wilbert, Lewis came from the lower forty-eight and his fur parka, still a bit stiff in its newness, gave him the appearance of a gorilla. But the beard and the parka seemed to match his tattoos. And Lewis chewed dynamite and pissed napalm like all Marines, Wilbert thought with pride.

"Ovah heah," Lewis said softly.

Stiffening, Wilbert swiveled around on the sled, "What is it?"

"Ovah heah."

Wilbert walked over to stand next to Lewis, who stood motionless, studying something ahead like a trained sniper.

"Did ya hear something?" Wilbert asked.

"No sir," Lewis whispered, "but I saw something."

Wilbert Gin spotted something too, but at first, he didn't know what it was. "Did ya see that?" He pointed towards a tree line nearby.

Lewis shook his head, "No sir, didn't see ah thang."

Then Wilbert spotted the round lights again. No, not lights, more like lime-colored glowing objects, round and the size of marbles. A short ways out among the timber, the glows floated near the snow-covered ground.

"I see 'em now," Lewis said. "That looks like chem glows, but round."

Wilbert knew what his grandson spoke of—like the glowsticks children liked, chem glows were used by the military for low-level illumination at night, dimmer-switch versions of spotlights.

"I don't believe that's what that is," he said. Though he'd heard and seen a lot of things in the wilderness, these glows were the strangest. And it worried him; he'd never encountered glowing eyes before, that's exactly what they looked like and they didn't look natural.

"Grandpa," Lewis said. "Could that be ole Goose and Skidder, trying to spook us?"

Wilbert hoped that Goose and his weird friend had sense enough to get out of the wind of the blizzard. He knew that Goose wouldn't be up to Halloween tricks, because a man could get shot stone dead in the wilderness for even attempting to scare somebody. All wilderness trappers and people who lived in the wilderness knew but four things. They were always lonely, always hungry, always lost, always scared.

"No. It's not Goose," Wilbert said. "He's got better sense. Best we leave, though."

They returned to their sleds and as Wilbert pushed off to take the lead, he looked back, watched the glowing eyes as they moved through the twilight forest. At that moment, he estimated a half-dozen sets of the eyes, maybe more, trailing their sleds. And now, Wilbert could see more than simply eyes.

Lewis yelled, "Grandpa, watch out!" just as Wilbert felt his sled suddenly slow and then halt. He whipped his head around and saw that his dogs had stopped at the edge of a gorge. Only the Alaskan Huskies' attentiveness had kept him from running off the edge.

Distracted, he looked back again and the glowing eyes were wider now, closer. With them behind and the steep drop-off ahead of him and Lewis, there was no way to outrun them.

Lewis must have figured it out too; he leaped off his sled and moved to stand next to Wilbert. They both stood in a moon-washed space at the edge of the gorge.

Wilbert not once took his eyes off the hulking silhouettes with glowing eyes that moved through the stark, twilit shadows. He simply began easing his hand toward his gun, muttering, "Git ya rifle, Lewis, shoot to kill."

"What tha hell *are* them things?" Lewis said.

"Don't know son, we're 'bout to find out, though."

Half hidden in the dark timber, the silhouettes with lime-colored orbs for eyes bounced and steadied, then sprang out of the shadows straight for them. They hopped like kangaroos but croaked out a noise that no kangaroo or any known creature ever made.

"Dear God," Wilbert breathed, frozen in shock.

The Huskies yapped and strained at their reins.

He shouldered his rifle, yelling, "Shoot, Lewis, shoot," fired point-blank and knocked a spectral silhouette down. It bounced back up.

Lewis fired almost simultaneously, pumping several rounds into them before his rifle jammed. He dropped the rifle, reached down, pulled out his knife and motioned to his grandpa to do the same. Meanwhile, the Alaskan Huskies put up the good fight.

Wilbert Gin and his grandson didn't want to die without a fight and that's how they died, swinging rifle butts and thrusting their knives to the very end.

CHAPTER 12

By the kindness of God or the luck of the Irish, Clayton still breathed, when he wouldn't have thought it possible to see another sunrise. He lay in the sled, breathing cold air while the train of Huskies raced over the snow among the trees. Ordinarily, he would've been enthusiastic riding in a sled, would have enjoyed watching the view rush past him, but he'd slept after Palafox fed him gruel.

And for a reason beyond his grasp, he was still alive. Not just living, but he seemed to have crossed a medical threshold. Yes, he had aches and soreness, was reminded of this when he summoned enough strength to shade his eyes from the sun's glare. But his fever was gone, along with the deepest of that unrelenting pain and what replaced them felt nearly like awe. All he saw right now, he wanted to sketch. Being an artist was his life's ambition. Was. Once, in a fit of passion, he said he would cut off his leg to be an artist, to be able once more to separate shades of blue and green. Not anymore. Now he realized there were some things not worth the sacrifice to have what you've always wanted. Viscerally, he'd changed and it hadn't announced itself with a flash of light or with a startle but instead came as a puff of wind, as when a door suddenly opens.

The trees slid by and the sled seemed weightless. He was grateful he could see the carpet of snow over the sloping, forested terrain. The most important thing he was grateful about, he still had his leg.

Since they'd been traveling, stopping only to rest, not once did Palafox broach a question about his sketches, though she spoke of other things. Granted, he dwelled in a state of vagueness. Nevertheless, he wondered if her motivations were benign and her only motivation was to keep him awake and talking, or if she feared talking about his sketches would bring up his equally intriguing question about her telling him the wolf on her arm was a birthmark, which simply couldn't be true. It had to be a brand of some sort he decided, not a tattoo, because tattoos were done with ink. Though he could be wrong, what he'd seen appeared burned into her flesh, just like the mark on Tuma's arm. The only thing certain, he had to be guarded about anything else he disclosed to her, at least until he could figure out her intentions toward him, or until they were out of the wilderness, in a very public place.

Wincing against the ache it brought in his neck, he eased his head around. With her parka and the coral-colored fur over her face, Palafox could have been mistaken for a bandit in the wilderness. As she guided the sled, the Christmas jingles on the sled sounded strange, but added a little sweetness. He made a mental note to ask her at their next stop why she'd placed the tiny bells on her sled. In the meanwhile he didn't have to concentrate on the route, or watch for stop signs or any other conspicuous warning. The Huskies simply raced, it seemed reckless racing, on a twisted route among trees placed so tight that the sled seemed to lightly shave off their bark in its passage. Though he could have endured the journey forever, impatience plagued him and he hoped they were well on their way to the winter campgrounds by now.

It wasn't a long time before the train of Huskies jerked the sled and raced along a shoulder of a ridge. To the left, a frightful drop to the white treetops below. The sled increased speed near the ledge. Clayton gripped the sled's frame while it bumped and slid over the snow and snaked among the trees.

The sled crunched snow as the steep ledge became a plateau high on a mountainside. Just ahead, a steep granite cliff appeared as if it had frozen in the process of falling. Countless icicles hung flush against the grayish rock. Some of the ice had boiled out of the cracks in the rock and become frozen glass. Clayton didn't suppress his instant desire to sketch the sight but stored it away in his mind for another time.

The sled slowed until it stopped. He looked at the leaning cliff above them and felt a sense of dread. If the cliff broke off they were dead; they were less than a hundred feet from the leaning cliff.

Tuma's sled pulled to a snow-covered brush pile abutting the rock-face cliff. He stopped the sled and hopped off.

To Clayton's right, stacks of wood, a wide, rectangular lean-to and snowdrifts on both sides. Three dogsleds sat marooned under the lean-to. A thick scattering of doghouses and three other lean-tos were in the vicinity as well, these shielded by tall timbers. On the left, two hundred feet out, he saw the top of a steep gorge and past it, a serrated mountain range sat ready to vanish in the haze surrounding it.

As best as he could tell, the immediate vicinity seemed the kind of setting routinely used by people, except for what was noticeably missing. He saw no campfires, smoke, or any sign of life, human or canine, other than them. He lay in the sled and wondered if they'd reached the winter campgrounds. And if so, why it had been abandoned.

Palafox stepped around the sled, flashed a grin while she removed the furs from around her neck and face, "Can you see the shelter?"

Clayton squinted and looked everywhere. He didn't know what to search for: a house with a hot tub or an igloo, a teepee, a yurt, he had no clue.

"No," he rasped out.

"Watch!" she said and hurried away.

Tuma joining her on the way, she snow-marched to something he had noticed, the massive snow-covered brush pile against the icy cliff. They huffed, grunted, pulled, dragged brush and limbs away and stacked them off to one side, revealing a black half-oval opening, wide as a car length.

Obviously a cave entrance, but Clayton wondered why they went to the trouble of camouflaging it. The topography and tricky path didn't offer itself for easy discovery by happenstance or by a wayward wanderer. *But better safe to lock the door,* he figured, then noticed Palafox and Tuma disappearing into the mouth of the cave.

After a long minute, the thought of them never emerging crossed his mind. Soon, his mind had convinced him that even if he did manage to go inside the cave to look for them, some kind of nightmare beast waited for him inside it. The dark opening gave him little comfort as he tried to talk himself out of the notion.

Palafox exited the cave and hurried to the sled, "We gotta get you inside."

"Is this the winter campgrounds?"

"No," she began dusting the powdery snow off her parka, "we're at the shelter. We'll stay here until we know if the mountain pass is passable."

"How long will that take?"

"Maybe three or four days, no more."

"How long have we been traveling?

"Two days," she said, "let's get you inside."

Clayton nodded in agreement, felt frustrated because he knew if they were at the winter campgrounds, he'd be that much closer, maybe only a matter of days, before they'd take him to a village and he could get medical care.

The cave was better than being out in the cold wind and snow, at least. Was he afraid of the dark? Not really, but he didn't like the confinements of a cave or the darker-than-soot dark. These things brought memories and he didn't want the experiences, the genesis of those recollections, to resurface. He had the scars to remind him, those were enough; every fiber of his body felt strung tight as cables that might snap if he suddenly moved.

Once they removed the packed snow off his leg, he saw the top of his left foot but not his ankle still in its binding. The color of the skin looked positive. He wished he could be as cheerful about going inside the cave.

"Put your arm over my shoulder," Tuma said, "put your other arm on my daughter's shoulder."

When Clayton did, Palafox nearly stumbled over Snow Wolf. "Move, move," she said and Snow Wolf obeyed. Clayton noticed, with some alarm, that Snow Wolf seemed injured; the animal limped away, favoring her right front leg.

With his arms over their shoulders and around their necks, Clayton hopped across the snow on bare feet, then into the cave. The cold rock-slab shocked his feet as much as the spoiled-onion-and-hog smell inside traumatized his nose. He breathed through his mouth the best he could, but couldn't do anything to protect his feet.

It took a moment before his eyes adjusted to the blackest dark he could ever recall seeing; by the time his vision recognized dim light, they had guided him to a roughly constructed bunk. A mild ache in his left ankle didn't last long once he had his weight off his left leg. The bunk's legs creaked and wobbled, then adapted to his weight. With his palm, he felt the smooth fur of pelts arranged to create a thin mattress.

As his eyes adjusted to the dusky light, he felt his bony ribs, examined his bony fingers and skinny arms, quickly figured he might weigh a hundred twenty pounds now, down from the hundred and ninety he'd carried into the wilderness.

Palafox and Tuma hung an animal hide at the cave entrance, apparently to be used as a flap door. The white-and-beige hide probably came from a caribou, he contemplated. The flap swept back and forth with an asthmatic wheezing as it rubbed across the gray-rock floor.

Tuma plunked logs into a dug-out place and got a fire going. Clayton wondered how long it took to dig out the solid rock to make a flume and pit for the fireplace, decided it took a very long time.

The fire began to tinge the walls with the luster of light buttery yellow, making them glisten with aged, yellowish, shellac coloration. The ovate ceiling held several small stalactites seemingly ready to drop and impale him.

Against the wall near the fireplace sat a larder with shelves. Bowls, gourds, brownish plates, big and small bowls rested on the shelves, stacked on one another in no apparent order. He saw no cans, packages or food articles that he could recognize.

A split-log table with benches rested almost at the center of the cave. Three more cots and a half-dozen chairs were arranged throughout the space, with no seeming intent. The furnishings impressed the notion that one had to make do with what one had.

Nothing was visible at the back of the cave when he entered. His amazement came when the firelight, weak but growing, helped him see that area anew. All kinds of furs, perhaps thousands, were packed together back there like colorful suits at a men's clothing store. The furs extended from ceiling to floor from wall to wall, so tightly they allowed no view of the cave's back wall.

That explained the hog-and-spoiled-onion odor. Considering the huge number of hides, he wondered if the cave was used as a stopover place for fur trappers, or a storage depot. The amount of space inside the cave didn't lend itself to housing many people. At a guess, no more than twelve could sleep inside the cave, but that number would be cramped.

The cave was every bit a cave, dark, smelly and stuffy. But for him, right now, the cave was nothing less than a penthouse suite even if he didn't like being inside it, the best natural protection against the harsh elements of the arctic wilderness.

Gradually, the fire's luster flooded the cave's walls with a buffed, mellow radiance. As the walls illuminated, details of chiseled carvings, patterns, became visible on the walls. He gazed at them, amazed that the geometric symbols were similar to the ones he'd sketched in his journal while traveling down the mountainside.

He let his eyes slide over one, then the next, and chiseled lines on one particular shape began to appear.

It couldn't be ....

Yet, it seemed it was. The wolf woman's outline displayed in the radiance as if her outline had suddenly rushed into the cave and burrowed itself into the wall, to become as prevalent as the hog smell in the air.

The entrance flap stirred, it seemed as if the cave exhaled and inhaled like a living thing.

His pulse quickened, though he felt no fright with the unexpected sight of Wolf Woman, only an uneasy "This is crazy" kind of sense. He steadied his unexpected anxiety by breathing slow, reminding himself it would be easy for his claustrophobia to overpower his senses at such times.

The reminder helped, just not enough. Clayton wasn't prone to superstitions or portents in everything he sensed or saw, but for reasons he couldn't explain, he sensed a bad omen inside the cave. He closed his eyes.

Heard the flap swish.

He opened his eyes.

Palafox stood in front of him, smiling.

His pulse went wild.

"Lay down and rest," she said. "I'll gather some animal skins, they'll keep you warm."

He nodded, "Okay."

She turned and hustled to the furs that hung at the back of the cave, stooped, heaved up a brown hide and rested it on her shoulder. Without a pause, she grabbed another hide and tucked it under her arm, then rose and ambled around a chair in silent footsteps toward him. Her shadow slid over the wall and a scrap of hide dangling from under her arm trailed through the dust behind her.

An unexpected draft hit his bare skin. It raised the tempo of his pulse. He didn't move, but became aware that he had only a sense that an existence breathed against the bare skin of his throat. He slumped backward on the bunk. The buffed glow on the walls, the furs at the back, the onion smell, the symbols, the dark, they all oppressed him. He didn't belong here. He had to get out of here. If he had to pick up the sleds and carry them on his back, he was going to get the hell out of the wilderness.

CHAPTER 13

She was glad they'd had good sun days for the most part for the past five days, but Palafox thought the snow seemed unusually deep for this time of season. The snow sank her to her knees in places and she stooped underneath tree limbs weighted with snow.

The scent of the green needles of the trees came into her nose. She blotted her chapped lips with her parka sleeve, noticed the fine hairs of the sleeve's fur were worn down.

After she got her energy, she slogged through the snow to the cave's entrance. She shoved the flap aside and went in.

She had wondered if Clayton was asleep, but he lay awake, his head on his right arm and shading his eyes with his left hand. He had no pelt on him from his waist up. His spiked hair, hairy chest and beard that hid his face made him look like a thing of wildness.

He rose and rested his bearded face on his palm, rubbed his eyes with his finger, yawned.

"Very cold," he said.

Arms crossed over, hands moving rapidly to create friction heat, she said, "it's freeeezing, burrrr."

He grinned, "Trying to be funny?"

"Kinda."

He rubbed the bridge of his nose. "I haven't seen Tuma lately."

She stepped to the table and didn't answer, or look at him while she took off her mittens and placed them on the table.

"How long's he been gone?"

She adjusted her mittens and kept her gaze on them.

Of all the questions he could've asked.

She finally answered, "Four days."

"Four days! ... Where's he at?"

She turned and said, "He went to the mountain pass."

"I'm ready to leave."

"Me too," she said.

"I can't eat any more soup."

She glanced at him a moment then looked at her mittens and adjusted them evenly.

At least he's well enough to complain now.

She said, "You'll go hungry, that's all we have."

His face went still and he slumped back on the bunk. His hand floated over his brow and he rocked his head as though he watched an object swing back and forth.

"What's the matter?" she said as she folded her arms across her chest and leaned against the tabletop.

"Do you feel gloomy?"

He took his hand away from his brow and raised his right knee under the hide and rocked it, slow.

"Listen," he said. "It's not that I'm ungrateful to you and Tuma and for all that's been done for me. It's just that I'm trapped in endless sleep. You can't go on giving me soup that makes me sleep. I've gotta get out of this place, I've gotta get my strength back."

She was surprised by the rapid-fire aimed at her. She got the message all right, even if he said it lightly. He wasn't angry and that didn't surprise her. His voice was soft but she detected stress in it. Seeking a way to cheer him she knelt to unwrap his foot.

"It's true. The soup makes you sleep," she said, and focused her attention on his left foot and leg.

The bad color of his foot and leg had gone and his pink skin looked healthy on the top of his foot. He'd lost all his toenails, but his ankle and hairy leg had little swelling. The scabs on his leg and foot were healing well. She was pleased with the progress and his improvement. She knew he would get well if the grizzly wounded him. She leaned back and looked at him.

"Daylight is short," she said, and smiled. "It fools the heck out of me to wake and it still be dark outside."

His eyes leveled on her, "I've gotta eat meat. And exercise."

She stood and stepped back to regain her balance, simply looked at him.

He turned away and gazed up several moments, rocked his knee under the pelt, before he turned and fixed his eyes on her and lowered his chin.

"I need to move around."

"You're not as strong as you think."

"I'm strong enough."

"You're not. We'd be in plenty trouble if something happened to you out there," she pointed outside the cave. "We would freeze or starve to death trying to keep you alive."

"Yeah! Well I'm sorry. We're all dead in a hundred years anyway."

She raised her arm and pointed outside again, "It'll take less than a hundred hours out there."

"Okay," he said, "maybe I should keep my mouth shut. But I can't sleep my life away. I've gotta get strong. I've gotta leave here. I've gotta eat meat, lots of meat."

She grabbed her mittens and held them several moments then laid them down, lifted reluctant eyes to his, "Your leg and foot are better. Wait at least another day or two, all right?"

"No. You don't know what it feels like to wake up and not know how long you've slept, not know where you're at, not know if you're surviving or just occupying space—"

She snatched her mittens off the table. She didn't know what to say to him but many things ran through her mind. She stared at the mittens and laid them on the table, quiet.

Then she faced him, "You don't own those feelings, you know. I want to leave as much as you do. I know what it feels like more so than you, all right?"

Clayton jerked the pelt off his bare legs and swung them off the bunk. Wincing, he sat up on the edge of the bunk. He pulled the hide over his lap. Then he grabbed the bunk's frame with both hands. He bit the corner of his left lip with his top teeth, steadied his gaze at her, leaned back and his shoulders steadied. He remained silent for a few moments.

"I've gotta do something or go stark raving mad eating soup. Another mouthful and I might lose it."

She knew his disposition wasn't because of what she had done, but she had spoken the truth: soup was all they had to eat. Unless the elder brought in a kill, boiled dog might be their only source of meat. The worst part, every dog was needed to pull the sleds. The Huskies had to have their food too, for strength to pull the sled.

She knew if they don't leave soon, they're are in big trouble.

She didn't want to say that and she couldn't fault Clayton for wanting to get strong and eat meat, but he was way too eager to move around on his leg and foot.

She looked at his caved-in stare. She said softly, "Just wait a few more days, or at least wait until the elder returns."

"Listen," he exhaled. "I've gotta get my blood circulating. I gotta exercise."

There she was, forced again to choose between what she knew was the right thing and what he wanted to do. For as long as she could remember she faced problems straight on, but she had little energy left. For a moment, she thought he would break his leg and that would teach him a lesson and she didn't have regrets thinking that either. Nothing she said had convinced him to stay put. He seemed dead set on doing exercises. She resigned herself to help him stand, although she felt like tripping him or shoving him down.

She said, "I still don't like this, Clayton. An injury to you now could keep us here and we couldn't survive, none of us would. The snow and cold are just beginning. You don't know what real cold is like yet."

"My condition isn't life-threatening anymore," he said and reached out and took her hand for support. His hand was warm. She helped him stand; his skinny, bony legs wobbled.

Each step he got stronger as she helped him to the table, he resisted when she tried to help him sit down. He limped around the table without her help. He was half-naked in the warmth of the cave, but wore the flimsy fur shoes she had made for him. After the tenth trip around the table, she could tell his muscle tone was coming back to his arms, back and chest. Perspiration started to glisten among the scars on the sleek, pale flesh of his upper body. She was impressed with his vigor and spirit and even his refusal to let her help him.

The exercise did him good, his disposition seemed happy and energetic now. She lost count at twenty trips around the table, but at last he sat on the bunk, breathing fast.

Finally he said, "Let me ask you something."

She sat on the bench at the table in front of him. All their conversations had been one-sided because he'd been sick, his voice croupy and crackly, but now his voice was vibrant and distinct, that man's voice that wasn't too hollow-log or too weak, but clear, soft and strong, the kind of man's voice a woman felt good and secure with. His words were not quick-draw, or too slow either.

She smiled, "What you wanna talk about?"

He sighed, but peered at her with steady eyes, "I'm curious about the symbols on the wall."

"What you curious about?"

He stroked his beard, which showed a thin streak of white hair along his angular jaw. He glanced at the symbols and drawings again.

"Their meanings," he said, "what does Wolf Woman's posture mean?"

"I've seen you staring at her since you've been here," she said. "No one knows the origin of the designs or symbols. They've always been here. Many, many generations of the Tacoma clan have used this cave. I've been coming here since I was a child, though we've never stayed this long near the sacred valley in the winter. Our people used to stay in the caves for winters, but not anymore, you know," she leaned forward, "sometimes, I feel as though Wolf Woman, as you call her, wants to speak. What Wolf Woman has on her face is called a Kinarog, a wolf war bonnet. Our people went into battle wearing wolf war bonnets. Wolf Woman is called Yau, and her name means 'spirit of the wilderness.'"

"Oh," he said and glanced at Yau then back at her, "you superstitious?"

"Not that much," she said, "are you?"

He shifted on the bunk, uneasy, "Some. Amazing how the lines seemed burned and perfectly grooved in solid rock."

She smiled, "You're an artist, too. I saw your drawings, the crow, the tree and boulders in the stream, I hope you don't mind I looked."

He lowered his chin and looked at her from under his eyelids, "You read what was written."

"No," she said, "the words were smeared and the lines on some of the drawings smeared too. From wetness. All the drawings didn't smear though. The drawings were the best part, I hope you don't care that I peeked at your drawings."

"Of course not. You're the first person who liked my sketches." A grin came to his lips.

"I know that's not true, your drawings are good." She said this, though she felt the drawing of the crow was awful bad. "I was surprised that you drew Yau with signs. I asked myself where you had gone to find Yau, since you hadn't been in this cave." As the drawing of the crow had been bad, she felt the drawing of Yau was outstanding.

The kindness left his eyes and seriousness came to his face. He glanced at Yau's image on the wall for several moments as if he was in thought.

She felt he wasn't going to answer her and she had to know.

"Where did you find Yau to draw?"

He turned to her and his eyes seemed cold. Finally, he said, "On the mountainside near the lake." His eyes never left her eyes, searching them.

She thought a moment, though her knowledge of that place was deep, she didn't know the place. She peered at him and smiled, "I bet the drawings of Yau you found were recently done by an artist having silent fun."

He looked at her and his expression seemed impatient. A few moments went by and he didn't seem to care to answer.

She wanted to keep his spirit high and decided to change the conversation. She relaxed and smiled, "I bet you showed your drawings to everyone after you done them."

Clayton seemed distracted as he shuffled the pelts on his lap. He glanced up. Eventually he said, "Maybe, why?"

"A young girl in our clan is an artist, and everything she draws she shows to our people. Artists like to show their drawings don't they?"

He didn't have a smile on his lips but instead he licked his lips, folded the pelt and glanced at Yau, then stared at her.

"What's remarkable about Yau is that the image here and on that rock formation, shows her with a leash or rope attached to something that's been defaced off the rock. I believe the two Yau etchings are similar, especially the snouts and the rope or leash. The etchings had to be done by the same person."

"Probably a coincidence don't ya think?"

"I haven't the slightest idea," he said, "but it's not likely, it's too incredible."

"I believe so too, if that's what you saw." This time her smile was borne from friendliness, "Clayton, you know what I've never had?"

"What's that?"

"A drawing of me. Could you draw me?"

He studied her a long time. The silence made her nervous. At last, he said softly, "You bet I can, but I don't have pencils or anything to sketch with. But I'm glad you saved my journal."

"Journal!" flew out before she thought clearly.

"The book," he said.

"Oh!" she said, and then chuckled. "You had me confused."

He lifted his chin and his eyes seemed to brighten, "Wait. Why not? I can sketch with charcoal."

She was caught off guard, "You can? Can you truly draw me with charcoal?"

"I've never sketched anything with charcoal before," he said, "but ancients used charcoal all the time and I don't see why I can't."

His eyes seemed excited and he grinned wide. He looked almost like a young boy who speared his first fish or who guided a sled for the first time.

"I would be pleased," she said. "You see, when I looked at Yau in your book, snow got on the lines and the drawing of Yau smeared and so did some of the symbols. I was going to tell you but I forgot. I hoped you could use me as a substitute for Yau to keep in your journal. Some of the other drawings are fine."

He stared at her several long moments, "It's all right. You're better for the eyes."

"When can you draw me?" Saying this, she felt a little rush of tingles over her arms and neck.

His eyes grew wider and his brows lifted. He tugged at his right ear. "Any time you like."

She glanced at the nearly finished parka that she'd sewed for him. She looked back at him, "I'll finish your parka right now. Then can you draw me? I've never had a drawing of me." Nervous in a way she had never been, she said, "You're not too tired are you?"

"I'm never too tired to draw the beautiful," he said.

She averted her eyes and couldn't say a word. She stood slow and bumped the table when she did. She grabbed her mittens off the table. Then she didn't know why she held the mittens.

"Where ya going?"

She didn't look at him, "No place."

She returned the mittens to the table. Suddenly she felt the cave had become too warm with her parka on. She went to the flap and shoved it aside to exchange the musky smell inside for the scent of the needles of the trees. She thought she heard a bird tweeting.

It was the first time she had heard a bird song in the cold of winter and it brought very good luck to hear one. The immense joy she felt was as though the radiance of the sun had suddenly shined on her face for the first time.

She shifted her gaze, sweeping the branches, pausing at places where a bird might sit to sing. She listened. She thought about her man who waited for her return, wondered what he was doing or if he was thinking of her. She tried to keep back thoughts that she knew to be untrue, but she couldn't.

After several moments, she stole a glance at Clayton from the corners of her eyes, saw his image in the glow, his face hidden behind his beard; eyes stared at the ceiling with the back of his bushy head on his arm. He gave her a glance. She turned away and back to the outside, scanned the branches again.

Her thoughts came in currents to carry her away. She listened for a repeat of the bird song, wished for it. She also wanted to walk down the path to the running brook and wade in the water to wash her face and hair. But, the water's surface was frozen, covered with ice and snow. She was twenty-five seasons and no one had ever said she was beautiful. It was her very first time to hear that one word spoken to her by a man. The worst part, there was no arm to hold onto.

Finally, after she got her thoughts in order, she went to the fireplace and put logs into it. She smiled at Clayton with her best of best smiles. She wanted to hurry and finish his parka and get the journal before he changed his mind to sketch her. Men did that sometimes, get a woman excited and not finish. Before she could halt the words, she said softly, "Thank you."

Clayton's eyes warmed as he slowly raised his chin. Composure came to his face as his chin lowered. Then his eyes opened, surprised, "thank you?"

"Yes!" she said. "I mean, I meant, thank you for saying—" The words she wanted to say caught in her throat and she held them back "—that you'll draw me." she smiled through numbed lips. "Let me pull the parka across your back and then I'll fetch your journal."

Whenever she saw the ugly scars sliced into his flesh she cringed, felt his pain. She knew one thing: the grizzly didn't put those scars on him, because a grizzly had claws. The wide purple scars on his back seemed to have been done by a knife. Especially the one long scar from his left shoulder continuously across his chest to his hip. That was surely a knife cut.

But why would someone cut him like that unless they wanted to bleed him out, to end his life?

"I'll be back," she said.

He nodded slowly but he never looked at her.

She left the cave to get his journal.

Outside in the snow, she stopped, thinking she heard something. The corner of her eye glimpsed little more than a shadow, then other shadows appeared and darted between tree trunks. They were dogs. For an instant, she felt very hungry, but then she realized what the sight meant: someone had to be dead.

CHAPTER 14

The Huskies raced toward the lean-to and their legs seemed like many branches of trees in a fierce wind. Then she saw the elder and the other sleds pulled behind the elder's sled. People had to be dead to abandon their sleds. She felt her heart beat in her ears. By the empty sleds' black handles, she knew the sleds the elder towed weren't one of their people's sleds.

She wondered about the people who owned the sleds, but her mind was full and her smile happy while she walked to the elder to tell him the news about what Clayton had said, that she had the information the elder wanted. And the elder would tell her if the mountain pass was blocked. She hoped not. Though even if that was his answer, she could breathe and sleep better knowing.

The elder was stooped over as she walked up, just coming out from under the lean-to, just finished unhitching the dogs from the reins. He straightened up and pulled his parka sleeve down, held the reins.

Smiling, she said, "Where did you find the sleds?"

The elder looked solemn, "At the edge of a gorge. It was a fight there."

He handed her a big knife. Her heart sunk.

"Hide the knife," he nodded at the cave, "don't let him see it."

She glanced at the cave and back to the elder, "I spoke with Clayton."

The elder froze and stared at her. His eyes wanted to know.

She told the elder what Clayton had said. The elder stood as if the cold froze him, gaze unblinking, the reins slipped from his hands. When she finished, his face was that of a man meditating.

"Do you know where Yau is located on the mountainside?" she asked.

He looked at her, questioning. He shook his head slowly, then he peered straight into her eyes, "It's a new sign made by Yau, to mark the territory of the sacred valley. Each generation searches for her signs."

Palafox wasn't sure what he spoke about, "Please tell me what this is about."

"They're coming," he said.

She sighed, thought a moment, spoke slowly, "But, the council of elders says that no one knows when the travelers will return."

"No one knows but the Great Spirit and Yau," the elder said, "It's written there would be signs for the people." He spoke this while he put his mitten on his right hip, as though he had an ache. "It's been many generations since the last travelers came to take the gift from us. We've been over every mountainside, every hill in the sacred valley and this is the first warning sign. There will be many more signs for the people as time draws nearer."

This, she had heard of since her first memories, but never thought beyond it. Now her heart trembled at not knowing.

"What will we do?"

"What our people have done since the sky formed. We will lead and defend the gift for the good of the people," a weary sigh and then he said, "We must leave right away. We must inform our people of the discovery. A snow slide blocked the mountain path out, we must go way around. Remember well the path we go out on, Daughter."

She didn't know the trail around the mountain pass. Only the elders and a few others knew that trail. All she knew, that meant another week's journey in the cold wind and snow.

"Go around! We don't have enough food," she said.

The elder scanned the horizon, and didn't seem to hear her.

"I'm afraid now," her voice trembled.

His dark eyes were hard as he lowered his chin and peered at her, "You should be afraid. We should all be."

She was terrified to ask but she had to. She nodded at the cave, "What about him, now?"

The elder took a deep breath and looked down. "At some point, he'll draw Yau and the language," and then he looked at her with eyes that wanted understanding, "he'll show them to others. Others will come to the sacred valley in search and we'll have complications. And more will come, and more complications. There would be no end, no stopping it, we have no choice."

Palafox's breath caught in her throat. She shook her head slow, as if she could shake away what he had said. She felt as if her mind was suddenly paralyzed and couldn't think beyond what was hinted. She felt light in her stomach.

The elder took a heavy draw of air, nodded, "It's for the good, Daughter." Then he stretched out his mittens, grasped the reins and started to clean the black-handled sled. She stood over his hunched form without moving, shocked from seeing what looked like blood, almost black, smeared on the sled's frame.

She pushed down the swelling in her chest.

"Not him," she said, her words slurred, "he won't remember, let him go."

The elder leaned back and peered at her, "Did he say anything about his leg and foot?"

"No," she said and shook her head, "not a word."

The elder seemed to consider this as he sighed and looked down for several moments. Then he peered at her, "It's what we do now that will decide our future."

She felt as if a friend was in a desperate fight with a wounded moose. She felt helpless, unable to prevent tragedy. She tried to dismiss the notion in her mind but couldn't. She blurted, "He'll resist every moment."

"I've thought of that. Sure, he'll fight. But in the end, it will be the natural order of things that must guide us in every way, dealing with him. If we fail, another will come, then another. If we fail, it will be the end."

She sighed and looked down, but then raised her head and peered at the elder, "He wants to leave, nothing more. Let him go."

"No!" He rose abruptly then shifted the reins in his hand. "Much is at stake, Daughter. We must leave here in two suns, no more."

She looked at the cave and wiped her nose with her mittens, "He's not strong enough to take on a long journey, none of us are, we must have food—"

"We have no choice. The signs in the trees and in the wind say another blizzard is on its way. We can't stay this high up. And it could be generations before our people found the first warning sign and we would've missed the temptation."

Air sucked into her mouth. She shuddered and stepped back.

"It just can't be," her voice trailed off in disbelief.

"Yes. Yes and there will be four others."

She remembered the first statement of the scripture. "No one can decipher scripture after the first statement."

The elder nodded, confirming, "The forces of evil can read and quote the scrolls, anyone who can read can quote the scrolls for their purpose. The confirmations are passed down by whispers. The force of evil comes in many disguises, in many forms and in many ways to deceive us. To seize the gift and its power. There's more to the scroll's tenets but I cannot share it with you, Daughter."

Stunned at the revelation, she simply refused to accept it. She knew each temptation had a specific part in the scroll to identify them, but no one was able to decipher the symbols or their meanings. And that explained a lot of things, many things about the council of elders.

"This is a mistake," she almost spat out.

"No," the elder's head shaking vehemently, "the council of elders is aware, knows all the signs and what they mean. The knowledge cannot be written in language."

He then raised his arm and pointed at the cave, shook his arm and said, "That man will decide our fate by what we do, or don't do, or what he does or doesn't do. We don't know which. We cannot take chances, nor can we interfere in the natural order or course of things.

He could be the force of evil sent here to seize the gift or he might be the first temptation."

Once, she believed in the scroll and the warnings about the temptations. Now she considered them fantasy stories. In disbelief, she muttered without thinking, "The First Temptation, the council said the temptations come in pairs."

He glanced at the cave and back at her. He whispered, "Yes. But he's the first, we believe. We don't know if all the temptations are to come in pairs."

"But how can we be sure? Wouldn't a temptation know?"

"No. Temptations don't know they're a temptation. Only the force of evil knows they're a temptation. The forces of evil spirits are clever and smart."

"But how can we be completely sure?"

"By the first warning, of Yau. " He quoted the scroll's tenet. "He shall enter the sacred valley bearing a gift of another, destroy a great beast, take heed for he shall bear the Saluuette's mark …"

"There's more to this tenet," he said, "but I cannot share it with you."

The second and third lines were in symbols. She knew the first part of the tenet and now the second. What she wanted to know was the third.

"What convinced you?" she said. "He's just a man, and this might be a coincidence."

The elder looked at her. He didn't smile.

"No. It's not a coincidence. The gift bestowed upon our people came with a terrible warning. Are you willing to chance that this man might be a coincidence or misunderstanding, knowing the consequences if he's the force of evil?"

She shook her head, lowered her face, and mumbled, "No, none of us would."

"The temptations don't know the signs that authenticate them," the elder said. "Only the temptations sent by the force of evil would try to fool us. Only the council knows the signs and the confirmation. Many things known to us should never be written in language. To do so would unrest men's minds and that would not be good. We must act and behave as we would. To do otherwise will complicate matters for us all, forever more. The Great Spirit cannot be fooled."

She looked up at him, "What are we going to do?"

"As I said. Make ready to leave."

That was why the elder had been acting so, so strange; he was convinced that Clayton Spears was the first temptation, or was sent by the force of evil. She refused to believe this. Clayton was a mortal with blood as red as hers. And all he seemed to want was to leave the wilderness.

She didn't believe in the temptations scrolls in any way.

But she wasn't telling the elder how she felt. She didn't want to think or discuss it further. She had noticed the elder didn't have a kill and she had to make something to eat. She wished they had meat to eat, that Clayton had never come into the sacred valley and that she hadn't stayed.

"We must have food," she said wiping her nose with her mitten.

The elder looked at her kindly, "Did you make the tribute for the grizzly's spirit with the colors?"

She nodded, "Yes. I had to use his tattered dungarees for some thread but I finished the tribute *and* with all the colors."

"Good. Good, Daughter. I'm hungry for meat. Make ready to boil dog. We must celebrate the tribute to the grizzly's spirit and the final confirmation sign. We shall know soon enough if this man is the first temptation, or if he was sent by the force of evil."

She sighed and looked off. Then she turned back and peered at him. "How can you know for sure, how can we *know*?"

"I cannot say, Daughter," he said, and smiled warmly. "You mustn't worry. You mustn't harbor fear. It's a great thing for our people. It honors our people to defend the gift. It's a great thing to fight against the force of evil, it's a good day if he's the temptation."

Fighting unfamiliar tears, she said, "What can we do if he is?"

"Nothing at first. The force of evil has a mortal's body. We will leave here, when we get to the bottom of this mountain it will honor our people to destroy him." He removed his mittens and cracked his knuckles, grunted like a bear as he did so.

She flinched and tried not to let him see her trembling. She wanted no part in this affair. Unless Clayton turned out to be the force of evil. Then, she'd be the first to put a stake in his heart.

"This could be one big coincidence and one big mistake. Mistakes have happened in the past," knowingly pushing to keep the closed subject open with the elder.

"No. No mistakes have been made in the past. We're not so easily fooled. The force of evil has weaknesses in a mortal's body and— I can say no more."

He stared at her and his stare made her unsettled. Then he moved his face slightly to peer into her eyes, as if he searched for some telltale sign. His eyes seemed to possess magic or senses beyond his sight, for she sensed he was immune to her resistance to fight back.

For a moment, neither of them moved. Then like a fool, she dropped the big knife he had given her. When she squatted to grab the knife, he stepped on it. She rose slow and gazed at him, frightened.

He just stared at her for a long time. Then he stretched out his mitten and grabbed the knife. He stared at her for several long moments more before he handed her the knife again, never once losing eye contact. With every bit of inner strength, she maintained a calm face and stared back even as she wondered if the elder suspected her as a force of evil spirit.

He smiled at her, slow, as if he knew something or had read her mind, though she knew he couldn't. Then, without speaking, he shifted his gaze to look out over the wilderness.

She followed with her own eyes to the clouds that brooded at the horizon of the snow-white land. A wind blew through the trees above them and the treetops quaked without a sound as the last brightness of the day was sinking out of the sky.

CHAPTER 15

In the churchlike silence, Clayton greedily gulped down a hindquarter of boiled dog. The idea of eating dog meat didn't sicken him as he'd imagined it would. But then, it wasn't the first time he'd eaten exotic meat. Besides, hunger did that to a man, made him not care about the source of food that quelled his hunger pangs.

After he ate his gut full, he laid on the bunk and put his hands behind his head and stared at the barreled ceiling of the cave. Eventually, he slid into a state that no longer confused him but confounded him.

His failure to make sense of the questions that Palafox asked him about his sketches created a mystery where no mystery was before.

It had to be a ridiculous notion, since thousands of peculiar carvings and sketches existed throughout the world. What significance were his sketches to her, what were the undercurrents to her questions? But for the first time, he wondered if he'd stumbled onto something he shouldn't have.

Yet he couldn't shake the feeling that he was caught in some strange web of deception. She asked seemingly simple questions and he answered them. Well, most of them. He truly hadn't trusted her since the first time she asked him about his sketches.

Everything about Palafox seemed like one mystery after another. The news about leaving for their winter campgrounds didn't lift her spirits as much as it did his. In fact, she seemed unmoved while she was giving him the good news. It was like she dreaded the return to her winter home.

The other thing, she seemed eager about was him sketching her. Now, she seemed less enthusiastic. Perhaps she was nervous about having him sketch her? Perhaps this was truly her first sketch?

After she gave him several piles of charcoal to choose from, he'd filed and rubbed the best pieces to fine points with a knife. He was pleased to see that each piece possessed a unique dark-colored shade when he wet it with his tongue. The various shades of charcoal would add an okay quality of light and shade to the lines of his sketch. He was happy about this.

He sat on the edge of the cot. She stood at the table in her parka with her right mitten on the table, almost in a pose but natural enough to work for his sketch. She smiled but it didn't beam. Tuma sat on the bench on the other side of the table, watching with a cautious expression.

The eyes were his favorite part on a face to sketch. He couldn't sketch Palafox's eyes because they seemed off somehow. Squeezed, without her actually squinting them.

"Your eyes seem red and swollen, are you all right? Change your mind about the sketch?" His words carefully chosen to draw out an answer, at least a clue.

Palafox smiled and said, "Sure, I'm fine. It's the fumes from the burning logs. The fumes irritate my eyes, but they'll clear up after the logs burn a little while longer. Do my eyes look too bad for you to draw?"

Her face seemed to brighten, this time.

"No, not really. I can manage," he said, and looked down and continued to sketch her. The fumes from the burning logs irritated his eyes to tears at times too. He hurried to finish the sketch.

When he was done, he offered the journal for her to preview. She accepted it with a big smile, laid it flat on the table before allowing her eyes to drift downward to see it.

An instant later, she drew back. She chuckled. She turned around, then leaned over to examine the sketch closer. Her voice rising in a nervous giggle, she squealed and covered her mouth. But then a curious expression came over her face, as though she tried to subdue something in her mind. She giggled nervously this time, drew back slowly, and then leaned forward again.

"I don't look like this, do I?"

"Why, what's the matter?"

She looked at him, her smile was warm. Then she looked back down and used her forefinger to trace the drawing.

"Am I like this, do I really look like this?"

He could tell she seemed happy, he felt happy for her. And relieved that she seemed happy.

"Yes, you do. I hope so."

"Let's see," Tuma said with a grin. "Yes, it's like you, Daughter."

She turned to him, then back to Clayton, her smile gleamed, "You make me beautiful."

"It's because you're beautiful," he said.

"Thank you," she said. "Can you draw the elder?"

He glanced at Tuma, who gave a tight nod, then said, "Why not?"

He sketched them four times apiece, together and individually. In the process, he discovered a genuine friendliness he hadn't experienced in a very long time. They smiled and the joy in their eyes seemed genuine. He was delighted the charcoal sketches worked out.

Everyone seemed happy though Tuma's reaction wasn't the same as Palafox's. Tuma was reserved and didn't say much about his sketch, he just grinned a lot. Their grins, chuckles flattered him. He didn't think he was a good portrait artist.

When the entire session was over and Tuma had left to see to the Huskies, Palafox sat across the table from him. She stared at him for a while, then smiled and said softly, "I made something for you." She adjusted her parka. She ran her fingers through her hair, and smiled the entire time. "I'll be right back."

Before he could react, she rushed to the hanging furs at the back of the cave and retrieved a folded fox pelt. Nodding at Tuma, who had just returned from outside, she went to the fireplace and turned her back.

"Don't look," she said. "Close your eyes."

Clayton closed his eyes.

"It'll be ready as soon as I can tie this one little thread," she said and approached the table where he sat.

"You can look," she said.

Clayton opened his eyes.

Palafox held a in her hand a bear claw necklace. They were like browns, black, grays, maybe reds, yellows, or maybe orange embroidery. White stitching had symbols like circles, triangles, and rectangles, stitched together with tiny and colorful beads along the eight six-inch claws. The claws were polished to a high sheen and attached to a thick leather half-moon-shaped loop. The fine embroidery went another six inches before the claws were attached.

"Wow," he said.

"Go on, take it," she said, and grinned wide. "It's yours, go on, take it. The claws are from the grizzly you killed. It's the tribute to the grizzly's spirit. The necklace is yours."

"I've seen pictures of bear claw necklaces," he said, trying to control his excitement. "But I never thought I'd see an original one. What a beauty!"

"Wear it, put it around your neck," she said, her eyes bright.

"Are you sure you want to part with this?" he said. "It's a beauty."

"It's for you."

"I'll wear it proudly," he said, and hung the necklace around his neck, adjusted it so it would fit over his sternum. He inspected the eight black claws and admired their sheen, certain that a skilled jeweler would fail if they tried to duplicate such artistic work.

"It must've taken a lot of time to sew and make," he said, glancing at her, then at Tuma, who stepped around the table.

"Not so long," she said with a glance at Tuma. "I started polishing the claws from the time we found you."

"I can't ever pay you what this must be worth."

Tuma plunked on the bench, leaned forward, and smiled, "Each brother who kills a great grizzly earns the right to own a grizzly claw necklace. Only a mother, daughter, or sister of the Tacoma clan is permitted to make a grizzly necklace, as a sacred tribute to the grizzly's spirit. It makes the grizzly's spirit proud."

Clayton thanked Tuma politely, and said, "I'll treasure it and wear it."

They talked a short while and he felt warm and relaxed. Not so for Palafox, who seemed to have returned to her earlier odd lack of enthusiasm. Plus, she went outside frequently and returned. He assumed the boiled, greasy meat they'd eaten didn't agree with her.

Palafox returned to her spot on the bench and it seemed her eyes were teary.

Tuma laid his big hands on the table and said, "May I see it?"

Nodding, Clayton removed the necklace and handed it over.

For a few minutes, Tuma examined the necklace and seemed quite pleased with it. Then he laid the bear claw necklace in front of Clayton and rubbed the beads, then each claw, with his forefinger. As he did, Clayton sensed a change in either the room, or the elder, but couldn't say what or why. Suddenly he felt tense as Tuma looked at him.

Tuma twisted on the bench and straightened his shoulders as he leaned back from the table. He raised his eyes and the scar on his right cheek twitched his thick brow.

He grasped the bear claw necklace and examined it. He placed his fat thumb, the one with a long thumbnail, on the beads of the bear claw necklace.

Tuma said softly, "Brother, can you recite the colors that you see 'mongst other things on this bear claw necklace where I have my thumb?"

Befuddled, Clayton glanced at the necklace and then at Palafox, who sat with big doe eyes.

The quiet and stillness cast an air of deception where deception wasn't before, it seemed to squeeze the cheerfulness out of the air. The warm air inside the cave seemed to go cold. He lifted his eyes and stared at Tuma's poker stare.

Then a woofing chorus filled the air outside the cave. Even to Clayton's inexperienced ear, the Huskies were barking territorial barks, warnings to not come closer.

Palafox's eyes went big. She jumped to her feet. "Someone's coming," she said, in a fast sinking voice.

At the same time, the legs of the bench scrubbed the floor as Tuma stood. He stared at the entrance. But then his expression changed, as though something had only then occurred to him, he shoved the bear claw necklace over the table to Clayton. With one fierce glance at him, Tuma grabbed his spear and hurried outside, Snow Wolf following him.

Palafox followed until she stopped at the entrance, held the flap to the side with her forearm, peeked outside. Without speaking, without looking in Clayton's direction, she turned and raced to where the furs hung at the back of the cave. Scarcely had she reached where the furs hung than she turned and raced to the larder and scanned the shelves. Hardly had she done that than she returned to the entrance to once more look outside. Then she pivoted and scampered to where the furs hung again. The few light bumps and taps made by Palafox under the hanging furs were as distant thunder.

He did the only thing he felt capable of doing at that moment. He grabbed the bear claw necklace and draped it around his neck. He stood and trying to do too much, too soon, dizziness came over him and he wobbled. He did the only thing he could do, he collapsed on the bunk. He listened to faint sounds inside and outside the cave. His pulse quickening.

CHAPTER 16

Clayton didn't need the service of a mystic to know that Palafox was troubled. The shadows seemed as tense as he was. She burst out of the hanging furs, unrolled a brown pelt and a knife flashed. She dropped the pelt and hurried around the table.

He sat up on the edge of the bunk, "What's going on?"

"We gotta visitor." She extended the knife. "Here, hide it."

He clutched the knife by the blade, "Fill me in."

"The visitor could be a cutthroat."

"Where are your guns?"

"We have none."

He winced. No pistols or even a rifle? Incredible. The only potential weapons he'd seen were axes, knives, hatchets and spears. With all the prospects of danger in the wilderness, all they had to defend themselves with were knives? It was too fantastic. He shook his head, "You expect me to believe that."

She sighed, and said, "Our people left with the guns, they were too far ahead for us to catch up, it was my fault."

He looked at her, "A knife won't do a hell a lot of good, especially against guns."

She sighed again and fumbled with her mittens, "I'm gonna hide in the furs, if anyone comes inside don't look back at the furs, all right?"

"Got ya. Maybe it's just someone lost or passing through."

"We can't take chances, things happen all the time in the uplands and no one can explain what happened."

She turned and raced to the furs, twisted sideways, squeezed through the furs until she was out of his sight again.

He turned his attention to the Jim Bowie knife, shifted it so he held it by the handle. The bone-handled knife fit his palm nicely; it had good feel. The eight-inch blade had good balance. He licked his thumb, rubbed the knife's edge, shaved a bit of hair off his forearm.

Amazing something like a letter was carved on the handle. He wet his thumb, scrubbed what seemed like dried blood off, figured it was blood from an animal. It didn't stop the sinking feeling in his gut when the letters "WG" began to appear on the bone handle. Likely, initials.

After a few minutes, he wedged the knife to its hilt between the frame of the bunk and the cave's wall, covering the knife with an inconspicuous pelt. He practiced grasping the knife for a half-minute.

A knife was close and personal.

He didn't want to think past that.

The barks of the Huskies swelled outside and sounds indicated sleds approaching. He listened to faint voices in the dark. Dogs snarled and growled. Men's voices rose, then raucous laughter. A self-amused giggle mixed in the growls. "Stop," a man's voice said. A dog squealed, yelped. Like one of the men had kicked the dog to silence it.

Clayton never trusted anyone who abused animals or who didn't love animals.

Through an opening in the flap, flashlight beams highlighted tree branches and the dim image of at least two people walked toward the lean-to.

A short time later, Tuma entered the mellow light of the cave. Behind him came a burly man, not tall but squatty, bloated around the midsection, followed by a short man.

The fat man strolled like a conquering Viking. He stopped and rolled his shoulders, scanned the décor and nodded, sniffed the air. His grin reminded Clayton of a frog eyeing a tasty insect. The man saw Clayton on the bunk and he nodded, still grinning.

Clayton returned the nod with a tight grin.

The fat man wore a parka pieced together from some grayish-furred animal, frayed and topped by an outsized fur hood that encircled a reddish beard with a black streak. The man's head appeared to bud off his parka. His baggy trousers seemed mushroom brown, with dark stains on his right leg. His trouser legs were stuffed inside wide, knee-high boots. Inside his parka, a wide brown belt studded with brass, on the right side a holster with a pearl-handled pistol. The fat man never stopped grinning as he gazed around the cave.

The other stranger was a lanky man though short in stature. His parka, also frayed, seemed too big for his body and was ripped in places. The lanky man's shoulders slouched and he bounced on one foot, then the other while he hugged himself, blew mist through his mouth and nose as he rubbed his parka-clad arms, "Boy howdy, it's cold," came from his squeaky voice. He also wore a grin on his weasel-beaked face and his Spam-colored skin was pitted with pockmarks.

The fat man held the air of someone who had money even though his dress said otherwise. The lanky stranger could've passed for a man riding the rails wearing all he owned.

The two men glanced at each other and at every article in the cave, including the shadows. At first, it seemed the men were getting an idea of the cave's layout, but after a series of facial gestures, stares and grins, it seemed more like they were scoping out the cave.

Clayton's pulse raced. He breathed to calm his heartbeat. He looked away and pretended they weren't there for a moment. Maybe he was being paranoid. He looked back.

The fat man shot a glance at Clayton again, then turned and lumbered to the hanging furs.

Through the corner of his eye, Clayton watched him grab a handful of the furs, pull them to his face.

The man nodded, turned with a grin, "Not bad, not bad ah'tall, Tuma."

That said, he shuffled quiet along the perimeter of the furs, looked up and down the hanging furs. He stopped and grabbed more furs and smelled them, nodded in approval.

Clayton held his breath and prayed that Palafox stayed perfectly still because the fat man stood right where she had entered the furs to hide.

CHAPTER 17

The fat man turned from the furs and lumbered across the floor, plunked onto the bench at the table.

Clayton breathed a sigh, tried to relax.

Moments later, Tuma introduced the strangers. The fat man with the paunch and wide belt was Goose and his lanky cohort was Skidder.

Clayton greeted them cordially with a nod and tense grin, then intentionally avoided the conversation they were having with Tuma. Instinct told him Tuma wanted to do most of the talking anyway. Though he felt edgy, he concentrated on presenting a relaxed demeanor.

"A comfortable setup you got here, Tuma," Goose said, and grinned wide. "It's cozy, right nice."

Skidder flopped on the bench next to Goose. "Um-hum, warm too."

Tuma said, "I've lived all my life here in the uplands."

"That a fact," Goose said, "I can see that, by all the designs on the wall, look there, Skidder." Goose pointed at Yau.

Skidder chuckled as he stared at Yau's image with a smirk Clayton couldn't figure out.

Tuma said, "What ya boys doing this high in the uplands this time of season?"

Goose chuckled and leaned back, then slumped forward with a wide grin and folded his arms on the table, "We'd hoped to put some trap lines out, but I can see by the number of furs hung up back there, there might not be enough game left here to trap."

"I know that's right," Skidder said.

"It's kinda late in the season in the uplands to trap game," Tuma said. "Lowland flats are the best territory to trap in the winter."

"Um-hum," Goose said, twisted on the bench, removed his arms, folded his arms across his chest and eyed Tuma.

"We got sidetracked, say, three months or so ago, might've been longer. But, somebody stole Skidder's traps and furs. So, we decided to pitch in and try to find the men who stole his goods. We smelled smoke and saw ruts in the snow, decided to follow the ruts to find the source, and for other reasons, too. We kinda hoped if we come across somebody, they'd be friendly and kind enough to put us on the trail outta here—"

"Don't forget," Skidder said.

Goose looked at Skidder, "I won't." Then he continued, "Me and Skidder figured if the folks were friendly, we'd talk about a little partnership for the duration of our stay in the uplands. An extra two hundred traps could mean a lot more furs, provided the men weren't the same men who robbed Skidder."

Tuma crunched his shoulders. "At daylight, I'll point y'all to the path out, we don't have room here," Tuma said, and in a friendly way.

"Much obliged," Goose said. "No use in us staying if no game's here, right Skidder?"

"I know that's right."

"I gotta spit," Goose said. "Would ya mind if I spit in your fireplace, Tuma?"

Tuma nodded, "Okay."

Clayton watched as Goose spat his tobacco plug into the fire and it sizzled. Goose took his hands out of his mittens and seemed to scrub his teeth with his fingers. Then he spat in the fire again, again and again.

Goose stepped to the table and slumped on the bench, "By the way, Tuma, if you don't mind my saying so, when we went to the lean-to, I counted nine sleds under there but not enough dogs in the pens to pull all those sleds. I'm in need of a jeep sled to haul supplies. I'd like to buy a sled if you'd be kind'a enough to sell me one."

Tuma inhaled and crossed his legs, "The sleds belong to other brothers, I expect them back anytime."

Goose leaned back, "Anytime, that a fact."

"I hear that." Skidder reached out and removed his mittens from the table.

Goose grinned and looked at Clayton, "What happened to the fella on the bunk, he don't look well?"

Tuma glanced at Clayton. "He killed a grizzly in a fight."

"That a fact. The grizz must've roughed him up pretty good."

"He'll be all right," Tuma said.

"A fine bear claw necklace you got there, bud, did the claws come from the grizz you killed?"

Clayton nodded, "Yes."

"Don't suppose you'd sell the necklace for a fair price?"

"It's not for sale."

"It's a damn fine bear claw necklace, bud. Best I've seen."

"I know that's right," Skidder said.

"Thanks," Clayton said, nodded with a grin to be polite and friendly.

Goose stretched his arms over his head and yawned, "Oh, me." He glanced at Skidder with a broad grin. Skidder buried his face on his parka arm on the table. His shoulders shook from giggling.

Goose smiled at Tuma while he spoke, "Those sleds under the lean-to, how did ya come about the two sleds with the black-painted handles?"

Tuma's eyebrows twitched. "Why?"

"If you looked on the frame, you'd see the letters 'WG' carved in the frame on the right side."

Tuma uncrossed his legs and his shoulders straightened, "I saw the letters."

"The letters are initials and 'WG' stands for Wilbert Gins. He had a habit of carving his initials in everything he owned. That's my dad's brother and his grandson Lewis was with 'im when they went missing, say, a week or so. We've been searching for 'em ever since."

The knife ...

Clayton turned away. He dreaded to think that Tuma and Palafox might be thieves. He hoped he was wrong but he couldn't rule the possibility out. He also didn't want to think about the scenario if Goose found the knife braced between the wall and his bunk.

"Where they go missing?" Tuma asked.

The lines on Goose's forehead got deeper and darker, "I'm not proposed to point fingers, but it's reasonable to say they went missin' 'round here. How'd my uncle's sleds end up in your possession, friend?"

"I found the sleds at the edge of the gorge," Tuma said. "I took the sleds because they were turned over, covered with snow, looked abandoned."

"That a fact."

Tuma nodded.

"See anybody?"

Tuma shook his head, "No."

"Where's the gorge?"

"A long ways," Tuma said. "A place you don't wanna go."

Goose raised his chin and chuckled. Finally, he said, "What happened to the traps and furs? The dogs that pulled the sled? I know Uncle Gins had furs with 'im, because me and Skidder transferred a thousand dollars' worth of furs to his jeep sled, say four or five weeks ago. Before we traveled into the uplands and the blizzard caught us with our zippers down."

"I saw no furs or dogs, just sleds," Tuma said.

"He's a lying bastard ain't he, Goose?"

Goose turned to Skidder and said, "Be quiet."

"Tuma, Tuma," Goose said, and shook his head in a curt way. "Your story how the sleds found their way into your possession wouldn't satisfy anybody. My uncle wouldn't abandon his sleds and walk out of the wilderness carrying three hundred traps, furs, and dogs. You look like a smart man, and I'm not saying what ya described isn't the truth, but you understand my suspicions, friend."

"Yes. I hope you understand my impoliteness," Tuma said. "I believe you have overstayed your welcome. So, if you'll go, and take the black-handle sleds with you."

Goose and Tuma stared hard at each other. Clayton felt the air tense and he lay uncomfortable on the bunk. His hands were on top of the caribou hide, Skidder watched his every move.

Goose reached into his right parka pocket, pulled out a steel trap, tossed it on the table in front of Tuma. "This trap came from the sled under the lean-to. See the initial 'WG.'"

"I see the letters," Tuma said.

"Explain how you ended up with his trap, too?"

Tuma's posture stiffened. "Like I told you, there were no dogs or furs, just three traps in one of the sleds."

Goose stared at Tuma and kept his arms folded on the table. "Word been going around for years about prospectors and trappers vanishing in the uplands with everything they own. I know you're a reasonable man by looking at ya, but, Tuma," Goose shook his head in disgust, "some of those furs ya got back there are better than two, three, four year old. Some of those furs could belong to Skidder, Uncle Gins, and God knows who else. I believe you're trying to blow smoke up my ass."

"I heard that," Skidder said.

"Time for y'all to leave."

Scarcely had Tuma said this than Skidder scooted around the table and steadied an automatic pistol against Clayton's head. A serious black nine-millimeter automatic pistol.

Skidder stared at him.

Clayton said, "Easy-easy, now-easy."

Skidder cocked an eyebrow, "Don't flinch, keep ya paws where I can see 'em, fella."

"Easy-easy, we can work this out," Clayton said.

Skidder threw back his head and chuckled, "Get a sled full of this fella, Goose."

"We don't have time to mitigate, tie him up, Skidder." Goose held his pistol, its black barrel pressed at the base of Tuma's skull. "This pistol's got a hair trigger," Goose said, "a slight jar will set it off, so stay right tight old Eskimo, steady old man."

Skidder kept the barrel against Clayton's head.

"Get on your feet, fella," Skidder ordered.

Clayton stood and Skidder shoved him.

Clayton turned to Skidder, "Take it easy-easy."

"Stand still and put your hands behind ya back, fella."

Clayton put his hands behind his back, "I couldn't wade my way through soapsuds—"

"Shut ya poormouthing," Skidder said, tied Clayton's wrists, then forced him to sit on the bench.

Goose spun Tuma around. Barely had Goose begun binding Tuma's wrists than Snow Wolf walked inside the cave.

The wolf hunkered down and bared fangs.

Skidder hopped out in front of Goose and shot Snow Wolf dead.

Goose's head turned to the furs. The legs of the bench scrubbed the floor as Goose squatted behind Tuma. Not yet finished tying Tuma's hands, he shoved the pistol to the base of Tuma's skull.

"The wolf was a pet," Clayton said.

"Ya hear that, Skidder?"

"Huh."

Goose raised his head above Tuma's and whispered, "I heard a noise back there in the furs, like the way a rabbit squeals. And something moved. People are hid back there, Skidder."

Skidder banged his head with his left hand. "My ears ring, I didn't hear ah'thang."

Goose waved the pistol at the hanging furs, "I mean it, I saw somebody back there in the furs."

Skidder raced and hid behind the table and Clayton, raised his head up above Clayton's shoulder. Skidder said, "Come out from back yonder, we know y'all's back 'ere, come out before somebody gets it real bad."

"We know ya' hidin' back there, come out," Goose said.

"Want me to shoot in the furs, Goose?"

"Hell no, a bullet'll ruin lots of furs." Goose jostled Tuma's shoulder with his free hand, "How many hid back there, old Eskimo?"

Tuma shrugged.

"Last time, old Eskimo, how many hid back there?"

Tuma said nothing, folded his hands on his lap.

"Where your guns?"

"My brothers have the guns, they'll be back anytime now."

Skidder kept the cocked pistol against Clayton's head. "The old Eskimo lying ain't he, Goose?"

"Shut up."

"Fella, who's back yonder?" Skidder said.

Clayton ignored him.

"I said who's all back yonder?"

Clayton sighed and Skidder slapped him across the face.

Clayton shook the daze off and the gray spots in his eyes went away. He spat blood to the floor from his busted lip. His face and lip felt stinging hot. He tried to blame it on the slap. He calmed his breathing the best he could.

"How many hid back yonder, fella?"

Clayton looked down. Skidder shoved the pistol barrel underneath Clayton's jaw until his neck stretched back, "I said how many back yonder, fella."

"Skidder," Goose said softly, "put the fella in front of you, go back there and cut them ropes the furs hang on. If they had guns with 'em back there, they'd already got the drop on us."

"Get on your feet, fella."

Clayton stood.

Then Skidder grabbed Clayton's hair, pulled his head back and shoved the pistol into the base of his skull.

Clayton shuffled over the floor, wrists tied behind his back, the pistol's barrel against his skull. Sweat from his forehead burned the corners of his eyes.

Skidder stopped him at the edge of the furs and made him stand still, whipped out a switchblade and sliced the ropes holding the furs. One line dropped, then another, and another.

Palafox shot out of the furs and raced for the mouth of the cave. Skidder sprinted after her, chuckling, caught her at the flap. She tried to wiggle free of Skidder's bear bug. Her legs plowed the air.

"Let go of me!"

At that moment, Tuma shoved Goose to the side and lunged for Skidder's gun.

Skidder released Palafox, grabbed Tuma in a headlock, growled and cussed while he and Tuma wrestled for the pistol. Then Palafox exited the cave in a run.

Before he realized what he was doing, he was running to knock Goose down and give Palafox time to get away.

Goose spun around and caught him around the neck, yelling, "Whoa, fella, you're trying to spoil the fun," and forced him onto the bench.

Goose seemed to enjoy the tussle between Skidder and Tuma. "Woo-woo, Skidder, ya better hogtie 'im before that ol' Eskimo whoops up on your ass."

Spraying cuss words, Skidder bounced and wrestled with Tuma like a rider being thrown around by a bull. Then a noise came that sounded like a paper bag had popped.

In the stillness following, Tuma doubled over and grimaced, holding his stomach. He took two jerky steps and plunked onto the floor, rolled over on his back. He grimaced again, but he didn't mutter a word, just gasped. He didn't move again. Tuma watched death coming as the gun's smoke rose up around him.

CHAPTER 18

Skidder stood over Tuma with the pistol along his side.

"You idiot," Goose said, "go catch that Klooch."

Skidder looked up slow. He glared at Goose. Finally, Skidder said, "Don't call me names."

Goose said, "Go fetch that Klooch, you nincompoop."

Skidder stared hard at Goose for several moments, but then turned and walked out of the cave.

Goose stepped to Tuma, who lay in a small pool of blood and shook his head, "This old Eskimo had it coming, that's restitution for stealing furs for years, probably killings, too. He won't be robbing anybody else."

Though confused and shocked, Clayton heard Palafox outside saying, "Let go of me. Stop! Let go!"

A moment later, Skidder dragged her back inside. He manhandled her to the table, jerked her parka down behind her to restrain her flailing arms and then tied her wrists behind her back.

Then Skidder reached around and grabbed her breast with his bony hands, at the same time he ground against Palafox's butt. Instantly, she drew back, wheeled and kicked him, but missed what she aimed for. Her kick landed hard on his thigh.

Skidder raised his hand, smacked her across her face.

The lick snapped her head back.

"Don't you hit me," she said, and tried to kick him again.

Goose chuckled, "You've gotta a little spit'n wildcat by the ass now, Skidder."

Skidder frowned. He grabbed her and shoved her against the table, placed his hand on her head and tried to push her face into the table's surface.

Before Clayton could think straight, with his wrists tied, he got off the bench. Skidder, taken by surprise, didn't have time to do anything before he used his shoulder to send Skidder airmail across the floor.

Goose grabbed Clayton from behind and flung him into the table. Clayton bounced and collapsed to the floor, but was only there a second before Goose jerked him up and pulled him around to bring them face-to-face.

Eyes squinting, Goose grabbed Clayton's chin and squeezed.

"Fella," Goose said through gritted teeth. "If ya do that again, I'll take personal interest in seeing that ya beg for somebody to shoot you." He shoved Clayton to the floor.

Skidder giggled.

Clayton felt a mule kick the side of his head. His mind tumbled in darkness, then shut down. Clarity returned in slow motion and sounds were eerie, confused. He shook his head to clear the fog that blurred his vision, saw wide gray boots inches from his face.

Grunting, Goose jerked him off the floor and made him sit on the bench with a hand pressed down on his shoulder.

"Don't move, fella," Goose said.

Releasing his hold on Clayton he went over to Tuma, cut the pouch away from Tuma's neck and emptied the pouch's contents on the table.

Colored rocks, a cone-shaped metal spear point four inches long and the jade jewel, still on its lanyard, tumbled out. Goose grabbed the jade and inspected it, rubbed it, then shoved it into his parka pocket.

Palafox sat on the bench across the table from Clayton. She glanced at him a moment then pressed her face on the table. Her shoulders began to tremble.

Goose pointed outside, "Get that wolf and the old Eskimo outta here, hide 'em in the snow. Others could arrive before we leave."

"Ya gotta help," Skidder said.

"Shut up, ignoramus."

Skidder glared at Goose, "I done told ya, I don't like it when people call me names."

Goose grabbed an armload of furs and went outside. When he returned he made Clayton stand. Smirking, he lifted the bear claw necklace off Clayton's neck, put the necklace around his own neck and adjusted it while he admired it.

Clayton glanced at Palafox, who sat with her face on the table, he thought about the knife. If Goose found the knife against the bunk, his uncle's initials on the knife, they were doomed, if they weren't already.

Goose led Clayton away from the table, then walked around him. "What happened to my uncle and nephew?"

"I don't know."

"That a fact."

Clayton nodded.

"You're mixed up with this ring of thieves aren't ya?"

From the corner of Clayton's eye he saw Palafox raise her head. "We're not thieves."

Goose's eyes shifted to her, "Shut up."

Palafox put her face back on the table.

Clayton didn't say anything, but he now knew what bad luck felt like when it sank all the way to the gut on the slowest route.

"How did 'ya come about that purple scar across ya chest, fella?"

Clayton didn't mutter a word and didn't intend to.

"You killed the man that cut ya didn't you, fella."

Clayton stared.

"Ya say ya don't know anything about anything, and ya here with these thieving Eskimos."

"They saved my life."

"Umm-humm, I don't believe you."

Clayton spat blood from his busted lip. "Why's that?"

"I'm asking the damn questions, fella—"

"Goose's got college," Skidder said.

"Shut up, you idiot."

Skidder glared at Goose, "Don't call me names."

Goose shoved Clayton back onto the bench, stared back at Skidder, "What ya gonna do about it, bovine?"

Skidder's eyes narrowed and his hands seemed to quake.

"What ya staring at Skidder, you don't know what bovine means? Come on. We got work." Goose took an armload of furs and ambled toward the entrance. "Idiot," he mumbled as he brushed past Skidder.

"Don't call me names ya hear me, college words hurt my head."

Goose stopped at the flap. He turned, "Umm humm, we got a word for that, too." Chuckling, he went outside.

Skidder watched Goose exit, then turned to Clayton.

"What ya starin' at?"

Clayton kept his eyes locked on Skidder.

Skidder's weasel-beaked face held no emotion and both his cheeks seemed blemished more by the hard cold.

"You better stop starin', fella, or you're gonna be real, real sorry." He whipped out an eight-inch switchblade while he spoke.

Clayton looked at the floor, wanted to run from these lunatics.

Skidder grabbed Clayton's hair, pulled his head back and pressed the switchblade against his throat. Skidder's breath smelled like something had died in his mouth.

"I'll slit ya gawd-dam throat, fella," Skidder said.

Clayton shuddered and held his breath. He told himself Tuma's death had been an accident and that Skidder wouldn't harm him unless Goose told him to or Skidder lost what sanity he had left. He tried to remain calm in spite of the trembles and prayed that Skidder would stop before he got carried away.

Skidder let go after a long stare down, closed the switchblade, grabbed an armload of furs and glanced back at Clayton as he exited the cave.

Clayton listened to sounds trail away over the snow, but knew both men would be back. He couldn't see the slightest possibility for escape. Injured or not, how could they escape? Impossible without divine intervention, he didn't believe in such things.

Then he saw a chance so thin it wouldn't cast a shadow. The knife wedged against the bunk held their lone hope. He had to get them to put him on his bunk.

He turned and looked at Palafox, whispered her name.

Palafox shrugged and kept her face on the table several moments before she raised her head. Her eyes were swollen and glistened.

"I'm real sorry about Tuma and Snow Wolf," he said, and in a low voice.

She closed her eyes and sighed. She opened her eyes and stared at him. "None of this would've happened if it weren't for you." Her lips quivered.

She was right. He took a deep breath and exhaled slowly.

"We don't have lots of time," he said, "when they've loaded the sleds, they'll make their getaway, they won't leave witnesses to a killing, they're hard cases, it's all or nothing for—"

"What can we do tied like this?"

"Help persuade them to put us on our bunks before they—

"You're a fool, with the elder gone we don't stand a chance."

He glanced away. Seconds passed before snow crunched near the mouth of the cave. She glanced at the entrance, gave him a knowing look, and pressed her face on the table.

"Shhh," she said, "be careful."

Goose and Skidder entered the cave, pistols in hand at their sides. They stopped to scrutinize Clayton and Palafox seated across from each other. Goose shoved his pistol in its holster, barked, "I don't wanna hear one peep from none of y'all."

Skidder stepped to the hanging furs, grabbed an armful of furs and jerked the line strung across the back. The last row of furs dropped to the floor, exposing the cave's back wall. Even in the dim light, Clayton knew what it was when he heard Goose gasp.

Wide gold seams, nine of them, each at least a foot across, like wide columns in solid rock, glistened from floor to the ceiling that stretched twelve feet or more above the floor.

Skidder realized it a second later. "Gol-lee," he said. The pelts fell from his arms into a pile at his feet.

Everyone in the cave gasped. Except Palafox. She didn't move and kept her face pressed on the table. She rocked her head, slow.

"Gawd almighty," Goose said, a wide grin came to his red-bearded face. He put his mittens on his hip. "Gawd almighty."

Skidder spun around, did a stumbling tap-dance through the pile of furs, stepped on the bench where Clayton sat and landed on the tabletop with both boots.

He kicked the bowls and plates off the table as he danced, shouting, "Gol-lee we're rich, Gawd almighty we're rich. Yippee. Woo-hoo!" Eyes wild, he whipped out his pistol, waved it in the air. "Woo-hoo. Gol-lee. We're rich, we're rich, boy howdy we're rich, Gawd almighty we're rich sons of bitches." Skidder danced, shuffled and kicked his boots in the air. "We're rich-Gawd almighty, we're rich...." He giggled the entire time, as if caught in some strange warped computer loop.

Clayton felt nauseous. He wanted to knock Skidder off the table and grab the pistol and would've if his hands weren't tied. Without any bravado, he knew if he got his hands on a pistol ... he didn't want to think about it. He and Palafox didn't stand a chance, they had no chance, none at all.

CHAPTER 19

"**S**top it, Skidder! We got work," Goose said, and he wondered if Skidder's mind had finally dissolved.

Skidder stopped dancing and looked at him.

"We've got work, Skidder, check their hands, make sure they're good and tied. Tie their ankles too. And put 'em on separate bunks. Set her at the far bunk." He pointed at the other bunk. "Watch 'em close. Don't let 'em talk or signal each other while I think things out."

Nodding, Skidder shoved his pistol in its holster, leaped off the table and got to work.

Goose had no compunction against killing everyone in the cave for this much gold. That crazy-ass Skidder left him no choice. Out here in the wilderness, one thing separated hunters from prey, the gun and only one law applied if you stole from another man. As slow as he was, even Skidder understood that.

No way would the idiot keep his mouth shut about the gold. If they returned with a sled full of gold, unwanted attention would soon follow. He could lie about where he found it, leave it at that, but Skidder's big mouth would start flapping the second he encountered a bitch with a little dope, whiskey and piece of ass to offer. Next thing, Skidder would be in some police station, the police would know about the gold, the murder and Goose's part in it and that just wouldn't do.

Only one way for this mess to go away. Skidder had to go last, of course. If he had Skidder throw the bodies into the gorge, they wouldn't be found before the thaw. If they weren't then, which was likely, by next winter the bodies would be gone. In the meanwhile, he and Sissy could take a long vacation someplace, anyplace she wanted to go. Heck, all this gold might fund a big shindig of a wedding. She wasn't the first who'd wanted to marry the Goose, she'd wanted to get married for five years now.

How much gold could he haul on four sleds with one driver and thirty dogs pulling? Maybe five or six hundred pounds and that meant a truckload of folding money. Skidder would help load the gold too. The plan wasn't free of problems.

Tuma's friends might appear before they finished loading up, but by then, the bodies would be in the gorge. Easy to pretend he and Skidder had just arrived too. Might even offer to help in the search for Tuma's group. But if he got away before then, with the hawk coming, no way his sleds could be tracked in the snow, nor could anyone put him at the cave.

The third problem seemed less worrisome. He could always sneak back for more gold, but finding his way back into the uplands would be difficult. He'd worry about that later. He needed to get going and be loaded and gone by daylight. Just as surely, there'd be no ball and chain for Goose over a fool.

"Skidder, come here," he said, and looked at the gold.

"I'm not leavin'," Skidder said. "Not without as much gold as I can haul. And that bitch."

"She does have nice tits. Not too big not too small, just right. And nice hips too, don't she?"

"I know that's right. I'm first, I don't like messy seconds."

"You can have the Klooch all to yourself, Skidder. I don't want any of that Klooch."

"Really?"

"Sure," Goose whispered. "She belongs to you, all to yourself."

"Oh man, this gets better and better."

"Skidder, you're forgetting one thing, Tuma's friends are liable to show at any time, so we don't have much time. We need to load the sleds with all the gold the dogs can haul, then hightail it. You can shoot the fella and the woman and chunk their bodies into the gorge. Even better, take 'em to the edge of the gorge, untie 'em and shove 'em off. The fall'll kill 'em both. That way, it would look like an accident if someone found the bodies."

"Then we're in cahoots fifty-fifty?"

"It seems we are now," Goose said, but saw something he'd never seen on Skidder's face before: a flicker of intelligence. "Of course we're fifty-fifty, we're good friends aren't we, partners first and foremost aren't we?"

"I know that's right, just don't double-cross me."

Goose faked an expression of hurt on his face. "You surprise me Skidder, you're not kinda threatening your partner already are ya?"

"All I gotta say is don't double-cross me. Don't claim what's mine. It's not a threat, just don't pull any slick stuff on me with all your college words, they hurt my head, what's mine is mine."

"Do you have a better idea for what to do with 'em?"

Skidder shook his head, "No."

"We can't stand here all night. Tuma's friends are liable to show any moment, then we'd be in a shootout and there's no cause for it."

Skidder leaned forward, "But, I want the bitch before we leave."

"Skidder, we don't have time for that, not now."

"I wanna take her along with me on the trail out, just for a while."

Goose shrugged. "As long as you deduct the hundred pounds she'd take up from your part of the gold. After we've loaded the sleds, you can do what ya want. Just think, a piece of ass anytime you want, it'll be like you're married."

"I heard that, dadgum it, this gets better and better," Skidder said, softly. "Why don't we go ahead and shoot the fella, or jest tie him to a tree outside, let him freeze solid while we're loadin' the sleds, it's cleaner that way and he'd still last until the thaw."

"That sounds like experience talking, Skidder."

"What do ya mean?"

"Never mind."

"No, what did ya mean?"

"I meant that was an okay idea you have. Wished I thought of it myself. Keep 'em alive until the very moment we start to leave. Then we either tie him to a tree in the woods or just shove him off the gorge. Makes no difference to me how you kill the fella before we leave. But, your idea to tie him to a tree is real smart. We can do that just before we leave."

"Why can't we tie 'im to a tree now?"

"Won't work. We gotta keep 'im alive until we start to leave. In case the old Eskimo's friends show up. The fella and the Klooch can be our bargaining chips. That way, the old Eskimo's friends might understand this ole Eskimo stole the furs, traps and sleds. Of course, his friends could be in cahoots and helped him. But we'd have the evidence of that too. They'll have to go along with us to avoid a shootout. So we keep 'im alive until we leave."

"Better and better." Skidder extended his hand. "Put it here, partner."

Goose shook his hand, smiled proud and patted Skidder on the shoulder, "Bring the sleds out front. I'll root around here to find something to work the gold out of the wall. Bring the axes inside, shovels are in the jeep sled."

"All right."

"And oh, drag the old Eskimo near the edge of the gorge while you're out there, but don't chunk him off just yet. Just cover him with snow real good, make damn sure to cover all the blood trails outside in case those friends come along. Don't forget to do the same thing with the dead wolf."

"Sounds like a plan, partner," Skidder said.

"You tie up the fella and the Klooch?"

"Yep, hum-huh, sure did."

Goose nodded. "Well partner, what ya say?"

Skidder broke out in a chuckle, "Let's get'ah move on it."

Skidder headed outside and as the flap closed over the entrance, Goose walked over to the fella.

"Get on the bunk."

"What's this about?"

"Shut up."

He got some rope and tied the fella's ankles again, checked the knots to guarantee the ropes were tied tight and strong. It would take Superman to break the ropes and this fella wasn't Superman.

"Lay down on the bunk."

"All right," the fella said. "Can you put the animal hide on me so I can keep warm?"

Goose wasn't without compassion. He believed the fella wouldn't cause any trouble. Skidder had kicked the snot out of him and busted his lip right nice-like. That'd make anyone think twice before trying anything. Still, he lifted the animal hide and patted the other hides down for a knife or pistol. He didn't feel anything like that, so he covered the fella with the animal hide, then covered the smelly Klooch too after he checked the ropes tied to her ankles and hands.

Does anyone here ever bathe around here, smells like a bunch of wet animals inside here ...

Before he covered her, he thought about pulling off her parka and getting him some. A bitch like her liked it rough, he could tell by her disgusted look at him. That kind of look always excited him, experience told him women were always excited when they were forced into it. Most of them anyway.

Goose felt satisfied after he checked the ropes that the man and woman couldn't escape while he and stupid-ass Skidder worked to dig out the gold. After that, load the sleds, then go with Skidder to take the fella and the Klooch to the edge of the gorge. He still didn't know if he'd shove Skidder off or plug him, but decided to let Skidder decide, if he could let him. He'd do that for him.

CHAPTER 20

Working as quietly as he could, Clayton took advantage of the animal hide and dim-lit shadows to conceal his moves and twists. Thanks to Goose's clumsy pat down, the knife had shifted positions.

He had no idea where the knife was, even if it was still wedged between the cot and the wall. He maneuvered his hands and repositioned his body to locate the knife wedged in the frame.

He never took his eyes from Goose and Skidder, who were busy piling furs to one side of the wall until the stacks looked more like mounds of clay than hides.

They'd just begun the task of chipping at the gold seams in the cave wall. They shot casual glances at him too, while they worked. Even when they stooped over, he could tell they watched him and Palafox from their side vision.

Light from the fireplace and the few candles scattered about caused the image of Yau on the wall to move at times. Goose and Skidder would look back, startled, huddle and whisper, then get back to their work. Each time Goose swung the axe it hit the wall with a wallop, bits of rock and gold zinged through the air and ricocheted off the wall. He'd chuckle and say, "Hear that one Skidder? Sounded like a bullet didn't it?" And the bona fide parrot would giggle and repeat, "I heard that."

With an axe, knife, shovel, they banged, chipped and mined the gold. Eventually, Goose splintered the axe handle, resulting in several minutes of swearing. After the loss of the axe, they dug out the gold using hand-sized logs to pound their knives and the axe blade, into the seams.

Skidder snorted and grunted while he dragged pelts loaded with gold. Other times, the little minion carried a pelt like a bizarre, grim version of Santa to where the sleds sat at the entrance.

He had glanced at Palafox several times; a shadow lay on her face, he couldn't tell if she slept, or was in a daze staring up. She didn't react to anything the two men were doing.

While Goose and Skidder worked, he lay on his left side and maneuvered until he finally located the bone-handled knife, still wedged in the frame. After an hour or more of sweat and painful maneuvering, he managed to dislodge the knife.

It took another hour to position the knife to cut the rope binding his wrists. Just in time, too. His fingers were so numbed, if he hadn't cut the rope when he did, he would've lost the feel of the knife.

The numbness soon left, he exercised every muscle to improve the blood supply to his fingers and hands. He felt the knife sticky in his palm and realized he'd cut his fingers. Undeterred, he slowly drew back his legs and cut the rope from his legs and ankles.

He knew the best element of attack was surprise. Even a split-second could mean they lived or died. He worked out a plan to use the knife to grab a pistol, turned the plan over in his head, concentrated on defensive angles, from them standing at the foot of the cot to them standing above him.

If he got his hand on their pistol, there was but one way Goose or Skidder would take the pistol from him. It was all or nothing for both him and Palafox. The dimness of the cave, the sweat, the spoilage on his tongue, the feel of dampness on his flesh, the fireplace casting shadows, the logs burning slow, the designs on the wall, the surreal shadows, and the sinister voices whispering reminded him of a time in his life.

A lifetime ago, he spent two days in another cave. He didn't want the memory to intrude on him, now or ever; determined to force it back into the past, he looked over at Palafox.

He'd tried more than once to catch her eye, but she wouldn't look at him. As before she remained quiet, as if in a daze, she didn't move or acknowledge he was even there. She stared at the ceiling.

He felt she was still in shock over the killings. He felt sad for Tuma and Snow Wolf too, but his fear that they would not survive had pushed his sadness aside.

Exhausted from freeing himself and hashing out the situation for a long time, he finally dozed. He awoke feeling lucky; Goose and Skidder still worked feverishly. The pounding and clacking went on until he saw daylight through the flap. Goose and Skidder's chuckles and giggles were more frequent and he knew why. He felt the sleds were about loaded.

Goose and Skidder seemed in good spirits when they exited the cave. He lay on his left side and watched Skidder attach a rein to the harness on the Huskies. He could see a slice of the sky through the partly open flap.

After Skidder finished, he went in the direction Goose had walked, toward the gorge. He could tell the direction from the sounds of crunching snow.

Perhaps Goose and Skidder might leave and not harm them; if they meant them harm, it was logical to think they would have already done it. With this thought it was easier to breathe, to even feel somewhat optimistic.

"Palafox," he whispered. "*Palafox.*"

She kept her gaze at the ceiling.

He tried again, "I got the knife free."

She never moved. He had to get her attention, had to tell her his plan to keep them both alive long enough to leave the wilderness. This was his mission in life, now.

Perhaps two minutes passed before voices rose with passion and fervor outside. He heard Goose say, "Idiot," then several moments later he heard him say, "Imbecile," followed by both men's shouting and yelling for perhaps half a minute. Then a quiet came to the outside, the kind of stillness that signaled a storm.

Snow crunched, Goose shoved aside the flap and huffed his way through, stopped and glanced at him on the bunk. For a second, Clayton thought Goose seemed troubled.

Mere seconds passed when Skidder eased the flap open and poked his head inside the dim cave. His bearded face had a twisted smirk. Goose went to the back wall and didn't look over his shoulder. Skidder slipped behind Goose.

Clayton pretended sleep and peeked through his eyelids. He was sorry Palafox hadn't come out of her fog while he had a chance to tell her his plan. But if they put their hands on him, he would use the knife anyway. He'd stab the sky if it laid a hand on him now.

Goose stood at the gold-laced wall, spread his mittened hand over the gold seam. He turned and glanced at Skidder a moment. Then he turned back to the gold-laden wall.

Just loud enough for Clayton to hear, Goose said without turning to Skidder, "Stupid to take the woman, Skidder, there's another hundred pounds easy, right here."

Clayton had seen what Goose couldn't. Skidder had slid the automatic pistol from his belt. As Goose finished speaking, Skidder patted Goose on the back.

Clayton closed his eyes at the instant Goose turned.

Bang!

Clayton opened his eyes to see Goose's body stiffen and tilt back, saw his head collide with the floor, heard the ill-sounding thump.

CHAPTER 21

Skidder straddled Goose's twitching body and raised the pistol.
Bang!

Goose stopped twitching and lay still.

Gun smoke shimmered near Skidder at the back of the cave as he lifted his foot to stand next to the body.

Skidder was about to come after them now. Clayton was certain of it. Shoot Palafox and him in the heads and make off with the gold. He tried to keep his panicked mind calm and a frightened eye on Skidder's every move, every action.

Skidder snickered, coughed and covered his face as he did. He whipped around and seemed to scan the cave, then he grinned and looked back at Goose as though satisfied about killing a trophy worthy of praise.

He raised the pistol and aimed at Goose again, mumbled "Pow-pow," and snickered again. He shoved the pistol in his belt and walked toward the front of the cave.

Skidder's shadow rose off the floor and slid across the wall; it had no form. Until it skulked over to Palafox. Skidder's Spam-colored face smirked while he fondled Palafox's breast and he giggled that strange giggle.

"Stop, stop it," Palafox said.

Skidder leaned back, covered his mouth and snickered. Then he hurried back to where Goose lay on the floor. He mumbled incoherently, snickered again and again.

Clayton squeezed the knife. God had brought two adversaries to one. He needed seconds, prayed to God to give him seconds.

With that maniacal giggle, Skidder went to the fireplace. Clayton didn't believe one moment that Skidder was bothered by anything, even their presence. Maybe that was why he hadn't already taken his gun to them. Maybe in the excitement, he'd forgotten about them.

Skidder will kill us both in time.

That part wouldn't change unless Clayton changed it. He watched as Skidder added logs to the fire and turned his back to warm up.

Skidder scanned the cave, oblivious to him and Palafox while he picked at his scraggly beard, then burst into an uncontrolled snickering fit. He leaned forward, holding his mouth in some self-amused game.

Until he froze. He raised his weasel-beaked face and turned toward the back of the cave. "That right," he said, drew his pistol fast, like a cowboy in quick-draw showdown, crouched and pretended to take shots at the shadow on the wall. He did this at least eight or nine times. Each time he drew the pistol he crouched, grinned, snickered and mumbled "Pow, pow, pow."

All the while Clayton watched, refusing to take either amusement or distraction. He had to lure Skidder close without tipping him off or pissing him off. Barring that, if Skidder left the cave, he would ambush Skidder at the entrance.

Skidder shoved the pistol into his belt, removed his parka and dropped it on a pile of furs, frowned and giggled, rolled his eyes. Then, something different happened.

He mumbled to himself a voice that was still male, but not his. Then his voice changed, became softer and high-pitched. A woman's voice.

Though Clayton couldn't quite make out the words, it sounded like Skidder was having a quiet conversation with someone. The voices sounded like two people, with Skidder as the go-between.

While Clayton was trying to figure this out, Skidder shook as if surprised or startled by a sound and scanned the cave as if unfamiliar with it.

Something else, when Skidder giggled, when he made weird facial gestures or moves, the shadows behind him shifted, but not in harmony with his movements.

Skidder swiveled his body to peer at Clayton and stood that way for a moment, as if figuring out something.

Suspecting that Skidder was sizing him up for the kill, Clayton stopped looking at the shadows and kept his body still. His legs cramped and his calf muscles stiffened. It took everything he had to not jerk when Skidder suddenly snickered and grabbed his parka off the floor and began examining his parka as a mother gorilla might inspect her infant, plowing the matted fur with his hand, then reaching up to do the same thing with his hair, which drooped and twisted under his grasping, squeezing fingers.

Clayton didn't have the strength to wrestle with Skidder for more than a few seconds and seeing him now, he doubted Skidder could be reasoned with. Nevertheless, he had to lure Skidder close in some way. And he had to do it soon.

He suspected why Skidder was letting Palafox remain alive. But he knew he couldn't allow Skidder to have his way with Palafox, not so long as he had a breath.

Without warning, Skidder hurried and stood over Palafox. His bent-over shadow covered her.

He fondled her. "Wake up, ole Skidder boy is here," he said around a giggle.

Palafox shifted her body to avoid his hand. "Don't touch me, stop it!"

Skidder mocked her in that high-pitched woman's voice, rocked his body and repeated several times, "Don't touch me." Then his voice shifted to baby talk while he grabbed her breast again, "Let's have some fun."

She tried to jerk away again, couldn't. "I said, stop it."

Clayton cringed. Her bunk was fifteen feet away. He'd never make it before Skidder could grab his pistol from his belt. Unless he wanted to be a kamikaze, he had to be patient. He had the best element of attack in surprise, he couldn't waste it. Most of all, he had to remain calm or risk Skidder shooting him from a distance.

Skidder moved his hands over Palafox's breast. She squirmed, twisted her body. "Stop it, stop, stop it!"

Skidder mocked Palafox in the feminine, high-pitched voice, repeating, "Stop it." Then his voice changed to his own and again came that inane giggle as his shoulders quaked in amusement.

Then Skidder went silent, braced his hands around her face and seemed to examine her eyes. "Dumb Klooch," he said, but in that strong, gravelly deep male voice. He released her face and returned to fondling her breasts and thighs and this time her crotch.

Palafox resisted and squirmed, but could do little more with her ankles tied and her wrists tied behind her. She made kicking motions with her legs, at one point managing a knee between his legs.

Skidder retaliated.

Palafox tried to avoid being slapped but her efforts were no good. Skidder slapped her continually with his open hand and the worst of it, Skidder's giggle heightened each time he smacked her.

Clayton heard the smacks from where he lay, bit his lip and squeezed the bone-handled knife until he felt he'd crushed it. As soon as he was free, his first action would be to rip Skidder's lungs out. But he couldn't rush Skidder, not yet. He had to wait until he was certain he'd catch Skidder off guard. Waiting for a moment of opportunity to take Skidder on was the worst feeling.

Then Skidder stopped slapping her. Then he took his switchblade and cut the rope off Palafox's ankles but left her wrists tied behind her back. Avoiding her weak kicks, he dragged her off the cot and shoved her toward the table.

Palafox muttered incoherently; now Clayton could see dark trails of what looked like blood under her nose and on her chin.

"Please." The word languished in the air. "Please." Hunched and stumbling forward, she moaned, "I beg you, please."

And for the first time since his encounter with the grizzly, Clayton felt totally, entirely alone. All alone, he'd hoped Palafox's silence meant she, like him, was marshaling her resources for either escaping, or killing Skidder, as soon as she had either chance. He'd clearly been wrong. The death of the man she called the elder and her beloved pet had taken her fight, or was it the beating?

Clayton lay on his left shoulder and faced them, watched Skidder pushing her toward the table while she mumbled pleas for him to stop, heard Skidder's giggling reminders that he had a gun and it would please him very much to use it. Half Clayton's body felt as numbed as his mind. The knife seemed to sweat cold blood in his hands.

Skidder grabbed Palafox and bent her over the table, held to her back with one hand and with the other hand roughly yanked her parka outfit up. Palafox maneuvered her body around and shoved Skidder to the side.

She hopped toward the exit, her voice trembled, "Keep away, get away!"

Skidder skipped across the floor and giggled, hiccupped as he did so, easily grabbed her, spun her around and tried to kiss her. She resisted with her shoulder, earning blows to her head and face. She drew back, leaned against the wall. Gasping like someone drowning, she blurted, "Stop you're hurting me, help me!"

Skidder grabbed her hair and shoved her back to the table, giggled as he bent her over the tabletop and pulled her undergarments down below her knees.

"Damn," Skidder said, and giggled, "I ain't never saw so much hair on a women's legs, this oughta be fun."

She angled her head around to him, "No. Please."

Clayton held his breath, bit his tongue. His earlier resolve evaporated. His face felt hot. He exhaled to calm his pulse.

"Let her go, man."

Skidder froze for several long moments. He craned his neck and stared hard.

Clayton stared back.

Finally, Skidder said, "What did ya say, fella?"

Clayton glared without saying a word.

Skidder stared with a predator's detachment. Finally, he raised his left arm slow and lifted his right forefinger.

"You're startin' to get on my nerves." An ugly grin spread across his face. "Be there in a sec."

Clayton knew his attempt to bring Skidder close to him might've just failed. Now, he felt sick in the stomach.

Skidder tied Palafox's ankles to the table legs, ending her chance at another escape. Her parka pants were down at her ankles. As Skidder rose, he deliberately traced her legs with his skinny fingers. He stopped.

Palafox seemed to inhale, exhale, then she seemed to hold her breath. The air tensed.

After long seconds, Skidder turned and narrowed his eyes on him.

"I don't like being watched and I don't like people who use college words neither, they hurt my head."

Skidder whipped out the switchblade, held the shiny blade at arm's length and poked the air with the tip of the blade. He rolled the blade in the air.

"I'm gonna flatten your eyeballs, fella."

Skidder giggled and stepped slow toward him. All the time stabbing the air and rolling the switchblade.

"You the man all right, Skidder," he said, as calm and soft as he could. "Slapping a woman with her hands tied, at least be man enough to use your switchblade on me."

Only a few steps away from the table Skidder hesitated. The ugly grin left his lips. His face stiffened. He looked down several moments then he glanced back at Palafox.

Clayton exhaled his trembles, pushed down the swell in his chest. The hide covered him midway to his stomach. He held the knife at his tailbone, as if his wrists were still tied. He was all in now. He would either die or live.

Skidder stared at him. Then glanced back at Palafox again. Then looked back at him. A weird grin lazily spread across his face. He closed the switchblade and shoved it in his trouser pocket, grabbed his pistol from his belt.

Hardly had he breathed than Skidder raced to the bunk and stood above him with a pistol aimed at his right eye.

Palafox, watching, said, "I—"

"Shut up, I'll be there in a sec, baby," Skidder said, and lowered his weasel-beaked face.

"It's over, fella, get on your feet."

In that moment of insanity, Clayton had one clear thought; though Skidder's eyes on him spun like mag wheels in a fog, this was the first time he could recall Skidder speaking an entire sentence without giggling.

He didn't take his eyes off the black barrel inches from his eye, but couldn't ignore it when Skidder repeated.

"On ya feet, fella."

Clayton calmed his breathing the best he could. "My wrists and ankles are tied, remember, you tied me up." He didn't want to show any fear, but his words trembled in spite of speaking as softly as he could. The knife trembled, wet in his hand.

It seemed an eternity while Skidder studied him, as if deciding whether he had or hadn't tied his ankles and wrists. Finally, Skidder shoved the pistol inside his belt and grabbed the animal hide, snatched off the hide.

Clayton looked past Skidder, "Run! Palafox! Run!"

Skidder whirled around to Palafox.

Clayton swung the knife. The blade glanced off Skidder's hip and buried into his left side all the way to the handle just above the hipbone.

Skidder blurted as his head snapped back. "Oh!"

The next instant Clayton stood with a death grip on the knife inside Skidder. At the same time, he grabbed for the pistol with his left hand. At that moment, Skidder grabbed for the pistol with his right hand. Clayton's momentum hurled them backward.

They crashed into the table, locked together. They dropped on the bench, rolled and hit the floor with Clayton on top of Skidder.

Skidder's cheeks ballooned as his pain-ravaged eyes widened, body squirming in contortions. His hands pinched and clawed, trying to squeeze Clayton's windpipe.

Clayton felt Skidder's struggles weaken and he wrestled free of Skidder's hand, jerked the knife out and sank it into Skidder's midriff. Blood spurted hot against his fist.

Gurgles puffed from Skidder's mouth as anguish floated in his eyes. He withered, tried to breathe. His face quivered, then a rasp of air and he went limp.

The deed was over with, done, finished.

Clayton whiplashed back to reality. And to the shock that he'd killed another man, though this feeling was lessened by his knowledge that Skidder would've killed him. He didn't regret it. Nor was he going to lose any sleep over Skidder's death.

Without reason, or at least any reason he could have explained, he felt his gut roil with nausea. He didn't feel glad, though he didn't have regrets, yet he felt sick. Skidder wasn't the first man he'd killed to live, but the other killings were different. The others, he'd had a license to kill and a combat-hardened heart.

It was the smell, he realized. He'd never gotten used to the smell that brought the gut sickness only known to men who killed. He knew then something he'd doubted for a long time. He had a conscience.

He grabbed the knife and jerked it out, wiped the blade on Skidder's trousers. Somehow he managed to stand, stood over Skidder's lifeless body, trembling, for a time that couldn't be counted in seconds or minutes or even hours.

When time began again for his weary mind, he went to Palafox, still bound to the table, cut the ropes off. She lifted her head, turned her eyes to him as though she only then recognized him. She stared, mute.

What he saw was the survivor of a twelve-round slugfest. Where her bright eyes and smiles once were, he saw lips split in two places, both eyes puffed and her right jaw bulged.

She stepped back from the table. She rocked her hips and pulled up her undergarments. Her lips barely moved, then she spun on her heels and made a wobbly sprint outside, into the snow and midmorning sun.

He didn't go after her but instead slumped on the bench. With a heavy sigh, he leaned his head back to let troubles drip from his head.

He lost his grip on the knife. It clanked when it hit the cave's floor. And then, dead silence.

He sat there, head down, gnawing his fingernails, waiting for the shudders and trembles to go away.

He was happy they were alive. The two goals he couldn't lose sight of were regaining his strength and leaving the wilderness on the fastest route available. He would do whatever it took.

He smelled death's odor again and choked. He got on his feet and walked outside feeling awful sick.

CHAPTER 22

Palafox kept telling herself she was safe but she kept running to get away. She'd been terrified many times, but that cutthroat touching her was the most terrifying experience of her life.

Finally, she stopped. She sank onto the snow and leaned against the tree. So often before, her thoughts about the elder and Snow Wolf helped her to feel safe. This time, thinking of them made her thoughts cold.

With the elder gone, she couldn't pretend the scrolls were crazy tales anymore or turn blindly away no matter how she tried to tell herself that. Her doubt concerning the scrolls had changed her. What was she going to do—or have to do, now?

She went over everything she could remember that happened since they'd found Clayton, she felt worse, not knowing if he was or wasn't a temptation.

Daylight faded and she hoped there would never come a time when the hand that feathered the sky died. She got to her feet and walked toward the cave.

When she got within sight of the cave, she saw Clayton through the woods. He was leading four of the Huskies as they dragged the big man over the snow.

Clayton dropped the reins and pointed a gun at her.

She darted behind a tree and wondered if he would shoot her and wondered where he had gotten the gun. She waved, frantic.

At last, he recognized her. He lowered the gun, glanced around the site and slung the gun on his shoulder.

She let go the snowball she had pressed against the swelling on her face and walked to him. The dead man on the snow, a trail of blood oozing from his body, unnerved her, but it was Clayton's gaze that drew her, at the way it hinted at something she couldn't place.

He wore the parka she sewed for him. In the fading light, the parka was a coppery shade and the parka itself gave him broad shoulders. His brown hair and black beard seemed blown by the wind, but not the colorful bear claw necklace and the jade jewel he wore around his neck. His steady stance and gaze could've passed for a warrior's.

His eyes roved her and steadied on her face. "Startin' to get worried, are you all right?" he said.

She was far from all right, but nodded. "You?" The swelling on her lip and jaw made the word sound flat. They stared at each other in silence.

"You need medical attention," he said.

He was wrong. She wasn't hurt, but frightened. His gaze hinted that he knew that.

"I'll be all right," she said and covered her busted lip with her mitten, then added, "You saved our lives."

"We're in trouble if the law finds out."

"It's just you killed him when you did," she barely got the words over the lump in her throat. "Where ya find the gun?"

He limped to keep from falling and tugged the reins for the Huskies to begin moving. "It's a rifle," he didn't look at her though she followed him, "I found it in one of the sleds."

"Where ya going?"

Clayton pointed to the forest; his eyes didn't meet hers. "Out there, it'll be dark soon, I'll bury them tomorrow"

"We can't bury them."

"Huh," Clayton stopped, "what do you mean?"

"We burn them."

"What?"

"We burn them."

"You can't be serious."

"Serious as fire. The earth is hard, full of rocks here. Let the wind take their ashes to the deepest gorge where no sunlight can touch their ashes, let their ashes stay there."

He looked off and stepped away, holding the reins leading the Huskies. She rested her mitten on his arm. He stopped and looked at her with steady eyes.

"We gotta do this," she said.

"Have you smelled human flesh burning?"

She shook her head, "No."

"It's unforgettable."

"I don't care."

He shrugged and handed her the reins without looking at her. "Do what you have to do." He turned away. He seemed to have the weight of life in his limp toward the cave.

She called after him, "Wait."

He stopped, glanced over his shoulder and gave her a bland-faced look.

"Thanks for saving our lives."

He barely nodded and seemed to frown. He turned away and continued to walk toward the cave.

"Wait," she stepped out of reach of the dead man and followed Clayton, "wait!"

Clayton stopped and turned. She stepped to him. She didn't want to ask but they had to know.

"Did you find the elder and Snow Wolf?"

"Do you want to torch them, too?"

She didn't like his insinuation. "No. But we must return them to the sacred valley."

He watched her fumble with her mittens.

"You all right?"

She let her arms fall to her side, "Just a habit."

"We all have habits."

"You noticed mine."

His eyebrows lifted. "Yes, it's lying."

"Huh?"

He wiped his busted lip. "You know what I'm talking about, don't act surprised."

"I've taken care of you while you were very sick," she said. "Took care of your needs, fed you. Me doing that don't give you the right to say what you like to—"

"Naturally," he said and his jaw clenched, "sorry little lady, but I want to leave here on the fastest route, so if you'll show me the direction to the mountain pass or nearest village, I'll gladly be on my way at first light with you or without you."

"Do you have a wish to die, we'd be dead in a week!" she said. "The elder said a blizzard is on its way, the dogs have to eat, there's no food to keep us alive."

"Yeah right," he said, his words grinded through his teeth, "it's easy to take a man's possessions when he's dead. I found this rifle in one of the sleds, along with lots of food and other articles."

"Th…the items belong to the crazies."

"That's a lot better. Any other truths you've forgot to share with me, tell me the truth for a change." He pulled out the knife she'd given him and pointed to "WG" carved in the bone-handle. Bloodstains were on the handle.

She stepped back out of his reach.

He put the knife back into his parka and looked at her. "Do you know what would've happened if they found that knife on the bunk? Were you tryin' to get me killed?"

She shuddered and felt weak, "No."

"Where did you get the knife?"

"The elder gave me the knife when he returned, he told me there was a fight at some gorge."

"What kind of fight?"

"What do ya want me to say, Clayton, that I asked the two wilderness crazies to come here? I don't know who the knife belonged—"

"Maybe so, but I'm ankles deep in your little game," he said.

"What do ya mean, game?"

He adjusted the rifle sling on his shoulder. "It's time to break bread off the same loaf," he said. "You want to know something pretty bad to orchestrate that little charade about the sketches and Yau. Don't put my life in danger again without my permission, all right?"

"I don't know who the knife belonged to."

"Yeah, I can't think of one reason why you wanted to know if I showed my sketches. It makes perfect sense, you want to protect something. Why did you want to know if I showed my sketches, or if I had a companion with me?"

"I didn't want to know," she said. "The elder wanted to know."

"Why?"

"The elder wanted to know exactly where you found Yau to sketch and exactly where you found the green stone you had. His woman wore the stone when she vanished four seasons ago. He wanted to make sure no one was with you when you entered the sacred valley."

"Why didn't Tuma ask me?"

"He never got a chance to ask more than he did because you were too sick with the wilderness fever. I can't say any more."

"Why not?"

She looked up at him, eye to eye. "Reasons. I got reasons."

"What a lousy, smacking cop out."

"Maybe it is," she said. "I don't feel like talking, all right? I'm sad, tired, I'm hungry, I'm hurting, I feel sick. Dirty. I'll feel this way until I burn the crazies, all right?"

He looked at her in silence for several moments. "We can talk later," then turned to leave.

"Stop, you can't just walk away, I'm all right. Stop."

He did, then just glanced over his shoulder at her with another bland-faced look. She stepped to him and wiped away a lock of hair that had blown into her face.

"Say what you have to say. I'm all right, I get sick when I think of being tied up and the killings and other things. I'm over it now, say what you have to say."

He fixed his gaze on something over her head. Then with a sigh, he lowered his eyes to her. "We can talk later."

"I want to talk, now. I'm fine, I'm all right, I'm fine. I'm sad, that's all, I'm all right, can't you see that?"

Clayton didn't reply quickly. When his green eyes again met hers, he said, "There's enough gold inside the cave to start a war. That's why you hide it."

"My people have little uses for gold. We only use gold when it's necessary and that's not often. To my people, gold destroys a man's spirit and—"

"You could use some gold to buy some damn rifles," Clayton said and rubbed the side of his forehead. There was swelling there she hadn't noticed before. "Rifles and pistols, why haven't I seen guns? And, where did all those furs come from?"

"I already told you about the guns," she said, "my people find abandoned sleds loaded with furs in the sacred valley when they return at the thaw."

He frowned, "So you find them? What about the people?"

"No one knows what happens to 'em," she looked off his stare. "They wander away or get lost, no one knows, what do you want me to say?"

"That doesn't seem possible, you expect me to believe—"

"You can ask any question you like but that won't mean I will answer, I might not feel like—"

"That's fine, just don't put my life in danger or set me up as a patsy again—"

"I didn't set you up—"

"Which way do we need to travel to reach the mountain pass or the nearest town or village?"

She looked away a moment, swallowed, then looked back at him. "You're not exactly alone," she said. "I want out too, but alive. More so than you. But ya gotta trust me first."

"Yeah, right," he stepped back, dismissing her.

"It's our only chance," she couldn't tell him the truth. Too many other matters were important for her to sort through first.

"I'm gonna regret this," he said. "Why should I trust you?"

"We don't have time. The blizzard won't stop, we're both exhausted, I want to find the elder and burn the crazies and rest, load the sleds with what we need and leave here—"

"I'm like a duck, flat footed, don't much give a quack if we leave now, or tomorrow," he said. "This place has got me rattled, I feel like my skin's shedding."

He exhaled, "Consider this. If you burned the men, your conscience might bother you later. Wait a day or two and simmer down—"

"Simmer down. Simmer down? I'm fine, don't you see that I'm fine? I'm all right, I tell you, I'm fine."

He sighed, and said, "I'll bury 'em tomorrow."

"That won't happen. I won't sleep while the dead men are outside. I won't sleep. Another thing, if a blizzard suddenly appeared, we're dead and so are the dogs that pull the sled. Nothing can survive the cold and deep snow this high on the mountainside."

"What's wrong with the cave? It provides good protection against the snow, wind and cold."

"When a snow slide drops from the cliff and blocks the entrance to the cave you won't think that."

Clayton turned and looked at the leaning cliff above the cave entrance. Palafox continued, "Snowdrifts get as high as the roof on the lean-to here, and you have lots to learn."

Clayton looked strange, but his eyes brightened as he spoke, "Well, I've learned one thing, it's not wise to trust you."

She resented what he said, but in truth how could she blame him? He was right. She said, "For one thing, you gotta know how to guide a sled, and the right way to harness Huskies."

His brows arched, "Oh, I think I can handle a sled."

A flock of squawking black birds flew into the gorge. The birds wheeled in one big circle, flapping wings as they lit in trees above the gorge.

Palafox felt her heart beat skipped. She'd never seen a flock of birds in the winter this high on a mountainside.

The wind lightly lifted Clayton's tangled, messy hair as he watched the birds. When he turned his gaze back to her, his breath rolled out of his nose and mouth, like smoke. She stared at him and her stomach begged her to step out away from him.

Finally, he said, "I'll search for Tuma." He turned and hobbled over the snow, but then stopped and turned to face her, "It's not a crow."

What was he talking about? "What?" she said.

"My sketch. The sketch is an eagle," he grinned, and said, "not a crow."

"Eagle, all right. Eagle, eagle, all right," she said and didn't smile.

He turned, walked to the cave and waved his mitten in the air over his shoulder.

She'd worry about how she felt another day and at another time. She'll burn the wilderness crazies whether he liked it or not. She kicked a clump of snow like it was his head, it felt very good when she did too. She was the keeper of her conscience and not anybody else's.

She started to look for a wide, open spot to burn the crazies, to take her mind off the scrolls and other things. She couldn't tell him she didn't know the way around the mountain pass that they were stuck and might not survive. She took a deep breath and decided she was too tired to think now. Instead, she would use the sled to haul the wood to the spot she had selected.

After unhitching the madman from the reins, she started for the lean-to where the dogs were penned. It wasn't long before Clayton came out and followed the trails in the snow. A short while later, the black birds in the tree swooped away and squawked when Clayton approached the edge of the gorge.

He stooped and wiped snow off something. After her second or third glance, she saw him stand up and shoulder the rifle. He glanced at her.

She believed he'd found the elder; she dropped the wood and hurried to him. Apparently, he saw her coming toward him.

When she was close enough she saw an unusual look on his face. She sensed his expression was about finding the elder and Snow Wolf dead. Who wouldn't be afraid of death?

He held his mitten out, "Stay back."

She moved closer to him, "You find the elder?"

He nodded.

"I want to see him."

"No," frowning, he shook his head, "no."

"I've seen people dead before."

"It's not that."

"I want to see him."

"No," he shook his head again, "you really shouldn't see him."

She stared at him for several long moments, then started to step away. He snared her arm. She glared at him.

He said, "You're upset, he's not a pretty sight."

"Death never is," she said, and dropped her eyes to his mitten on her arm. When she lifted her eyes again, she saw the elder's arms half sticking from the snow.

"Take your hands off of me."

Clayton released his grip on her arm.

She turned and hurried to where the elder's arms were above the snow. When she approached the elder frozen like he was in the snow nothing could have prepared her. There were dark pits where once his eyes were.

She covered her mouth to stop the scream inside it. But her mind wouldn't be quiet.

Run away, get away....

She turned to follow her mind's command.

CHAPTER 23

Clayton had wondered how much Palafox might be disturbed by the sight of Tuma. Now, he knew.

Her face strained as she collapsed against him, wrapping her arms around him as she buried her face into his parka. He embraced her to comfort her and she drew back. Her eyes glistened.

"What happened to his eyes?" she said, and wiped her cheeks with her mitten.

Clayton couldn't find any words to comfort her. He knew Tuma's eyes were cut out. It could serve no good purpose to mention it now. He felt a stab of remorse but not pity for Tuma and Snow Wolf, naturally, and sadness. And who wouldn't feel that?

Looking into the distance, he saw no sight he was interested in, no sight to store to paint one day. Only one thing was bedded inside his head, "I've gotta get out of this place."

Palafox wiped her nose with her sleeve and sniffled. Her eyes squeezed nearly shut, "We'll leave after we burn them until there's nothing left."

Her voice had lowered and it didn't sound like her; every word stretched to the breaking point. She dropped her mittens to her side, took a wobbled step back, peered at him with a look that sent chills over him and reminded him their time spent caring for him had delayed the journey out.

"Burn them," she said.

Clayton realized her emotions were tangled in a gutful hate. She seemed consumed, entrenched by it. He'd seen men's emotions in lockdown before. He grabbed her shoulders and shook her, "Snap out of it." Her eyes remained slits, she didn't seem to know him.

He shook her again, "Snap out of it, stop."

"Burn them."

"Snap out of it," he shook her shoulders lightly as he said it. She still seemed dazed.

He didn't know what to do, had not been around a woman whose emotions were charged up like hers seemed to be. So he did what instinctively came to him.

Moving with awkwardness, he embraced her, pinning her arms. At the same time, she pushed against him with her arms and elbows, tried to free herself by kicking him.

"Stop," he said, "control yourself."

She continued her struggle to break his embrace. He held her tighter, until her fight to free herself was useless.

He felt the intensity of her emotions start to give way.

"Shhh," he said, "shhh, it's over, it's over, shhh, it's over."

Her fight slowed then he felt her relax. Her breathing slowed and her trembling almost went away. He let her go.

She took several steps back. For uncomfortable moments, she peered at him in silence. It seemed her mind tumbled over on itself and her face softened.

"I'm sor-sorry," she said, and looked down.

"Nothing to be sorry about."

She lifted her eyes to meet his, "I meant I'm sorry."

She coughed and looked down again, but he could tell she still watched him. "It's all right," he said.

She took a deep breath, glanced around as if to confirm her whereabouts. She expanded her chest as though calm had enveloped her, shook her head slow and closed her eyes for several moments.

Then she regarded him in silence, until she broke it, "I can't explain what got into me. I have work."

She stepped past him, toward the lean-to, as if nothing happened. Without moving, he watched her walk to the woodpile. He went to the cave and entered, the rifle clutched in his right mitten. He wouldn't be caught again without the rifle or a knife in his possession. He sat at the table and took stock of their situation. The fact they were isolated didn't bother him for the moment. They were safe in the cave. It provided protection against the elements, at least until the blizzard came.

First, the provisions from Goose and Skidder's sleds meant they could survive maybe three weeks without hardship. Second, the intensity and the duration of a blizzard could compound their problem if they remained at the cave. Then what?

He suspected they were vulnerable to the blizzard if they stayed or tried to get out of the valley to the nearest village. He wondered what trouble would come if the blizzard struck while they were on their way to the mountain pass. If the blizzard hit before they reached the mountain pass, the passage over the mountain range could be blocked. That meant one thing: They had to leave right away if they expected to reach the mountain pass before the blizzard.

And there were other good reasons to leave. He'd suspected danger the first time he entered the cave. That sense still lingered inside him.

He'd felt Palafox had tried to conceal the truth from him more than once. He had to trust Palafox, what choice did he have? She had the advantage. The idea made him wary, he wouldn't follow her blindly.

It wouldn't be easy to get Palafox to come clean, to spill the truth or say why she'd been hiding the truth from him.

Maybe by tomorrow night, he might learn that he was paranoid and there was no mystery about his sketches. Not likely. There was more to her story and whatever it was, she wasn't willing to tell him. He sensed this, just as he intuited she didn't trust him and didn't like him but instead tolerated him.

He didn't know if he liked her or not, hadn't thought about it either way, just that he had to be careful to not get close to or be distracted by her.

Her motivations or reasons didn't matter though, so long as she showed him the way out of the wilderness. His mind's one track: reaching the mountain range at the horizon, then escaping the wilderness forever.

It constantly befuddled him, his goal of the mountain range in the haze. All he had to do was walk or sled to it. Yet the way things had gone so far, nothing was simple or what it seemed.

To add to his apprehensions were his ankle and leg. Although aches and the occasional pain were the norm for the healing process, his leg and foot, horribly damaged and with a devastating infection a short time ago, seemed fit. This amazed him.

It's one fat mystery how gas gangrene could have improved for the better...

He was dead tired. He thought Palafox's physical condition neared exhaustion too. There was madness in the idea of burning the men, but cremating was the same thing wasn't it?

Perhaps his thought was driven by guilt, that she needed his help, needed some offering of thanks from him. She'd suffered enough. In spite of how tired and miserable he felt, he decided to go outside and help her stack wood to burn the men. He grabbed the rifle, slung it on his shoulder and exited the cave.

CHAPTER 24

Palafox wondered about Clayton as he helped her stack wood. He spoke hardly at all. He looked weak, she knew they both were.

They hitched the reins to the madmen and the Huskies dragged their bodies near the woods, where she and Clayton strained to hoist them on the great woodpile. They spoke in spare mumbles, as if they knew what each other thought, worked this way until after dark.

Clayton found a can of kerosene along with another rifle and other food articles in one of the sleds. Despite his earlier protest, he poured the kerosene on the wood for her. She retrieved one of the cigarette lighters found in the sleds that belonged to the cutthroats and set the wood on fire.

Clayton covered his nose and mouth and hurried away, toward the cave. When he reached the flap, he shot a side-glance at her and went inside. She watched him then slowly returned her gaze to the fire.

Survival didn't frighten her the most now, but the sense of uncaring did. She added more wood to the fire.

She walked over the snow and her caribou boots made no sound. She stopped and shielded her face from the heat, drawing deep breaths of air scented with kerosene and smoke. The air steamed and snapped as fire rose off the logs. The entire wilderness, silhouetted in the dark, looked on fire. A wolf howled in the distance and she felt like running until she dropped dead.

Her brush with death had profoundly changed her and not for the good. Perhaps she had uncaring inside her all along. She realized, for the first time, she could kill without feeling.

CHAPTER 25

Palafox leaned against the cave's entrance, peering at the sky and the treetops. No wind and the sky clear. She felt uneasy for many reasons. They were leaving for the sacred valley at first light tomorrow.

The past three days, they'd spent waking time sorting through the supplies the wilderness crazies had in their sleds, keeping most of the articles they found. Knowing they couldn't feed them anyway, they let some Huskies they wouldn't need go free. They'd worked and loaded the sleds they would take on their journey to the sacred valley.

What surprised her was how quick she'd grown to depend on Clayton. Knowing she still had decisions to make, she feared that. She watched while he placed several pairs of snowshoes on the sled under the lean-to. She turned and went to the table, knowing she had a lot to think about.

She sat at the table to fix her necklace, broken in the struggle with the madman. The swelling on her face and eyes had gone down a lot.

From the bench, she looked at the rifle leaned against the wall at the entrance. Clayton's bear claw necklace was spread out on the table. She grabbed it and inspected the colors. She wondered.

Then she started to work on her necklace, a special gift from her man. What was she going to say to her man? How could she explain what had happened to her?

Clayton entered the cave and sat at the table across from her.

"Why pull a sled loaded with wood when we have an axe?" he said. "I made a handle for it."

"When we stop to rest in the sacred valley," she said, "the axe blows attract animals."

Clayton's eyes glittered with interest, "What kind of animals?"

"Mostly arctic wolves," she said. "We must take care not to make sounds more than necessary and be choosy where we stay in the sacred valley. Or start a fire. Arctic wolves can smell smoke from a long ways, too."

Clayton folded his arms on the table, "Just what I need to think about, my throat being ripped out while I'm asleep."

"I don't believe it's that bad, at least I don't think it is."

She stood and hurried to where they had rehung the furs to shield the gold in the wall.

She worked on her necklace, but glanced at Clayton while he rolled a cigarette with tobacco and papers he found in a sled, then lit the cigarette with a lighter. The cigarette looked pregnant.

The only way she'd smoke a cigarette was if she knew she was going to die within a day. When she felt the moment was right, she nodded to a pile on the table.

"Can you hand me the two green beads?"

"Sure." He searched the beads on the table, stopped and held a bead up, "Is this one green?"

She felt an unexpected tension in her throat. She searched his face, and saw a face calm, not puzzled.

"No," she said and pointed at the pile of beads, "do you see the blue ones right there? The green ones are next to them."

Clayton sighed heavily and said, "I can't distinguish between blues and greens. I'm color-blind."

"Oh." She stood, aching in her knees and belly. She didn't look at him,

"It's all right," she said.

She stepped to the table, grabbed a green bead but dropped it onto the table. Clayton slammed his hand on the rolling bead.

She winced.

He held the bead up and rolled it with his thumb and finger.

"What color is this one?"

"Green," she said.

"It feels like a pebble."

"Yes, it's a pebble."

"Interesting."

"Hand it to me," she said.

Grinning, he handed her the bead. She strung it onto the necklace and began hurriedly stringing more beads. In the process, she dropped two of the blue ones.

Clayton watched her shaky fingers. He puffed out smoke from the cigarette.

He said, "I believe we're ready to go at first light."

Her mind tumbling back to the elder's last words, she nodded without looking at him, stood and turned to go out of the cave.

"Where ya going?" he said.

"I'll be back."

He chuckled then said, "You better, I plan to leave at first light."

She ignored his comment and hurried outside. Once she was clear of the cave, she walked to the lean-to where the sleds were parked.

Clayton's color blindness wasn't known to her or to the elder, the significance of his color blindness added more complications to sort through. The elder wouldn't have asked Clayton about the colors in the necklace unless that was the authentication. She wondered if the colors had to do with the Great Spirit's blues, greens, reds and whites.

She paced around the sleds, slapping the handles and leaving a deep trail in the snow. The pacing didn't help. Her thoughts remained unsettled like her racing heart.

If Clayton didn't know the colors, that meant only one thing. He was the bad temptation or was he? More important, what was she going to do now?

Then she noticed Clayton stood outside the cave. She wondered if he saw her pacing. If he did, it must've seemed strange to him.

Aiming to not show him her unease, she pretended to inspect the loaded sleds. As she stooped to adjust the snowshoes tied on the sled, she heard his footsteps crunching over the snow. Why did he have to come to her now? She took a deep breath to calm her pounding heart, stood and smiled at him.

He stopped, "What ya doing?"

"I'm restless and trying to stay busy," she said. "It'll be dark soon."

"I loaded what you said to load."

"I can see that."

"How far is the mountain pass after we stop at the sacred valley?"

"A few days. I'm too sad to think now." She nodded at the brown tarp that covered the elder and Snow Wolf, "I'm glad you found that to cover them."

Clayton nodded. "I've said this before," he said, and his eyes went over the tarp while he folded his arms and unfolded them. "I'm truly sorry about Tuma and Snow Wolf."

"I've been tryin' to make sense of what happened to us," she said. "When we speak of the elder and Snow Wolf I feel sad," she looked away then back at him. "Let's not speak of them again." She couldn't explain it, but she was suddenly purged of sadness.

"All right," Clayton said. He turned and limped over the snow to the cave.

She watched until he went inside. He seemed so earnest, she found it hard to believe he could be a bad temptation. Yet what did his color blindness mean? She could go wilderness crazy thinking about the possibilities. She knew, as all her people knew, she had to do what was right. None of her people in her position would stop until they determined if he was a temptation. It seemed like she balanced on a ledge of a cliff.

She had only one thing she could do. Once they reached it, she'd take Clayton deep into the sacred valley and lose him some way. Should he follow her deeper into the sacred valley, the Mueumonds will find him for sure, that would be the end of him. She would be in danger too, until she reached the Saluuette's territory and the sacred forest.

The sacred forest. Her only chance to survive the winter. But she'd have to kill a big animal to survive. Yet, what would she do if she lost Clayton, if he found the sacred forest by mistake? The Saluuette wolves would scare him off before he found it, though. All her thoughts troubled her greatly. She grabbed her forehead and flung any thought out for a while.

It wasn't long before she smelled the scent of salt pork. She'd never tasted meat as good as salt pork. She liked it raw, thought it chewy and sweet.

She returned to the cave to eat and rest. After they finished eating, they talked for a short time of their plan to leave at first light.

Clayton sat at the table, pulled out cigarette papers, reached into his parka pocket and pulled out an object. An object she could barely believe he held. He had a Saluuette point. The spear point was made from the Great Spirit's sled. All her people had one.

"Where did you find that?" she said.

Clayton's eyes searched her eyes, "Find what?"

She nodded toward it, "That point you're holding?"

"Oh," Clayton turned the Saluuette point over with his fingers and examined it, "I wondered what this was it feels like iron. I found it on the floor."

She held out her hand, "It's a spear point, hand it to me."

He gazed at her, "Why?"

She wiggled her fingers, "It belonged to the elder, hand it to me."

Clayton looked at her for several moments, until he at last smiled and laid the Saluuette point in her palm. She tucked the point away in her parka. He couldn't ever know what the Saluuette point was used for. She would think about it later.

Clayton stood, went over and with his finger traced the lines that outlined Yau. He glanced over his shoulder, then turned back to Yau. "You've never told me what Yau's strap holds that's been defaced off the wall."

She straightened in her chair, "I thought I did."

"No," he shook his head. Then he stepped to the table and plunked down onto the bench.

She saw nothing wrong with sharing some things now. "Yau holds a strap, and it's said the strap was attached to some kind of beast-animal used in ancient battles."

"That's interesting," he said as he folded his arms on the table, the cigarette between his fingers, his eyes brighter. "What kind of animals and battles?" He turned his head and blew out smoke. Then he picked at something on the tip of his tongue.

"I don't know," she said. "The battles happened many centuries ago, just crazy stories of the beast my people talk about. The tales scare me though."

"I can't imagine you afraid of anything."

"I wake up afraid," she said.

Clayton chuckled, "Me too." Then started with sincerity, "After we bury Tuma and Snow Wolf in the sacred valley—"

"We don't bury them, we lay them out on the snow so their bodies can give back to those we've taken much from."

Clayton looked at her without expression, "I never thought about a funeral that way."

She wanted to change the conversation, "Let me ask you something."

He removed his arms from the table, "Ask away."

"What exactly brought you here? I mean to the sacred valley."

"Why do you call the wilderness the sacred valley?"

"The sacred valley is a place, a very specific place that the Great Spirit walked when the Great Spirit formed the sky. What brought you here?"

"I was at a dead end. I had nothing to do or hold me down. Nothing grand or earthshattering. I had a friend who was from Alaska, he always talked about fishing the Yukon and lakes in the wilderness. I thought I'd come here and check it out for myself."

"No other reason?"

He shook his head.

"Where's your friend?"

Clayton withdrew his eyes and turned his face away from her. He took a slow draw off his cigarette. He turned his head and from the side of his mouth, he blew smoke out, like his insides were on fire. He didn't look at her.

She brushed the hair out of her eyes. She decided to move off the conversation, "Clayton. If you see a moose or caribou, you must kill it for food. If we're in the sacred valley and you kill one, we must load as much meat and fast as possible in one of the sleds and leave. The arctic wolves and other things will smell the blood, or hear the gunshot, they'll come in hunter packs at a deer's speed. We've gotta kill at least two big moose or two caribous to survive."

Clayton leaned back, "Wait a—wait, you talk like we're staying the winter in the wilderness."

Palafox's insides fluttered at what she was going to say. She had to think of something fast, "Oh, don't be silly, our journey over the mountain pass will take four days from the sacred valley, then another three or four weeks to the winter campgrounds. That's if we don't get caught in the coming blizzard. A blinding blizzard will stop us, it could be days or weeks before we can move again. All the big animals are leaving the sacred valley for warmer weather."

Clayton bit his bottom lip, leaned back and glanced around. His eyes returned to hers and searched them.

"You're hiding something."

"Don't be silly."

Clayton scowled, leaned back and folded his arms over his chest. "Let's have it," he said. "I thought we'd agreed to break bread from the same loaf. And here you are, hiding the truth about something."

"Do we have to talk now?"

"Damn right," he said, "if my life's in danger."

She winced inside, "Your life is not in any more danger than mine, we should get rested, this might be the last shelter over us for a long time."

She wanted to be earnest with him, but how could she? He gave her an impatient look, grumbled something under his breath and then stood, grabbed the wide-beam flashlight and hurried out of the cave.

She listened to the sounds as he walked toward the lean-to. Then tears rolled down her cheeks. She wiped her cheeks with her mittens and listened. She didn't hear any sounds in the snow now.

She didn't have the strength or desire to continue to deceive him. She didn't like herself, ached and felt sick inside. She knew what moved her to tears—she didn't have a man's hard heart—but she might have to have one.

What was more important, her feelings, or protection of the sacred forest and its gift? Her heart was one way and her mind the other way. She knew what had to be done.

She had to take him deep into the sacred valley and in some way lose him. Then he could go his own way, temptation or not. He saved her life, here she was figuring a way to destroy him.

She glanced at the rifle leaned against the wall.

CHAPTER 26

After they camouflaged the cave's entrance, they were on their way. All during their preparation, Clayton wondered if he could handle a sled pulling another loaded sled behind. Palafox had trained him well though; it didn't take long to get a feel for the Huskies and steering a sled.

They skirted the dense timber and continued through the sparse timber where the dogs could maneuver. Though he felt reasonably confident, he didn't ignore the dangers of guiding a sled in the wilderness.

One small boulder or snow-hidden log could foul the skids of a sled. They didn't have tools to shape a new skid, or the time. His objective was to keep the Huskies on the ruts left by Palafox's sleds.

In his mind, the Huskies seemed made to order to pull sleds. In fact, he felt the Huskies liked the experience as much as he did. He wasn't worried about being lost, he felt they were already lost, at least he was. The only relief he experienced was when he saw the mountain range out there in the haze. From what he could determine they were headed straight for it.

As dusk came on the third day, he noticed they were traveling in the opposite direction of the mountain range. Finding out the reason would have to wait until tonight, when they stopped for the night to rest. Riding apart from Palafox's sled, both their heads fully muffled against the cold wind, meant they couldn't talk while the sleds were moving.

The dogs picked their way in the surreal glow of the starry night. After several hours, it was too dark to see. They pulled the dogs around them in a wagon-train formation, sat together in the snow and fed the dogs with dry dog food they'd found in one of the sleds.

He noticed that standing for hours on the sled had caused a slow burn in the muscles of both his legs. It was a relief to sit and relax, though he could never be fully relaxed in the middle of the arctic wilderness. A glance up revealed that.

Palafox looked at him. A shadow covered her eyes and he recalled that she hadn't seemed in the mood to talk over the course of the last three days.

"Let me ask you something," he said.

At her nod, he asked more for conversation than anything else, "Why do you have those chimes and little tiny Christmas bells on your sled?"

"I found the Christmas bells and wind chimes near our winter campgrounds and put them on my sled to scare bad spirits." She said the last part with a light chuckle.

"That explains a lot."

"You don't believe me?"

"I believe you but did you hear something?"

"No," she said and her eyes widened, prompting for more.

"That sizzling sound," he said, and looked up. "Wow. It's the northern lights. The aurora borealis. It's the first time I've seen them."

Palafox peered at the northern lights for a few moments. Then she said, "Some call them the northern lights but we call them the Great Spirit's breath, that's what the Tacoma clan call them."

"Never thought about the northern lights that way," he said. Gazing at them, their name didn't matter so much. The lights were ethereally beautiful, like a reddish and white fogged breath of ribbons floating down out of the dark starry sky.

After several minutes, he felt he had to know, "I was wondering. We were headed toward the mountain range at the horizon for two days. Now it seems we're traveling in the opposite direction. Why is that?"

Palafox stared at him, then took in a breath that became a deep sigh upon its release. She poked the hot coals in the fire with a log.

"We had to take the trail around a deep gorge to reach the sacred valley."

"Oh," he said, and felt satisfied about her explanation. "Are we making good time?"

She nodded, "Yes. And, I want to say something."

He tried to not let her see him tense, "What?"

"We must kill a moose, or caribou."

He relaxed and stroked the fur of the dog nearest him

"Are you worried I'll miss? We talked about that."

"I know," she said and studied him for a few seconds, "I just felt like talking about how important it will be to kill a big animal. The dogs must eat meat every day to stay strong. The dog food won't last very long. Another thing, when we enter the sacred valley, we can't make many fires, they must be small and covered up with snow after we heat our meal and we must be very, very careful at all times."

Clayton nodded but didn't reply. He saw no sense opening up a conversation they'd just had several days ago about a fire in the so-called sacred valley. Her comments really didn't make much sense about a fire. The last time he'd heard, animals were still afraid of smoke and fire.

They chatted awhile longer, then huddled close together near the fire, he watched her eyes until she rolled over and went to sleep. He woke when he heard the dogs moving around. The wind wasn't blowing and daylight was coming to the wilderness. They broke camp and were on the way again.

It was near midday and hardly a breeze when they traveled down a draw, then along the shoulder of a great range. They came upon a slope where the steep, snow-covered terrain was rough for the Huskies, they continued along until they reached the bank of a huge snow-shrouded lake.

He watched as Palafox glanced back at him and held her mitten over her head, the signal for him to stop. He slowed the sled until it eased to a halt beside her, grabbed the rifle and stepped over to her.

She scanned the area, then raised her arm and pointed across the frozen lake, "Where the forest starts out there, is the beginning of the sacred valley."

Clayton followed her into the sacred valley. The place they stopped to have the ritual burial for Tuma and Snow Wolf was, well, not that spectacular in his opinion. In fact, it seemed an ordinary location in the thick forest of conifers.

He didn't know what he expected to see, perhaps some grand view of the wilderness. But one thing was obvious, it was still and quiet in the woods except for the sounds they made walking on the snow.

After he helped Palafox slide Tuma and Snow Wolf's bodies off the sled, she waved a hand when Clayton asked where to move it. "They're fine here," she said. "Normally we place our dead naked on the ground, but the elder's too frozen for that now."

She took the branches of conifers, waved them over Tuma's face and body. She mumbled something in a chant-like song.

He stood back and listened, noted her shoulders trembled with her crying that gave way to a sustained, mournful whine that rose and fell. She mumbled something over and over.

He liked Tuma and Snow Wolf and felt much sympathy and heartfelt sorrow for them. It was sad and in a way scary because of how quiet the area was surrounding them. But what really frightened him were the macabre corpses. Tuma's arms reached up and his legs were drawn up, almost like he walked on all fours in the air.

The entire process of the ritual burial took less than ten minutes but it seemed a lot longer. When Palafox stood and motioned back in the direction they'd traveled, her eyes were dry but very red now.

It took a half-hour to return to the frozen lake.

She stepped off the sled and walked to him, "Stay behind and do as I do and keep your rifle ready to shoot a moose or caribou. We're in the sacred valley. Keep your wilderness eyes open all the time for anything that moves in the daylight."

He kept the rifle ready all the time and wondered why she told him that. His annoyance at the repeated reminder faded when he noticed that frost had become thicker on her eyebrows.

"All right," he said.

By the time he slung the rifle on his shoulder, hopped on his sled, grabbed the reins and got the dogs moving, she was at least fifty feet ahead and her sleds were moving fast.

They changed direction regularly as the sleds moved over the terrain. The sun balanced on the mountain range when Palafox held up her mitten and pointed across a barren terrain, to a forest line of mostly conifers at least a half-mile away.

They exited the forest and started across the slope, which to him seemed similar to a ski slope. All thought ended when they reached midway; the snow under his sled trembled once, then again, the once silent wilderness filled with a rumbling.

Fear gripped his spine when snow rushed down the incline, toward him. Hardly had he braced himself than his sled was swamped by a wave of snow. The impact sent him, dogs and sleds pell-mell down the slope. The churning snow felt alive as he rolled and tumbled in the tongue of the monster snow slide.

CHAPTER 27

In some maniacal surfing contest, Clayton got pulled under, then pushed up, violently. Blinded by the snow pounding his face and head, in a scramble to regain control, his body arched back.

The world around him became gray and the air silent as he was buried under the relentless snow wave. His mind shut down for a few moments, then it felt he moved in slow motion.

Just as quickly, he shot to daylight and felt air under his body. His arms and legs worked automatically as he rolled and tumbled in the churning snow. In the confusion, a chorus of pitiful squealing— the dogs—and Palafox's scream mingled with snaps and pops that sounded like bones crunching.

He tumbled in an inky darkness, then the sense of any motion stopped. The air became silent and still. And he felt pressure against half his body. He couldn't breathe. He was smothering. He strained his body. He strained again and broke free of the snow, gasped for air that was scented with the green wood of conifers.

Clouds of mist and fog prevented him from seeing more than five feet in any direction. He was disoriented, until he heard soft plunks come through the fog. He had no idea what was making the sounds.

He tried to scramble out but the snow had packed him in tight. The left half of his body was stuck. Frantic, he grabbed the knife out of his parka and started to hack at the snow.

He realized he still had the rifle when its sling cut into his shoulder. The rifle was sideways across his back. He looked for Palafox and didn't see her, the dogs, or the sleds in the fog.

"Palafox!" His voiced echoed.

More of the plunking sounds, then he heard, "I'm down here, hurry." Her voice echoed, elusive and feeble through billows of fog.

Clayton couldn't see her. He chopped at the snow and panic helped him finally dig out his upper body. His left leg remained stuck. Looking hard and frantic around him, he spotted the handlebars of a sled several feet away. Just the handlebars.

He tried to calm his breathing to hear any sounds under the snow. By their muted barks, a few seconds later he realized all the Huskies were buried alive. There was nothing he could do for them. Regret stabbed him.

"Say something, Palafox!" There was silence for a few agonizing moments before he heard, fainter than before, "Down here."

With much effort, he extracted his leg from the snow. Pain and numbness kept him from feeling it, much less knowing how badly he'd injured it. He lay on his stomach and elbow-crawled through the fog, in the direction of her voice.

To get a fix on her location he called, "Say something, Palafox!"

"Down here," she said, fainter still. A person could scream every second for the rest of their natural lives in the wilderness and never be heard. He knew this from near deadly experience.

"Don't move, stay put!" he crawled over a tree trunk half buried in the snow. Then he heard the *plunk* sounds again, at last learned their source: chunks of snow the size of softballs and basketballs tumbled down the slope, hitting half-buried trees or other obstructions.

After thirty or forty yards of crawling, he spotted a half-buried form in the fog. Palafox laid on her right side, facing downslope, already at work, scooping out snow with her mittens. She panted and exhaled with each scoop.

That she seemed all right released the anxiety locked in his chest and he breathed much easier, but he didn't feel safe. Without delay, they had to get off that slope before it shifted again. Seeing him, Palafox settled back.

Her brown eyes wide and tortured, "Hurry," she said. "We've gotta save the dogs."

"They're gone," he said. "Are you hurt?"

"No," she said, "hurry."

It took several minutes before he freed her and in a desperate scramble to get off the slope, they crawled horizontal across the slope because they couldn't see the timberline in any direction through the fog.

Not far from where he found Palafox, he saw a section of the buried tarp and expended the energy to dig it out. Hardly had he secured the tarp than the snow under them heaved a sudden tremor and the plate of snow shifted down eight or ten feet, spinning him around.

Together, they made a feeble scramble until they saw the timberline, gathered strength with their new direction and crawled to it. Using each other for support, they managed to stand.

Palafox's voice strained, "What are we going to do?"

"We'll manage," he said, and dusted snow from his parka. "Let's get away from here—"

"We gotta save the dogs—"

"I told you they're gone," he said. "Let's get the hell outta here."

He grabbed her arm and pulled her along in a stumbling jog. He heard her sobbing but had no breath to say comforting words. After several hundred yards, though winded, he felt they were safe from another avalanche; the terrain wasn't as steep here. He pointed to the snowy ground and motioned her to sit.

She sank to the ground, drew up her legs, buried her face in her mittens and rested them on her knees. She sobbed and rocked slow, back and forth, grieving.

Clayton's grief could wait. His thoughts flooded with a thousand things as he left her alone and walked away to cut green limbs to build a fire. He felt that was the best thing to do, since a fire would bring them physical comfort.

When he returned with an armload of limbs, she had packed snow around the tarp so they could sleep in relative warmth. She talked in circles about saving the dogs, getting the sleds out of the snow and not making a fire. He wondered if she'd suffered a concussion.

Her eyes lingered on his face. Her face seemed to strain to not cry. "What are we gonna do?"

Finally, he said, "We'll be all right, I have the rifle and we have cigarette lighters and candles, we won't go hungry. We're lucky." He started to tremble and shake uncontrolled when he realized just how lucky they were.

"I'm afraid," she said, "let's go look for the dogs—"

"Listen, they're gone, nothing will bring them back, all right?"

She looked back at him and wiped both sides of her face with the heels of her mittens. The color had seemed to drain out of her face, but she nodded and sighed.

Dark closed around them and they didn't make a fire after all. They propped against trees, with the tarp with snow on top of it for warmth. Late in the night, in a half-dream sleep, he heard a hum and realized Palafox sobbed quietly. The depth of her sob suggested she was unreachable.

What was a man to do about a sobbing woman? He didn't know how to comfort her, or if he even could. What could he say that would make a difference? No words he had could soothe over the whole spiraling course of events that had fallen upon them. His best hope was that she'd work out her troubles alone and without his intrusion.

He tried to pretend he didn't hear her sob but he did. And she couldn't know what her sobs did to him. He could feel his heart thumping when he covered his ears with his mittens.

Deep down, he felt he was the blame, the guilty party. He stayed awake and listened to her sob for the longest time. Then her sobs got softer, then she became still and quiet.

There was nothing else for him to do but sleep, but when he did, the fear he'd felt came tumbling in a dream, as if he were falling from a great height. He woke in alarm, realized where he was and drifted back to various states of restless sleep.

He languished that way and trembled with a sick hopelessness at their chance of survival. He awoke, for good, long before daylight and before Palafox opened her eyes.

They followed their trail back to the slope. When they approached the edge of the incline, they stopped and looked over the destruction caused by the avalanche. To stand in its midst and not be amazed was impossible.

A quarter-mile of forest, obliterated. Trees bent, broken and partially covered with a spread of debris and snow.

How did we survive?

The air was scented with green wood in every breath; it was easy to imagine the forest had gone the way of warm flesh and died.

Palafox looked at him, shook her head. She wiped her eyes, "Poor Huskies."

He nodded and couldn't speak right then. But he felt pity for the animals. Finally, he said, "It won't take long for us to leave after I find the sleds. You stay here. Take the rifle."

She grabbed the rifle and held it but didn't speak.

The handles of one sled still jutted above the snow. He crawled until he reached it and worked feverishly, digging out the snow to reach the goods in the sled. Once he did, he hurried to grab what he could and stacked the canned food, dried beans, coffee, sugar, a wide-beam flashlight, candles, two small pots and his journal, among other items, onto the tarp. In all, he made five trips across the slanting terrain to the two sleds he'd found.

He'd failed to locate two other sleds, the lanterns, or the can of kerosene; he swallowed his disappointment and crawled off the slope, trying to tell himself he was lucky, that he'd recovered more than he ever dreamed he would be able to. Yet, he knew it wasn't enough to sustain them for long.

At midday, they hauled what they could and walked down the terrain to what Palafox called a frozen brook that would take them part of the way to the mountain pass.

"The best way to escape the wilderness is to find a frozen stream and follow it," was all she'd said in explanation. With no choice, he'd nodded and followed her.

The weight of the articles they carried on their backs was light compared to the weight of survival on his mind. There was no reason to feel optimism about their chance of walking out of the wilderness, but he couldn't allow his thoughts to go in that direction or they would surely perish.

Instead, he focused on the chance of killing several big animals, then finding cover and being holed up until the early spring. They had sufficient food to last at least ten days without putting themselves on rationing. With enough killed meat they would survive longer. He decided to instead take each day one at a time or go crazy. Then he decided the latter would be the best course for him.

The streambed was narrow and winding. Though he hadn't expected any greenery to survive in such cold, plants and other flora overgrew sections of the frozen brook. The growth slowed them down at times. Nevertheless, he felt they made adequate headway in spite of the weight they lugged on their backs.

Palafox avoided small talk and remained unusually quiet, accepted the weight she carried without complaint. For reasons he couldn't explain, she seemed more than just nervous about the possibility of not finding food. She was friendly but seemed preoccupied, edgy. She would stop walking, stand motionless and study the slightest of sounds.

She was especially tense in the dark and often woke him unintentionally when she startled herself awake. His worry grew that she might've suffered a concussion, especially when she began to complain about headaches at times.

Palafox noticed it first, during one of her stand-and-listen sessions, but he immediately felt it too. Toward the end of daylight on the fifth day, they began to feel a light breeze, but in the distance. The wind noises were faint at first, but soon began to sound like a distant-but-approaching sea and the air was turning colder.

His initial thought was that the wind and cold were both odd, because the sun had shined bright for the past five cloudless days. They continued to walk. A laborious process in the snow and the problem was, physical exertion didn't occupy his mind enough. The likelihood of success was remote if they didn't kill an animal soon. In his mind, he wondered if Palafox feared the same thing.

At dusk, she slapped his shoulder with her mitten and pointed toward a steep bank, to what looked like a depression in it. Not an avalanche, he decided. The snow around it hadn't been disturbed.

He grabbed the wide-beam flashlight, left the frozen brook and climbed the bank, stooped to enter the chest-high, diamond-shaped entrance.

Once inside he stood, careful to not bump his head and shouldered the rifle. Palafox had followed him, her steps almost soundless.

A short passageway led to an open space. He shined the flashlight and couldn't see much at first. The beam highlighted what appeared to be a pile of limbs and sticks. The objects were covered with dust but appeared arranged with purpose, one atop another. The arrangement was roughly four feet high.

Someone had used the cave, maybe stored up some firewood. No surprise there. But the limbs were stacked in a way that seemed, well, odd.

He stepped back and observed the arrangement critically. He turned to Palafox, who stood peering at the limbs. He nodded at the stack, "Is it my imagination or is it just a pile of limbs?"

Palafox shook her head, "No," stepped to the limbs, "it's not that simple." She lit a candle, squatted and inspected the arrangement with her mitten. "I've never seen anything like this."

"What better place to stay," Clayton said and adjusted the rifle sling. "It's dry wood. We can make a decent fire, rest a day or two, hunt, get our strength back."

She stood up slow, held the candle at arm's length and moved it over the arrangement of limbs. She stepped away from it, then another step back and stood still.

He was just about to speak, to ask her what she'd seen, when she turned to him. Her face drifted in and out of a shadow.

"This is a birthing cave," she said in a low voice.

Clayton considered what she said and nodded.

"No doubt," he said, flippant, "it's a nest of some sort."

Her face stiffened, became grave. She took a steady breath, "This is no place for us."

He didn't feel the same way.

Then a crackle came from the trees outside; the wind had begun to blow. He shifted his attention to the wind.

CHAPTER 28

Clayton listened to the wind outside and wondered if Palafox felt the same way he did.

"The winds are worse, we should stay inside the cave until this blizzard clears out," he said.

Palafox seemed reserved, her expression almost strange in the candle's glow. Her eyes began to move around the stacks of limbs, "I don't see another way, but I don't like it with all these limbs."

Clayton felt she was being paranoid, but turned when she did and they exited the cave. The forested hillside acted as a barrier against most of the wind, but not the sounds. Here, the wind sounded like a freight train. By the time they'd returned to the cave, snow was shooting among the conifers like it had been blasted from cannon.

He used the tarp to cover up the entrance to the short passageway leading to the cave's mouth. Candles and a small fire made the remaining space comfortable. After the interior warmed up, he smelled the faint odor of a horse stable, alien to the wilderness, but he got used to it along with the smoke in the air.

They relocated the stacks of limbs to one side of the cave. He chose one side, Palafox the other to stow their meager belongings.

After they ate, he felt weariness overtake him and couldn't resist the call of sleep.

He awoke with a start, surprised to see Palafox standing near the tarp. He hadn't heard her get up. He raked hair out of his eyes and lifted his head, was about to speak when she pressed her finger to her lips and nodded at the tarp. He listened, but didn't hear a sound out of place. Moving quietly, he grabbed the rifle and scrambled to his feet, then stepped to stand next to her.

"What's going on?" he whispered.

She looked at him with a strange gaze, "It sounded like pick, pick— listen."

He wondered why he didn't hear the same sound.

"Probably the wind," he said.

She hugged herself as if she felt a chill. "Something's out there."

He listened and debated if she'd really heard anything. Then a measured crunch-crunch, crunch-crunch continued uninterrupted up the hillside, until the sounds stopped near the mouth of the cave.

Every instinct told Clayton no sane person would approach a dim-lit cave during a blizzard in the dark without vocalizing their presence. He gripped the rifle tighter.

CHAPTER 29

Clayton kept the rifle barrel pointed at the tarp while he tried to think. He ruled out a grizzly. They were in hibernation. And the noises on the snow didn't sound like a moose, or any four-legged animal that walked. It sounded almost like someone walked with a bum leg.

He stared at Palafox several moments, nodded for her to move away from the tarp. She stepped silent until she stood behind him. She said, "What do you think it—?"

He raised his hand for quiet. The same instinct that told him it wasn't an animal said that whatever stood outside could hear them talk and was about to enter the tunnel-like passageway into the cave. If he heard a noise inside the passageway, he'd fire through the tarp. He steadied his happy finger on the trigger.

A minute went by then maybe two. He began to feel whatever stood outside wasn't interested in attracting attention. Yet, it hadn't left. He would've heard it leave.

Then a faint clack, clack, clack mingled with other sounds outside. The clacks came five times, then silence.

He tried to tell himself he trembled because of the cold, but that wasn't true. Why, he couldn't have explained, but he got the notion that a person might be half-frozen outside, unable to speak, trying to send a message by bumping limbs together.

On one level, his conscience wouldn't let him shoot through the tarp without knowing what he was about to kill. Each moment seemed more agonizing than the last, like counting seconds, waiting for a live grenade to go off. Panic swelled inside him until he felt he might get hives or black out from not breathing.

He nodded to Palafox to hand him the flashlight.

"What are you doing?" she said.

He didn't answer her or take his eyes off the tarp. Blindly, he felt for the flashlight until he had a firm grip on it, then eased the tarp to the side. He shined the beam.

Immediately, something left the vicinity. The sound was of hooves thundering down the hillside toward the frozen brook a short distance away.

Startled, Clayton lowered the rifle and clicked off the flashlight. As he did, a squeal, a dog or wolf's, mingled with croaking somewhere at the brook. After a few seconds, the poor animal hushed mid-squeal.

Palafox's breath hitched and she looked at him, unbelieving.

Then another croak, this one fearsome as a lion's guttural grunt, came once, twice, three times. It was celebrating its kill, or perhaps warning others to stay away.

Clayton tightened his grip on the rifle. He hadn't heard anything like the croaks before, but to him, they sounded like noises produced by a mature animal. His conscience didn't bother him now, just the opposite.

After a minute, he turned and looked at Palafox, "What kind of animal croaks in the wilderness?"

Palafox looked at him with guarded eyes.

"There are bad things—very bad things—in the uplands in the winter."

He asked a few more questions but he wasn't getting anywhere. Her silence was clear, ominous. One thing was certain; she was visibly frightened and her fear surrounded him like the smell of a wet animal. Why was that? What kind of animal would cause her to be afraid?

He couldn't spend mental energy on that right now. He pushed his suspicions back and returned his attention to the sounds outside.

A few minutes of listening revealed no other out-of-place sounds. He felt certain the croaking animal remained in the vicinity, near its kill.

He eased his finger off the trigger, clicked the safety on. The sigh he heaved was forced, didn't make him feel any more at ease.

The night was far enough along that daylight was maybe an hour or two away. But it was hard to get any sense of time where he was. The nights were long, sometimes the nights crawled by.

He eased the tarp to the side and shined the beam. No eyes shone back, nothing suspicious in fact.

Palafox grabbed his elbow. Her eyes showed worry. "Don't go outside," she said.

Just that. No explanation of why she said it. He guided the flashlight beam outside and onto the snow. "Just animals," he said as he bent over and stepped through the narrow passageway, exiting the cave to stand at the entrance, the rifle locked and loaded.

The wind surrounded him immediately, vibrating his parka like fangs ripping for his flesh. The arctic cold was almost like breathing air in a freezer and the cold bit the skin on his face and neck, bringing goose bumps.

Snow was falling heavy, but what took his entire being were the signs of beaten-down trails on the snow at the mouth of the cave. Two trails went down the hillside toward the frozen brook. One trail went up the hillside, above the cave.

He couldn't make out the individual tracks, so he twisted the flashlight up and along the terrain. The chrome light didn't highlight an animal, or eyes shining. He saw nothing out of the ordinary, in fact, yet, still wary, he decided to shoot anything suspicious.

After a minute, he felt that some kind of animal had wandered into the vicinity looking for shelter, only they got to the cave first. *Which means the animal must've left the area.*

Or did it? But he knew soon it wouldn't be finicky about its source of meat.

He trained the flashlight back up the hillside for one last look. A blur of a shadowy enigma leaped over the flashlight's beam.

The enigma virtually flew with the grace of a panther among the swaying trees, moving swiftly, near silent even with its size. It plopped on the snow and loped through the dark, almost as if it hadn't been there.

In his shock, Clayton decided what he'd seen seemed too damn nightmarish to be anything real, more like a surreal trick of light and shadow.

The few times before, when he'd let his guard down, came close to disastrous for him. He wouldn't stand around to find out what kind of animal it was. He grabbed the flashlight he'd dropped and scurried back inside the cave.

The moment he entered the cave's poor light, Palafox blurted out, "What's wrong?"

What should he tell her? What could he tell her? He didn't want to alarm her unnecessarily, what he'd seen was implausible. The panther-like figure had to have been an aberration, one rooted in a trick of light and shadow. Or a mysterious illuminated enigma that would've caused nonbelievers to believe in monsters.

In the second he had to come up with an answer, he decided the best answer to avoid frightening her was to dodge her question.

"I thought I saw something," he said, which was true.

"Like what?"

What, indeed? He stepped to his bedding spot and paused to answer over his shoulder, "It looked like a windblown shadow."

She sighed and stepped to the tarp, eased it to the side, but then turned and peered at him for several moments.

"It's getting daylight, we must leave on the first sunny day."

Not waiting for his reply, she stepped to her bedding spot, grabbed her mittens and flopped down. She glanced over at him. She didn't have a calm way of hiding her dread, he noticed.

"I've got the rifle locked and loaded," he said. "There's nothing to fear."

It was easier for him to say that than to try to explain the aberration. He wasn't positive he could've explained the vague shape, other than to say the outline seemed to shimmer. He couldn't shake the enigma out of his head if he wanted to.

All that was left to do was wait for daylight. After a half hour, he tired of standing and sat on the dirt floor across from Palafox. The small fire and candles separated them.

They talked aimlessly about locating to another area after the snow stopped falling so hard. He sensed she was preoccupied with something, something she wanted to tell him, but for some reason couldn't, or wouldn't. All along, he felt she knew what kind of animal that had croaked but wasn't saying. Why was that? If she were hiding something, something that seemed to terrify her, why not share that with him, so he could help her, help both of them?

"An ear has compassion," he said, and forced a grin he hoped looked friendly. "Wanna talk about what's on your mind?"

"I suppose you're still wondering what it was that croaked," her voice sounded more assured than before.

He was glad to see the change in her.

"Yeah, it crossed my mind a time or two."

She didn't smile or frown when she said, "I've thought through this a couple of days, when I remembered the elder made you a member of the Tacoma clan. Because of that, I felt maybe you had to know, and—"

"Know what?"

"What we're up against."

He sighed. "By all means, brighten my darkness."

"Once I tell you, it's your responsibility to not share what I'm going to tell you with anyone outside our clan," she said. "Lives will depend on it."

Why the secrecy?

But now that she was finally talking, maybe the less he said the better.

"You shouldn't tell me."

She looked at the small fire and he wondered for an instant if he'd overplayed his hand. Genuine concern colored her face, almost as if she couldn't believe it had come down to this. Without making eye contact and as if it were a passing thought, she said, "It's important that you know."

He got a sick gut feeling.

"I don't need to know, don't tell me—"

"Our lives might depend on you knowing."

She didn't look at him, though he looked at her for several moments. At last he said, "If you didn't already know, I place a hell of a lot of value on my life."

"I know this might sound outrageous," she said, "but the croaking you heard outside a while ago that was a Mueumond. The Mueumonds are the reason my people don't stay in the sacred valley during the winter months. We haven't for centuries."

Clayton said, "I guess it's safe to say the Mueumonds aren't charming neighbors?"

She gave an impatient huff at his attempt to lighten the mood. "There are things in the upland wilderness not meant for round eyes to know about. The Mueumonds aren't neighbors and really not animals either. The Mueumonds are things, very bad things."

CHAPTER 30

By now, her tendency to avoid specifics was beginning to grate on his nerves. But she got his attention all right. Even so, he wondered if she wanted to frighten him more than he was.

"You're pulling my leg," he said, "they're not real."

"If the Mueumonds were a myth, I wouldn't be telling-"

"And may I ask what kind of things are the Mueumonds?"

"Let me finish, all right?"

"Then crack the egg. Try making sense for a change."

She stared at him with eyes that wanted to bite.

He nodded half-heartedly, though his frame of mind wasn't ready for any of her nonsense, of any more delays in telling him what he needed to hear.

Her eyes softer now, she said, "The Mueumonds hibernate in the summers and emerge in the sacred valley in the winter. Only at night, or on cloudy days in the winter. They stay in woods in the winter, where sunlight can't touch the snow on the ground. The Mueumonds won't hunt food on any sunny day in the winter and that's the best time for us to travel."

She stared at him for several moments and sighed.

"I know this sounds outrageous. It won't be simple for us because winter is just beginning and the Mueumonds aren't mindless, they're relentless killers and—"

"Killers? Get outta here."

"Do you wanna know or what?"

Seeing true anger on her face, he decided to drop the sarcasm and nodded.

"All right then, listen carefully. The Mueumond's eyes are sensitive to the sunlight, to bright light and to firelight. They hibernate like bears, but only in the summer, then molt off all their fur and hair. It's said the Mueumond's skin turns pink after molting, so their skin blisters in sunlight. The Mueumonds can smell blood miles away in the sacred valley."

"A phenomenal sense of smell," Clayton said. He didn't want to stick his neck out on a fat hunch she'd gone stark raving mad. He didn't want to make a snap judgment. He couldn't dismiss the facts. For one thing, he couldn't ignore two events as fiction. He had heard something unexplainable, had seen something frightening.

He stood and stepped to the tarp. One thing he knew he had a rifle. One bullet to the head would drop any animal in the wilderness.

"Where you going?" she said.

He'd traveled so far, endured so much, but now a mysterious animal might have their number. Deep inside, he grew angry. And then, he began to wonder. He turned and looked at her. She sat as before, looking at him with her parka arms folded.

He said, "Why didn't you mention these critters before now?"

She sighed, then started slowly, "I did. It's the beast that Yau holds with a strap. I told you about that at the cave. The beast got loose during battles and bred with something brought here to battle my people, over territory in the uplands many, many centuries ago."

He shook his head, annoyed.

"You can't expect me to believe a bizarre tale like this, come on." He stepped to the nest of limbs and grabbed a nice stiff one. A thought flashed though his head, too quick to consider seriously.

He glanced at her and couldn't believe it—she was sulking. Hurting her feelings was the last thing he wanted to do.

"Clayton," she said and her expression softened, "the Mueumonds have reduced my clan from over a thousand to less than a hundred over the generations. My people have suffered thousands killed by the Mueumonds. A Mueumond grabbed my only brother. He was just twelve seasons. He only walked away from the light of the campfire to pee." She tossed her mitten behind her; it hit the wall and dropped to the floor, "And like that, he was gone. Sometimes at night, when my mind is still, I can hear my brother scream and it fills my ears. Even the elder's woman went missing, in the middle of the day, just four seasons back. What's strange, Clayton, is where you said you found the jewel. The elder's woman had to be running for her life to travel that far. No wonder we couldn't find her."

Clayton nodded, snapped the limb in half and laid the two pieces on the fire.

"I'm sorry to hear about your brother and people. But if unorthodox animals existed in the wilderness, why haven't people escaped and talked about them? The only animals in the Alaskan wilderness that are dangerous I read about were a bear and a moose."

She leaned back, seemed to relax again.

"Did your book say wilderness trappers or a snow slide would kill you dead, too? No one escapes the Mueumonds once you're in the sacred valley in the winter, like we are now. The Mueumonds hunt humans. That's why my people find sleds with furs and other items in the upland at the thaw. During the Gold Rush, it's said thousands of people, dogs, cattle, mules and horses went missing in the uplands. They went missing because the Mueumonds got them. And only five seasons ago, the elders began to suspect something terrible about the Mueumonds. Want to know what—?"

"Of course I do."

"They believed the Mueumonds are adapting to sunlight. And that the Mueumonds' population has increased each year for several centuries. The elders are frightened that this is a terrible sign for bad things to come."

His earlier belief turned to doubt.

"Your story doesn't add up. Why would anyone come into the wilderness if the Mueumonds were that dangerous?"

She glanced away and adjusted her necklace. "I've already told you, the Mueumonds hibernate in the summers in the sacred valley. They don't emerge until the first snows. And rarely leave the sacred valley. Besides, we have our reasons for returning to the sacred valley at the thaw. Reasons sacred to my people. And important. And no, I can't tell you." She shook her head. "I really, really can't."

He wondered if one of the reasons was to find sleds with furs, to cover up evidence of the Mueumonds, or something else. He reached up, rubbed his eyes, then his beard. "All right. Your reasons are important. But staying alive's important to me, damned important. And I'm not sticking my neck out for your reasons."

Things were adding up. Starting to come together, just not in a neat little puzzle. But he'd figured out enough to decide to sleep with a knife in his hand and keep the rifle locked and loaded.

Yet he didn't want to upset Palafox anymore than she seemed to be.

"Listen, I want to leave the wilderness safely and alive, that's all I want, all right?"

She nodded and wiped her cheeks with the heel of her mitten.

"For agreement's sake, let's say what you're telling me is accurate. What kind of animals are we dealing with here? I mean, how do the Mueumonds act and look?"

"You won't believe me if I told you."

He forgot his earlier vow, "You're probably right, but I'm sure you're going to tell me anyway, just so you can scare the irises off my eyes. And if I don't ask, you might not tell me till it's too late or next year sometime. So go ahead and brighten my dark mood right now, why don't you?"

The sarcasm flew over her head, but she got his question.

"I've never seen a Mueumond alive or dead, but I'd like to see 'em all dead. I've heard 'em croak more than a few times too. Several men were attacked by the Mueumonds and saved by my people several generations back. The men talked about how they survived.

The Mueumonds attacked in the middle of the night. The men saw shadows, they called them very strange shadows. The shadows, they said, were more like outlines that seemed to waver. Like a mirage, but the shadows were solid." She swallowed hard, "The men said if you're close enough to see a Mueumond, you're dead. It's said that the men who survived the attacks went wilderness crazy. That boils, sores and swellings developed on their skin from wounds. It's said the men died in a painful way. But, there's something else that happened to the men and it's only whispered about."

Clayton nodded, "May I ask what the whispers were, or do I wanna know?"

She averted her eyes and her voice trailed off when she said, "You don't wanna know."

"Good, don't hang the noose round my neck," he said, not sure if he spoke in annoyance, or relief. In a weird way, he suspected the worst. But he truly didn't want to know.

She looked at him and nervousness broke over her face. "I will say this, it's better to die than to survive with wounds inflicted by the Mueumonds."

"Exactly what are the Mueumonds?"

"I don't know. I've never seen one. I've heard them croak though."

"I just can't fathom that you've never seen one of those critters alive or dead," he said, trying but failing to keep the waver out of his voice.

"I'm not exaggerating. But I believe the stories that we must leave the sacred valley before the first snows. So we won't encounter them when they come out of hibernation. I heard one elder say that at the first snows, the Mueumonds flood the sacred valley like ants out of a disturbed mound."

Her story was so bizarre, a part of him desperately wanted to dismiss the Mueumonds as nothing more than a Yukon legend. But the prospect that the Mueumonds were real scared the hell out of him.

"You know this is peachy, just peachy."

She didn't reply right away but watched him, and finally she said, "I know none of this makes sense to you, we can split up if you like. Try our luck on our own. I can probably do better on my own anyway. How does that sound?"

"Loud and clear," he said. "Thanks for holding me in such high esteem. You certainly don't expect me to leave you with those critters on the loose and alone do you? Forget it. I'm not going anyplace without you, so you can push that foolish notion out of your head. Besides, where the hell would I go? I've been lost since the soles of my boots pressed the soil here. Besides, you know as well as I do the mountain pass is blocked by now. Even as I speak, snow is falling thick as clouds outside. At least three feet of new snow since yesterday. Are you tryin' to get us killed?"

Clayton was making a guess but even in the poor light, he saw her stiffen in surprise and her mouth open. Her reaction suggested she hadn't been serious about going it alone.

"Now that we cleared that up, we have to do something," he said. "We can't lounge here and get buried in snow. We should think about finding another place to hole up."

"We can't go anyplace if the sun's not out," she said. "Where could we hide where the Mueumonds couldn't find us? And we couldn't walk long distances in the fresh snow, and daylight doesn't last long, and light of day is growing short each passing day. Before long we won't have more than a couple of hours of daylight."

That didn't sit well, though he knew she was right; there was nowhere to go in the blizzard even though they were in a wilderness larger than Texas. And she was right about not traveling far. Even so, with the way events had gone so far, it was hard to know what to expect from her, or the wilderness.

He looked outside at Alaska's early twilight. When he began this journey he had a new life ahead of him, but now even the clouds seemed to be falling apart. Depression he thought he'd beaten rolled over him, threatened to bury him.

Her enlightenment about the Mueumonds was troubling. Especially one thing she said he couldn't ignore. In winter, in the sacred valley, no one escaped them.

Trying to keep safe wasn't going to be a cakewalk if the so-called Mueumonds were real. Yet on top of everything else, he couldn't stick his neck out on a hunch the creatures weren't real.

There was still something odd about her story, something that wouldn't let him go ahead and just accept every crazy thing she'd said. What was the reason she wanted him to keep quiet about the Mueumonds? Why'd she wait so long to tell him about them? Did her people protect the Mueumonds? Did the Mueumonds protect her people?

She'd known this all along and she seemed so afraid. What she had told him was incredible. Worse, he felt this was just the start of it.

He stepped over and plunked down across from her.

"You're not very encouraging," he said. "I'm suspicious of you, but I agree we couldn't travel far in this snow. You've been really good at stating the problem. Way I see it, we have to stay in the cave and defend ourselves until this blizzard blows out. Do you have any ideas on ways for us to do that?"

CHAPTER 31

Clayton's stare made Palafox wonder if he thought she'd gone wilderness crazy. She'd decided to tell him only what he needed to know, enough so they could try to survive. If he could see the Great Sprit's colors, it would be a lot simpler for her.

She had to find a way to stay alive long enough to reach the Saluuette territory and the sacred forest. The Saluuettes could establish quickly if Clayton was the force of evil temptation and destroy him on the spot. For herself, she didn't care. Only survival mattered to her.

The more she thought the less likely survival seemed. It was a fifteen or twenty-day journey on foot through the sacred valley to the sacred forest. *The Mueumonds will hunt us down the whole time. We'll both be killed long before we reach the Saluuette territory and the sacred forest.* She sighed to calm her nervousness.

"I can understand why you would be suspicious and I don't blame you, Clayton. But there's one thing I want you to trust me about, the Mueumonds are killers of the worst sort. We can't underestimate them a moment. I know this will sound silly to you even before I say it, but remember what I said? That the light of a fire hurts the Mueumonds' eyes? Our only hope will be to keep a fire blazing in the dark and we don't have enough wood inside to last a week. Besides, the smoke inside will drive us outside and the Mueumonds might be waiting. They might return when it gets dark and I don't need to say what'll happen if they get inside this smelly cramped cave with us."

Clayton said, "We have a wilderness full of trees. I don't know about you lady, but I plan to stay alive. I have a whole life, a new life ahead of me and it's worth fighting for. The Mueumonds will have to earn the right to stop me from getting out. And I've been thinking. What we need to do is send a message to the Mueumonds."

"You certainly talk the fight," Palafox said, feeling encouraged that he made staying alive sound easy. "What kind of message?"

"If the Mueumonds try to enter the cave, we kill 'em. This cave is a good defensive position, provided the Mueumonds don't, oh, unless they possess tear gas, or have to be shot with a silver bullet or something like that. I have over fifty one-hundred-sixty-grain pointed Core-Lokt bullets and they can put ugly on forever."

"Wipe 'em out and let the Great Spirit sort 'em out, is that what you have in mind?" she said and sighed a breath of relief.

Clayton chuckled, "That's about it."

"I read that once on a shirt. Not exactly that way, though."

Clayton grinned and hooked his hair over his left ear.

"There's one little thing that bothers me about what you told me about the Mueumonds. If they're as dangerous and aggressive as you've painted them to be, why didn't they attack us a few hours ago?"

This stunned her. He was right. Why didn't the Mueumonds come after them last night? Were all the stories she'd listened to from the time she was barely able to understand true?

She shook her head and stated the truth, "I don't know."

Clayton slapped his thighs with his mittens and grinned.

"Well, daylight's here, let's get ready to greet the what-ya-call-'em if they return at dark."

She grinned, and said, "Mueumonds. I'm with you, baby—" Her hand covered her mouth before she even thought. The word baby was something she'd read a woman called her man once. It had come out of her mouth, so naturally.

To her astonishment, Clayton stared at her with no expression of surprise or awkwardness in his eyes or face. Then he stood up.

At the same time, she stood clumsily and stumbled. Her momentum carried her into him. He caught her before she slammed facedown onto his boots and helped her to stand. He was smiling. Mortified, she feared he might believe she stumbled on purpose.

His grin faded and both of them fell silent. His smile was a nice smile. *What a wild man he is, with his wild beard and hair.* A warm sensation fattened her face and she felt at the fringe of something she couldn't place a name to. She waited with a look, a willing look.

Finally, he grinned again.

"Careful girl, easy to get off balance in here."

She winced and wondered how she got herself to this point. She had tried so hard to not like him. Her man's image flashed in her mind.

"Thanks," she said, and squirmed free of his strong hands and stepped back.

"No problem," he said. "I'll chop some ice out of the brook for water and coffee and think over a plan. Though I don't need much of one. This thirty-ought-six rifle will cause eyes to grow big or cause a bulletproof-thinking lunatic to raise the stakes."

"I'll make us coffee, something to eat, we'll need the strength," she said quickly. "Also to drive out the foul smell of this cave, could you roll me a cigarette? I want to smoke one."

His eyes narrowed, but in good humor he said, "You're crossing the line. Are ya smoking tobacco and drinking coffee at the same time?"

"I know. Sounds like fun that's worth fighting for."

"You're raising the stakes."

She gave him her best smile, "I'm all in."

He ducked out of the cave into the day lit wind and falling snow muttering, "Lord, Lord, Palafox. I need fresh air."

She chuckled. This couldn't be happening to her. One thing for sure, the moments he held her were too darn short. She admitted to herself the thrill that went through her. If Clay—what she'd come to think of him as, if only in her mind—if Clay had held her five seconds longer, she'd have done it. She felt like breaking every limb in the cave over her head for not doing it. Why didn't she go ahead, wrap her arms around his neck and kiss him with all she had while she had the chance? She might not get another time of natural innocence. Clay gave her hope that she'd see her man who waited for her. She sighed, telling herself that was enough.

But then, she thought about her man less each day, wondered if that was bad luck for her or good luck for him. She couldn't help herself, she'd just have to think about her man at another time. She had too many important matters to think about now, like staying alive.

She removed her bear claw earrings, grabbed a limb and snapped it in half like Clay had done and tossed it onto the fire, then another. Ashes scattered off the coals and she felt a brief sensation of warmth.

She tried to not think about their helpless situation, about how they were going to survive another night.

Or about the decision she'd have to make if they survived.

Instead, she concentrated on stories she'd listened to about the Mueumonds, focused harder on every detail of how to survive if they were attacked.

It was said no person known had escaped the Mueumonds once they made contact, but she wouldn't, couldn't allow that to intrude on her thinking. Just the light of the fire would hold them off until resources, exhaustion and hunger overpowered the victim. *Or at least that's what the stories say.*

It wasn't long before Clay returned. They spent the rest of the day eating, resting and talking over a plan to defend the cave, as he called it. She wasn't as optimistic as he seemed to be, but went along with everything he said.

He made two homemade spears for her and strangely, he said, "After forty-three bullets, we're the will-o'-the-wisp."

She didn't know exactly what he meant, but managed to keep her heart steady. The air inside changed as daylight slipped away.

As Clay stood peering outside, he turned, "Do you know how to operate an automatic rifle?"

She stood up and shook her head.

"Let me show you how to load the clips and—"

"All right," she said. She'd fired a gun before but not a gun like the one he had. She listened to his instructions and did what he told her, but by the time he finished, she had decided it was the best time to tell him.

"Clayton, I wish there was a better way for me to say this, but there's not. I want you to know if I'm bit or mauled by a Mueumond, please don't let me suffer. It'll be all right."

His face hardened. He adjusted the gun's sling with one hand and stared at her. Understandable that he didn't want to hear that from her, yet she had to assure him it would be all right.

She grinned. "We'll kill 'em all, won't we?"

He gave her a stiff jaw while he mumbled, "That's the spirit," then grinned and looked away.

The grin was forced, she knew. Just as she knew if a fight with the Mueumonds got to a hopeless point, there would be only one way they would get to her. Up to now, she had always believed and felt that all men were alike, but not anymore.

He seemed calm while he sorted through the bullets, examining each one, and while he sharpened the knife on a small rock he'd found in the cave. He even stretched back and took a nap. That he wasn't taking their situation seriously worried her, especially when he said, "Wake me when it starts getting dark." And so, she did.

After darkness fell, Clay stood outside the cave for hours. She was supposed to sleep but she couldn't. Every so often Clay returned inside to get warm, then would go back outside and stand at the entrance. Night crawled along slow.

With a new purpose, he entered the cave, slapping snow off his coppery-hued parka and said, "We've got a visitor or two slipping down the hillside, maybe thirty yards away."

She sat up. Clay removed the top half of his parka and quickly took the tarp down over the entrance to the cave. Only then did he stoke the fire.

Her job was to keep the candles lit and the fire going but not a blazing fire. She sat on the limbs, facing the entrance, feeling like a defenseless temptress on an altar, awaiting sacrifice to a pagan god.

Their plan was simple. She would sit on the stack of limbs and be bait, to get the Mueumond to hesitate or stop at the entrance. She was dressed for it and already vulnerable. Her parka and hood didn't exactly meet her thoughts of a sacrifice of purity she'd read about.

If I'm going to die, then let it be like ... never mind.

Perhaps reading her thoughts, Clay gave her the tarp to wrap around her. She wished he hadn't done that. She had a sinking feeling the tarp was a death shroud.

She caressed herself as she seated herself on the limbs.

"I'm afraid," she whispered.

Clay nodded without expression, "Me too."

She nodded, noticed her shadow laid crossways on him in the cave's warm glow.

He laid the flashlight down near his shoulder then lay on his stomach, behind some limbs, propping the gun against his shoulder and pointed the barrel at the cave's entrance. He pulled out the big knife and laid it next to his shoulder. His demeanor seemed calm, unmoved, but when he draped the bear claw necklace around his neck she saw his hands tremble.

She smelled his man sweat and with other smells in the cave; the air smelled with a stench of meat she almost tasted when she breathed. The little fire snapped sparks and the candles made her shadow bulky.

Clay glanced over at her, "Stay still and quiet."

She intended to stay still, but she shivered and her teeth began to chatter. She sat down in the fire's weak glow, her back against the wall, wrapped herself tight in the tarp and tried to squeeze herself to nothing, as her shadow had tapered down to nothing. She buried her face on her knees and breathed deep and slow.

The movement over the snow outside was unmistakable. She could have been wrong but it seemed more than one entity made the sounds. Something that sounded like steps to the entrance stopped.

She didn't want to look and didn't. It was a minute before she noticed the cold draft through the passageway had almost stopped. At first, she thought the wind had quit blowing. Then she heard the wind.

Fear washed over her. She looked up. She gazed at the dark passageway to the cave. When her vision focused to the darkness, there was nothing more than a subtle movement at the entrance.

A spiky shadow, lighter than dark, crouched and rocked, as though it were too beefy to enter. Clack, clack and a faint breeze drifted in the dark.

She barely breathed, "Clayton."

"Shhh, I see it."

The dark silhouette filled her line of sight and began to take on … *it can't be* … human shape.

She shrank back and quaked.

Two eyes opened, startling as a nightmare.

She screamed.

Clay shot it.

CHAPTER 32

The shadowy thing blew back, making piercing screeches as it seemed to flounce down the hillside. A clamor trailed out of hearing, then silence fell on the woods outside.

Could the thing be dead?

She trembled and couldn't have spoken if she had wanted to. And her ears wouldn't stop ringing. When Clay said something, she opened her mouth but nothing came out.

When she didn't reply, he turned and said, "When you scream it disrupts my concentration, just sit tight."

She tried to speak. She couldn't, any more than she could move. Her focus was so intense her vision blurred until she blinked it away, back to clarity.

When Clay leaned back on his knees, he fumbled with a bullet in the rifle. He twisted and rocked. "Crap," he moaned. He kept his eyes on the entrance, working fast. It seemed he strained with every effort to dislodge the jammed cartridge.

"Did you see the air glow green around the eyes?" she said in a small voice and felt a shudder all the way to her toes.

He nodded, "Cat eyes like those are for seeing in the dark, just sit tight, damn rifle."

Footsteps, followed by a shadow. Her breath caught in her throat. The imposing apparition crouched and seethed. Narrowed green eyes glowed, fangs gnashing, then rocked and started through the passageway.

She covered her ears and blurted, "Shoot, shoot!"

An ear ringing explosion flashed.

She screamed until the cave seemed to spin.

The shadowy thing blew back and crashed down the hillside, making snapping and popping sounds. There was something permanent and wretched in the screeches and croaks she heard as it did.

A few seconds passed, then the silence filled with a few croaks, then many, then the croak sounds swept through the woods like a herd of moose in dispute. The croaks became faint until silence returned.

When she'd heard those croaks at a distance, she was certain the Mueumonds were racing to the cave in a killer pack, that soon, she and Clay would be slaughtered in the cave. The noises were gone for now, but the feeling remained.

"Did you hear all those croaks?" she said.

"Just sit tight." Clay adjusted the rifle stock on his shoulder.

The wind wasn't blowing as strong as before, but the quiet didn't calm the pounding of her heart. Certain it wasn't over, that she and Clay were still under assault, she waited and listened. She tried not to show weakness but her legs were numb and she almost collapsed in fright when Clay asked her to take the flashlight. She grabbed it from him, sat down and again leaned against the cave wall.

The noises again, muted, but not obscured by the snow. Six, maybe more Mueumonds, she was certain that was what they were, lumbering straight up the hill. But unlike before, when the noises came in a straight, narrow trajectory, these seemed to come from all around the cave's entrance.

Panic filled her. The Mueumonds were lined up to charge the cave. She looked to Clay, but he lay still and seemed calm, watchful, he didn't seem to share her certainty.

The sounds went quiet outside. At times, she heard a crunch on the snow then silence, then another faint crunch.

She remembered the stories. They said the Mueumonds were relentless. So why didn't they attack, try to enter the cave? Were they afraid of the fire? Being shot? Were the stories even true? Then she remembered something else from the stories: Mueumonds were smart, cunning. And might be content to wait them out.

Yes, that's why they haven't attacked yet. They're smart.

Clay looked at her, his words lacked emotion, "It seems they're preparing to rush us. If the rifle jams, I'll do what I can, take the flashlight and run when you see your way clear."

"You just can't let them inside," she said, hoarse from screaming, but also from the emotion rushing through her at the idea of being left alone with them.

Instead of replying, he stared at her with the air of someone casually drinking coffee out of a tin cup. He turned and aimed the barrel at the entrance.

Perhaps he was resigned to his fate, but she wasn't prepared to die in a filthy, smelly cave. If she ran, it would be minutes, hours at most, before the Mueumonds caught up to her. She didn't have the stomach to fight to the death but her inner voice refused the notion of prolonging the outcome. She saw no point suffering in terror needlessly.

She scrambled up, grabbed her spear; Clay watched her but said nothing. She returned to the limbs and leaned back against the wall. She decided to fight if she had to if for nothing else, for her brother.

Hour after hour after hour rocked by until finally, Clay stood and turned.

"Hand me the flashlight," he said.

She did what he asked.

"You can't go outside," she said, and wondered if he'd gone wilderness crazy too.

He didn't acknowledge her but instead stepped slowly to the entrance, the rifle at his waist and the flashlight in his left hand. He shined the flashlight beam outside.

The darkness outside filled with seething sounds all around the cave, coming from what sounded like a half dozen directions at once. Heavy thuds were followed by sounds of limbs cracking and popping. But these sounds were moving away, as though the beasts were fleeing through the forest. More than surprise, she felt relief.

Clay stepped back, keeping the rifle pointed at the passageway and the flashlight shining through it.

"They're frightened," she said, "the flashlight—"

He shook his head. "It's getting daylight," he didn't take his eyes off the entrance, "they'll be back."

CHAPTER 33

They watched daylight arrive and it was a forever process. Stories or not, Palafox felt safe in the daylight even though it was cloudy. Immediate survival looking more certain now, she was able to turn her thoughts longer term, to what they were going to do and how they could survive if the Mueumonds returned.

Clay didn't object when she followed him to stand just outside the cave entrance. Even as they crept outside she didn't want to go, but decided to be another set of eyes and ears. The snow was ruffled up in some spots, packed down in others, with many distinct trails leading off in all directions.

The patch Clay stood over was stained with blood. He shook his head and frowned, looked at her, "You see anything peculiar about the blood?"

She studied the frozen crimson pool.

"Yes, it seems foamy like," she said, and felt even more panicky though she didn't know why.

Clay nodded, "I thought something seemed different."

They walked down the hillside, following the thin crimson trail on the snow. The trail zigzagged between trees and crossed the brook up along the hillside.

No doubt in her mind, Clay wanted to see the Mueumond he believed he'd killed. She didn't want to see one. She was already afraid of them dead or alive.

What she wanted was the sun out, so they could at least try to make a run for safety. The desire was hope. With the daylight so short, they wouldn't make it to the Saluuette territory before the Mueumonds caught up to them. She shuddered, not from the cold.

Not far across the frozen brook, the crimson trail ended at a wallowed-out spot on the snow. The spot had snow furrowed, piled up and dug out all the way to a bed of brown leaves, twigs, ferns and needles from the spruce next to it. Frozen crimson was strewed and splashed and had frozen while dripping down tree trunks. It was apparent something went through death throes here. One crimson trail led away and wound up the hillside, into thick woods and brush.

Clay removed his mitten and picked up a strand of hair, rolled it between his fingers while gazing at it.

"It's thicker than our hair. Has the texture of monofilament line," he said and looked up at the sky. He seemed to nod strangely.

Palafox followed his eyes. The slate-colored clouds looked like pregnant sows.

He handed her the strand. She accepted the hair but wasn't amazed by it as he'd been. She had seen thick piles of such hair in circles near the sacred forest a number of times, no one in her clan could explain what the hair was doing there. She said nothing, just inspected the hair, which was spotted with orange, brown and white.

He scooped up a handful of the snow covered with bloodstains. He sniffed the ball and dropped it before pulling on his mitten, glancing around the woods as he did.

"The animal's mortally wounded." His gaze seemed to go along the trail to the thick woods.

"I'm not walking up there," she said.

He shook his head, "I'm not either. One thing's certain, they bleed."

"Huh."

His brows arched, "Meaning, they can be killed. And I suspect the Mueumonds know it on some level, just like most animals do. Notice anything about the tracks in the snow?"

"It's the first tracks I've seen of the Mueumonds," she said, and it was the truth.

"Five toes, with the third toe longer at the back. Unless the animal was sliding, it seems to have talons like a bird of prey."

"We should return to the cave," she said, remembering something. "The Mueumonds could be hiding in mounds of snow. It's said they do that on dark cloudy days in the winter and jump animals when they walk by."

"Or ambush people," Clay said, and narrowed his eyes at her. "You certainly know a lot about the Mueumonds for someone who hasn't seen one."

"Only from stories told by my people—"

She saw a familiar movement and waved her hand to get his attention. "An arctic wolf," she whispered. "One of the fiercest wolves in the upland wilderness, though Saluuette wolves are fiercer."

The arctic wolf was sniffing the trails along the ridge just above the cave. It stopped next to a tree and glanced warily at them.

"Maybe a scout, probably smelled the Mueumond's blood," she whispered. "The arctic wolves hunt in packs and fight the

Mueumonds, the Mueumonds hunt and fight them too. Hurry, shoot it. We need the meat."

He grabbed the gun off his shoulder and held it at his waist.

"What, a healthy wolf?"

"Shoot it."

Clay shook his head, "No."

"Why?"

The wolf wheeled, bounced and vanished in the woods and haze.

Clay didn't look at her. "Look at those trees." He nodded at trees to his left.

She saw three trees that looked like lightning had struck them. Long lines of bark were absent from their trunks, about six feet up. She didn't puzzle over the mystery, she knew claws had torn the bark away. Then her eyes fell on what was wedged in the fork of the tree. The wolf's head rested in a fork of lower limbs, and its body had been eaten to its shoulders. The wolf's eyes had iced over.

She swallowed. Her stomach churned.

Clay's focus on the corpse was as if he were in a trance. Finally, he said, "The more they eat, the better."

"What do you mean?"

"An empty belly is fiercer."

"Don't get any strange ideas," she said, and her heart beat a tiny bit faster.

"Just the truth," was all he said in reply.

When she looked back at the dead wolf, she observed something dark in the fork of another tree behind the corpse. Blinking her eyes against the bitter cold, she made out a sled-sized, reddish piece of some stringy globular material.

"Is that what I think it is?" she said, and pointed.

"I'm not sure. Could be a half-eaten ribcage of a big animal and a hindquarter, I don't know what that other stuff is, just that it's foul-looking." He pointed at some brown-and-red gunk hanging from two limbs that she didn't see before. Then she saw five other trees with globs of stringy meat and hides of animals in the forks.

She said, "Why would the Mueumonds hang mangled dead animals in a fork of a tree, other than to keep it away from wolves?"

Clay shook his head, "I don't know, unless this vicinity is used as a trap for another animal, a lure of some kind, maybe. Or the carcasses are used as a warning to not trespass. You see anything odd with the carcasses in the trees?"

Palafox scanned the lumps of meat hanging.

"I don't see anything, let's get away from here—"

"The carcasses should be covered with snow."

She stopped her turn, voiced the same conclusion, "That means the carcasses were just put there."

"Perhaps. With all the tracks and the blood trails, maybe the snow hasn't had time to cover them. There's a minimum of two hundred pounds of bone and meat in those trees. It's there to serve some purpose."

She winced inwardly. He was right of course. She wondered about the significance of storing meat in trees, but couldn't understand why the Mueumonds went to the trouble. She and Clay didn't talk about the possibilities long before they hurried away.

When they returned to the brook below the cave, Clay began jabbing ice out of the frozen brook with the knife while she provided another set of eyes and ears to stay alert to their surroundings.

Finally, he shouldered the rifle and shuffled up the hill toward the cave carrying an armful of the ice chunks, loaded so heavily he seemed to rock as he walked. She filled her arms with all the ice she could carry and followed.

After they ate and had coffee and cigarettes, he worked on the gun for a while, hoping to fix the problem of jamming bullets. Then he lay down and went to sleep. At no point did he say more than a word or two, even when she asked a question.

When it was her time to rest, she found it hard to sleep, troubled as she was about so many things. It was daylight outside and she didn't expect any Mueumonds would show up during daylight. She relied on the stories she'd heard most of her life.

She believed she was in a doze, heading for full sleep, when she felt something settle gently onto her face, and thought she heard a thump.

She opened her eyes.

Clay slept.

It was becoming dark outside.

She felt another touch, the feeling like snow when it lands on a face. She wiped her cheek. On her finger was a speck of dust and dust drifted in the dim glow from the lone candle.

She listened.

Something seemed to scratch on the wall of the cave. It came again, pick, pick, pick.

A quiet panic began to fill her.

CHAPTER 34

The scratching abruptly stopped.

Courage borne of fear forced her to sit up.

The scratching resumed, lazy in its work.

She wondered if the Mueumonds were able to dig. Then she pondered if they had strength to claw through solid rock.

The scratching stopped briefly, then a faint, so faint pick, pick filled the air again.

Afraid to move more than she already had, her eyes drifted to Clay and back to the wall. She watched him sleep and wondered if she should wake him. When the scratching's pace quickened, she stood and stepped to where he lay.

So he wouldn't make any sound, she slowly pressed her hand over his mouth. Barely had she touched his lips with her palm than his hand shot up and she felt the sting of the knife against her throat.

When the tremors subsided in her she whispered, "Listen," and as he pulled the knife away, she turned her head toward the sounds, "somethin's clawing on the wall."

He sat up quickly, grabbed the rifle and stood. He peeked outside.

"About an hour till dark," he said.

He stepped to the wall and pressed his ear to it, listened for several moments. He took a pace back. "The scratching's stopped," he said, and stood there to examined the wall.

She wondered what he was up to and was about to whisper her question when he removed his mittens, wet his fingers with his mouth and rubbed the wall, then rubbed his forefinger and thumb together as he looked at the wall again.

He said, "I don't like the looks of this."

"What, what—?"

"This wall has been mudded."

She shook her head, confused, "I don't under—"

"I never paid that much attention to the wall before now," he said, "the light was too poor and the way it feels the mud on it, it reminds me of a dirt dauber's nest."

Wasps? Dirt daubers went through her mind and a shudder went through her body. From where she sat, she couldn't tell the difference between ordinary rock and a mudded wall. The wall was smooth in places, chipped, cracked and gray almost like solid rock. Was he saying that instead of rock, the wall was covered with mud? Why?

One look at his worried face suggested he had the same question she did. Finally, she said it out loud, "The Mueumonds outside are planning to keep us inside the cave? To store us in here, like for food?"

He nodded and his eyebrows arched, "It's a good possibility. It's even possible the carcasses in the trees are meant to feed what's on the other side of this wall."

"It makes perfect sense," she said. "The Mueumonds wanted to hoard food in this cave and discovered us. Why else wouldn't they be as relentless as the stories say?"

"I wouldn't know about that," Clay said. "One thing seems apparent. Whatever's on the other side of this wall will claw out, if it's tonight, tomorrow or whenever. They'll be hungry when they do, we're practically dinner for them. You're right, this might be a birthing place or an incubator chamber." He shouldered the rifle.

"Or the Mueumonds use this place to hibernate," Palafox said. "No wonder the men and elders of my clan couldn't find the Mueumonds in the summers and—"

"What!"

She nodded, "Yes. The men and elders of my clan hunt Mueumonds while they're in hibernation in the sacred valley. To destroy with fires, spears or poisons. It's been centuries since my clan destroyed a Mueumond in hibernation though. They can't find them. And the elders saw this as a very bad sign of things to come."

"Why didn't you mention this before now?" he asked.

"I saw no need. We're in great danger here."

He sighed, "We could be in the middle of a dominion of 'em. This place could be honeycombed with them. We've got to vamoose, pronto."

Palafox felt her pulse jump.

"I wished you hadn't said that. Don't you believe we'd be better off if we took our chances inside the cave, at least until daylight tomorrow? Then leave. I'm not optimistic we'd see another day if we're forced out now, it's nearly dark. The Mueumonds will hunt us until daylight."

"How do you know that?" Clay said.

She blew out a frustrated breath.

"I told you already. Each generation has their stories and we learned from their mistakes so we wouldn't repeat the same mistakes."

For the first time, he bit his lip. He said, "Look, there's no need to keep holding out on me like you've been doing. If we have any chance to stay alive, you have to tell me everything and I mean everything that might help me understand these things."

Everything? No, never.

But, she realized that in trying to protect her tribe and herself, she had probably held back more than she should have.

"All right. The Mueumonds are a crossbreed of two animals. Each was bred for war, they got loose and bred together. For countless centuries, my people have tried to control them, destroy them with poisons, forest fires, killing them in hibernation. If you ever hear of a forest fire in the wilderness in the summers, it's because my people set it, to kill and trap the Mueumonds. You can name it and my people have tried it. The Mueumonds keep coming back stronger and wiser. They seem to adapt to whatever we do to destroy them. And there's a lot more about the Mueumonds than you would care to know about. I don't feel we should waste what precious little daylight we have discussing that right now. We should take our chances inside the cave until daylight tomorrow."

He nodded, "I agree, but can we hold on that long?"

He held up a hand, went to the opening and peeked outside. When he returned, he was squinting.

"Okay. I suspect the Mueumonds won't willingly expose themselves to fire, or being shot, if they want to keep us inside. But it's a matter of time before something pecks through. And if it's tonight, I'm sure the Mueumonds outside will make an effort to keep us inside. Then we'd be—"

"Trapped like rats in a burrow," she said.

"It might come to that. We have a lot against us, but we should have a plan to escape if it comes to that." He glanced at the pile of limbs. "How about this? If they push through the wall tonight, we can use the limbs and set the cave on fire to buy us time. We have enough wood to plug a section of the wall if they claw through and enough limbs to start hell's inferno inside this cave—"

"I'm up to it," she said with a weak smile. "Let's greet the Mueumonds with a warm welcome. Let's wipe 'em out. The only problem it won't take much smoke to drive us out."

He sighed, "To where they'll be waiting outside."

"Yes. Either way, it seems we're trapped if the Mueumonds come through the wall tonight."

He nodded a silent yes, "It's a gamble all right. Every instinct tells me we should leave now, while we're not under duress. But there's reason to wait. The thing is I've been through several pressure cookers before where the best plans failed. We can't panic. Our plan should be simple if we have to run away in the dark. We won't have time to do much. We can use the flashlight to blind them and kill them if necessary. Then we'll have to trust our instincts from there."

"I was afraid you might say that," Palafox said. "But what choice do we have?"

"It's a gamble either way. But above all, we can't-" He smelled the arm of his parka. "Our parkas smell like smoke. The Mueumonds just might confuse the smoke for a fire. All animals are afraid of smoke and fire. That might be the break we need if we have to run in the dark. We have to be cautious about the use of the flashlight. The batteries won't last indefinitely…."

They batted their plan around a few minutes longer and decided to stay the night. They discussed the possibility of being separated in the dark if they had to run. Clay indicated the brook could be a place for them to hook up if they became separated.

They took turns staying awake and listening. There was only one thing she knew now it was dark and the wind gusts were loud.

Some time passed before things settled down outside. She grew weary, then exhausted as time dragged along. The clawing on the wall had stopped before dark and still she couldn't sleep.

Then a vibration on the wall startled her. She had moved away from the scratching wall before dark and now something was picking and scratching against the wall she now leaned against.

She held her breath. She stayed calm to make sure she wasn't dreaming. Finally, she jostled Clay's boots to make sure he was awake.

He looked around, as if he wasn't sure where he was. He turned and looked at her.

She nodded at the wall behind her and he nodded back.

When she began to ease away from the wall, an incredible force slammed her back against it.

She screamed.

CHAPTER 35

The force of the impact transmitted to her teeth then with a startling suddenness, her parka jerked beneath her chin.

She tried to scream. She couldn't breathe. She gasped, kicked and twisted. She grabbed what she could and pulled down and strained to breathe.

Clay had scrambled to his feet with his knife. He quickly cut her free and pushed her away.

Palafox lurched to a stop and turned only to see her parka hood sucked through a fist-sized hole in the wall. In the same instant, a powerful arm covered in grayish skin and auburn hair came speeding out of the hole, black curved claws extending.

The claws made a whooshing grab for Clay's head at the exact instant he ducked.

She grabbed a spear and shrieked as she swung it. The spear smacked the arm and it withdrew through the hole, its claws fighting themselves.

Clay's eyes were hard when he shoved the rifle barrel in the hole. His face twisted when he said, "Grab this!" and fired the rifle.

Sounds erupted from behind the wall. Clay stepped back and snatched the flashlight up, shined the light through the narrow hole, shot into the hole again and stepped back.

"Put the limbs on the fire, get ready to run!"

Finally, Palafox got control of her shakes. She grabbed an armload of limbs and laid their tips on the fire, knowing they now had only a short time before the smoke made it impossible to stay inside the cave.

She turned partway and covered her ears as Clay raised the rifle. An arm's-length flame shot out of the barrel when he fired into the hole again.

Crunching sounds emanated at the cave's entrance.

"The entrance!" she said.

She covered her ears again as Clay spun, the rifle still at his shoulder and a flame shot out of the barrel.

The next sounds were the growls of wolves and croaks outside, from somewhere around the brook, an apparent fight between the arctic wolves and Mueumonds.

In the same moment, Palafox saw a glowing eye in the hole. In her shock, she thought it seemed to be studying what they were doing. She aimed for the eye and flung the spear through the hole. She felt a jarring.

For an instant, she believed the spear pierced the eye of a Mueumond, then she felt a tug. She yanked back, but only half the shaft returned. It had been bitten off. She dropped the shaft and grabbed the other spear.

Clay covered his mouth and nose with his left mitten while holding the rifle with his right. He coughed against the rising smoke and said, "We gotta go!"

She watched as he grabbed up two limbs, their tips on fire. When he began to shove the flaming limbs through the hole, croaks and screeches burst forth behind the wall.

He stepped back and garbled out, "They're stirred up like a pack of rats." He waved at her and pointed at the entrance, "Get out, go!"

The smoke had made it hard to breathe without coughing, her eyes began to sting and water. She tried to blink the tears away to get better vision, but couldn't do anything about the dizziness that weakened her.

Engulfed in smoke so hot it felt like breathing fire, she squinted and battled through it until she stepped into the passageway. There, she reached down to grab up some of the supplies. She was stopped by Clay seizing her wrist. He shoved the flashlight in her mitten. In her peripheral vision, she could see the fire had begun to engulf the piles of limbs in shooting flames and smoke.

Clay's face appeared, close enough so she could the strain on his face. He choked out, "Run—I'm behind you!"

Hunched over, she bumped her head and shoulders in the tunnel passageway and continued forward, her hand outstretched in front of her, her mind consumed with breathing, getting air. She experienced an awkward-sleepwalking sense, stumbled and somehow managed to keep her balance as she kept moving, aware at any instant she could collapse and not get up.

She heard a wall crumble inside the cave, then two quick shots that brought crushing despair. But there was nothing else for her to do but save herself.

CHAPTER 36

She stumbled out of the cave into blackness cold enough to paralyze her at first. After a succession of coughs, her head spun until she thought she'd fall. Then the dark seemed to steady around her.

Her eyes were stinging and watering. She wiped and blinked away the tears. She raised her arm and shined the flashlight back and forth through the woods. Noises created by the sweeps were of something fleeing through the forest.

She coughed so hard she felt her stomach coming up. She turned the flashlight's beam through the smoke in the cave. Finally, her voice broke free and she yelled for Clay.

It was only moments before she heard a cough, then another cough as he stumbled out of the cave. He carried the rifle and pack loaded with their supplies.

"They're coming out of the wall, get the hell outta here," he said, doubling over between coughs.

Coughing, they stumbled and slid down the hillside. Not once did she lose awareness of the dangers around them; mindful that to lose her footing might mean her death, she pointed the flashlight everyplace she could. She heard several croaks and screeches, but they seemed to be coming from behind them, in the direction of the cave.

Once they reached the brook, they hurried on, though at a slower pace. Here, the flashlight revealed glimpses of glowing eyes on the wooded hillside above them on their right. When she directed the flashlight at the eyes, Clay fired two wild shots at them. The eyes disappeared.

She was consumed with fear, the type of fear she'd felt when they nearly lost everything in the snow slide, a far worse dread than when the cutthroat had touched her. Now, she was terrified.

They continued at a slow pace and spoke only about where to shine the flashlight. The farther they walked the less activity they heard. Still, the feeling they would lose their lives any moment stayed with her.

After they put distance between them and the cave, they fell into a strangely easy conversation about staying alive. Her hope rose when they talked about surviving to the next minute, to the next hour.

They stopped to rest at intervals. It was cloudy and the wind got stronger. Snow was falling now, she knew the Mueumonds wouldn't move very much because in spite of the clouds, the daylight seemed much brighter.

She tried to prepare herself for what they might have to face in the blizzard, a shortage of food and being pursued by the Mueumonds, but at moments she felt like weeping, thinking of all that could go bad. All the dangers were too much for her to think about but her troubles seemed always on her mind.

She didn't believe they had enough energy between them to keep a fire going, plus they didn't have enough wood, just tree branches.

Now she was glad she'd listened to all the stories on how to avoid the Mueumonds. Daylight was starting to fade and she needed to focus all her energy on staying alive the first night.

She gently grabbed Clay's parka arm. She said, "We should think about a place to spend the night, while there's enough light."

"What about a fire?"

"We don't have enough wood. You'll have to trust me on this, we need to find a log buried in the snow, away from the frozen brook."

If wasn't long before he spotted dead tree branches above the snow and the top edge of a big log.

She said, "We have to dig out the snow to the ground. Then we lay down on the ground next to the log. You on one side and me on the other side. We cover ourselves with lots of snow and green limbs of the trees around us. We can dig out a place under the log, so we can talk quiet. The stories say it'll work."

Clay shook his head, "Sounds farfetched to me."

"The main thing is our odor. We can use needles of the trees and rub them in our hands, then coat ourselves with sap on our faces, hair and parkas. Then we hide our tracks in the snow to this place and walk up the other side of the hill to throw them off."

Clay said, "The wind's blowing in the opposite direction from the way we walked. They'd have to be downwind to scent us, it might just work."

She was heartened by the renewed strength in his voice. "Could you make me another spear? Also, I want you to cut me a small limb, about the size of my finger, so I can jab you with it if you snore."

He did what she asked. By the time darkness closed in, they'd finished pulling snow on them and hiding their scent. She lay with her face against the log. She could feel Clay's warm breath against her face. That helped her feel safe.

Sometime during the night, she woke to a rumbling on the snow along the brook. At first, she thought a tree fell. When she heard the clacks and soft croaks she realized Mueumonds were running along the brook. Then the log quivered from weight, then a light clack, clack, clacking. She knew then a Mueumond had jumped on the log, hopped off and run down the hillside.

Before she breathed, she made sure she couldn't hear any other sounds. The urge to cough came; she swallowed it away before she breathed.

"Clayton," she whispered and there was no answer for several moments.

Then he said, "Shhh, sit tight."

CHAPTER 37

There was no relief from fear or hiding from the Mueumonds. The worst of it was the cold, wind and dark. The constant threat of the cold and snow and the Mueumonds were always present, even when Palafox had slept. She didn't really sleep; it had been more like a twilight sleep. They both were weak, exhausted and frightened as much on the tenth day as they were on the first day.

Palafox was concerned because she knew they should've already found the gorge to follow to the Saluuette territory. Once there, they would be safe. But she knew the frozen brook ran to the gorge and turned into a waterfall, but no gorge appeared.

She was taking Clay to the sacred forest. She couldn't lose him in the sacred valley as she had planned to do. Taking him there went against her clan's law and against all her teachings. She had no choice, there weren't any alternatives she could think of. But it still didn't make it right to take him there. This thought was on her mind while she walked ahead of Clay on the frozen streambed. It was just daylight when she heard something behind her and turned.

Clay had dropped to his knees on the snow. As she watched, he took the rifle off his shoulder, then his pack. He scooped snow from the ground with mittened hands, then held them close to his face. He grinned wide.

"Remarkable," he said softly. He stood and leaned the rifle against a tree, then walked to a tree limb and pulled the limb to his face.

What is he doing? It made no sense, but he seemed to be sniffing the needles sticking from the limb.

When he released the limb, he stretched out his arms and spun around, looking up. Laughing softly, he looked out through the woods with a kid's expression and spun around again. When he dropped to his knees a second time, he grabbed another mitten full of snow, peered at it and again laughed softly.

Was the cold driving him wilderness crazy? The way he acted increased her fear that a Mueumond had bitten him back at the cave.

She stepped close to the rifle and was prepared to shoot him if necessary so he wouldn't suffer.

Then he said, "I can see."

Bewildered, she only watched while he removed his mittens from his hands and looked at the pink skin, turning them over, his eyes glinting with wonder and joy. He quickly removed the bear claw necklace.

"I can see," he said, the broad grin on his face widened impossibly. "I'm serious. I can see greens, blues, browns, I can see colors, I can see." Still grinning, he looked at her, "I can see your parka, the colors. I can see the gray clouds, I can see."

She wasn't sure what to say to him.

"Ya-you can see colors?"

He nodded, "The white of the snow. The green needles. The mist in the air. The clouds. I'd forgotten how many shades and colors a single cloud has. I can see colors."

For the next half hour, she observed his celebration of his newfound sight. She knew what had cured his colorblindness and knew then he couldn't be a force of evil temptation. The mushroom from the sacred forest cured all sickness, diseases, infections, or injuries caused by nature or caused by the forces of evil. But the mushroom didn't cure diseases or infections caused by man. When Clay was very sick, the elder had instructed her to give him pieces of the sacred mushrooms in the soup medicine.

Palafox felt all along Clay was an innocent man who had strayed into the sacred valley. Seeing the proof of her rightness, she knew she would have to reveal a lot to him. Now, knowing his innocence, she felt safer in doing so.

But how could she explain the sacred forest and Arnaq? If they made it to the sacred forest alive, how could she explain her people of the Tacoma clan? With sinking heart, she accepted Clay's fate.

He can't leave the wilderness alive or dead.

If they made it through the Saluuette's territory, she would tell him a little bit at a time. She didn't want to think about all of that now. She was glad he could see colors. He was like a little kid and this made her heart swell happy inside.

On the eleventh day, one day since he had recovered his sight of colors, Clay seemed to have a lot more energy and marveled at everything. He talked briefly about going to art school and he talked about not being a trivial soul anymore.

She felt an ache when he talked about finding their way out of the wilderness and how he was going to eat a steak and have a thick vanilla malt milkshake.

She knew he could never leave with his knowledge of the sacred forest or of her people. Her people's whole way of life would be in danger of being discovered and destroyed forevermore, the sacred forest would be in danger forever if one word got out.

Many deaths would happen for those who tried to find the sacred forest and their blood would be on her. One man's life would be worth saving an untold number of lives. Just as certainly, she had to persuade Clay to stay, because she knew she couldn't do the unthinkable, how could she? She cared too much for him now.

After all, he had saved her life twice and probably saved her life in other ways. Even though he didn't show any interest in her, direct or otherwise, she cared probably more for him than she was willing to admit. And she had since they'd found him. But she also knew the Saluuette wolves would track him down if he tried to leave the wilderness.

She just couldn't let him leave. She had to convince him to stay of his own free will. How could she do that? She wasn't sure she could. He was too determined to get out of the wilderness. If they made it to the sacred forest alive, what was she going to do?

Around midday, every tree swayed and crackled as if wakefulness had gone across the wilderness at the same time. At a great distance, she barely heard the croaks, but she did.

"They're tracking us," he said and pushed back the hood of the parka to listen.

"It's cloudy and the sun's not out," she said. "It's at least two hours before dark."

"I'm not surprised, it seems twilight dark in the forest now." He looked around. "I'll stay here and try to throw 'em off."

"Listen, listen to me, Clayton," she said. "I'll help, it won't take long." She pointed to the right side of the brook. "Pee at the base of every tree. That'll slow 'em up and make 'em sniff around and it might throw 'em off on the wrong scent trail. You go up that way, I'll go this way and we'll meet back here in a few minutes."

"Sounds like a plan," Clay said. "With all the tree sap on us, it's amazing they can even smell us."

"The Mueumonds are far away but not that far, so don't take long," she said. "The Mueumonds are smart and cunning. They can't be fooled for long."

She went one way and Clay the other way. She went up and along a shoulder of a ridge, then down through a small holler and up along the side of a slope, taking time only to pee on tree trunks every hundred steps. Each shadow, each brush pile, she feared something crouched behind.

The noises returned, sounding like distant thunder at different locations in the forest. She stepped behind a tree and listened for several long moments, then began to run back toward the brook, keeping a constant vigil at her back, sensing that at any moment the Mueumonds would overtake her by surprise.

Before she did, she saw an open space through the treetops.

She jogged in the direction of the open space. The trees became thinner and she knew the gorge wasn't far. She found it, approached the edge of it, stopped at the edge and looked about.

She knew this area and the open spaces in the woods would make their progress easier, faster.

Then the croaks sounded, this time they were closer.

Daylight had grown weak. She didn't spot any of their tracks in the snow on the brook, but knew she'd come out below where she and Clay had separated.

When she did she saw he'd aimed at her, but then lowered the gun and started toward her at a fast walk.

She bent over, grabbed her knees and breathed fast and deep, finding it difficult to catch her breath.

"I got worried," he said as he walked up to her.

"I found the gorge, we need to go there, we might have a chance," she said, winded.

And then she noticed. There was a strange, very strange silence, a break in the pattern of the croakings. There was little wind, just an occasional rustling of frozen tree limbs. But none of that allayed her sense that the Mueumonds were fast closing the distance.

"I haven't heard them croak for at least five minutes," Clay said, searching her face. "Maybe it's enough daylight to make them stop and hunt for cover."

She looked up and saw the threatening sky, knew they couldn't waste time.

"I found the gorge and we gotta go there," she said, not wanting him to see how frightened she was or how she felt inside.

They left the brook and followed her trail back toward the gorge. When they arrived at the gorge, they sat down and leaned against a tree to rest with the gorge at their backs. Palafox knew to follow the gorge meant they'd be in the Saluuette domain before it got dark. Then the sacred forest in four or five days.

She removed her mittens and felt for the Saluuette points in her parka pocket.

CHAPTER 38

C layton wondered how much longer they should remain where they were catching their breath. The Mueumonds could be tracking them in spite of the daylight, it was near twilight in the timber because of the mist, clouds and tall trees.

"We should get going," he said. "Which way do we need to travel to the mountain pass?"

Palafox stood. "That way," she pointed down the gorge. "Let me help carry the supplies."

He undid the makeshift pack and as he started to give her some supplies to carry, several low croaks sounded, not far, maybe fifty yards directly behind them in the timber.

He turned and looked in that direction, then turned and stared at Palafox.

They each grabbed several cans and put them into their parka pockets and left in a hurry, leaving behind their food for survival. They began to move fast along the gorge, keeping the gorge in sight at their right.

Clayton searched for a place to hide and there were plenty, but where could they hide without being discovered? He glanced back over his shoulder to make sure nothing was about to overtake them.

The croakings came from all directions now.

He tried to keep his head above panic. His leg muscles and hips burned, his lungs starved for oxygen again. They didn't have a chance. He was about out of breath.

"We can't keep this up, we don't even have time to find a log to hide under the snow."

"I know," she panted out.

He hurried to the lip of the gorge, peered over and down. Not even snow clung to the steep and slippery-looking rock. He saw no painless path to the bottom. *Leap into the gorge* flashed in his head. Horrified at the thought, he shuddered and stepped back, took a deep sigh to release the anxiety locked in his chest.

He couldn't run anymore. There was little brush and little protection otherwise. What was the use? They were trapped and surrounded. The croakings were even closer than just a minute ago. He didn't want to spend valuable time searching for a place to hide when there wasn't any place.

"The chase is up, we have to take a stand here," he said.

She looked around, then back to him. "There's nothing here to hide us—"

"We keep the gorge at our back. The rifle has enough firepower to hold 'em off, it might buy us time to escape while we still have some daylight."

The moment he checked the rifle he discovered the safety and bolt were frozen as if they'd been welded. He realized he had nothing to work with now other than a rifle butt, knife and a spear.

He fumbled for his cigarette lighter and candle. Only a moment later, the snow crunched behind them. Instinctively, he turned to see what the noise was about.

A thick-haired animal with a spiked mane of long quills stood regarding them. It had a wide pear-shaped face and it stared a malevolent stare.

Clayton's heart hammered. He forgot his pains and his aching body.

"It acts like it doesn't see us," Palafox said.

He didn't take his eyes off the beast.

"It sees us all right, take the rifle, give me the spear."

She slowly handed him the stout spear and took the rifle.

"Now run. I'll follow your trail in the snow."

"I, no—"

"Run."

Though certain he was about to die, an artist's fascination took Clayton over, made him record each detail of the creature. The Mueumond's mane looked like twelve-inch, black-striped quills, spotted like an auburn zebra's might be, as though born of an orange marmalade gene pool. The creature still didn't attack, but it moved and its skin shifted; the gangly body seemed like it was in the process of metamorphosing to something else.

The transformation stopped. Its grayish hands looked scaly and ended in claws six inches long, curved like an anteater's claws that clacked, clacked.

The animal's prominent frontal lobe didn't seem like a mindless animal's, but instead one of intelligence. Its hairless, high and muscled cheeks looked designed for crushing bone and ripping flesh. Its green eyes were shaped like limes. Its rusty, yellowish-and-orange hair curled and hung scraggily off its body, like a musk ox molts. Its beefy legs were covered with tangled frayed hair like the ends of a matted grass rope. Its beefy body, the length and the size of a calf's, weighed two hundred pounds at least.

It flamed its lips over ivory canines five inches long, maybe more, that overhung its tubular bottom lip. Its front arms hung gangly, like an orangutan's.

The beast hissed like a powerful lion and mist shot out of its nostrils in a silver spool. Then it shook its head and the quills rattled as a gooey mess slung from its ivory fangs and cherry-red tongue. Clear strands of salvia dripped off a jaw like a Komodo dragon's.

Clayton tried to grab the knife from its sheath, chaos conquered his mitten.

A croak rose from the animal's throat, like a shrill from an animal's last throes. At that instant, Clayton realized Palafox still stood there, to one side and behind him.

"Run," he said, "I'll kill it and follow your trail on the snow."

He knew that was wishful thinking; he didn't believe for a second he could survive long enough to kill such a powerful-looking beast with a spear and knife. He just wanted Palafox out of his way so he could have a fighting chance and maneuver away from the beast. He knew he was in a fight for his life—and he would fight dirty. But why should Palafox also have to die?

This time, she obeyed, turning and beginning a stumbling run-walk in the knee-deep snow.

The beast snorted a thunderous croak that assaulted the forest. One step, then another and the beast crouched and moved forward, claws extended and clacking.

The beast's eyes shifted to Palafox's retreating form.

Clayton waved his arms and spoke to distract it, "Here! Here!"

The creature slowly curled its lips, showing its mouth full of teeth and fangs, then seethed a scudding steam that boiled into an eddy at its face. It straightened up on its hairy back legs and stepped forward. Six feet tall, the animal bowed up, muscles taut and alive as it stepped in for the kill.

Clayton had heard plenty about the Mueumond, but he had no idea what the beasts could do, or how fast. The creature was streamlined enough to be agile and quick. It had to be, to kill animals fleet of foot. Like humans.

With insidious croaks it shot forward, hopping like a kangaroo. It bounced with claws extended.

On instinct alone, Clayton leaped to the side and simultaneously swung the spear like a baseball bat. The spear smacked the Mueumond's head at its bushy eyebrows.

It stumbled, extended its hairy arms and planted its face on the snow. Its weight furrowed the snow to the lip of the gorge.

At once, it sprang to its feet. At that instant, the lip of the gorge gave way, taking the Mueumond with it.

"Oh man," Clayton said, and though he felt his entire body go weak, he immediately stepped to peer down over the edge of the gorge.

The hairy Mueumond flung its legs and arms like a crazed animal fighting itself in a slow spin. Snow clumps plunged alongside the beast, which was shrinking fast in its fall. In a sudden stop, it bounced, then wilted into a powdery plume of snow. It didn't move again.

He turned and stumbled into a flat-out run, following Palafox's trail helter-skelter through the forest of trees and brush.

He'd been jogging for maybe a minute when a croak sounded behind him. He cast a fearful glance back to see a single Mueumond make an explosive bounce, up and over brush. When it landed, snow blew up in clouds. It plowed through brush and snapped limbs off trees as it bulled through them. Its striped mane of quills fluttered like a scarf.

His heart pounded in his ears. The sight almost stopped his breathing. Helpless to outrun the beast, he stopped and watched as the Mueumond bounced and its green eyes glowed, heard it croak each time it landed and bounced in great leaps of at least twenty feet in the air.

Clayton's heart thudded as he faced the bouncing terror. He whipped out the knife, crouched for a fight to the death.

The first thing he noticed: this Mueumond seemed thicker than the last one, heftier. He was certain the Mueumond sprinting for him now was more mature and experienced.

The Mueumond hopped over brush with silver jets of seething mist boiling out its mouth. Then it exploded twenty feet into the air, snapping off a tree limb when it did.

Quickly, Clayton parried and swung the spear with an uppercut swing.

The Mueumond tried to avoid being hit in the air by holding out its arms to shield its face, but the spear walloped its forearms and chest. Stunned when it landed, it stumbled and staggered to keep its balance.

Clayton swung with all he had.

The Mueumond tried to avoid being hit again but the spear connected with the power of a bat. Clayton swung again, again. Each wallop cracked and fractured bone and damaged muscle in the Mueumond's arms and face.

The Mueumond stumbled, lime-green eyes dazed and disoriented.

Clayton swung the spear and smacked it in the head.

Instantly, the creature went into a cat-like freeze and collapsed. Air surrounded Clayton with an incredible stink of musk.

The Mueumond seemed to pant in shallow breaths as blood flowed from its quivering jaw and pooled on the snow. Then it let out a strangely mesmerizing screech, high-pitched and to Clayton's ears, filled with pain.

The next moment, as if responding to the Mueumond's screech, a multitude of croaks and spine-chilling screeches erupted in a flurry of tones that vibrated the air in the shadowy forest.

It seemed to Clayton like a series of thunderclouds had zeroed in on his location. If he was right, dozens of Mueumonds were coming in response to this Mueumond's call. And his heart and gut told him the Mueumonds were hemming him in. He sheathed the knife, clutched the spear and left the Mueumond on the snow to either die or survive on its own time.

He started a jog through the forest, following Palafox's trail along the sloping terrain with the gorge in view at the right. Even as he tried to keep up a steady walk, his endurance and strength ebbed.

When the exhaustion deepened to the point where he knew he'd have to stop soon, he jogged out of the forest and onto a great barren snow expanse that sloped downward. Despite his desperate mindset, the sight filled him with awe.

It looked like a great ski slope a quarter mile wide and at least a half mile down to the snow-covered forest, the expanse of the forest below looked like an entirely different country.

His movements cautious, he turned and listened, shot glances here, there, to each side and at the back. Still he didn't see Palafox's trail.

He yelled for her. He waited seconds and started back into the forest to find her trail.

"Wait, wait!"

"Where the hell'd you go?" he asked between breaths.

"You ran past me while I squatted."

"That's more than I need to know. Give me the rifle and let's get outta here."

She pointed, "Hurry, we need to get to the bottom of the hill and into the forest."

He grabbed the rifle and checked the safety, found it still frozen, so was the bolt. He slung the rifle across his shoulders.

Off they went down the slope. They immediately started to slide, spinning and careening uncontrolled halfway down the slope. He pushed, pulled and started to slide on his buttocks. He began to pick up speed.

In a few moments, he was traveling at a good pace. He steered with his left arm lagging behind him and controlled the speed the same way.

The croaks and screeches became fainter in the forest behind him.

He stopped fifty yards away from the forested line at the foot of the slope. Once he stood, he saw Palafox above him, sliding on her buttocks at a slower pace. The other sight took him aback.

At the top of the mountainside, there were at least a dozen marble-sized black objects, moving at a fast scurry along the slope. *They're Mueumonds, have to be.*

Oddly, they weren't behaving with the assurance and drive he'd observed before. They stopped and ran back and forth across the top of the slope, as though confused.

Palafox came to a stop, scrambled to her feet and dusted off the snow.

"We gotta go this way," she said, and pointed into the forest. Seeing his face, she glanced up the hill. "Please hurry—," she gasped and her mittens flew to her mouth. She stood with a blank-faced stare. Then she slowly poked the air toward the left side of his face.

"You're bleeding," her voiced trailed away.

He wiped the left side of his bearded face, saw blood and removed his mitten, felt around until he touched a small laceration along his jaw and neck.

"It's nothing, probably a limb scratched me," he said. "Let's go."

Palafox frowned, "A limb?"

"Yes," he said to assure her but he wasn't sure. "Let's go."

She seemed reluctant to move for several moments. Finally, she sighed and spun around, he followed as they jogged at a slow pace. He dreaded the notion of entering the forest, after feeling so free in the snowy expanse.

After a minute of jogging, they entered the darkening grouping of the largest trees he'd ever seen. The snow on the ground here looked innocent of any activity by man or animal, what might have seemed innocuous any other time only seemed dark and foreboding. The giant firs and spruce, some he judged eight to fifteen feet across, looked four stories high, as a forest might have looked at the turn of the eighteenth century.

They kept vigilant and walked the terrain until they came out onto a snow-covered hillside that ended at the beginning of another hill. He looked at the base of the two sloping hills.

Palafox turned to him, "We've gotta follow that frozen stream."

* * *

Now at the stream, Clayton looked up and down it, thinking it was like a narrow snow-covered highway about forty and fifty feet wide, with banks three feet high.

"Let's keep moving, we still have at least an hour of light," Palafox said. "Can't say we're safer now, but we're in Saluuette territory."

CHAPTER 39

While they walked, Clayton wondered about the so-called Saluuette territory. Palafox had explained it as a place where big wolves dwelled and a territory the Mueumonds avoided most of the time; the Saluuette wolves would kill or run the Mueumonds away.

"The Saluuette wolves are friendly to most people," she'd said. "And not to worry."

Yeah right, he was worried all right. But about her. For some reason, she hadn't seemed herself since they escaped the Mueumonds. She exhibited far more energy than he ever had and she acted friendly enough, but something else seemed on her mind besides the gravity of their situation.

More than a few times, she watched him curiously like he would suddenly vanish. A prospect he wished he could do, considering their circumstance. He began to feel uncomfortable around her. Although he felt their fragile pact of friendship remained, she seemed afraid of him now. He couldn't explain why. He wished she would air out her brain.

On the third day since the Mueumond attack, they were down to their last can of corned beef and hash. Clayton suggested they eat only a quarter of the can and Palafox agreed. She took her meager portion of the hash and gulped it down.

She said, "I want to tell you something."

He was simply too exhausted to speak, but he nodded.

"If you see a wolf, don't make a threatening move, all right?"

He looked at her, wondering if she'd lost her mind the way she'd lost her bear claw earrings.

"In case you've forgot, we're outta food," he said.

She nodded, then fidgeted in her parka pocket. She pulled out a cone-shaped iron point.

He remembered the point she'd asked for back at the cave, her telling him the cone point had belonged to Tuma.

She said, "When you're approached by a wolf take off your mitten and put this Saluuette point in your right hand. Make a fist with a portion of the point sticking out over your thumb, like this." She demonstrated. "The wolf will smell your fist and it'll remember you."

That did it. "Have you gone nuts?"

She chuckled and said, "Not yet." She extended her mitten with the cone point.

He gave her an impatient look, but accepted the iron point and casually put it in his parka pocket. He wondered what the Saluuette point was about, again wondered why she suddenly seemed full of energy.

They began walking and he followed her, hardly aware the wind had slowed. It seemed he passed time taking a step, and another. When he glimpsed an odd circle of black on the snow along the small hill at his left, he stopped.

"I see something."

She glanced over her shoulder, "We don't have far to go."

He followed her up the bank and over the snow, stepping cautious between the trees, pausing when he spotted three trails on the snow. The tracks were Mueumond and fresh, probably made within hours. The answer soon appeared before him in the three scorched-black circles that contained smaller circles of hairs, bits of fur and quills.

It was almost as though the Mueumonds shed their hair into three neat circles. The Mueumonds' flesh and bones, including the hides, seemed to have dissolved.

A weird disquiet settled in the pit of his stomach. He raised his head and looked at Palafox. "Something very bad happened to three Mueumonds here, just hours ago."

She nodded as she spoke, "I've seen piles of hair like it before, but never on snow. The elders tried to explain the rings of hair by suggesting Yau kills them, but the elders really don't know."

Clayton stepped to a tree and knelt to inspect its bark. "The bark's scorched but no snow is melted." He stood and turned to her.

"We find piles of hair just like this at the thaw, we don't need to be here," she said, and her eyes were dark.

"Do you believe the elders?" he asked.

"I don't know. What can you make of the hair and quills in the rings of scorched earth?"

She wants me, me, to find a solution to a circle of hair, when her own people couldn't explain it?

He grabbed a mitten full of the hair and examined it, dropped the hair and dusted off his mittens. He came straight to the point, "I can't say. Obviously the Mueumonds had a bad night. It seems intense heat killed them and apparently not a hair was singed."

"We know that," Palafox said. "It's always the same."

He sighed and scanned the nearby timber.

"I have a feeling the Mueumonds aren't the baddest animals in the wilderness. There's something worse, far worse than the Mueumonds. Whatever killed the Mueumonds killed them dead in their strides."

She counted the trails with her mitten, "I see what you mean, there's no sign of a fight or them trying to run, or trails leading away." Her eyes were big. "They died together and at the same time."

"I suspect the villain was above them, perhaps in the trees...." He looked up and scanned the trees, "It happened so quick, the Mueumonds never knew what hit them—"

He looked back at her, "Almost like a bolt of lightning disintegrated them in an instant. What's remarkable, no hair was singed. That's inconceivable, even in a lightning strike there's evidence of burning."

She stepped back and looked up at the trees, lowered widened eyes to meet his. "These Mueumonds might've been scouting for us."

"Hard to say. If whatever killed the Mueumonds has us in sight, we'll never know. You say you find circles of hair like this when you return at the thaw?"

She nodded in agreement and said, "But not all the time, I don't see all the rings of hair, others find them too and talk about them. Let's leave here, I'm afraid."

"Not so fast. Why is it surprising to find circles of hair in the Saluuette territory?"

She straightened, "Because the Saluuette wolves defend the territory. They either kill the Mueumonds or drive them off in the winter. The number of Saluuette wolves has declined for generations.

The elders believe it's Yau that kills the Mueumonds now and not the Saluuette wolves, let's get going."

He nodded and hoped he'd managed to hide his suspicion that she wasn't telling him everything she knew about the phenomenon, or anything else. He wondered if the force that killed the Mueumonds was a form of microwave energy that destroyed tissue.

He understood that death strikes every living thing. A part of him felt when his time was up, then let it be this quick. He was shell-shocked by the apparent incineration of the Mueumonds. He didn't feel an ounce of pity for them, but a part of him felt the violence that killed the Mueumonds was obscene.

What he found more worrisome was the prospect of an attack from whatever killed the Mueumonds. He scanned the trees with utter absorption as they walked back toward the frozen streambed.

Until a movement up ahead caught his attention.

CHAPTER 40

Beneath the towering trees rested a huge gray boulder, on top of it stood a wolf. This was a huge silvery-blonde sable wolf with a bushy, lead colored tail that wagged slowly. A truly fearsome glare seemed like the wolf's greeting.

Clayton's first instinct, run. "Oh man," he said, and gripped the rifle.

Palafox hurried to him and grabbed the rifle before he managed to take it off his shoulder.

She said, "Don't make a threatening move no matter what happens."

"It's meat," he said, and wondered again if she'd lost her mind.

She turned and stepped cautious toward the big wolf and stopped several yards from the boulder.

He wasn't sure but he sensed the wolf watched him more than Palafox. Then the wolf leapt off the boulder and snow jumped at its feet when it plopped onto the snow. It got its balance and stood steady. Its ice-blue eyes seemed to stare grimly.

He watched with increasing despair. Then Palafox said without looking at him, "Take your Saluuette point and do like I told you and hold your fist out in front of your waist, don't be scared."

He trusted what she said though he had no way of knowing if she knew what she was talking about. He was scared all right and thought about the rifle again until he saw other wolves. These wolves were cream sable, silver sable and lead–colored, and they all seemed healthy and plump.

The wolves appeared out from behind tree trunks and brush. Now a half-dozen wolves surrounded them. The wolves were truly magnificent and powerful-looking.

He focused his attention on the first wolf, whose ice-blue eyes remained on Palafox. The wolf took a careful step and lowered its head, its ears straight up.

Palafox removed her mitten and pulled up the sleeve of her parka on her left arm, revealing the birthmark on her forearm. Or what she'd told him was a birthmark.

He felt no surprise when the wolf sniffed her arm, scenting the so-called birthmark. Then the wolf stepped cautious toward him. The only sign the wolf was aggressive came from its ice blue eyes. When it lowered its head the other wolves came and stopped at the edge of the frozen streambed. They slowly lowered their heads and flashed their fangs without a sound.

He sensed the wolves were primed for an attack. To not unduly excite the wolves he spoke softly.

"The wolves don't seem happy."

"Don't move," Palafox said. "The Saluuettes are curious."

A part of him trusted what she said. When the huge sable wolf stepped in front of him, it seemed to frown. Before he could blink, the wolf had his fist in its jaw. He felt the wolf's fangs bear down on his skin. He didn't move. He was afraid to blink. The pressure stopped before it broke his flesh. The wolf released his fist, stepped back, back again. Then it wheeled and bounced through the woods. The other wolves fell in behind the big wolf and they ran through the woods until they were out of sight.

Palafox turned with a wide grin. "Those are Saluuette wolves. They fight against the Mueumonds and travelers."

Still catching his breath, he wondered if he'd ever get out of the wilderness. "What's this about? The ritual with the Saluuette point made my flesh crawl. Am I going to be bit on the neck and turned into a wolf, or sprout fangs and crave blood?"

Palafox's eyes were friendly. "Why would you say that?" she said, and smiled. She raised her left arm and motioned for him to follow.

Palafox glanced over her shoulder. "You're going to see the sacred forest, it's the reason we're here, the reason we exist, the reason my people are the way we are. Everything will be all right, just wait, you'll see, you'll be happy here."

He nodded and didn't reply. *The reason we exist?* What did that mean? Where was she taking him?

Finally, he asked, "What's a traveler?"

She stopped and waited for him. Then she said, "They're ancient warriors who vowed to return centuries ago, to take the sacred forest from us."

Her reply sounded foolish. "Listen, whatever. What happened with the wolves wasn't like swatting a fly and forgetting about it."

She studied him for several moments. Finally, she said, "Quit being so mistrusting, just keep the Saluuette point on you at all times."

He felt she pretended the wolves were as normal as breathing. He glanced back over his shoulder to see if the wolves followed them. If the wolves were out there they didn't want to be seen.

He kept moseying forward noting how the brush and ferns here seemed different. The entire forest seemed ancient, primeval, the likes he'd expect to see millions of years ago.

They stopped on a bank of a little pond. It was frozen along with a four-foot waterfall. Palafox pointed across the frozen pond, "Do you see anything different?"

He blinked his eyes to clear the fuzziness, but what he saw didn't change. There was no snow on the ground. No frost, either. What he stared at seemed like an olive-green forest in any season other than winter, Definitely not like a forest in the arctic wilderness. More like a jungle. A creepy-looking jungle.

He wondered if he could believe his eyes.

CHAPTER 41

An illusion might explain this fantastic jungle near the Arctic Circle but this place was no illusion. This place looked like a tropical jungle.

"This is crazy," he said, and wondered if he indeed was crazy.

Palafox looked at him eagerly. "Feel the ground with your hands."

His sense of touch required a few moments to adapt to the change. What he felt was warmth, pleasing warmth. "This is crazy," he said, and leaned back up. He stood and pulled on his mitten trying with all his might to think logically since the forest before him defied all logic.

If the jungle was an illusion, it was one hell of a convincing one. He wasn't going to argue with where he stood.

He looked all around, trying to see all at once, all of his senses waking slowly to the dramatic differences between five minutes ago and now. And, between reality and this, whatever this place was.

"This is fantastic," he said, and looked around. "What is this place?"

"You're in the sacred forest," she said. "The Great Spirit left this forest to my people, as a gift to us and proof of his existence."

He wasn't so shocked when she said that. He wasn't going to say what he thought. He nodded and smiled to be polite. He felt there was an answer. There had to be an answer.

His first notion was volcanic activity inside the earth warmed the ground. This was plausible, since Yellowstone National Park was the same way. He couldn't think of any sensible alternative for a tropical forest in the middle of the arctic wilderness. But here he stood in a tropical forest in the arctic.

Scanning the area more leisurely, he noticed a variety of amazing plants, with long and narrow-spade pea-green leaves, knife-blade leaves of olive and broad heart-shaped leaves, arrow-point leaves, cinnamon and chartreuse leaves. A variety of smaller and therefore more subtle burgundy, indigo, lemon and mint green nestled among other plants of all sorts and sizes.

A botanist's paradise ... hell, an artist's paradise ... a gardener's paradise...

An incredible variety of plants and trees were every place he looked. He couldn't help thinking this jungle fit right into a forest of ancient myth.

She bade him to follow her and his awe of the place kept him from challenging her this time. When she led him through a small opening in the trees, he stopped. As hard as it had been to accept the forest, he literally couldn't believe this next sight.

Growing among the mint-green ferns were five, no six ginger-topped mushrooms, if mushrooms could be the size of picnic tables and waist high. The mushrooms' trunks were a yellow-squash appearance, each about four feet thick and each covered in prickly looking thorns about two inches long.

Palafox took a knife and cut four plate size chunks out of one mushroom, smiled before she took a bite of it and chewed. Her eyes never left him as if she was taunting him to believe what he was seeing.

Palafox offered him a piece of mushroom. "Here, you'll like this," she said. "The Great Spirit gave my people these mushrooms as a divine gift, proof of his visit here and his existence."

While he ate, she talked away. She said, "The mushrooms not only provide us with nourishment but also they cure all things, diseases, infections, injuries caused by nature and especially those infections, diseases and injuries caused by forces of evil. The mushroom will not cure any diseases, infections, or injuries caused by man. The only place these mushrooms can grow is right here on this very spot. No other place on this world can these mushrooms grow. Don't you find that miraculous?"

He stopped chewing and she stared at him in a curious sort of way. He nodded to be diplomatic and began chewing again, but mentally disregarded her comments.

He would call the mushrooms amazing because of their taste, but not miraculous. For one thing, she couldn't have been all over the world or over every inch of soil, so how could she claim there was nothing like this any place else? Besides, it wasn't the first time he essentially ignored what she said. He took another bite and chewed, noting it had a flavor of beefsteak, chewy and sort of tough.

"Hmm, good," he said, "it tastes like meat, the more you chew. I've tasted it before." Rather than waiting for her reply, he took another mouthful. He was hungry.

She nodded, watching him with that same curious look.

"Yes, I cooked them for you in the soup when you were very sick with the fever. The people of the Tacoma clan called these Iraluq, meaning moon. But I call them mushrooms."

"You're funny," he said, and smiled at her.

Then his knowledge came so fast, he stopped chewing. Didn't he have gangrene and didn't it cure itself? Didn't he have a crushed ankle and didn't it mysteriously heal itself … and didn't his color vision return? His color vision's return was particularly amazing. The doctors had informed him he'd never regain it. One doctor went so far as to suggest he would lose some vision as he aged because of the head wound he suffered in combat.

Now he began to wonder. How could he argue with the facts, or dismiss what Palafox told him, as anything but the truth? He couldn't dismiss what she told him as wishful thinking, not all of it, how could he? He believed there might be lines of truth to her story and it gave him chills.

Palafox handed him three plate size chunks of mushrooms. "Here, put these mushrooms in your parka for us to eat later," she said, "eat all you can, but the mushrooms aren't enough to keep us alive. We must have meat and lots, lots of it, walk with me."

He followed her, willing to swear he strolled in a lush equatorial jungle. In spite of all its magnificent implausibility, he suddenly got a sense he was being watched. He knew the feeling well.

He looked around and quickly realized something wasn't right. Of all the variety of plants, it occurred to him he hadn't seen a single flower. That odd circumstance puzzled him as much as the tropical temperature. With each step, a deeper mystery brewed in his head.

They'd walked the distance of a football field and still no sign of other life. Clayton neither heard nor did he see a bird, a flower. He found this fact more than amazing, but incredible.

He felt this tropical environment should be infested with spider webs, insects and ugly worms, among others. Yet this forest seemed absent of even the peskiest things. He'd seen not one gnat, fly, mosquito or spider.

He sensed the forest seemed too in balance and in harmony, almost similar to landscape art, or a poem devoid of its heart and soul. He began to feel bad vibes.

They walked out of the suffocating closeness and onto a bare-granite-slab formation the width of a football field and just as long.

Out front of and on the great granite slab, gray vapors rose from what seemed to be small vent pools. No brush or bushy plants grew on the slab; it was just a bare slab of continuous rock.

To his left, maybe fifty or sixty yards away, a pond of about a half-acre was bathed in a diffused light; thin steam lifted off its surface. He wanted to, needed to, but he held back the urge to sprint to the pond and dive in.

And no bird I know about looks like that ...

He pointed to the pond. "Did you see something over there?"

"I wasn't looking over there," she said.

He took another look at the pond. Satisfied nothing was there he walked toward a foot-wide stream that cut a trough about a foot deep through the solid rock before going to the timberline, a fast-twisting snake out of view at that point.

He stepped across the stream and knelt.

Beneath the surface, lime-green algae, most a foot long, swayed side to side in the current.

He cupped his hand and tasted the water. The water tasted metallic. A persimmon-like bitterness clung to his tongue and gums, almost numbing them. What an unpleasant shock. He spat the water out.

He stood and looked around. Some water in the smaller pools seemed to boil a chalky liquid. At some lesser vents, what turned out to be small artesian wells, mounds with the appearance of yellow anthills were built up around the little puddles of water. He felt the yellowish mounds were a type of sulfur.

The sudden possibility of poisonous gases made him think the place could be dangerous. He turned to rejoined Palafox and they walked to the pond near where the curious forest began again. The fishbowl-shaped pond's water seemed about waist deep, deeper farther away from the bank.

He looked at his reflection and was astonished. Even his own mother, God rest her soul, wouldn't have recognized this caveman out of the macabre, with this beard and the parka on. The water felt bath warm. He wanted to jump in parka and all.

He stood and Palafox walked toward an unusual sight at the mouth of the pond, a black and rusty-red boulder with a slight gleam to it. The boulder was the size of a single-story ranch house and as wide as it was tall. Near it lay several gray boulders, some round, some smooth as a tabletop.

He kept his eyes glued on the rusty-black boulder, noting the surface was pitted and scooped out in places. Metal articles seemed attached to it.

Something clicked in his memory.

Yes. It had to be. He stopped. He hadn't seen anything like it, but was certain. The rust-colored boulder was an iron meteorite.

CHAPTER 42

"An iron meteorite and it's magnetized," Clayton said.

The objects he'd seen on the meteorite were a bunch of rusty pots, picks, shovels and axes, all seemingly glued to it. Some axes and shovels still had wood handles, but most had decayed. Other objects were crosscut saws, small and large cast iron frying pans and pots used at the turn of the last century.

Palafox turned to him and her face seemed puzzled. "An iron meteorite. Magnetized?"

"Yes."

"This is the Great Spirit's sled," Palafox said, and smiled.

"What?"

"The Great Spirit's sled."

"I thought you said that," he said, and stepped around it absolutely amazed. The same petroglyphs on the cave wall were on the smaller rock boulders. The woman's body with the wolf's head and the spear, Yau.

He removed his mittens and traced the spiral with his fingers. "Amazingly, beautifully done spirals."

"Those are rings, not spirals," Palafox said. "When rings fly away from the sun, the rings will be seen for a long time in the sky. It's the sign of the Great Spirit's return."

"That sounds like a warning, Palafox."

"No, the rings mean the Great Spirit will return. All the elders of the Tacoma clan agree that's the meaning of rings here."

"Who made the rings?"

"No one knows. Some elders said the rings were made by our people, other elders didn't know."

"Absolutely amazing, this meteorite might be worth millions."

"Millions?"

"Lots of wealth."

"You're the third person who has seen this place that was not born to us."

"Some outsider or wayward person would've found this place by now, either by air or by exploring," he said.

"Not so far," Palafox said, glancing away so briefly, he couldn't be sure she had.

He looked up. The gray mist blocked the view to the heavens, but horizontally he could see a long, long way. They were in a trough between two great mountain ranges; a deep, steep-walled mountain basin and the ranges surrounded them.

It was a fantastic sight that normally would've had him reach for his paints and brushes, but he wasn't on a sightseeing tour. Nevertheless, the sight aired out his brain for several moments. He could never get used to such beauty. What true artist can? But he had to. He was in the middle of a mystery, the kind that might mean he lived or died. But there were so many ways to die inside. He knew this to be true.

Without his color vision each day he woke the sun highlighted nothing worth painting. He had a renewed life ahead of him now. If there were reasons for all things happening, then let it be.

"No wonder you can't see this place," he said, "the mist shields the place from above."

"Only in the winter does the mist stay high above the trees," Palafox said. "Yau protects the sacred forest from outsiders, she's a spirit, and those who found the sacred forest never survived to talk about it. They all became lost in the wilderness and perished, at least that's what the stories say."

He didn't want to draw her attention that he had very much heard her. Too much was at stake. He decided to change the subject.

"Have you seen Yau?" He asked this while he walked, slow and wide of the iron meteorite, stopping only to kill time pretending to inspect it.

"No," Palafox said, "the elders say no one has seen Yau, but I feel she exists though."

For a moment more, Clayton feigned his inspection, but he was thinking about how he could find his way out of there.

He said, "Where did the saws, shovels, pots and pans on the great spirit's sled come from?"

"Our people found the shovels and stuff in abandoned sleds," Palafox said. "The Mueumonds got to the people who wandered into the sacred valley in the winter."

Clayton nodded. He continued to step slow and wide around the meteorite. He lifted his eyes.

A jaundiced membrane the size of an overblown beach ball suddenly loomed and bobbed in the air two feet away. Five exposed dark purple vessels branched along the sides of the membrane and over the hair to the crown on top. Hanging from the oval's sides were three four-feet-long black tentacles. At the ends of each tentacle were hard-looking objects shaped like footballs but the size of tennis balls. And the shock of thick white hair on the looming object made it seem joltingly alive.

If there was ever a time to run this was definitely it.

CHAPTER 43

"Ho-ly crap," Clayton said.

Palafox grabbed his arm, "Hold on. You're afraid after all you've been through."

Clayton wondered what kind of far out creature this was.

"Got that right, sweets," he said, "what is that thing?"

"Arnaq is not a thing, but a being with a spirit," Palafox said, "don't be so jumpy. Oh look. That happy round-sun color means Arnaq's hungry."

Moving slow and careful, he stepped out of reach of Arnaq's tentacles, not once taking his eyes off it.

"Hungry for what?"

Palafox chuckled lightly, "Food. Give Arnaq some food."

"What?"

"The mushrooms. Go ahead, give some to Arnaq."

Unsure what would happen next, he extended his mitten with the mushroom at the tip of his fingers toward the bobbing creature.

Which raised a tube-like tentacle and with one fluid motion wrapped his wrist, tight. The tentacle had scales like a snakeskin. Arnaq grasped the mushroom with another tentacle, a translucent tube about four inches in circumference. Fluids and bits of mushroom shot through the tube until the mushroom dissolved in seconds.

"Arnaq eats mushrooms and hanging fruits," Palafox said. "Some fruits are not good to eat though. So don't eat any fruit without asking, okay?"

He nodded halfheartedly. He hadn't seen any fruit.

Palafox said, "Arnaq will take tiny bits of meat if it's boiled just right. You could say Arnaq is clear about how she likes her food."

Arnaq's tentacles released his wrist. "Nothing like being finicky," Clayton said.

Palafox looked at him with her aloof brown eyes and began to explain Arnaq's eating habits. He listened and began to wonder what Arnaq was capable of. He suspected he had to walk a delicate balance between getting out and staying alive. It wasn't like him to not ask questions, though. "Are more, er, Arnaqs around?"

"No." Palafox seemed disappointed. "Once, there were three, but many generations have gone since we've seen another Arnaq."

One of the first things he'd noticed: Arnaq didn't seem to have eyes, but dots like miniscule black freckles. "How does it see?"

"Don't know. No one knows but Arnaq."

He wasn't surprised. He felt Palafox painted a benevolent Arnaq—but he wasn't so sure. "Does Arnaq understand what we say?"

"We believe Arnaq understands some of what we say but communicates with colors like blues, greens, reds, pinks and yellows, among many other colors in geometric shapes that we have no name for. Arnaq uses shapes like a triangle and a rectangle to get her point across. We believe a gray color in a triangle means not sure, frightened, or apprehensive. Or that Arnaq's perturbed about something."

Clayton didn't feel comfortable saying what was on his mind. One thing was certain: if Arnaq could read minds he'd surely be dead by now.

Arnaq bobbed and leveled with Clayton's face, then the creature raised its tentacles and placed one on each of his shoulders. Arnaq slowly floated level with his face and pressed against his forehead like a kowtow ceremony.

When Arnaq moved in close, one of the first things he noticed was the air filled with the scent of basil and the air seemed static. He'd smelled the basil fragrance before and knew where he'd smelled it. Near the rotting grizzly. Now he suspected that Arnaq might be more than an alien life form.

When Arnaq pressed against his forehead, he almost came undone. But nothing happened. He sensed something strange from Arnaq. He sensed a welcome.

Arnaq felt like a warm elastic rubber against his face but seemed to have sandpaper skin like a shark. He couldn't see into Arnaq's interior sphere whatsoever. Arnaq withdrew its tentacles from his shoulders, bobbed and floated slowly to Palafox.

"Forest green in a rectangle means Arnaq likes you," Palafox said, and smiled.

He half grinned. "Nothing like a square right off the bat," he said, and tried to stay calm. Tried to not reveal what he suspected.

Palafox stared at him questioningly.

With a low humming sound, Arnaq's sphere changed into velvet yellow.

"Arnaq wants more food," Palafox says, "that's what the yellow color in a circle means, we think."

"Incredible," he said, and then grabbed another hand-sized mushroom from his parka and held it out.

Arnaq arched its right tentacles and the quickness in the way Arnaq grasped and dissolved the mushroom sent shivers through him.

"Don't be frightened," Palafox said.

She was right on target. He was physically shaken. Although relieved she believed Arnaq liked him, the million-dollar question was, what did Palafox know about Arnaq that she hadn't told him?

For now, he'd set aside that she didn't tell him about this creature long before now. But she had adequately gauged his fear of Arnaq.

"Where did Arnaq come from?" he asked.

Palafox slowly stroked Arnaq's white matted hair.

"No one really knows." Then she spoke to Arnaq, with a tone of affection, almost like baby talk, "You're lonely aren't ya?"

Clayton had so many questions he wanted to ask but right now wasn't the best time to ask them. He wasn't sure he should ask any more questions than he had to.

Then Arnaq changed to a deep-sea blue and descended slowly until it leveled with Palafox's face. It flashed several shades of blue inside a nested rectangle, circle and triangle. Then its right tentacle seemed to tenderly wrap around Palafox's right mitten.

"Arnaq senses danger," she said.

The effect of the colors in Arnaq's sphere were eerie. For a moment, he sensed Arnaq had either read his mind, or Arnaq's intuitive powers were incredible.

He glanced around, "Danger?"

Palafox ignored him but she spoke as if she spoke to a person and told Arnaq that Tuma and Snow Wolf were no longer with them. Arnaq's body formed two triangles of light blue, then deep-sea blue filled the sphere. Pulsating blues, greens and reds flooded Arnaq's sphere and vibrations filled the air as if a soulful song played.

"Arnaq knows the elder and Snow Wolf are gone now," Palafox said.

"That's not possible," he said, "Arnaq understands what death means?"

Palafox nodded as she spoke, "Don't know, but I believe so."

Arnaq flashed blues and when the colors flashed, a scintillation of chills flooded over Clayton's skin. The longer he observed Arnaq the more convinced he was that Arnaq expressed complex emotions with colors and that Arnaq experienced a kind of remorse or unhappiness after learning about Tuma and Snow Wolf.

He could hardly believe anything such as Arnaq could exist anywhere. Even though the creature seemed fragile, he believed Arnaq was capable of many things—and he didn't plan to stick around to learn what they all were.

When Arnaq removed the tentacles from Palafox's mittens, a pale blue covered the entire sphere. Then Arnaq floated up.

Palafox stretched out her arm and gently pushed the air with her mitten. "Go, leave us," she said.

Arnaq floated up higher, then zipped through the air without a sound and a chilly energy rushed across Clayton's face. Astonished, he said, "Shame on you, I believe you hurt Arnaq's feelings."

"Not really," Palafox said, "all my people have their own special way of talking with Arnaq. I understand Arnaq sometimes and sometimes I don't, and sometimes Arnaq understands me and sometimes Arnaq doesn't."

Arnaq returned to its former sharkskin color, then metamorphosed to match the canopy of green leaves and seemed to vanish in the foliage.

While Clayton tried to spot its shape in the branches, he asked, "Is Arnaq male or female?"

Palafox chuckled. "Don't know. No one knows. You might say Arnaq is an it … if an it exists then Arnaq is an it, but I believe Arnaq's female because she pulls up all the flowers here and does something with 'em. Arnaq won't let flowers grow in or around the sacred pond or anyplace else in the sacred forest."

"No doubt, Arnaq's female," he said.

Palafox's smile disappeared from her lips.

He thought she was going to say something but she stared at him as if he had a hole in his head. After a few moments she said, "You know, the sacred forest belongs to Arnaq as much as it belongs to the Tacoma clan. Arnaq's entire world is here at the sacred forest, Arnaq couldn't stay alive at any other place. If she goes too high she'll burst and if she leaves the sacred forest she'll die."

He didn't believe a word Palafox said. He sensed that Arnaq was the proverbial four-thousand-pound gorilla, paddling through the wilderness, tearing limbs off trees whenever and wherever it liked.

"I believe Arnaq is a lot worldlier than I would care to know about," he said.

"Some in my clan believe the same thing. While others believe Arnaq's a smart pet that performs tricks with colors and nothing more—but who knows—C'mon. Being an artist an' all, you'll probably be pleased and possibly enlightened at what I'm going to show you."

She began to amble along as if she strolled in a secure suburban park on Sunday evening. She stopped and turned and looked at him with one of those "aren't you coming?" smiles.

"C'mon," she said in a chirpy voice.

He wasn't reading a story about a strange place where the impossible seemed possible. He was up to his neck in the middle of one. He believed he had to walk light and talk light from here on out.

Palafox jabbered freely as they ambled along. The unfortunate fact was that she said nothing that would help him understand this incredible jungle or Arnaq. He was in too much denial to think beyond where he stepped.

Palafox took him to a location in the sacred forest where strange-looking trees grew. Some trees were nicely shaped, as if they were pruned. She told him this place was where Arnaq got her food.

It seemed all the trees here had fruits. Some fruits were shaped like pears, others like gourds and some fruits were the sizes of watermelons and cantaloupes. The odd fruits were the color of tomatoes, melons and pineapples among others. Aside from the bizarre amount of variety, the place reminded him of a fruit orchard.

When he stepped around a tree, he stopped and stared. *What am I looking at?*

It was a tree of flaming fruits.

CHAPTER 44

Clayton's eyes were glued to the fruits on fire but shifted when Palafox went to the lowest branch and snapped off one of the flaming fruits. It was the size of a honeydew melon, but it seemed to have a light blue and yellow flame emitting from the fruit's cantaloupe-hued skin. She whipped out a knife and loped off the top of the fruit, the flame slowly extinguished. She smiled as she stepped to him.

"Here," she held out the fruit, "you might like this Jaspose fruit."

He stood motionless. Finally, he grasped the fruit. Amazingly, the fruit didn't radiate heat or feel unusually warm. Now that his shock had ebbed a little, he noticed the smaller fruits on the same tree didn't seem afire. He figured the flame emitted by the fruit wasn't really a fire; perhaps it was similar to light that radiated no heat.

He stared at Palafox for several moments. No alarm or other emotions showed on her face, except perhaps anticipation. Finally, he felt the fruit was safe to eat. Why go to the trouble to poison him with fruit? Her perky smile was already doing that.

He swallowed the juice from the Jaspose fruit as if drinking from a coconut, discovered that the juice had a watery taste of honey. The fruit's pulp was a sky blue. He took a cheek-full of the pulp and chewed, found it sweet, juicy, almost like lemonade with honey.

Palafox nodded, as though seeking his approval of the fruit's taste. "The Jaspose fruits ripen only in the winter and only every fifth season. You're lucky they're ripe, okay to eat."

He nodded with both his cheeks full. He wiped juice off his beard with the sleeve of his thick parka.

"I've never tasted anything like it."

She smiled. "I'm glad you like it," she said, and took a deep breath. "These Jaspose fruits won't be enough to keep you alive. These fruits are Arnaq's only food. Arnaq's not greedy but you can't eat all her food, we must have meat."

"I understand," he said, not caring he spoke with his mouth full. He noticed she didn't say, "they" she said, "you" and never once mentioned herself eating the fruit. He wondered why that was or was he being paranoid?

She showed him the good fruits to eat and the fruits to avoid. They carried on small talk until she finally led him away from there, saying she had something else she wanted him to see.

As they walked, she talked non-stop, mostly about Arnaq. The more she said the more he suspected Arnaq might be an alien life form. And that it possibly reached earth on the iron meteorite and evolved over billions of years. But he decided another possibility was plausible. When the oceans receded from the Alaskan territory, Arnaq's species had to adapt. That would make Arnaq a terrestrial species, evolved not unlike other species, not unlike dinosaurs. That would make Arnaq a terrestrial being. After all, Arnaq resembled a squid, though certainly a strange one.

Another thing he thought about was either the Tacoma clan protected this place and called it sacred ground, or Arnaq protected and provided for them. Plus, the mushrooms and the incredible jungle made him wonder, *What are a strange creature, and a strange jungle, doing in the middle of the arctic wilderness? Could they be by happenstance?*

But what was the probability that Arnaq and the jungle could emerge, exist, unnoticed in the arctic wilderness? A quadrillion to the tenth power to one? It was just too incredible to think about now.

One thing was certain: a fortune was here for the taking if the mushrooms could cure infections and diseases. Yet if the mushrooms were real, wouldn't the entire civilized world know by now? He suspected the knowledge of the mushroom and sacred forest hadn't reached the civilized world because no one survived after discovering this place. Once again, he repressed the impulse to ask questions about the mushrooms.

After walking five minutes, they arrived at a place he realized was a cave entrance, though it was partly hidden by foliage. A harder look and he saw not one, but two oval entrances.

Palafox smiled and said, "We call this place, the cave of knowledge."

Clayton nodded to be polite, trying to take in what he was seeing.

At the entrance were stacks of candles, a wood barrel of torches and a barrel of black liquid that looked like tar. Palafox grabbed several torches and lit them, then handed him two lit candles and a torch. They went into the left entrance.

Clayton stepped quiet behind Palafox, straining to listen to the whispery sounds. The cave's temperature wasn't as warm as outside but not uncomfortable. He narrowed his focus until his eyes adjusted to the glow inside, glancing off the granite wall.

A short distance in, they stopped. Palafox lit several more candles. The light spread, filling every crevice and nook in the cavernous room. The stone walls seemed to light up with a soft orangey glow, reminiscent of a campfire's radiance.

The glow was pleasing and the air seemed easy to breathe, although he could smell a kind of dampness. Once he stopped, a strange whispery sound filled his ears and the unsettling rhythm of the whispery noise seemed almost like the cave was breathing.

When his eyes adjusted to the afterglow, one of the first things he saw were books. And books. And more books. He felt he'd entered a sanctuary of books. Stacked on the floor were piles of books, head high. On the walls were shelves and shelves of books. The walls were covered with bookshelves, each shelf crammed full of books. Heaped on the floor in front of them were stacks of what seemed like very old books covered with dust.

He moved farther into the room and turned his eyes to Palafox, "Must be thousands of books here, how did you come by all these?"

Her brows lifted, "English missionaries brought them on sleds into the wilderness for years, from the 1870s to the 1900s. They died in 1905, the Tacoma clan mourned the loss of the Prescotts for an entire season."

"Pity," he said. "How did they die?"

"Old age."

Clayton stepped between the stacks of books, noting they were covered with dust. Then he saw a stack of books that looked different from the others. One of the books had almost a dark green color. He picked it up, flipped through the pages and turned to look at Palafox.

"Shakespeare?"

"Quick, my tablets, my tablets," Palafox said, and chuckled.

He wondered if she wanted to play a game. No matter. He wasn't in the mood.

"That's from Hamlet," he said.

"Oh, you've read Shakespeare?"

He put the book back, then quipped, "It was required reading."

"I didn't like Romeo and Juliet," she said, and smiled.

He nodded but didn't look at her. Suddenly, he felt the sacred forest and the Saluuette territory were as treacherous as Shakespeare's plays, that the only happy ending was to stay alive long enough to escape this place and the sacred forest forevermore.

"You read many of the books here?"

Palafox raised her arm toward several shelves, "Lots and lots. All the books on that shelf, and others too."

She listed her favorite books. The quantity and quality of books dampened his half-baked notions about her. Then he noticed another stack, this one neater than the others, arranged in three rows about waist high. These books looked like the types of journals used for recordkeeping.

He grabbed a journal and flipped through some pages. The hand printing was exquisite, with each letter perfectly shaped and printed. Hardly had he begun to read than Palafox lifted the book from his hand and dropped it back on the stack, began to carefully straighten it back in alignment with the others.

Without looking at him she said, "These belong to the Prescotts, the English missionaries. We're not permitted to read 'em."

He looked at her, wondering why she'd said this in such a quiet, almost shy voice. It was clear he'd overstepped some line.

Then she poked the air with the candle. "C'mon, this way," she said, and turned, stepped away.

He wanted to be a pleasant guest.

"I'm behind you." He glanced at the stacks of journals as they exited the huge room of books.

He followed her into another pathway, one that emerged in another chamber room. This room, a smaller version of the first room, held a lesser number of books. His attention was drawn to symbols and petroglyphs on the pitted orangey-glowing walls, where stickmen were drawn with wolves or dogs fighting. Several animals displayed antlers and amazingly, looked like dinosaurs.

Dinosaurs with antlers?

He was fascinated by the petroglyphs frozen in the rock until he began to notice one group of petroglyphs was greater in number than any other. This one displayed wolves, or perhaps dogs.

Palafox raised her arm and pointed to a set of petroglyphs. "My people used only spears and arrows to hunt for ages." She began to point to each petroglyph, as if a story was frozen in each action and in the images' life-and-death struggles.

"See these drawings?" She pointed to one grouping. "They stuck an animal with a spear, then the young wolves wrestled the big animal down so men could rush in and kill the animal with spears and arrows. But the wolves did the work. The elder's scar on his face was caused by an antler. It stuck him while he wrestled a big moose after the moose was wounded when he was young. He suffered broken bones in his shoulder, leg and ribs too."

"I can only imagine the injuries," he said, "I wouldn't wrestle with a wounded thousand-pound animal."

"If you're hungry enough you would, a man's blood runs red-hot."

She continued to explain some of the petroglyphs of the wolves, stickmen and animals. After several minutes they exited the room.

If they'd stayed longer, he would have surely gotten into a discussion about what he suspected that his fate was in her hands and he shouldn't underestimate her.

Another thing gnawed at him too. Had he arrived at her clan's winter campgrounds, or was this place a pit stop on the way to it? Naturally, his suspicions had to take a backseat to keeping the talk light. He didn't want to get on her bad side.

He felt his life greatly dependent on being cooperative in every way. He racked his brains on ways to find answers to his questions without any interference from Palafox. But he did not want to learn any more than he had to about the sacred forest, Arnaq or Palafox's people. He felt bad vibes from the beginning and he couldn't explain why.

He followed her, raising the torch and stepping cautiously. When he passed by another dark chamber, odd dark shapes in the room stood out in the backwash of light. He stopped.

Palafox kept walking, her torch above her head, the glow fading. In a few hurried steps he was inside the chamber. He raised the torch high.

Four, maybe five dozen parkas were hanging on ropes. Lined up against the wall were four rows of sleds. On some sleds were spears, standing up at the handlebars and troughs, the part of the sled shaped like feeding troughs for cows.

The hanging parkas and stored sleds reminded him of the first cave he stayed in. He felt a sense of dismay. Suddenly he felt a cool displacement of air around him. Startled, he turned.

Palafox stood in the shadow, regarding him in tense silence. As she bit her bottom lip, crazy as it seemed to him, fangs seemed to protrude over her lip. Then the fangs were gone.

He squinted to focus clearly, held his breath and stared. The fangs were there and then not there, indeed, he imagined them?

Palafox shook hair out of her eyes. A mounting recognition came upon her face. She lowered the torch. Her eyes went dark and pinned him against the wall, smoke began to coil around her like a serpent.

He looked hard at her mouth, but her mouth didn't look like anything more than a mouth. Yet her eyes kept him tacked against the wall.

She raised her chin slow.

He felt a rush of chills.

"My people made the sleds and parkas."

His heart sank quickly. Did he believe her? No.

CHAPTER 45

P alafox wondered if Clay was scared. "Don't be afraid."

He stared hard. "Where are your people?"

She winced. "My people aren't here at the sacred forest at this time of season." She wasn't telling him the truth. Some of her people were here and their appearance would scare him. What outsider wouldn't be scared to know the truth about her people? One thing she was glad about, her man wasn't here. He would try to destroy Clay. How could she explain things to her man? Now, she wasn't sure she cared enough to explain things to him. One thing she felt sure of, she didn't want her man as her mate like she thought she did. She knew how she would spend the rest of her life and her man wasn't a part of her new life now. She'd changed and maybe for the good.

Clay pressed his mitten to his brow and shook his head. "This is your winter campgrounds isn't it?"

She wasn't telling him everything just yet. "No, we're still a very long way from the winter campgrounds. This is the sacred forest and we're safe here until the thaw provided we can kill a large moose or caribou before they all leave the sacred valley. We must have meat and soon."

Then he stared at her with a kind of disbelief in his eyes, and said, "What do you do at your winter campgrounds?"

She had to think fast. "Lets see, we watch television, sleep, eat, sing songs, tell stories, play games."

She wasn't telling Clay the truth. The sacred forest is the winter campgrounds for her people in their third term. They're hid in this cave and at other places in the sacred forest. She believes her people already know Clay is here. She's sure in some way Arnaq let them know. Arnaq watches over them and protects them. Her people will avoid Clay until they're sure he's not going to leave.

She felt Clay accepted her little fib. It was pointless to tell him the truth and she wouldn't just yet. He had much to learn about her clan first.

She was afraid to reveal much to him, because he might try to leave the sacred forest and the Saluuette territory out of fear. That would cause her great anguish. Probably more than she could bear. She had to be positive he wouldn't try to leave before she explained things to him, explained everything. Things never intended for outsiders to know. She didn't want to make a mistake. Others had made mistakes, she knew about the mistakes and the horrific end of those in spite of what the elders said.

The elders said the mistakes never happened. Blamed the rumors on weak words among gossipy women. In time, she came to know that the word "mistake" was used instead of names for those who tried to escape, to tell the world about them and the sacred forest.

She pushed the thought away because it was too difficult to think about all of that now. She longed to unburden herself, but when she told Clay the truth about everything, it might sound worse than anything he could have imagined.

She looked at Clay and he stared back at her. When she raised the torch and began to step around the sleds. He followed her and seemed curious about everything he handled, especially the spears. She told him the sleds were used to haul dead animals and used for journeys to hunt the Mueumonds. When she told him, he asked if she went on the hunts for the Mueumonds.

She said, "Women can't go on hunts for the Mueumonds, it is forbidden, but I'd like to go. But the elders say the Mueumonds can smell women long before they can smell men. Then the Mueumonds become difficult, troublesome and hard to kill, so the elders say."

She didn't feel Clay was satisfied with her explanation, because he asked, "Why troughs on the sleds?"

She explained. "When men go to hunt the Mueumonds, they haul meat and other supplies so they won't have to hunt for food and the Mueumonds at the same time."

Something in what she said drew his interest. He wouldn't let go. He continued to look at her awkward-like. Finally he said, "Interesting, rather convenient and ingenious."

She couldn't imagine why he said what he did so to satisfy herself she said, "Convenient?"

"Just thinking out loud," he said.

She studied him as much as he studied the troughs. He felt the sides and shook the troughs for sturdiness. She couldn't decide why he seemed so fascinated with them.

"Something about the troughs?"

"No, no, just sorta odd."

"What ya mean?"

"It's nothing."

"What?"

"It's nothing," Clay said, and pushed his mitten out for her to lead the way out of there.

Not knowing what he wanted her to say, she stepped into the pathway and decided to take him into another chamber room, one he'd surely see at some point because they would walk by it a lot.

As they walked, she told him she didn't want him roaming around the cave alone. She explained the cave had a complex system of narrow passageways, some that went for days under the mountains and it was easy to get lost forever which was true.

"Some passageways are dangerous, cave-ins and such," she added for emphasis. He listened, but only agreed not to go inside the cave alone.

What she didn't tell him, though, was that some chamber rooms hadn't been used by her clan for centuries. They were many relics in some of the chamber rooms, some relics kept in some rooms were not meant for outsiders to ever know about. And relics in some passageways and chambers she didn't want to know about. She felt all living things had their little secrets and places, to keep the good from the bad.

She was telling Clay a half truth about the cave. What she didn't tell him, deep inside this cave some of her people in their fourth term were in seven very large chamber rooms at the very moment. She knew her people wouldn't venture out with a stranger inside the sacred forest. But, her people had to eat. At times, they made forays into the sacred valley to feed.

When she came to the entrance into the chamber room that she wanted to show Clay, she hesitated. She couldn't explain why she felt reluctant to go inside. But she wanted Clay to see the room, knowing he would like it because he'd seemed fascinated with the drawings on the walls. She reassured herself, telling herself Clay's fascination with the drawings and the troughs were the effect of his artistic curiosity, nothing more than that.

She lit candles on the tables and lit two more torches. She walked to the farthest wall and traced the grooves with her fingers, thinking of a way to tell Clay some history about her clan. This was the best way and the best time for him to learn and understand things about her clan and their way of life, before she explained more history to him.

When she turned to face him, he was looking over his shoulder at the entrance.

"Hear something?"

Clay turned and stared at her but didn't say a word.

She stepped around the table. The glow of her candle lit up the cavern's floor near the wall. Near the floor were the Kinarogs, stacked on shelves.

About twenty or thirty of them, she didn't count them all. The long, slender snouts with jaws opened wide had white fangs, holes for eyes and massive, broad heads with long bushy and straggly brown-and-black grayish hair that spiked much higher than the pointed ears. The wolf heads were fearsome and frightening, even to her. They looked almost alive.

She stooped over and took one of the wolf heads, adjusted it. She turned to face Clayton and held up the Kinarog.

"These are war bonnets," she said. "It's like the one Yau has on all her drawings and picture graphs. They were used as battledress many, many centuries ago. My people wore them, to fight the travelers who came into the sacred valley to seize the sacred forest to gain possession of the mushrooms the Great Spirit left us—"

"I've heard enough," Clay said, "let's vamoose."

"Wait," she said, "I want to tell you some history of my people."

He adjusted the rifle strap over his shoulder. "Make it snappy."

"There's nothin' to be afraid of in this chamber," she said. "The wolf bonnets have jaws and teeth of bones. The bones come from moose, caribou and mountain sheep—let me share this story about the war bonnet and about Yau—"

Clay looked at her with a weary look of an animal. "This better be good. I sense something's wandering in the passageway."

While she looked at Clay, her vision caught a movement of something go by the entrance. She felt her breathe hitch. She knew it was one of her people caught outside and trying to return to one of the chambers inside without being seen. She listened to sounds of running along the passageway heading deep inside the cave.

Clay had turned to listen to the sounds too. He removed the rifle from his shoulder and clicked what she believed was the safety on the gun.

She had to move quickly. "Clay, don't be disturbed, that's probably Arnaq going to her bedding area. She does sleep in the cave."

Clay had a serious war face. He nodded slowly.

There was only one reply she could give to put Clay at ease. She nodded and said, "There's nothing, except the wind and Arnaq inside. And the deeper you go inside this cave the worse the sounds will become so don't go exploring alone."

"You won't have to worry," Clay said.

She half smiled. "Let me tell you some history of my people. When our people were brought here by the Great Spirit, other clans and other people were not here, so say the elders. Strangers, invaders began to roam the sacred valley in search of the sacred forest. For many, many centuries, bloody battles were fought to protect the location of the sacred forest and the sacred mushroom from the travelers and others. Many have perished for the protection of this sacred land." She raised the candle, stepped along the wall and pointed to picture graphs and carvings on the wall. She pointed at one etching, "See this drawing?"

He nodded.

"These symbols say when our people went into battle, they went into battle dressed with the war bonnets on their head to fight against the travelers. Our people were losing the fight, until they took a strange beast with them that was given to our people here at the sacred forest by a spirit. All people of the Tacoma clan had to have a symbol of a wolf on them, so the beasts could tell who their keepers were. My people also took with them hollow logs to bang, to attract the beast. The beast would hear the sounds of the hollow logs beating, would go into the sacred valley and kill everything they found in the vicinity of the banging logs—"

"Is that why you don't chop wood in the sacred valley in the winter?"

"Uh huh," she said, and was surprised he remembered. "The sad part, when people become lost in the sacred valley and after they lose their voice from hollering for help, their last efforts are banging a tree with an ax, in hopes a person will hear the blows and come to save them before they die. But what happens in the sacred valley in the winter, the ax blows attract the Mueumonds. Even today, if trappers or explorers stop to rest and chop wood to build a fire in the sacred valley, the Mueumonds hear the ax blows, and, well, you know now what happens next."

"Quite a formidable defensive system, " Clay said.

"What ya mean?"

"Oh nothing, just thinking out loud again."

"That's not it," she said.

Clay covered his mouth and muttered something when he coughed but she couldn't make out the words. Sensing his disbelief, or perhaps his disapproval, she said, "We despise the Mueumonds, we all do."

He stared back.

After several moments, she calmed enough to gather her thoughts to continue. "My people were immune to attack by the strange beasts, because of the wolf seals on our arms. My people would find the travelers camped, and beat the hollow logs. Soon, the battles turned in our favor, until the travelers realized the beasts my people had were wiping them out. Then the travelers brought their own beast to fight the beasts given to us. Finally, the beasts got loose during battles and bred with each other. The beasts' offspring turned against the travelers, and turned against us. The symbol of the wolf on our arm didn't stop the offspring from killing us, just as our foe did. We called the offspring, the Mueumonds—"

"Interesting," Clay said, "but, I'd rather be in the pond bathing."

She ignored him and leaned against the table. "The Mueumonds killed many of our people, as they did the travelers. The travelers lost many warriors but before they left, they made a vow to return someday, to seize the sacred forest and the miraculous mushrooms," she slid back her parka sleeve and showed him the seal, the wolf symbol on the inside of her left forearm.

Clay watched her with an almost displeased look, "I've seen the so-called birthmarks on you and Tuma and they're identical. Call it what you like, it means zilch to me."

"The symbols of the wolf are the same," she said, "but we really don't call them birthmarks. We call them seals. My people of the Tacoma clan are not born with the seal. Something puts the seal on our arms. When a baby of the season is born, all babies of the season come to the sacred forest and when they leave, some babies have the seal appear on their arm before the thaw."

Clay fiddled with the rifle sling on his shoulder and seemed to sigh. He looked at her and said, "Surprise me. Say you don't believe that's strange." There was a sarcastic fury in his voice, then he set his jaw and narrowed his eyes.

The longer she stared at him the warmer her neck and face felt. "Yes, it's strange," she stopped and didn't want to say anymore just yet.

He glanced at the entrance again, then looked back at her with a frown on his face almost like he was physically ill.

"Will ya hurry it up?" he said, "I'm sure something is moving in the passageway of this cave. I believe I can hear it."

"You're hearing a wind draft in the passageway, nothing more," she said, and hoped that was all he was hearing.

He kept looking at her, anxious again. She was growing tired and needed support. She stepped around the table, then leaned against it and folded her arms. "What happened after the travelers left the sacred valley, the sacred valley became so infested with the Mueumonds, the Tacoma clan had to hunt for food and battle the Mueumonds at the same time. It was a losing fight for my people, because nothing the Tacoma clan had could defeat them.

"One day a young girl was found roaming through the wilderness. Women of the Tacoma clan brought her to the sacred forest and raised her. She grew to be the most beautiful woman of the Tacoma clan. One day she woke and had a symbol of a wolf on the inside of her left forearm, like the one we all have. One day her mate went hunting and was killed by the Mueumonds. It's said this beautiful woman put on a war bonnet and went out alone to confront the Mueumonds. It is said the woman beat the hollow logs and led the Mueumonds near the sacred forest. There, she destroyed the Mueumonds with some kind of strange spear with great power. No one knows what kind of spear, only that she carried what looked like a spear. No one in our clan ever saw her use the spear to destroy the Mueumonds. That's how the Saluuette territory came about, because she always took wolves with her on her journeys to fight the Mueumonds.

"The young woman did this repeatedly, enticing the Mueumonds to track her near the sacred forest, then she destroyed them. It is told all that was left of the Mueumonds were hair: no bone, no blood, just piles and piles of hair after she destroyed them.

"Then one night this young beautiful woman was in the sacred pond, bathing and singing, happy after battle with the Mueumonds.

She changed into a spirit. And to this day, she still kills the Mueumonds if they come near the sacred forest. I know this to be true, you've also seen the piles of hair. She truly kills the Mueumonds when they come into the Saluuette territory or get near the sacred forest, if the Saluuette wolves don't. Many Saluuette wolves have been lost fighting the Mueumonds."

She expected questions, but Clayton only shrugged and said, "Sacred or not, I'm in the mood for bathing in the pond. I haven't had a bath since I don't know when—"

"You didn't believe a word I said."

"Of course I did."

"It is the truth," she said, and it was the truth.

"I've heard enough," Clay said, "I wanna go to the pond, bathe, take a breather, try to relax for a change."

She never felt like slapping anyone, but inexplicably, she wanted to slap Clay into the next thaw. But she felt that for only a moment. She knew better than to strike anything. If she were in her fourth term and the way she felt now, she'd tear his throat out on impulse alone.

CHAPTER 46

C layton turned and stepped out of the room.

"Hey, wait, stop, where ya going?"

"I'm going to the pond," he said, and already begun to ponder why Palafox bothered to tell him that story. He wasn't going to be here long enough to warm a place to sleep. Once he recovered his strength, he was gone.

"Wait."

He ignored her, veered to the left and retraced their path along the passageway to the entrance.

"Wait." Her voice echoed in the cave.

The fresh air and sunlight felt good once he exited the cave and headed toward the pond. He was definitely in better spirits. He heard Palafox coming up behind. He stopped and waited for her. Her shoulders looked rigid.

"I felt uncomfortable in the cave," he said. "Now, I want to bathe, nothing more than that."

"That's it?" She stopped a few feet in front of him. Her eyes warmed. "It's said you leave your smile in the water." Without the slightest hesitation she turned and walked away.

"The water will bring a smile to my face, you can count on it," he said, and she turned and smiled without losing stride.

He pushed branches out of his way and limped toward the pond like he was dying of thirst in a desert. Yes, he wanted to bathe, but even more, he needed to be alone and figure out a plan on how to go about leaving this place and finding out what direction he should travel. But the direction wasn't as important as leaving, was it? He was lost already.

But his mind wouldn't let him stay on escaping for long. He kept going back to the story Palafox told him. Did he believe her? Yes, to some extent he did. He felt there was a fine string of truth to her story, but there was always some truth to all tales wasn't there?

Another thing, he was convinced now that Palafox's people or at least some of her people provided for and protected the Mueumonds. He wasn't convinced that Palafox had the vaguest notion of this. The real story might be a neat little cover-up played on her people by her own people.

When he reached the pond he hid the rifle under some moss and kept the knife to shave off as much of his beard as he could and cut away hair on his head. He got naked.

He peeked around the iron meteorite, confirmed he was alone and did a belly flop in the pond that felt as warm as bathwater. He washed himself thoroughly with chalky mud, shaved off his beard nearly to his skin and cut as much of his hair from his head as he could.

As he spread mud on his face and on the inside of his arms, he inspected both his arms to ensure no wolf seal had suddenly appeared on him. He saw none.

After he finished his hour-or-so bath he felt invigorated, empowered and light on his feet. Dripping, he stepped out of the pond and had eased around the iron meteorite when a movement caught his attention.

Standing close to his rifle was a coal-black wolf. The wolf stared and didn't move. Its eyes were sea blue.

Clayton froze. The wolf wasn't the same one he had encountered earlier. Wondering what kind of mess he'd gotten himself into, he glanced at the rifle, which was only a few steps away, but he sensed the wolf wouldn't let him near the rifle. He held his ground and stared back at the wolf.

Then he saw another movement and it was another wolf and it watched. The rusty wolf began to wag its tail and the black wolf, as if cued, sat down and laid its snout on its forelegs in a submissive gesture. It made no sound.

Clayton tried to make sense of what was happening. It seemed the wolves were more than friendly, but submissive. He raised his right hand, palm forward in a gesture of friendship. The wolves made no move, just stared.

Although uncomfortable, he grabbed his parka and pulled it on. He tried to act nonchalant about the presence of the wolves but the fact was…at any moment, the wolves might pounce.

Since the wolves hadn't attacked yet, he decided to finish dressing. He never lost sight of the rifle, half hidden under the moss. After he finished pulling on his boots, he stood. He looked at the rifle and glanced at the wolves. He sheathed his knife.

As if they'd read his mind, the two wolves stood and lowered their heads. When he grabbed for the rifle, the wolves bounced through the brush and were out of sight.

He stood, trying to understand what was going on. He heard a rustle behind him.

Startled, he turned.

A flash of muscle and red fur knocked him on his back. The wolf put its front paws on his chest and bared its fangs. Slowly, it sniffed the scratch on the side of his neck, raised its head and its fangs flashed, as if it was readying to bite.

Before he could move or even dry out, Arnaq came out of nowhere, flashing gray and black. The creature lifted the two-hundred-pound wolf and hurled it into the brush. The wolf sprang up and snarled. Just as quickly, it wheeled around and vanished in the undergrowth.

Then Arnaq flashed blue and hovered above Clayton sprawled out on the ground. When Arnaq floated lower, it took two tentacles, eased them under his shoulders and effortlessly hoisted him to his feet.

For a moment, he felt he was going to die.

Arnaq bobbed and moved close enough to touch him. He caught the fragrance of basil. Arnaq put its tentacles on his shoulders and greeted him with a bump to his brow, then flashed basil green in a rectangle, a sign of apparent greeting.

He felt a peculiar sensation vibrating over his skin. He didn't know why, he didn't feel threatened by Arnaq, yet he was scared.

More than that, he felt there was more to Arnaq than he cared to know about. He felt the less he knew actually increased his chances of making it out alive. He was distressed over what happened and he wanted answers, but how could he get them?

"Thank you, Arnaq," he said, "I wish you understood me."

Arnaq flashed wondrous shades of blue and greens in triangles and polygons. Strange as it seemed, he felt the creature had understood him.

Arnaq wrapped his left wrist with a tentacle and tugged at him. It seemed the creature wanted him to go with it.

He took a step, then another, in the direction she—it was easier to think of it as "she"—wanted him to go. He glanced back at the rifle. He didn't want to leave the rifle but he did. Arnaq seemed pleased that he followed in tow, though he only had the colors she flashed, blues, crimsons and corals among other colors, to indicate this.

He followed her through the sacred forest. After five minutes, it seemed he was on a nature walk with her. In so many ways, he was attracted to the tranquility and peace of the forest. But in no way was he distracted by its beauty. He stayed vigilant, but now he wasn't as frightened as he was before, or thought he would be.

He did, however, wonder where Arnaq was taking him, had just thought of Palafox, of what she might be wondering when he disappeared, when he saw an opening in the trees ahead. And he knew, without knowing how or why, that he was about to exit the sacred forest.

He stepped onto ground that looked too well maintained to feel like wilderness. Here, there were few ferns and scant brush. The ground was cinnamon-colored but strangely, this didn't surprise him. Whatever it was, this location wasn't an ordinary place.

Up ahead, large poles stood upright, not unlike telephone poles back home. Except these were the color of sawdust and maybe twelve feet in height. Each pole seemed evenly spaced from the next one, perhaps fifty feet apart, forming a circle under the large canopy of trees. Clayton could clearly see that each shaft had petroglyphs burned into the wood, though he couldn't tell much about them from where he stood. The layout of the poles reminded him of an arena.

Next was a sight just as astonishing and if he hoped to stay alive, one that required his full focus—there were many colorful reddish, rust, brown, black and blond wolves, some lying on the ground, others standing or walking. Other wolves were barely visible in the brush at the edge of the sacred forest. Some wolves stood at seeing him, others stayed in their places, appearing not to care about an interloper's arrival. He knew they were Saluuette wolves because of their size.

Why had Arnaq brought him to this place? After a few moments, he suspected he knew the answer.

CHAPTER 47

When he stopped, Arnaq gently tugged on his left wrist. Clayton knew she was directing him to keep stepping forward, but it was too hard.

He swallowed back the nausea of fear. Telling himself he was safe, he took one step forward, toward the open arena surrounded by poles. The first step made the next, then the next one easier. Until he saw the skulls atop some of the poles. The skulls stood out like trophies and for the most part, seemed of animals. There were, however, some that looked remarkably human, yet something didn't look right about them. The jaws seemed too elongated and the skulls too flat on top to be human.

A snap and a soft snarl came from behind. Startled, he turned to see without losing his stride.

Regarding him through sparse ferns and clumps of brush were five Saluuette wolves, standing together as if frozen in place. Daunting in appearance, their pointed ears were alert atop bushy heads, their eyes a fixed gaze. In the chill air, their breath seemed to boil from their black nostrils.

Though he was able to keep moving, the fear returned, overcame him. He sensed the wolves were eager to rip out his lungs. He didn't want to sustain eye contact with them and turned to see where Arnaq was leading him. What was this all about?

But how is she to know about round eyes or what goes on in their heads. When he reached a round, flat rock buried in the soil surrounding the poles, Arnaq released his wrist and floated to the edge of the sacred forest. There she hovered, flashing an array of colors in a rush of shades and shapes.

The flat rock he stood upon was the size of a washtub and its surface also displayed petroglyphs. Too terrified to risk not remaining aware of the wolves, he only glanced at the petroglyphs.

The Saluuette wolves watched. He began to step away from the rock. With his first step, the wolves jumped to their feet. Their reaction and demeanor were obvious; he was to stay put. He stepped back, moving slow and stood on the flat rock. He didn't move again.

He felt naked, frightened of what would happen next. But in a flash of insight that made him nearly topple over, he realized, wasn't it the same way for most of his young life? In many ways, living with a drunk was one of the loneliest and scariest feelings. In his youth, he trembled from uncertainty and fear all the time of what would happen next.

Just like now. The wolves were edging toward him

Many, not all, but some of the Saluuettes were huge, burly and scarier-looking than the others. With each breath he inhaled, the air was loaded with the odor of wet leather while the Saluuettes smelled him, sniffed his boots, mouthed his mittens. Unlike a herd of cattle or robots, their eyes were expressive, wild, unpredictable and hard as iron.

After a few minutes, he sensed the wolves were only there to learn his scent. What comfort he took from that ended when he saw the burly Saluuette wolf that had attacked him at the pond.

The wolf gave Arnaq one glance and then stepped near him. It stared at him for a moment, but then narrowed its eyes, threatening or warning, Clayton wasn't sure which. He prepared for whatever fate the wolf had for him.

Then the wolf simply turned and trotted away.

The other wolves continued sniffing him, walking away, then returning to sniff at spots they apparently had missed before. He concluded Arnaq led him there for the Saluuette wolves to learn of his scent. Why else would he have been brought there?

Then came the most awesome sight of strange beings, he'd ever seen. Immediately he wanted to run but he knew he couldn't. These beings were people caught in some kind of metamorphous. They walked in a half shuffled. Their joints, limbs, arms, legs looked deformed.

They began to come out of the sacred forest in a procession, half walking on legs and half walking on hands and feet turning into hairy paws of animals. They were transforming to wolves. They wore animals hides of all colors and hair sprouted off their flesh.

When this group of twenty five or thirty crowded near him, he noticed one thing about them, they seemed friendly in their posture toward him but it was in their eyes. Their eyes showed pain and when they crept around him and in front of him they displayed a kind of affection by pressing their heads against his body almost like wanting to feel his body's warmth. Some touched the bear claw necklace as though it was a sacred thing. They made fascial gestures and seemed in horrid and tortuous physical pain. It was easy to identify the females.

When one female made a gesture for wanting food he grabbed a mushroom and held it out. That was a mistake. Arnaq swooped in and took it from his hands and flashed colors that made these beings cow. These beings slowly returned to the jungle and vanished.

Although he was frightened by the presence of the wolves and half people he wasn't as frightened as he thought he would be.

He had no clue, couldn't figure it out. In one way, he didn't want to know. But one thing was clear: Arnaq was in charge. The former was why he was here, the latter was probably why he was still alive.

The get-acquainted meeting lasted ten minutes more before Arnaq came over, tugged at his arm and led him away. As he allowed her to draw him with her, he asked himself, was this meeting arranged as a kind of warning, or was it to demonstrate compassion for her pets, the Saluuette wolves? He had no answer.

When Arnaq led him back to the pond, she flashed wondrous shades of colors, he assumed it was an exchange of how swell she enjoyed their visit together. By then, having decided that fear had no purpose anymore with her, he decided he liked Arnaq and told her that. Then she floated away and vanished in the branches of the trees.

He grabbed up the rifle and hurried to find Palafox. Should he tell Palafox what happened? Uncertain that he should, he decided not to. But he wanted answers.

After searching for her and calling for her several times, she failed to answer. He decided she was either sleeping or indisposed.

By that point, his thoughts had moved on. He had a hunch. He believed he knew where he could find some answers.

CHAPTER 48

Returning through the sacred forest, Palafox was thinking that Clay was spending a lot of time washing. She stepped out of the forest and called his name, several times. He didn't answer.

Concerned, she hurried to the pond. He wasn't there, as he had said he would be. She looked around, called for him again and listened, wondering where he could be.

Would he have gone alone into the cave to search for her?

She raced to the cave, grabbed up a torch, lit it and went inside, stepped quietly into the room of knowledge. Clay was reading something. Reading the journal of the English missionaries. She wanted to scream.

When she halted, he jerked and jumped to his feet; the stack of journals became unsettled and almost tipped over. She studied him as he tried to keep the stack from falling, noting how he looked almost cocooned in his parka. Finally, when he'd steadied the stack of journals, he looked at her. A shadow obscured most of his face.

She breathed deep. Finally, she said, "Why are you here?"

"Take it easy," he said, "had nothing better to do."

She felt her muscles grow tight in her body. She looked at the stack of journals and back at him.

"Where ya been all this time?"

"Here," he said.

She stepped toward him but stopped. She looked at the stack of journals and hurriedly counted them in her head. She looked back at him. At her gaze, he adjusted the rifle sling on his shoulder.

"You been here all this time?"

He finally nodded.

"You don't look the same with all your hair gone from your face and head," she said, to change the course of the conversation because she was furious.

He nodded.

"Daylight is nearly gone," she said. "Tomorrow, we must leave before dawn to hunt and to—"

"I'll be ready."

"We need rest." She looked over the stack of journals. The journals weren't supposed to be here in the first place. She recalled there had been much strife among the elders over the journals. She wasn't in the know about the controversy; she could only guess. If she had her way, she'd burn the journals until the wind scattered the ashes.

"I have something to ask you," Clay said.

"What is it?"

"It'll be best if you'll be upfront with me."

She sensed she had to be careful. "What do you want?"

"The truth," he said. "How old are you, and exactly what are you?"

She had thought she might, but she felt no surprise at his question. She felt he already knew the answer, just by the tone of his voice. For a moment, her mind was visited by mistakes made in the past. She knew once she revealed matters to him, her responsibility increased dramatically. Only when she was positive he wouldn't try to leave, only then would she trust him enough to tell him everything and to show him everything here.

"You won't understand," she said.

"One way to find out," he said, with a tone of impatience.

Finally, she said, "We age like your people until the fifteenth season, then it takes ten seasons for our kind to age one of your years."

Clay made a throaty sound, "That makes you pretty old."

"Old enough to think for myself, we shouldn't talk about this right now."

"Why not?"

"So much you must learn about my clan first," she said, and she began to feel weak, thinking he already knew important things from reading the journals.

He said, "You need fresh genes—new breeding stock for the Tacoma clan. But you can't without Yau putting a, what did the Prescotts call it? A seal of a wolf on the left arm of the men."

"We keep to our own kind," she said. "No one in your world would understand what and who we are." In truth, her clan never welcomed outsiders.

"I think I understand," he said, "the Prescotts' journal said it takes five terms, or ten seasons, for the transformation to take place. What term are you in?"

There was little doubt now, he knew, she didn't want to answer. She watched his eyes as she slowly pulled her parka above her belly, to just below her breasts. She wanted to show him the length of the blonde hair and to show modesty. It must've seemed that way to Clay because his eyes switched to her eyes. She really wanted Clay to be visually excited by the sight of her body.

"I'm in my second term," she said, and wanted to add more but in a delicate manner. "The third term can be halted if I am with child, but it will resume fifteen seasons after birth of a child. But if I have a second child the body processes stop completely. All the long hair falls out, the deformation of the joints and face reverts to the way we once were in just two seasons. Then we can never become a Saluuette wolf, we become Noctoids, which means we become servants to the Saluuette wolves. We help them in the summers, to gather food and stockpile it for the long winter. We feed them and take care of their needs such as taking care of their wounds, generally take care of them."

"It must be excruciating pain to go through that process."

"Only when the process reverts back is it painful. Some don't survive."

"I'm sorry." He seemed conciliatory.

Her heart calmed. "Don't be," she said, and took a deep breath of relief. "Not all my people go through the process. It's selective. We consider it an honor to protect the sacred forest and what it grows." The idea of becoming a Saluuette wolf frightened her. The idea of losing her mind, thoughts and feelings wasn't a pleasant thought. On rare occasions she'd confessed her feelings to her closest friends and they felt the same way. She wanted to become with child and she wanted Clay's child. Deep inside her she knew the only thing worse than becoming a Saluuette wolf would be living without Clay. Now, the prospect of losing him seemed assured if he learned the entire truth about her people being a race of wolves.

"Spoken like a soldier," he said, "once you metamorphose to a Saluuette wolf, do you have the capacity to mutate back?"

"No," she said, but she wasn't willing to tell him everything now. "Once you become a Saluuette wolf you stay that way until you die, either in battle with the Mueumonds, old age, or getting shot by a scared hunter. It's the same as when you grow old, you can't revert to your youth's body on a whim. We simply age differently and go through a different aging process than your people do."

"I'm sorry," he said.

"Don't be."

"What I don't understand is why Tuma didn't become a Saluuette wolf. He had a seal on his arm."

"He was bit by a Mueumond," she said, "a fact you didn't read but it's recorded in one of the journals."

He locked eyes with her, not letting go. "I find that amazing," he said. "But you told me your people hadn't killed a Mueumond in centuries. So how could Tuma have battled the Mueumonds?"

"Think about how old the elder was by your time. This is how elders become elders. They must battle the Mueumonds and receive a wound, learn much knowledge."

She wasn't being completely truthful. There were other considerations, many more. One of them was, how could she tell him that if he had a seal, a woman of the Tacoma clan who bit the inside of his lower lip until she tasted his blood would change him to be like them if he'd ate the Jaspose fruit? She couldn't tell him that, because he might never want to kiss her of his own free will. Free will was the prerequisite and so was the seal on the arm. Only a woman of the Tacoma clan with a seal could cause a man with a seal to become like them with a bite to his lower lip. A fact the Prescotts never learned, to record in their journals.

Right now, she'd love to taste his hot blood, she'd love that kiss. She could almost taste his blood by his man smell. Her mouth watered each time his smell drifted to her sensitive nostrils. But why didn't he find her desirable or want to kiss her? Was she not attractive? Maybe his sketch of her wasn't beautiful, as he had said. Maybe he just said she was beautiful just to make her feel warm all over.

"Reading between the lines," Clay said, "the Prescotts suspected the elders protected the Mueumonds, but they found no proof."

"That's not so," she said, and stepped closer to him.

His brows lifted. "It'd certainly make better sense to keep the Mueumonds alive, to fight your so-called enemy, the travelers—or maybe the Mueumonds are used to protect the sacred valley? To keep nosy people away from the sacred forest?"

"No," she said, and now she was struggling with the conflict inside her. His conclusion was exactly the same one she'd reached some time ago about the elders. What were the elders afraid of?

Clay said, "We didn't have any trouble stumbling into Mueumonds—"

"I know," she said. "We never return to the sacred forest on the trail we used. But they'll find our sleds when they return. C'mon, we must rest."

"Not so fast," he said, "I suspect you would rush back to the sacred valley at the thaw. No wonder people vanish in the upland wilderness without a trace."

"That's only a small part of it. We must kill a moose or caribou before they migrate to warmer weather, we must eat meat, so c'mon," she said, and grasped his arm to lead him out of there. One thing she knew, she was going to burn those journals.

The very moment they exited the cave, Arnaq flew in and began bumping and shoving them back inside the cave with her tentacles. Arnaq's hair was now black, a youthful, shining black and she was flashing blacks and grays. Palafox was too shocked to resist Arnaq's clear demand that she and Clay return to inside the cave.

CHAPTER 49

No explanation would come from Arnaq. Once they were well inside the cave, Arnaq left the entrance.

Clay seemed shaken. "What was that about?"

"I don't know," she said, "I've never seen Arnaq behave this way."

Clay stared at her for several long moments. Then he stepped toward her. She stepped back against the cave wall. He stepped closer. He put his hand on the wall above her head. He leaned slightly forward. There he was towering over her.

She stared up at him.

He nodded toward the entrance and said, "What's that about outside?"

"I don't know."

"Don't give me that."

"Why would I lie? I truly don't know," she said, and realized his man odor hung heavy in the air surrounding her.

When she smelled his manly odor the thoughts in her mind went wild. Her mouth filled with saliva. She had to swallow. She didn't want to duck under his arm and walk away. She sweated like the cave wall. She wanted him to take her right there and at that moment. But Clay seemed more interested in the sounds outside.

Clay just stood there staring down at her. Time seemed to crawl by as they talked quietly for some time.

When they decided to exit the cave again she didn't want to go. Her passions had become like unshaven outlaws. She wanted him in a bad, very bad sort of way. She wanted to tear off his parka, smell his flesh, his arms, and belly. She wanted to take him to the pond and wash his back. Then she wanted to slowly lick the water off his long, tone, muscled legs. But it was not to be.

Finally, she staggered a little bit, and panted as she exited the cave with Clay. When they did, it was dark, though the dark night of the sacred forest is more like a very early twilight.

They were afraid to walk far from the cave. It wasn't a long time, when they stopped near the sacred pond, before they heard croaks and cries of wolves, out there in the wilderness. Palafox recognized the squeals of the Saluuette wolves—and that the wolves were deep in the Saluuette wilderness fighting Mueumonds.

Clay did as well. He turned to her. Even in the dim light, she saw the tension in his face.

"It's a fight between the Mueumonds and wolves," he said.

"Don't say that," she said, "we've lost so many Saluuette wolves over the years."

"From those sounds, you're bound to lose more tonight."

"I don't want to listen." Her heart twisting inside her chest. "Let's return inside."

"I'm not sleeping inside," Clay said, "not with that fight out there. The Mueumonds might break through the defense—"

"The Mueumonds have never reached the sacred forest, ever, and they won't tonight," she said, and at that moment, in the distance, a strange blue light flashed in the darkness, then another blue glow flashed, then another and another.

"Whoa. Whoa!" Clay said.

"What is—? Oh, look!" she said, "there's another pop of blue. I don't know—"

"Shhh, listen," he said and turned to her, "you know perfectly well what and who is wiping out the Mueumonds out there."

Then she realized, "Yau."

Clay shook his head, "Right, call it what you like, but she's definitely bringing pee on the Mueumonds."

Bringing pee? What is he talking about? "Pee?" she said.

"Slaughter," he said, and angled his head to apparently hear better. "An ugly slaughter and it's the Mueumonds who are being slaughtered."

"Oh."

The cries and croaks swelled with fervor and passion that troubled her. This was her very first time to stay at the sacred forest during the winter but others had, but never wanted to stay again. Now she knew why.

The cries of the wolves out there in the darkness were painful to listen to. It seemed they'd been going on a long time, but she told herself it wasn't all that long a time; it just seemed that way to her. She placed her hand on her stomach, but still it tumbled.

She was just about to tell Clay of her feeling: that the Mueumonds were fleeing and the Saluuette wolves were chasing them down, when he said, "Sounds like the Saluuette wolves are pushing the Mueumonds back—listen, the croaks are fading, like they're on the run."

"Good, uh, good," she said, "I told you they'd never reach the sacred forest."

He turned and looked at her, "Don't be too optimistic, things can turn on spit."

She wondered what he meant.

Before she could decide whether to ask, he muttered something under his breath, shaking his head. She decided not to say anything, so intent he seemed on listening to the fight, which they both did until there was just a sad stillness.

They talked a little while, until the wilderness became eerie quiet. Finally, he agreed to return to the cave.

She showed him the rooms of sleep and the bunks in each.

"I want you to sleep beside me," she said, and she wanted more than that. She wanted his bunk beside her from now on. She wanted his bunk so close she could curl next to him to get warm, so she'd be there by him if he wanted her.

He says, "I've had enough of caves."

"Sleep next to me," she said. "I will be frightened if you don't."

"You frightened," Clay said, "I don't believe anything can scare you."

Before she could answer, Clay went on and said, "I'd like my privacy for a change." He grinned, straightened his shoulders turned and walked away only to glance over his shoulder once to say, "Sleep tight."

So Clay left to sleep outside near the entrance to the cave.

But how is she to know about round eyes or what goes on in their heads. She wondered what she was going to have to do to get his attention. Maybe she wasn't attractive. He said she was but why doesn't he see that she desires him.

She finally bundled up on one of the bunks and lay thinking about all that had happened. She wondered how she could make him want to sleep with her, to give her a child so she could live her life with him. Go with him, stay with him, and be with him. She wondered how much more she should tell Clay in the coming days, the question still in her mind when sleep took her.

CHAPTER 50

For the next three days at the sacred forest, she and Clay were together a lot, except when they slept. Nothing worked to get him to sleep inside next to her. She even watched him bathe in the pond and the moment she walked up he seemed startled. He frowned and never spoke a word. He hurried out of the pond and went behind the Great Spirit's sled.

Then Clay began to act strange. She wondered if he was getting sick again. He wasn't curious about anything or did he ask questions. He seemed tired a lot. He would bathe in the sacred pond for hours at a time.

He would sit and stare at nothing for a long time too. He said little, but he was pleasant and agreeable when they did talk. She didn't disclose anything important because he didn't ask. But she felt something was wrong with him. She reasoned he'd eaten too many of the fruits, or ate one that was bad for him. But that did little to explain why he seemed broody and moody at times.

On the fourth morning just before dawn, she woke and pulled on her parka. They'd planned to go hunting for meat. Her body needed meat now. She began to crave meat as much as she craved Clay's body next to hers. She didn't want to go through the process and become a Saluuette wolf now. She wanted to have Clay's child. She'd do anything for that to happen. Anything to have him, now.

She went outside and stood near the spot where he slept. The furs were folded and stacked. She wondered where he could be. Had he returned to the cave without her seeing him?

She went back inside, didn't find him. But in the room containing the stack of journals, she saw right away one stack wasn't as neatly stacked as the others. She wondered if she was mistaken. She couldn't be mistaken. And the worst fear, the fear of the worst, overtook her.

She left the cave, walked to the pond and called for Clay. After many attempts, she didn't find him. She decided either he had left the sacred forest, or he was lost somewhere inside the cave.

When she exited the cave a third time, the second search also fruitless, Arnaq met her, flashing greens and blues. When Arnaq led her to a path, Palafox sensed from Arnaq that Clay had left the sacred forest.

She returned to the cave, grabbed a spear and carried it with her along the path out of the sacred forest, into the Saluuette territory.

Where the snow began, she found Clay's tracks. Following them, she began to follow and surprisingly, there were no tracks of the Saluuette wolves trailing him. That was good. That meant he hadn't been gone long enough for the Saluuettes to take after him.

She stopped and studied the needles of the spruce, noticed how they were closing together. She knew what that meant. Another snow-and-wind blizzard was on its way. Snow wasn't surprising, considering how high they were in the mountain range. The blizzard wasn't a good sign. A blizzard never slowed the Mueumonds. In fact, they became more active in the Saluuette territory then.

She didn't know how far she walked along his trail. She had so many troubles going through her mind, she lost her sense of time. One of which was what he was doing away from the sacred forest—she'd already explained to him how dangerous the Saluuette territory was in the winter and without her. He knew the dangers.

When she went down into a hollow, she realized his pace was slower now, his stride close together. Then she saw deep impressions in the snow. That meant Clay was either hunting, following the tracks left by a moose, or the moose was following him.

She hadn't gone far when she came out onto a knoll she knew well. He had apparently stopped to relieve himself here, then his boot prints meandered off to her left.

Then his voice filled her being, as did the sight of him.

"What are you doing this far away from the sacred forest?" he said. His parka hood was pulled over his head. He wore the bear claw necklace she'd made for him and the reddish colors on the necklace matched his cheeks.

The sudden pacing in her chest nearly closed off her voice. She felt the muscles in her face tighten.

"I-I can hardly catch my breath, you frightened me so."

He nodded and a moment of silence lingered between them.

Finally, she said, "What are ya doing out here?"

His gaze became a hard stare. "Time to take the walk," he said. "You weren't tracking me were you?"

She wondered if he'd been reading more of the journals, until she remembered she'd been with him every waking moment.

"I was worried you'd get lost," she said. "A blizzard is on its way and it'll hit like nothing you ever experienced, we barely have enough daylight to return without losing our trail, so c'mon, let's go."

The first arctic wind hit them both. Even the air had acquired a malevolent purpose. She had suffered the same fear each time she thought about having to stop him. The wind and cold squeezed all hope out of her.

Clay frowned, "What's the spear for?"

Her heart lurched. "What do you think it's for?"

He gave her a dubious look. "Protection."

"Yes," she said. "We really don't have time for an easy conversation, we must return to the sacred forest right away."

His brows arched. "I'm not returning. I've seen enough, read enough. But don't go worry your head, your secrets are safe with me."

She winced. "Are you sure? Are you really sure about that? The temptations in your world are too great to keep the sacred forest and mushrooms and my kind locked away and out of your mind forever. In so many ways, you'll become a prisoner of the secret. Sooner or later you are bound to talk. When you do, you put our way of life in danger of being wiped out. Our way of life has existed since before your civilizations made a footprint in the soil. If the outside world learned of our existence they wouldn't hesitate to destroy us, by disease or other means, just to gain possession of the mushrooms. Our existence must be kept a secret. That's why nothing is more important than keeping our way of life a secret from your world."

"Why did you lie to me all this time?"

"I didn't want to," she said. "I didn't know what else to do, what could I do? After the elder was killed I didn't know what to do. I'm caught up in something that's bigger than any human can imagine and here I stand, caught up between what my heart tells me and my clan's law says. I've suffered more than you can know."

The uneasiness remained on his face. "I only took eight plate-size mushrooms, enough to tide me over until I find real food. Trust me. I want to forget about this place, and you. Another thing—and I don't want to sound unappreciative for all you and Tuma did for me—but I do not want to suffer for your mistake in bringing me here."

What was she to say? There was no point in misleading him now.

"I didn't force you to come here," she said. "I've lived long enough to know the difference between men who seek evil and men who seek goodness. My only purpose was to help you get well. Then those wilderness crazies showed up at the cave and my feelings for you. Clay, don't do this."

She took a careful step toward him.

Clay arched his brows and angled his head slightly. He raised the gun. The barrel pointed at her belly.

She stopped. "Have you gone wilderness crazy?"

He gave her a fierce look. "There's a chance of it. The evil here seems to be you," he said. "Drop the spear and stand back."

She stepped back and did as he asked, knowing now that instead of sleeping, Clay had returned to the cave and read journals. Now, he knew she had to stop him any way she could. She couldn't live without him. How could she do that now? More, how could she make him see her real reason for wanting him to stay, to be her mate? Make him know that her want was not because of what he'd read anymore?

A feeble idea came to her head. She could try to stall him long enough for the blizzard to strike. She couldn't count on the Saluuette wolves, now that a blizzard was on its way. They never ventured out in a blizzard. Could she stall him long enough? She had to try.

She took a deep breath. "I'm not going to harm you. We won't survive the blizzard if we remain here, return with me."

Clay grinned and shook his head slowly. "The longer I stay here, the more wolf I might become. I'm not going to become a Saluuette wolf."

She forced her words past the air in her throat, "You can't become like us, you don't have a seal do you?"

"Not-yet," Clay said, "And I don't plan to hang around until one mysteriously appears on my arm."

"We can talk this out, ask me anything, I'll tell you," she said. "But you can't leave the wilderness with your knowledge of us."

"Yes, I read that," he said. "What I don't understand, the Prescotts were allowed to leave but they returned. What I don't understand was, why?"

"They wanted to be like us," she said. "And they understood what grew here was too much a temptation in their world."

"They helped decipher some of the scrolls. I read that part," he said.

She burst out, "They did other good things too."

Her nerves threatened her sanity. Desperate to end this, she said, "You know I've gotta stop you. Please return with me. No harm will fall upon you."

His eyes squinted. "Killing you can be arranged, sweets. I don't see the necessity of shooting you but so help me God—" He clicked the safety off the rifle and stopped talking. After several long moments, he said, "Your secret is safe with me. And I'm not so easily tempted you should know that by now."

"I don't know what you mean," she said, yet suddenly, she did. "Oh, you read something about a temptation, and now you think you're one, well, you're not. Please listen, you can't and won't survive."

"I'll give it the old college try," he said, and grinned.

"It's not even wise to think for a moment there's a slim chance of luck you'll escape. The Mueumonds and Saluuette wolves will track you down, even if you kill me. They won't stop hunting you day or night and when they find you, you'll suffer a horrific end."

"I read about that. And I've been wondering something. Answer this, why didn't y'all kill me at the cave?

She burst out. "Kill you. I don't know what you're talking about."

"God forbid," he said. "I was color blind when Tuma asked me to recite the colors on the bear claw necklace and that was a good thing. If I had known the Great Spirit's colors, greens, reds, blues, whites, and yellows, I would've been killed by Tuma."

She regarded him in total confusion. She had thought all along that if he could see the Great Spirit's colors he was a good temptation. Was she wrong? "How do you know this to be true?"

"Some of your scrolls were indeed deciphered by the English missionaries. Trust me, I would have been killed. That's all I'm going to say," he said.

She didn't know what to say. She had too many matters to think about, like stopping him.

"I couldn't harm you," she said, and pushed the swell down in her chest. "Don't do this, I don't want anything to happen to you, surely you believe me after all we've been through—"

"That doesn't cut any ice with me—"

"Do you hate or fear me that much?"

"Hate? I've never given it thought," he said, blankly. "But I do fear what you'll become."

She suspected he would feel this way. "I won't become a Saluuette wolf if I'm with child. I care for you and will do anything for you, please believe me."

There was a long moment of silence between them. She slowly smiled at him. "I want your baby, Clay."

Clay glanced away. When he looked back, he had an odd look. She noticed his cheeks seemed to have turned redder. He said, "I've felt all along that's what you wanted, a baby. What I want to tell you is not easy. It has always been hard for me to talk about my short comings and I have many but lying is not one of them. But I do want to end this so you can move on, and so I can get the hell out of here. So many times I wanted to tell you, tell someone." Then Clayton took a deep breath. "My wounds keep me from having children. I wish I had died in combat."

"Don't say that, Clay, I want to be your mate."

"I can't be truly happy," he said. "I would make any woman's life a hell. Celebrating the holiday's alone, birthday's alone. I'll come to grips with being alone but won't force someone else to bear that burden because of me."

Then she recalled the cuts on his body, the slashes, the horrible knife scars. She'd seen him naked and knew he had the red stick but the sack didn't look quite right. It never did. It always seemed empty and flat. Then she knew. She wiped the corner of her eyes with the heel of her mitten.

The wind was getting stronger and she didn't have much time. "Clay, the mushrooms will give back if your wound was caused by the forces of evil."

Clay shook his head. "Nothing can be done."

"The mushrooms are divine," she said. "They'll return what was taken from you. You are healthy and strong now, are you not?"

"I've never felt better," he said. "But, I'm afraid you've hooked your horse to a wagon with a burden."

"Do you feel different down there?"

Clay stood in the shade of the trees that moved slightly. He seemed stunned. He didn't answer. His cheeks were going redder than before.

Finally, a short grin formed on his lips. "You never give up, do you?"

"I don't," she said, and smiled her best smile.

Then almost imperceptible at first, she saw movement through the timber. She realized what it was: a glimmer of hope.

Heart pounding, she said, "Clay, there's a moose crossing the open area down there. It's heading our way." She pointed at the moose's location. "We need the meat, please, please shoot it for us, if not us, then for me."

He grinned, and she could tell he didn't believe her. He glanced over his shoulder, then looked back at her with surprise. He held up his hand to not move.

She gave him a hopeful smile.

He said, "I'll hear the snow crunch if you take one step."

Then he propped against the tree and aimed.

"Let it get close," she said, and took a step for the spear.

He glanced over his shoulder. "It's a bad day to test my patience."

She angled her body upright, watched the moose as it walked alongside the small hollow, then turned right and headed straight up the floor of the hollow, toward them.

That's the moment Clay chose to shoot.

The moose bolted through the thicket, snapping trees and limbs as it did, then fell.

"You got it," she said, and quickly leaned over to grab the spear.

Clay made it first. His booted foot on the spear, he said, "I'll take this." His calm tone held a threat.

CHAPTER 51

Clayton stood and stared at Palafox. Then he looked in the direction of the moose and wondered had he killed it? "I don't see it."

Palafox pointed down the draw, "It's laying right down there among those trees. Its legs are moving some."

She was smiling. No doubt about why. The six-hundred-pound moose could provide enough food to last months. In his happiness, in his excitement about killing a moose, the urge to leave right away left him.

He had to help her gut the moose, quarter the moose into manageable sizes to haul back to the sacred forest before the blizzard struck or before the meat froze or before the Mueumonds or arctic wolves smelled the dead moose. He couldn't leave her alone without offering assistance. Some might say he was being noble but there wasn't an ounce of nobility about it. After all, another blizzard was bearing down. And, he felt they had some unfinished business.

"We have to hurry, let's go get it," she said, and smiled wider.

He slung the rifle on his shoulder and hefted the spear in his hand. Together they descended the slope. Finally, he saw the moose lying on the snow among splatters of blood. They approached the animal's broad back.

Next thing he noticed was when it shot mist from its muzzle. He removed the rifle from his shoulder and walked within five yards of the wounded moose. The coup de grace was a part about hunting he disliked, but it was necessary.

"Stay here," he said, holding out his arm and the spear to stop Palafox from walking closer.

He walked another yard and stopped, stuck the spear into the snow, eased the rifle to his shoulder and aimed for the moose's neck. He pulled the trigger. Nothing happened. He aimed and pulled the trigger again, still nothing.

He lowered the rifle and looked at the bolt. The bolt had opened, but another round lodged behind the hull of the first round in the barrel. Immediately, he knew the hull had swelled inside the barrel and couldn't eject. He reached inside his parka and grabbed the knife.

The moose struggled up and stumbled, but kept moving through the saplings. It made ten yards before it collapsed. On its next attempt to stand on wobbly, slender legs, it managed only a single stagger before it fell onto its side. Almost immediately, it struggled back onto its legs in its effort to escape.

"Shoot!" Palafox said, and grabbed the spear, held it pointed at his belly.

Clayton looked at her eyes.

She grabbed a mitten-full of blood-splattered snow. She opened her mittens, sniffed the bloody snow, twitched her nose and closed her eyes as though she sniffed the aroma of hot chocolate. She opened her eyes and peered at him.

Truly frightened by her obvious pleasure at the smell of blood, Clayton wondered wearily if he was going to leave the wilderness alive, after all. Whatever fate awaited him probably wouldn't be pretty. He needed to get another bullet in the chamber quick, if for nothing else than to defend himself. He was more worried now than he'd been when he was inside the sacred forest with her.

Then a slow smile came over Palafox's lips. "It's getting away," she said, and stood and began to follow the winding path of blood droplets on the impressions in the snow.

Clayton nodded cautiously and decided he wouldn't turn his back on her again. Then he worked to dislodge the bullet. He watched the big moose stumbling away through the half-lit forest, then looked back at the chamber and realized the knife blade was too large to dislodge the empty hull.

He pulled off his mitten and quickly cut off a short stick from a nearby tree, hoping he could maneuver the stick inside the chamber better than his broad-bladed knife.

"Hurry," Palafox said, and walked on the winding impressions in the snow, following the wounded moose.

"Keep away from it," he said.

She turned to him never lost stride and said, "It's getting away. Hurry. C'mon!"

He began to jog behind her to stop her, never stopping his attempt to dislodge the brass casing from the chamber. A glance up told him she kept stepping toward the wounded moose.

What is she doing?

He said, "Stay back!"

The moose struggled up and collapsed, then just as quickly regained its footing.

"Keep away from it," he said, and was forced to return to his task. Moments later he looked up. Palafox hustled up to the moose as it struggled to get back on its hooves. She drew the spear back and shoved it forward. The spear glanced off the moose's tough hide. At that instant, the moose turned and, with one head butt, Palafox went down.

He watched in petrified horror.

The moose's next target was her midsection and with repeated grinding head butts, the moose began to drive her across the snow.

Seconds passed with aching slowness as he dropped the rifle and ran as fast as he could, grabbed the spear off the snow and sprinted for the moose. Instinctively, all his hunting experience guided him. He knew where to plant the spear for a lethal blow.

All the while, Palafox screamed and pounded the moose's snout with her mittens. The moose drove her through the snow until her body wedged sideways against a tree trunk, then twisted its head and tried to break her body in two.

At that moment, Clayton shoved the spear behind the moose's ribs and toward its head. The moose gave a whooshing outbreath and collapsed.

Clayton could hear the moose gurgling as he stepped to where Palafox lay. Splattered blood covered her face. Her body twitched and trembled. Her right arm lifted off the snow and froze in motion for several moments before dropping back to her side. She groaned in a pitiful way, as though she tried to wake up from a much-needed sleep.

Stunned, he didn't know what do or what to say for several moments. He was in denial and he felt as crushed as Palafox's body seemed. Finally, he knelt beside her and pulled her into his arms. She was limp. He peered into her eyes.

Her only response was a half-conscious, wordless moan.

"Why didn't you listen to me?"

Her eyes wandered in a half trance.

"Get me to the sacred forest," she said, in a voice broken and weak.

When he picked her up into his arms and stood, she grimaced. Her head rocked. "Put me down, put me down."

He kept lumbering and staggering forward the best he could.

"I'll get you back," he said.

"Clay," she said, and it seemed her voice was twenty yards away.

The wind had gained strength, the trees rocked and clouds of snow shot among the limbs of the trees. He could barely hear the snow crunch under his boots. This blizzard had a punch that made him fear this might be the beginning of the end, perhaps for them both.

With each step he made, he bogged down in snow halfway to his knees and found it troublesome to keep his balance carrying her.

"Try to hold me around the neck," he said.

A grimace seemed frozen on her face, but her olive skin faded, became even paler, as her tortured breathing lightened and her eyes wandered. When she passed out, he rested her on the snow and tried to think.

He couldn't get her back to the sacred forest before dark. He lifted her and carried her until he stumbled and fell. He sat beside her on the snow gasping to breathe.

He pulled her head in his lap, brushed her hair back. He talked softly, telling her everything would be all right. He didn't know what else to say to her. He cleaned her blood-spattered face with snow.

Her breathing came short and weak. Then she coughed and a grimace went across her face, followed by a serene calm.

Fearing she might be going into shock, he said, "Stay with me. Don't sleep."

She opened her eyes and they seemed to shimmer. "Get me—" She went unconscious again.

"God!" Flew out of his mouth with such force it shocked him.

CHAPTER 52

S he slipped in and out of consciousness several times more. Clayton heard no rattling in her chest or breathing and she didn't complain about pain, her legs and arms didn't seem broken. Believing she was in shock from the violence of the attack, that she could be having internal bleeding, he elevated her legs.

His firsthand experience with internal bleeding came from his experiences in combat. He knew in many cases nothing could be done for internal bleeding unless a well-trained doctor was on the scene. He'd seen a soldier die of internal bleeding and the sight was depressing.

But he didn't feel bloating on her abdomen. He listened for static sounds underneath her skin, which usually meant bleeding. Hearing none relieved him.

He squinted at the darkening sky. By default, she had given responsibility for her life to him. He took the duty seriously.

Lots of forest, too much forest, lay between them and the sacred forest. The flying snow had begun and the wind gained more strength. He wouldn't know the way back to the sacred forest if their tracks were covered.

He retrieved his mitten, the knife and the rifle. He walked to the moose and pulled the spear out of its body, examined it. It was covered with blood halfway up the shaft. The sight filled his mouth with saliva and the inexplicable urge to lick the blood off the spear. The sight and smell of blood was overpowering him. Though blindsided by amazement, he had the strength to stop himself.

The sickly smell of blood had always made him nauseous. Now blood seemed so right to him, why was this? Maybe it was his appetite for blood pudding. He'd eaten blood pudding several times and it was delicious. So it was the pangs of hunger. Or was it something else? After a few moments, he examined both his arms for a wolf seal and found none. In his relief, he remained mystified why blood seemed so, suddenly right. Unsettled, he decided to think about it later.

The scent of blood would be carried by the wind to the noses of predators, alerting them, attracting them to this place. He planned to not be in the dead moose's vicinity at dark. He had to hurry.

When he returned to where she lay, she rocked her head slow. He heaved her up and she moaned a little while he carried her up an incline to a location on the shoulder of the knoll.

The place he selected overlooked the bottom of the hollow. He felt the location provided some security from predators; being out of sight and downwind of the dead moose meant no animal at the moose could catch their scent on the wind.

He had to pile snow on her before it became too dark. Although the thought of a blazing campfire would be ideal, wood was buried under four feet of packed snow. The only fuel was the slender green limbs, not enough to keep a fire blazing. Instead of a fire, he used three of the six candles they had between them for light.

Palafox opened her groggy eyes. "Clay." Her voice wasn't as loud as a gasp, but startled him the same.

CHAPTER 53

At first, Palafox was muddled. She remembered daylight and now it was dark.

"Where do you hurt?" Clay asked.

"The moose knocked me senseless," she said. "Did I cry?"

He moved his face close to hers. "Where do you hurt?"

It was hard for her to get enough air for words without her chest aching. "When I move tenderness comes at my chest."

Clay took a snowball and placed it on her lips. She tried to take a bite but she didn't have the strength.

"Any pressure in your stomach?" he asked.

She reached down and felt her belly. "No. I was scared when the moose got me down then all went black. I didn't feel anything until I came to."

"I'll get you back," he said.

"Did the moose get away?"

He shook his head, "It's dead."

Gray blotches flashed over her vision.

"I shouldn't be moved now, it's painful to breathe." She met his gaze. "I don't want any harm to come to you, please believe me."

"Listen to you," he said, and grinned. "Of course I know that."

Of course I don't believe you either ....

"Mushrooms," she said, "let me have a small bit. Maybe food will help settle my stomach."

He handed over a tiny chunk of mushroom. She nibbled on some of it, but then froze at a plunking sound, as if a single snow clump had fallen from a branch and hit the snow. The sound came from the hollow below them.

She looked at Clay, "Hear that?"

He nodded, "Rest and sleep, I'll be here."

She just wanted to hear his voice. Him beside her was what she wanted.

"I know," she said, then coughed. It was painful to cough. Exhausted, she closed her eyes.

CHAPTER 54

Snow crystallized on Palafox's parka hood and the tiny sparkles quivered like miniscule stars in the twilight. Clayton tried counting the sparkles to relax his mind.

He worried and prayed that daylight would come quick. She could have broken ribs or a strain to her diaphragm. No matter what was wrong, it was paramount to keep her as calm as possible.

He couldn't dismiss the notion he was responsible for her injury. The mishap played over and over in his head, a senseless exercise that did little to trim the burden. The mindless seesawing kept him wired.

The wind became stronger by the hour. At first, snow fell light; now it was falling heavy again and covered them like a blanket.

The wind also brought strange sounds, of wolves baying in the hills, then others. They were a long way off, the best he could tell. The baying ended after an hour or so.

A few hours after dark, he heard sounds like scampering feet over the snow. He could tell by the crunch on the snow and by the soft growls that wolves had found the dead moose. It seemed he could smell the musk of the moose and blood in the wind.

Listening, he eased his mitten into his parka and squeezed the knife handle, but remained still.

Finally, he felt a presence in the air nearby. He didn't move.

Sounds of scurrying feet sprinted across the snow then down the incline. Then a quarrel erupted between wolves at the proximity of the dead moose. Anyone could tell the squeal was conceding its air. Then the squealing hushed, as if a guillotine lopped off its head.

The abrupt silence sent shivers through his throat. He sat up, but didn't otherwise move. Only his eyes roved the shadows out there, beyond the glow of the candles.

He reached for the rifle and worked quickly to remove the jammed bullet, but nothing he did loosened it. The cold had welded the bullets. He gave up and laid the rifle on the snow.

It wasn't a long time, maybe an hour passed, before strange shadows moved just outside the glow. The shadows probed, bolder and more frequent. The activity on the snow came from different directions surrounding them. Then silence enveloped the area.

Clayton's hands sweated. His feet sweated. He knew they were wolves and he felt they were about to attack. He removed the knife from the parka. He didn't feel cold, or anything for that matter.

CHAPTER 55

Palafox felt pain in her ribs when she came to and with each breath, but not as bad as before. At first, she thought Clay had left her alone. Then she saw him flat on his stomach within arm's length of her shoulder.

Thinking him asleep, she decided not to wake him. Then she heard a noise, coming from somewhere out in front of her. The sound first, then a blurry shadow shot through the timber and darkness.

"Clay."

"Yes."

"Did you see that?"

"Don't worry," he said.

I'm plenty worried. "It might be arctic wolves."

"Try to rest," he said.

"You don't understand. Arctic wolves kill for the pure pleas—"

At that instant, a dark shadow sailed over her like a narrow black bird.

Clay scrambled to his feet holding his knife, greeted the wolf midair, wrestling with it like a windstorm in the branches of trees. The wolf sounded, "irk-irk-irk" as it tried to stand, then it collapsed. It didn't move again, just lay with its tongue lolling out its mouth.

She didn't feel sorry for the wolf or feel remorse. The fight ended so quick, she hardly believed it happened. Just when she'd calmed enough to breathe, another wolf came out of the dark and attacked Clay.

The wolf's jaws latched onto his right parka shoulder. The man and the creature's heads were so close she could barely separate who was what.

The wolf twisted and growled to rip Clay's shoulder off. When they fell, they rolled and twisted like a snowstorm across the tundra.

A twist, a turn, and then the wolf "irk-irked" and collapsed. Clay put his foot on its neck and stabbed it again.

She couldn't breathe and didn't remember ever breathing. She could hardly catch her breath for there was no measure of time.

When she heard a snarl, she turned to see a shadow in the air just as it knocked Clay flat. Now on his knees, he twisted, trying to stab the wolf with his knife. The wolf leaped to the side and almost at the same time, it leaped for Clay again.

He caught the wolf in his arms, lost his balance and fell onto his back again. The knife flashed in the glow as he plunged the knife into the wolf's side.

The wolf leaped to the side and began to chase its own tail. Then it keeled over. It didn't move again or make a sound.

She felt her heart in her throat. She covered her face with her mittens. She couldn't watch, so simply listened to the wolf's growls and to Clay's grunts.

When she peeked through her mittens, another wolf had attacked Clay. They were spinning and kicking up the snow. She couldn't tell who was on top.

This was the way it was. Three or maybe four packs of arctic wolves had surrounded them. The wolves came from every direction. Some wolves ran across her body and attacked Clay at the back while he staggered and danced with another wolf among the tree trunks and rolled on the snow.

The wolves came one, two, three at a time and Clay fought them. He broke the spear in two, then the rifle's stock swinging it. He growled, grunted and yelled at the wolves to come back for more. The arctic wolves came after him, unafraid. He killed, maimed and wounded as many and as often as they came.

No sooner had she covered her face with her mittens than a growl came, this one right at her head. When she looked up, the yellow eyes of a wolf squinted back.

It felt like a noose tightened round her throat. She couldn't get a word out. She couldn't scream. She couldn't breathe. The wolf grabbed her parka arm and began pulling, jerking her down the hillside.

She resisted the best she could and tried to hit the wolf, but she barely lifted her arms. She knew if the wolf got her out of Clay's sight, he might not find her in time. She tried to attract his attention. His back was to her. She tried to scream, "Over here."

She tried to squirm free of the wolf's grasp. She tried to adjust her body to smack the wolf or throw snow in its face but she had no strength.

Then the wolf stopped sliding her down the hill. Suddenly the wolf bared its fangs.

At that moment, she could barely lift an arm to defend herself.

The wolf stepped forward and slowly lowered its head showing a mouth of ivory fangs, ready to rip off her face.

Couldn't Clay see or hear her? At the moment she felt herself surrendering to unconsciousness, wishing the Saluuette wolves would show up but knowing they never ventured out in a blizzard. She watched in a daze as Clay turned and ran toward her.

He jumped over her, yelling and swinging the big knife and the broken spear like a club. Finally, she heard a thump and a pitiful "irk-irk-irk" as the wolf that attacked her ran away.

Clay stepped to her and knelt. He wheezed heavily. He'd been bitten; he bled from several parts on his face.

"You okay?" he said.

"Yes," she said between gasping breaths. "You're wounded, hurt—"

"I'm all right," he said, and didn't hesitate to grab the nap of her parka and drag her back into the glow of the candles.

It wasn't a long time but it seemed like time had frozen before the arctic wolves stopped their attacks. The wind got strong and snow fell heavy through the branches. Clay lay beside her and in a moment he slept. He'd said little. She stayed awake and listened but she heard only the wind in the trees.

When the wind blew the candles out, she drifted to sleep. She didn't know how long she slept when she was startled awake.

She listened.

She didn't move.

"Ruup-ruup, ruup-ruup." Croaks in the wind. At that moment, she was sure of two things: Dawn was approaching and the Mueumonds were nearly on top of them.

CHAPTER 56

Palafox turned to see Clay beside her, covered with a light blanket of snow. She watched the outline of his face. He seemed in deep sleep. She wondered if this would be their last moments together. She lay there thinking of the once simple and predictable life she led until weeks ago. Now it seemed her entire life and way of life was collapsing round her like a tree falling over.

She turned on her side to be closer to him. She eased her arms over his chest, felt his slow breathing and finally felt at peace, watching him sleep.

Then she heard another croak, this one close, quite close to them. She didn't want to wake Clay to bring him out of his sleep.

When she heard the third and fourth croaks, she decided to wake him. He was their only hope. She slowly moved her face to his face and whispered.

He woke and was groggy for several moments, then he seemed to go back to sleep.

"Clay," she said.

When she put her mitten over his mouth, he mumbled incoherently.

"Shhh," she said. "Listen."

Several low croaks sounded at the floor of the hollow.

"Oh man," he said, "they're on the moose, we gotta get out of here."

"You go," she said, "I can't make it."

His bearded face turned to her, "We're downwind, but it's only a matter of time before they smell the dead wolves and blood here. Do you think you can walk?"

"We won't make it," she said. "We won't make it."

"Won't won't do, you gotta try," he said in a low voice. "The wind in the trees will mask our sounds until we can slip away. Can you crawl?"

She nodded, "I think so."

He was right. If they could remain downwind of the Mueumonds, they might have a chance to evade them until dawn arrived. Even then, she knew they couldn't make it to the sacred forest before dark, not in this weather. In spite of what was against them, she had to try.

"I can crawl," she said.

"Okay, let's go," he said, rolled away and slowly got to his knees. He peered in the direction of the soft croaking sounds. "You're gonna to have to show me the way to crawl."

She pointed.

They began to low-crawl and it was rough going. Each time she pulled her left knee up toward her chest to push back, it almost took her breath. She had broken ribs for sure.

They managed to crawl until dawn was upon them. When Clay stood, he helped her stand and she used him as support as they went forward. She limped yet felt stronger the farther they walked. But they weren't covering a lot of distance. The snow was deep and it was soft and falling heavy.

Finally, when daylight arrived it was dim among the trees, almost like a bright twilight. She knew daylight wouldn't last because of the clouds.

Within minutes, they both heard croaks behind them and the sounds were very close.

Her heart loaded down.

"We're still downwind of them," Clay said.

Palafox wondered if they were living their last moments.

"I don't think that matters," she said, "they're hunting us."

CHAPTER 57

When Clay looked around, his movements hasty, Palafox wondered what he was thinking.

"We must hurry," she said.

He sighed. "We can't outrun them."

She leaned against a tree. The wind whipped the snow in clouds around them. She could hardly see farther than a team of dogs pulling a sled.

Clay gazed in the direction of the croaking sounds. She sensed he knew it was over for them. From their noises, the Mueumonds were on the shoulder of the ridge, not far above and behind them.

With a weakened heart she turned, and grabbed his arm and looked at him. "We won't make it."

He stood still, surveying the vicinity. "We've got the wind on our side. We've hid from 'em before."

She squeezed his arm and wondered if he knew the misery and hopelessness of their continuing farther.

"We don't have time to find a downed tree," she said, "we can barely see as it is."

"C'mon," he said, "hold my arm, tight."

425

After a short time, he'd dug a shallow trench in the snow, on the slope of the hill near the base of a tree. The spot was downwind of the Mueumonds. He helped her slide into the trench and told her to stay still. When he said that, they studied each other for several moments. His eyes seemed almost lost, as though he was seeing beyond her.

The thought she'd had him to herself for so many weeks and he might go away now and never kiss her, filled her with much despair. She had pretended to herself she could kiss him at any time and on some occasions gently touch him. Now it all was coming to an end.

She shook her head, "Please don't leave me."

He blinked several times. "Neither of us will have a chance if we stay together," he said, and began to pile snow and conifer needles on top of her.

She knew he didn't mean he would dig another trench—there wasn't time. And no amount of persuasion could stop him. She felt a tug of loss, as though she was losing him forever. When he looked at her again, his eyes were wide. There was a deep hopelessness in his eyes.

She reached up and caught his snow-filled mittens, looked eagerly at him. "K-kiss me, Clayton," she said, and she wanted to kiss him with the kind of kiss that would make him want to return to her in spite of all dangers he might face. "Kiss me."

He stopped. He seemed astonished and hesitated. Then he dropped the snow and leaned slightly forward. When he did, she clamped her mittens behind his neck and pulled him into her arms. She looked briefly into his eyes. Finally, she kissed him with all she had. For a moment he didn't respond, then he kissed her back. Her heart throbbed to bite him, though she knew it would be the kiss of death for him. She had actually fanaticized about if they kissed for the first time. His kiss and the way he held her tight didn't disappoint her. They said time didn't stand still but it did when she deepened the kiss. She didn't want time to move forward again. She didn't want to let him go.

Clay wrestled from her clutch and drew back. He looked at her, breathing heavy. Then he looked away and began to cover her with snow, to pack snow on and around the hood of her parka.

"Come back for me."

He glanced at her and nodded. Then he began to hum a soft tune.

"Give me your word," she said.

He gave a weak smile, then looked toward the croaks and back at her, "I gotta get moving," he said.

"I love you, Clay," she told herself. She swallowed hard. It took all her will to nod. As he covered her face with snow it felt like death's cold face. Then her vision blurred. At the last moment, his face was clear to her. She felt him pat the snow over her chest and sounds of him running across the snow. Just like that he was gone.

She had always assumed that when she found the man of her dreams she'd … she couldn't think. She held down a giant swell in her chest. She knew if she started crying she wouldn't be able to stop. She knew she had to be quiet as a fish underwater. She fought the swell with all she had to keep it down.

It was only minutes after he left before she heard a low "ruup-ruup" and the sounds were suddenly in her blood. The Mueumonds were all around. They were about to step on her. For a moment she felt the Mueumonds had discovered her.

Then, faintly, she heard Clay yelling and it seemed he was banging limbs or hitting a tree trunk with a limb. She listened to the blows and to him yelling at the same time.

She listened to sounds of snow crunching and limbs snapping around her. A half dozen or more Mueumonds made sounds, "ruup-uup-ruupruupruup," as they left the vicinity at a brisk pace, in the direction of Clay's yelling.

She listened to the croaking until the sounds went abruptly out of her hearing. She strained to hear Clay yelling or banging limbs, but only the sound of the wind filled her ears.

She lay still as possible, yet her mind would not lie still. She believed Clay did what he felt was best. After all, she was still alive and hopeful. She knew after the blizzard blew out, the Saluuette wolves would comb the territory, in numbers, in search of the Mueumonds. Hopefully they would locate her in time.

Her worst fear, they would find Clay first.

If she returned to the sacred forest in time she could stop the Saluuette wolves from hunting him and perhaps, yes, she had to return to the sacred forest alive. She wondered if Clay could elude the Mueumonds long enough and if he was safe, until she finally went to sleep.

CHAPTER 58

The blizzard blew out, the limbs of the trees sagged with snow. The nights were black except for the backwash glow of white snow in the wilderness.

On many occasions in the dark, Clayton found his way by touch until he became exhausted. He covered himself with snow each time he slept, then wished sleep hadn't come, the nightmares about the Mueumonds finding Palafox were so bad.

The nightmares were almost every night and always the same: Palafox, standing with half her body gone, her brown eyes peering at him, accusing. Nightmares so horrible that when he woke, he wished either the Mueumonds or the Saluuette wolves would get the job done. He knew both were hunting him.

He made a promise he wouldn't abandon anyone again. But this wasn't the first time he'd made that kind of promise. In combat, he'd left a wounded friend, to move his squad out of harm's way. When they returned, his friend had died of his wounds. Now Palafox was on his mind and he was feeling awfully low when he stepped to the edge of the forest line.

And stopped.

Something white bounded into the shadows.

At first, he didn't know what the white ball was. Then he knew. Then his mouth began to fill with saliva. He went into a low crouch and went after the rabbit.

He was within steps of it and never saw it before the rabbit bolted. When he began chasing it, intending to clobber it with the spear, the odor of wet leather filled each breath.

Not the first time he smelled wet leather. The Saluuette wolves had caught up to him.

He hurried into the shadow of the boulders and back up, against the vertical rock. This position sheltered him from the sight of any animal above him.

Time ticked away. Then a shadow with pointed ears grew on the snow in front of him. The wolf, tethered on the edge, surely searching for him. He didn't look up. Why should he? The wolf couldn't see him.

Several minutes later, the wolf left. Clayton never saw it, but sensed it was a Saluuette wolf. Probably the same one that had tracked him for days. He wondered a lot about why the Saluuette wolves hadn't attacked, had no answer now either.

He assumed he was still in the Saluuette territory; the chest-high ferns and size of the trees suggested he was. From reading the missionaries' journals, he'd learned the Saluuette wolves would kill him if he tried to leave the Saluuette territory, or if they suspected he was trying to leave.

Somehow, his mind also just knew while he slept, that it was getting to be dawn and he always got up. Now, in the early dawn, he leaned against a tree, gazing across another snow-white prairie without life, where the topography gently sloped down a quarter mile to the forest line. By a chance, he saw movement out there and figured it was animals.

When he lost sight of them, he wondered if his mind was playing tricks. Yet he knew what he observed weren't apparitions.

For several minutes he looked for movement and finally set out across the snow plain, to the last location he'd spotted the animals. He rested there, then set out again, eating bits of mushroom as he walked.

He came upon a trench maybe fifty feet wide that sloped and wriggled like a worm toward the tree line below. After lumbering fifty yards on its shoulder, he finally saw the animals and a spotted brown-and-white caribou, bloodied, slumped on its flanks in the snow.

He noticed right away the wolves weren't arctic wolves, or Saluuette wolves. These wolves were small, at most fifty pounds. He decided to let them finish the job; why exhaust himself fighting the wolves and the caribou?

Although he was wary, the wolves did little to frighten him. As if with one mind, they stopped their assault and all their eyes turned on him. Their gaze was a message and unmistakable. He remained at a safe distance, on the shoulder of the trench.

In turn, the wolves continued their assault against the caribou's flanks. The caribou showed lots of heart to keep its place in the world. But the wolves were numerous and relentless. At last, the caribou lost its fight and the wolves jumped into an eating frenzy. It was like watching kindergarten kids at a banquet. One wolf, with a solemn air Clayton had noticed earlier, licked the caribou's snout.

Clayton felt no pity for the caribou. A part of him felt he was also fighting for his place in the world. He wasn't optimistic he could ever find Palafox, or the sacred forest, again. Yet there was no time to rest, there was no peace when you were on the run, only a fight to survive each conscious moment.

After an hour, the wolves' eating frenzy slowed. Clayton's hunger pangs were fierce now. All he had standing between him and starvation were three plate-sized mushrooms and the half-eaten caribou. Thinking of the latter, his spirits went high and he felt hope's glimmer. It was time, time to walk down there and take the carcass away from the wolves.

The wolves presented their fangs, snarled and threatened with half-hearted charges; their bellies were too full to mount a serious defense. He reached the carcass without much of a contest, happy the wolves seemed only annoyed about his presence.

He stuck the spear in the snow and began to cut meat away from the caribou. Any meat he could get his hands on he cut away. Hand-sized chunks, thick, short slabs of meat, he placed inside his parka. For a strange reason, the sight of the burgundy meat made him drool and he felt a strange urge to eat the meat right now. Finally, he pushed the impulse down.

Then stillness in the silence filled his blood with a terrible coldness. He froze, stooped over and listened.

No sounds. No wind. He leaned up, scanned the shoulder of the trench, then to the sides of him and all around. Where were the wolves?

He returned to his labor for food. He cut meat away from the ivory bone. When he was about finished, with all the meat he could haul cut away, a sickly musk filled each breath. The Mueumonds, breathing down his neck.

He slowly stood and eased his palm to the spear, yanked the spear out of the snow and spun around.

In the backwash of dim light stood two Mueumonds on the shoulder of the trench. They stared at him, their matted hair dangling, their frontal lobes and pinkish faces the stuff proverbial nightmares were made of. The biggest Mueumond began to amble down the slope, with the other Mueumond following. They were hunkered down, stepping straight for him.

Clayton's heart pounded. It was gut-check time. In minutes, he would be another soul who gambled and lost in the arctic wilderness. He would vanish without a trace, without as much as a footnote, after the Mueumonds were finished with him. One Mueumond, he could maybe take.

He wasn't a match for two Mueumonds. He'd been lucky before now.

He threatened them with the spear.

"Come on!" He was surprised the words came out at all, since he felt powerless to do anything.

The Mueumonds stepped in a slow and methodical crouch, predators slipping up on prey. Their luminous eyes glowed lime green in the air around their heads, their eyes fixed on his.

His legs were ready to give up on him. He wanted to run or vanish. He began to consider charging the Mueumonds, to get it over with. He swiped his mouth and took a deep breath.

At that exact moment, a snarling Saluuette wolf came out of nowhere. The wolf leaped through the air and knocked one

Mueumond down. Just as quick, the wolf bit the other Mueumond's head clean off.

He couldn't move, couldn't think, couldn't breathe, could only watch.

The next moment, the remaining Mueumond attacked the Saluuette wolf. The pair merged into one spasmodic ball rolling and tumbling crazily through the snow.

The Saluuette broke free and tried to run.

The Mueumond caught it with its claws and sank its fangs into the wolf's back. As if by some strange force, the wolf propelled straight up in the air, at least ten feet. Then the Mueumond bounced and caught the Saluuette wolf in midair.

By the time they slammed back into the snow, the Mueumond was ripping and tearing flesh off the wolf. Finally, the Mueumond tore away the wolf's left-front shoulder.

He felt impotent to help, to change anything, wanted to run, but suddenly he was sprinting to the Mueumond. When he shoved the spear into the Mueumond, the spear's tip came out its other side.

The Mueumond screeched and rolled into a writhing ball. Just as fast, it jumped to its feet and tried to pull the spear out of its side as it stumbled over the snow. It fell several times, then got back up each time. It continued its stumbling run toward the tree line below.

Just before it reached the tree line, three Saluuette wolves rushed out of the shadowy woodlands and attacked it.

Even from where he stood, he could see the Mueumond's fur, arms and legs torn from its torso. The fight was the most awesome display of animal savagery he'd ever witnessed.

When the Saluuette wolves finished, they stilled their bodies and, as one, peered in his direction. He didn't care, having accepted the notion he was dead.

He turned his attention to the fallen wolf that saved his life and felt shock; the bloody animal was the same Saluuette wolf that had attacked him at the pond.

He watched as the wolf struggled to stand, then collapsed onto its side. Where the wolf's left-front leg had been, only a black hole remained. He could see the wolf's heart pumping and the lungs ballooning and deflating.

It took its last breath. Moments after it stopped breathing, he saw each muscle in the wolf's body spasm, as if expelling a soul. Then its body appeared to be steaming. That's what it looked like steam.

He glanced at the four Saluuette wolves below they were running straight for him. He had his knife ready. In seconds he felt he would be dead too. He'd used up all his strength.

As if in the throes of a death wish he tried to swallow, but the feel of sandpaper in his throat stopped him.

Shoulder to shoulder, the wolves trotted up to within yards of him and the dead wolf.

A lead-colored wolf stepped to the dead wolf and sniffed at it, then raised its head and peered at him, its stare contemptuous. Then it bared its fangs and a growl filled the stillness. The other wolves walked timidly around him and sniffed. He tried to pretend he wasn't scared but he was. He tried to smile at the wolves but he couldn't.

Still he didn't run, couldn't run. It was one of those moments you couldn't run; nothing went through the mind and the only thing that went through the body were trembles.

In that moment, he had the insane thought that the Saluuettes weren't there to harm him they were protecting him. Even crazier, that would explain why he hadn't seen any Mueumonds since he left Palafox, only heard the Mueumonds, but always at a great distance.

Another thing, just as illogical: what was happening now disputed what he'd read in the journals. The Saluuettes might have been hunting him—but not to kill him. Rather, the Saluuettes wolves were his bodyguards.

But why? What was their motivation? This, he couldn't fathom. The course of events was too unexplainable, too amazing. He didn't have enough energy to blow out a candle flame, much less try to figure out the Saluuette wolves' motivation.

Only one solution hung in the back of his mind. Palafox. Palafox must have something to do with the Saluuette wolves behaving as protectors. Or was it Arnaq?

From where he stood, the half-hearted snarls came loud and clear.

Leave while you still got a chance. The thought made all the sense in the world to him. Why test his harebrained theories? Why test the Saluuette wolves' patience? He backed away, steps slow and careful. Then he turned and walked to where his parka lay near the caribou's bloody carcass.

He quickly pulled on the parka, recalled it was loaded with at least twenty pounds of the juicy burgundy meat. After he sheathed the knife, he stumbled away.

He hadn't walked far before he heard a crackling in the air and noises at the proximity of the dead wolf. He didn't want to know what was going on. The less he knew the better for his mental state. The air seemed charged with static electricity and the aroma of basil. He didn't look back to see what was happening. He didn't want to know.

He kept his eyes forward and kept slugging through the snow. Not far ahead was the tree line. He wanted to get out of sight, make another spear and roast some caribou meat. In spite of what happened to him, he felt a renewed spirit. He felt better now, but not safe.

CHAPTER 59

D ays and nights and weeks circled him like wolves; each day the circle shrank in bitter winds, waiting for him to stop walking.

He collapsed as if a sniper had shot him in the head. He lay there, curled into a fetal position, his blood feeling like mercury weighting down his veins, trying to summon the strength to stand back up. He lifted his eyes to the murky horizon. Nothing but miserable desolation before him. No prospects for food, only one hand-sized mushroom remaining between him and starvation. He'd never felt so weak. He was scared, but not enough to give up.

Finally, he pulled himself up to lean against a tree. He could see another hillside in the dim haze at the horizon and realized he was near the bottom of another miserable forest range.

Countless times, he'd believed at the bottom of each hill laid a frozen stream or river. His plan was simple: to follow the stream until he came out somewhere. Over and over again, it hadn't worked out that way. Always another steep ravine, gorge, mountain or hill, and he couldn't walk around those.

He stumbled forward, grabbing trees for balance. At the next one in the endless mounds of snow, he collapsed and rolled over and over again, then stopped. He stayed where he stopped rolling, lay on his back peering up.

He'd taken his last step. The last step, the summation of all his miserable efforts, of all his life, of all his despair and misery. He didn't have the strength to continue; he couldn't continue. He lifted his head for a last miserable look before closing his eyes to sleep.

What the hell?

A power pole with wire. That's what the vision looked like. He looked down. Tire tracks in the snow?

He listened, heard nothing. He took a bead to his left. A long narrow path seemed to go to the horizon. No power pole in that direction.

He stared at the other direction. That way, the path curved. He decided to walk or crawl to where the last telephone pole stood and go in that direction.

Groaning with the effort, he forced himself up and wobbled along the path, determined now to die on his feet. He couldn't stop shuffling forward. It was if some force pushed him forward.

He tried to wipe his face and felt a thin ice sheet that had formed on his brows and parka. He struggled for air to breathe. Then he realized his lungs might be turning to blocks of ice too.

He sensed if he stopped again, he wouldn't move again. He kept lumbering forward, staggering around another endless bend in the path. Then he saw a bead of yellow light through the trees, then a bead of silver light at his left and out front. His heart was full of elation and he kept slogging forward one step at a time.

What he felt wasn't happiness; instead it was a strange breath of relief. He tried to walk but his legs gave out and he fell flat on the snow. He crawled to the side of the path, lay there until he felt warm all over, warmth he knew meant he was freezing to death. It was difficult to catch his breath now, he knew he was suffocating. With his luck, he'd freeze to death within sight of the light. *What a lousy, rotten irony.*

He pushed himself up and the folds in his parka cracked with ice. Nothing was in his mind except take a step forward, then another step.

He saw buildings in the glow of lights and roofs with snow on top of all of them. He kept moving. Then he heard and saw a car on a street and the back end of the car boiled steam as it moved across his sight.

He shuffled forward until he came to another power pole, stopped and leaned against it. Then he saw a dumpster and lumbered across a narrow path to reach it, leaned against it. As his eyes focused, he saw a sign. It read US Postal Service. There were lights, lots of lights in the windows of that building.

A strange voice sounded inside his head: Get rid of the knife. He took the bone-handled knife that had saved him and put it into the dumpster.

He looked both ways; he didn't want to get hit by a car. But no cars roared down the snow-covered street, yet several vehicles were parked outside small buildings and several houses, Christmas lights in their windows shooting through like silver spears. He thought he heard Christmas jingles, stopped and looked around.

A dog barked. A car cranked up in the distance.

He shuffled across the street, toward the building. Now he could see shadows, of people standing in a line inside the building. He found the doorknob with his mittens. The ice that crusted his mitten made it difficult, but he had enough strength to turn the knob. His strength was at rock bottom now.

He stumbled and nearly fell as he stepped into the bright-lit room. A gush of warm air greeted his face and his lungs and the strong light almost blinded him. He shielded his eyes with his mitten.

A gasp rose. "What in the world," a woman's voice said.

He couldn't respond.

"My God," another woman said.

Another woman dropped a handful of letters and rushed from behind the partition. People stood like statures with facial expressions frozen in disbelief.

"What ya want?" a woman's voice said.

Then voices went silent in the room, as though he'd stepped to a podium to speak. He tried to speak but no words came out of his mouth, only a slight grunt. The truth was he was frightened; he couldn't find words to speak through the fear. He suffered tense moments before words finally rolled out of his mouth, hardly above a whisper.

"I'm lost, can you please help me?"

A stocky woman peeked out from behind the partition. She wore black-rimmed glasses and her hair seemed bowl-cut. She said, "I thought you were a bear."

Voices rose like a drone of bees from a hive.

A man clutched his arm and led him across the room.

"Here bud," the man said in a kind voice, "lay on the bench and don't move. Fetch some coffee somebody."

"Don't move" were the best words he ever heard. He lay flat on his back on a bench, gazing up knowing full well he would not get back up.

People's voices in support surged forward and outlines of people in the bright light crowded around him.

When he came to, a clashing of voices and blinding lights greeted him, and he felt someone place something metallic at his lips, which turned out to be a spoonful of the best damn liquid he'd ever tasted. After slurping down the soup, he passed out again.

When he came to, he was on his back and felt his body floating. Then a rush of freezing air hit his face and he heard the whirling chop-chop, a sound he recognized. He could barely open his eyes for the blinding light. Then he feared he was dreaming and dying at the same time.

"You're going to be fine, just rest and stay still," a young man's voice said.

"Where am I?" he managed.

"Breathe slow," the young man's voice said. "Don't talk."

Bags hung above him on both sides. Then, he knew he would be safe. He was in a helicopter and faces of men were over him, peering at him while they washed his face and neck with a warm wet cloth.

"He's got severe frostbite on his hands, face, lower lip and on his right ear," a man's voice said. "He's suffered an injury to his left ear—"

"Check his temperature and keep him warm," another man's voice said. "We can't do any more until we get him to the hospital."

He closed his eyes feeling lucky and thankful. During his half-dream sleep he heard voices: a woman's voice, a man's voice. He couldn't concentrate but he felt warm for the first time he could recall. And he felt he was going to make it.

A sensation of floating and when he came back down, he felt his body float onto a hard surface, a rush of warm air against his face, from underneath his chin and down, across his chest. It felt so warm, so pleasingly comfortable.

Lights blinded him; he couldn't see. Then he heard commotion and many voices like shattered glass, roaring engines and a sickly Pine Sol smell flooded each breath.

Then a woman's voice said, "What a beautiful bear-claw necklace."

"Get the parka off," a man's voice with an English accent close to his ear said, "Can you hear me?"

He nodded that he could hear him, but couldn't stay awake to speak. The silver lights blinded him and besides, it felt so good to sleep.

"What's your name?" the man asked.

For a moment, he had forgotten his name. He racked his brain. Then he remembered.

"Clayton Spears." He barely got his name out above a whisper.

"Clayton Spears," the man said, "you're in the hospital, in the emergency room at Fort Wainwright Hospital. Do you have relatives nearby?"

Clayton shook his head, "No."

In fact, he had no relatives to speak of.

He opened his eyes, tried to focus, stared at ghostly images like faces underwater. The voices stopped. The faces peered at him in silence. After a few moments, the faces turned away and disappeared.

He glanced around. Silver rectangular boxes with wires and beeping sounds. He knew what they were.

He went in and out, not sure about events or the activity around him but instead he listened to anxious voices, cheerful echoes, in and out of his head. Then the man with an English accent said, "Wrap his feet and hands, nurse."

"Dear me, look how long his toenails are and the hair on his feet and toes," a woman said.

People's voices quickly leapt from one person to another. The beeping sounds and voices began to drift farther and farther away. He was too exhausted to listen anymore.

He wondered about Palafox and if fate had brought them together. He knew now and understood there were truly things worth fighting for, waiting for. If Palafox made it back to her sacred forest, she surely knew her clan's secrets were safe with him, or he wouldn't be here. He liked to believe she trusted him with her secrets. But there were secrets worth knowing and there were secrets best left secrets. He suffered pangs of regret now that he didn't take time to get to know Palafox more than he did. He also knew if he had to go through the experience again, a chilling prospect, he would do the same thing again.

Inexplicably, he recalled the caribou's fight with the wolves, how the caribou fought for its place in the world. He wondered again if his survival was by fate or just plain luck.

One thing was certain; the events he had experienced changed his life and his outlook on life. He believed now that everyone needed a little help along the way. He had no fear now but he did feel out of place just the same. Grateful he was still alive, safe, toasty warm and in one piece, grateful he could see reds, blues, greens, yellows, purples, he finally drifted to sleep believing in miracles.

THE END

www.ingramcontent.com/pod-product-compliance
Lightning Source LLC
Chambersburg PA
CBHW051537250626
47157CB00001B/79